P9-CMY-222

LEWIS & CLARK LIBRARY
120 S. LAST CHANCE GULCH
HELENA, MONTANA 59601

LETTERS
FROM
PARIS

Center Point
Large Print

Also by Juliet Blackwell and available from
Center Point Large Print:

The Paris Key

**This Large Print Book carries the
Seal of Approval of N.A.V.H.**

LETTERS
FROM
PARIS

Juliet Blackwell

CENTER POINT LARGE PRINT
THORNDIKE, MAINE

LEWIS & CLARK LIBRARY
120 S. LAST CHANCE GULCH
HELENA, MONTANA 59601

This Center Point Large Print edition
is published in the year 2016 by arrangement with
The Berkley Publishing Group,
an imprint of Penguin Publishing Group,
a division of Penguin Random House LLC.

Copyright © 2016 by Julie Goodson-Lawes.
Readers Guide copyright © 2016
by Penguin Random House.

All rights reserved.

This is a work of fiction. Names, characters, places, and incidents either are the product of the author's imagination or are used fictitiously, and any resemblance to actual persons, living or dead, business establishments, events, or locales is entirely coincidental.

The text of this Large Print edition is unabridged.
In other aspects, this book may vary
from the original edition.
Printed in the United States of America
on permanent paper.
Set in 16-point Times New Roman type.

ISBN: 978-1-68324-158-4

Library of Congress Cataloging-in-Publication Data

Names: Blackwell, Juliet, author.
Title: Letters from Paris / Juliet Blackwell.
Description: Center Point Large Print edition. | Thorndike, Maine : Center Point Large Print, 2016.
Identifiers: LCCN 2016033915 | ISBN 9781683241584 (hardcover : alk. paper)
Subjects: LCSH: Women—France—Paris—Fiction. | Life change events—Fiction. | Sculptors—Fiction. | Large type books.
Classification: LCC PS3602.L32578 L48 2016b | DDC 813/.6—dc23
LC record available at https://lccn.loc.gov/2016033915

To the Goodson Girls:

Minerva, Betty, Mem, Suzy, and Jane.
Thank you for the joy, the gumbo,
and the gleam of mischief.

ACKNOWLEDGMENTS

Merci beaucoup to my ever-patient, supersmart editor, Kerry Donovan, who encouraged me to follow my heart and write about Paris. To my literary agent, Jim McCarthy, who is the best cheerleader a writer could have. And many thanks to the copy editors and designers and artists who worked on the finished product of *Letters from Paris*—you make me look good!

Thanks are due my friends and family in Paris, Provence, and the Franche-Comté, especially the Stauffeneggers, the Dartevels, and the LaCroix. Also to Francoise and Hubert Laugner, for the wonderful sojourn in Alsace! And thank you to my Southern family—the extended Goodson clan—for beautiful childhood memories, and for reminding this California girl what life feels like in Louisiana and Texas. Thank you to my father, Robert B. Lawes, for always being there for me and for teaching me more than he realizes. To Susan Lawes, who shared her early appreciation for art and reading with her bratty younger sister. Finally, to Carolyn Lawes, whip-smart and funny as hell, a true friend and writer's muse in addition to being my sister. Could you please move back to California, already?

As always to my author friends, who truly know

that special brand of writer-crazy, especially Sophie Littlefield, Rachael Herron, Victoria Laurie, Nicole Peeler, Adrienne Miller, Gigi Pandian, Martha White, Mysti Berry, Lynn Coddington, and Lisa Hughey. *Muchísimas gracias* to my assistant extraordinaire and *amiga del corazón*, Anna Cabrera. And to my ever-patient and supportive friends: Maddee James, Karen Thompson, Bee Enos, Susan Baker, Kendall Moalem, Muffy Srinivasan, Shay Demetrius, Suzanne Chan, Pamela Groves, Jan Strout, Chris Logan, Brian Casey, Wanda Klor, Cathy Romero, and Mary Grae. And to the entire Mira Vista Social Club, especially Oscar's parents, Sara Paul and Dan Krewson. And to Oscar, of course; I hope you'll forgive me for naming you Gertrude in this book. It's a writer thing.

In addition to countless articles and photos found in the shelves of the library and on the Internet, I pored over the pictures in Alex Toledano's *Paris in Photographs, 1890s* (Calla Editions, Dover Publications, 2015). I also especially appreciate the photography of Virginia Jones, which I used to remind myself of street scenes in contemporary Paris.

Thank you to Sergio, who drives me crazy, forces me to laugh, and makes me proud every day. *Et merci à* Eric, for endless dinners, bottomless glasses of wine, and unfailing love and kindness. Also, for correcting my French. One of these days I'll get the *"ou"* right. Then we can work on my *"r"*s.

Finally, thanks to the *Lorenzi Moulage d'Art* for inspiring me—and so many others—with their beautiful artistry, their death masks, and for keeping the tradition of mold-making and copying alive. If you're ever near Paris, don't miss it! It's well worth the trip, and you might just spy the face of *L'Inconnue* decorating their walls. And, of course, to the mysterious woman known only as *L'Inconnue de la Seine*: I enjoyed imagining a different ending for you. I like to think it might have been so.

You find me at work; excuse the dust on my blouse. I sculpt my marble myself.

—Camille Claudel

PROLOGUE
SABINE

February 27, 1898

He sleeps.
Sabine creeps across the dark studio before dawn, beseeching the silent faces not to betray her. They watch her every move, mute witnesses to her crime.

Slipping through the door, she winces at the scraping sound of metal on metal as she pauses to latch it behind her. Fog envelops her, the mist cutting through her threadbare blouse and underthings, wet needles of cold air piercing her skin.

Sabine thinks longingly of the two dresses she left behind in the cupboard. He'd bought them for her. They are the finest garments she has ever worn: one blue, one green. Made of the softest lawn, a material so lush and supple it beckoned to her the first time she donned the garments; often she would caress the skirt, reveling in the sumptuous sensations that tickled her palm. He teased her for that.

Take nothing with you.

She has donned the heavy black skirt and the thin gray blouse she wore when they met in the

13

square in Pigalle. When she thought he was her salvation. Before.

Her feet are clad in her ancient black boots. The dove gray shawl her mother had knit for her sixteenth Christmas is her only defense against the night's chill. She wears her hair pinned back in the style he likes: an old-fashioned twist on either side of her head.

As though she stepped out of another time.

Also abandoned is a gold armband, still in its nest of fine black velvet, in a blue box upon the nightstand. The tortoiseshell comb for her hair. Her little hand mirror. The candle stubs and pocket-sized book of sonnets, her sketchbook and charcoal. She even leaves behind the pillowcase in which she packed her few belongings when she fled her childhood home in the countryside so long ago.

Before Paris. Before she was an artist's model. Before Maurice.

Before.

The damp air stings her cheeks with cold kisses. Dim light from the gas streetlamps casts an amber glow on the cobblestones, glinting off puddles from last night's rain.

They seem to flash a warning: *You will never get away with it. You will never get away.*

Sabine keeps her head down, walking as quickly as she dares. Listening.

She hears water dripping from a gargoyle at the

side of the church. A horse whinnying a block or two away. A dog barking behind a stout wooden door. The tapping of her boots on the paving stones, echoing the pounding of her heart.

Her own harsh breathing is the loudest sound.

And . . . something else?

She freezes. Holds her breath. Listens.

Footsteps.

Sabine runs. Runs for her life.

She makes it as far as the quai du Louvre. To the Pont Neuf.

The bridge that crosses the Seine.

1

*T*his was probably a mistake, Claire thought to herself as she wrestled her luggage cart— why did she always choose the one with a wobbly wheel?—out the exit of the New Orleans airport. The sliding-glass doors *whoosh*ed closed behind her, cutting her off from the terminal's unnatural coolness and leaving her mired in the soupy atmosphere of July, Louisiana-style.

Louisiana. It occurred to Claire that had she been blindfolded and her ears covered, she would still know where she was. She could feel it, smell something achingly familiar in the air. Humid tendrils of heat reached out and wrapped around her, dampness whispering along her skin, greeting her like an old lover.

A lover she'd left many years ago with a mix of regret and relief, an abstract fondness tangled up with the fervent desire to move on.

Claire took a deep breath of the hot, moist air, blew it out slowly, and searched the vehicles vying for curb access outside of baggage claim. When she'd cosigned the loan for her cousin Ty's new rig, he'd told her it was "huge, black, and shiny." One good thing about having more cousins in Plaquemines Parish than she could count: there was always someone to give her a ride to or from the airport.

A small group of already inebriated twenty-something tourists, apparently intent on finding Mardi Gras out of season, jostled Claire on their jocular way to the taxi stand; she barely managed to grab her computer case as it was knocked from her shoulder. A drip of sweat rolled down the small of her back. She stood with one hand on her luggage; other than a few boxes of books and souvenirs she had sent through the mail, the two big suitcases, one duffel bag, and huge purse were all she owned in the world. She'd sold or given away the rest before leaving Chicago.

This was probably a mistake, Claire thought again. The phrase had become something of a mantra ever since her cousin Jessica had phoned the week before last to say their grandmother was at death's door.

"Mammaw needs you, Chance," Jessica had said. Claire's relatives knew her as Chance; their grandmother went by Mammaw. "She's speaking in Cajun; no one can understand her but Uncle Remy. And you know how *he* is."

When Claire received the call, she had been sitting in her climate-controlled office in Chicago, wondering what a person wore to the opera. Was her standard black office garb— perhaps dressed up with some chunky ethnic jewelry and a colorful pashmina—enough, or was this more of a sparkles-and-tulle situation? From the vantage point of her desk she could see acres of taupe carpeting and a maze of cubicles, old brick factory walls chicly renovated with skylights, and steel-and-glass dividers for "No-Miss Systems: A Software Company." She looked out over the muted officescape, imagining Mammaw's house and thinking: If Jessica's was a voice from her past, what was her future? A night at the *opera?* Really?

You're getting pretty big for your britches, Chance Broussard.

As her newly ex-boyfriend, Sean, would say: in this, as in most things, Claire was just the teensiest bit conflicted.

Claire finally spotted Ty's truck, looming large and new in a sea of smaller cars and dented pickups. Ignoring the blare of horns, he double-parked, hopped out, gave Claire a bear hug, then tossed her leaden bags in the bed of the truck like so much kindling.

Ty drove toward the small town in Plaquemines Parish where they had been raised. They chatted a little about her life in the "big city," his new truck, the job situation out on the oil rigs, and the precarious state of Mammaw's health, but further conversation soon fizzled out. Claire's relatives worked hard, disdained complainers, saluted the flag, and enjoyed their football. When they started drinking, the young men might get raucous and the old folks were prone to spinning long, involved tales in which layers of fact and fiction, history and fantasy merged and overlapped. But unless they were in storytelling mode, her cousins remained largely silent, their thoughts and hopes and dreams kept locked away under sweat-stained New Orleans Saints or Ragin' Cajuns ball caps.

So Claire was free to watch the scenery—flat, full of brush and low trees and crisscrossed by creeks and bayous—and to ponder.

After hanging up with Jessica, Claire had finished up the day's work, talked to her team supervisor, and hurried to meet Sean for a drink at the latest trendy lounge, a former dive bar that had been revamped with an ironically 1950s décor à la Frank Sinatra and the Rat Pack. They ordered craft cocktails made with locally sourced ingredients that took about ten minutes apiece for the bewhiskered "mixologists" to produce and that cost easily four times as much as the drinks had in the bar's former incarnation.

After their cocktails arrived, they settled in at a table and Claire told Sean she had given notice at No-Miss and was going home to take care of her grandmother.

"Just like that?" Sean asked, a stunned look on his handsome face, grapefruit-bitters-inspired cocktail held aloft halfway to his mouth.

"Well, as soon as they can replace me at work."

"But . . . what about me? What about *us?*"

"I . . ." Claire trailed off. The sorry truth was, she hadn't thought much about Sean's reaction to her sudden news.

Of course he was important to her. Claire cared for Sean. A lot. They'd met not long after graduating college, and Sean—an Evanston native—had introduced Claire to the wonders of city life. Sean took her to fancy restaurants and cocktail parties; he taught her how to hail a cab and gripe about the El and stroll through the Institute of Art while making the appropriately erudite comments. With Sean by her side, Claire developed a taste for Thai food and Ethiopian food and learned to eat raw fish—who knew?— at sushi bars. She even became accustomed to paying the equivalent of an entire breakfast back home for a simple cup of French roast at the chic café on the corner near her downtown office. They were young and well paid; it was fun.

But lately Sean had been pushing for more. Their friends were starting to marry, settle down and buy houses, have children. Claire liked Sean and enjoyed being with him. But there was something lacking.

For years she'd been driven: first to get out of her small hometown, then to finish college, then to get a job, then to make more money. Now what? Sitting hunched over her keyboard ten hours a day, going out to trendy clubs on the weekend, able to afford a nice place to live and new clothes, and getting her hair done in a salon . . . was this what she had worked so hard to attain? Claire used to be able to lose herself down the rabbit hole of her work: writing code, beta testing, and resolving glitches. But now she wondered: Did any of it matter in the long run? *Is this all there is?*

And when she tried to picture herself settling down with Sean and starting a family, she felt the waters closing over her head, her lungs screaming for air. She felt like she was drowning.

"Tell me what's going on, Claire." Sean had covered Claire's hand with his, squeezed gently. "You get one phone call and suddenly you're ready to give up your whole life here in Chicago? I'm sorry your grandmother's not doing well, but she's getting up there in age, right? It's not unexpected, is it? Couldn't you just go for a visit, like a . . . ?"

Like a normal person, Claire finished his thought in her mind. But no matter how much she might enjoy expensive cocktails, Claire had never felt normal in Chicago.

When she'd first arrived at the University of Chicago, a scholarship kid fresh off the plane from Louisiana, Chance had stuck out like a sore thumb. She wore the wrong clothes, sported a frizzy home perm two decades out of fashion (according to the blunt but sympathetic assessment of her roommate, Zoey, who was from New York City and knew about such things), and spoke with an accent as thick as a cloud of *moustiques* over the bayou on a warm summer evening.

At first she had found everything—the chatty students, the scholarly professors, the city traffic—intimidating. Just as she had at home, she spent her nights hiding in her room or studying in the library.

But after a few lonely weeks Chance had made a decision. After all, she hadn't fought her way out of Plaquemines Parish just to let life pass her by. So she applied her formidable study skills to observing the behavior of the other girls: their wardrobes, their intonations, the way they giggled and joked about boys, and about life in general. How easily they reneged on promises, how they said yes when they meant no and no when they meant yes. How they never sat down for a full meal but ate only stalks of celery with peanut butter one day, huge bowls of ice cream the next.

She started introducing herself as Claire instead of Chance, and learned to drink and smoke, to flirt and "party." She told long, rambling stories about her hometown that her friends found hysterical, and made a feature of her "quaint" bayou accent. For the first time in her life, Claire succeeded socially as well as academically. The poor little Cajun girl managed to make some friends, attract a few boys, and still graduate cum laude. She landed a good job as a software engineer in

Chicago with a starting salary that was more than she had ever thought possible, a small fortune by the standards of Plaquemines Parish, where everyone had said: *That Chance! Just look at her now! She's the American Dream, that one—coming from nothing and making something of herself.*

But it had been years now, and Claire no longer felt like she was living the dream.

Claire used to ask why she hadn't died alongside her mother when she was little, when Lizzie Broussard's ten-year-old Ford veered off the road and landed upside down on its roof in the bayou. And Mammaw always said: *The Lord's got something special planned for you, sha—you mark my words. Your mother's voice reached out to rescue you—it was a miracle.*

But now Claire asked herself: other than the size of her paycheck, was she really better off than if she had taken that refinery job back home straight out of high school and grabbed a beer with the gang down at Charlie Bob's after work?

Claire knew what Sean's answer would be: a resounding *yes.*

And yet.

"Mammaw isn't just a *grandmother,*" Claire found herself saying to Sean. Trying her best to explain. "She raised me. She saved my life."

"I know how important she is to you," he said, his voice gentle. "And, of course, you should *absolutely* go see her. Take a couple of weeks, claim some family time. In fact, I could do the same and go with you."

Claire smiled and sipped her cocktail. "You said my hometown reminded you of that movie *Deliverance*."

Claire had never seen the film but she understood the reference.

"For you, I'd be willing to risk it," Sean said with a chuckle.

Claire knew he was glad to see her smile, that he assumed he'd won the argument. Sean was a nice man, easygoing and thoughtful. But he was used to Claire accommodating his desires. Honestly, she didn't much care whether they went to the symphony or the opera, or ate Vietnamese or Thai food for dinner, or went to the museum gala or the festival of lights at the harbor. In all these things, Claire was happy to let him choose. But this was different.

"I'm not happy in Chicago, Sean. It's not enough, somehow. It's hard to explain, but . . . I want something else."

"So you're going to move back to Plaquemines *Parish?*" He was getting angry now, pressing his lips together, his words taking on a clipped edge. "You hate it there. How many times have you told me that you never fit in, that you wanted something more out of life? You worked so hard to escape—how can you even *think* about going back?"

"It's just for a while, so I can be with Mammaw. Jessica says it probably won't be long now. I'll figure out something from there. I might even come back to Chicago—I really don't know. I'm sorry, Sean. You're a wonderful man. I just—"

"This is a mistake, Claire," Sean cut her off. "You're making a mistake."

"You may be right," she'd conceded.

Probably it *was* a mistake. But it was her mistake to make.

Ten days later Claire boarded a plane and headed to Plaquemines Parish, where they drank cheap coffee laced with chicory, no one even thought about attending the opera, and Claire—with her fancy college education and big-city ways—now stuck out like a sore thumb.

2

W hy is there a tree on the roof?" Claire asked as Ty pulled up in front of Mammaw's house.

"Storm came through coupla days ago," said Ty, peering at the greenery atop the little white clapboard bungalow. "Anyway, it's just a branch."

"Still," Claire said. "It's a very *large* branch."

"First I seen it," said Ty with a shrug. "I'd take care of it now but gotta get back to work. Prob'ly Remy's on it."

Uncle Remy came out of the house at that moment, smiling, gray haired and slightly stooped. In photos of him as a young man in his uniform, Remy had a broad smile and kind brown eyes. He had been a gifted mechanic, could fix anything ever since he was a very young boy; everyone said so. But he'd returned from Vietnam with a head injury, and even though it seemed like he'd healed on the outside, inside he had changed. He'd moved in with Mammaw and never left.

Mammaw always called him "slow." She said it right in front of him, and Remy never seemed to take offense. It wasn't until Claire had gone off to Chicago that she started to think there might be something wrong with saying things like that. Remy's "slowness" had always seemed a fact of life, like being tall or having curly hair; she had never thought much about it as a girl. He was Chance's best childhood friend—her only *real* friend. He was a hide-and-seek champion, and could even be talked into playing Barbies if she promised to play checkers in return.

"Hey!" Remy called out, shuffling down the broken concrete path. "Come see! It's my Chance! We missed you, Chance!"

She jumped out of the truck and ran to give Remy a hug, holding on for a long time. He smelled slightly of mothballs and spices, an achingly familiar scent that spoke to her of home and gumbo and family.

Sean was probably right; this whole idea was likely a mistake. But *this*—this moment—was worth the trip.

"We're gonna have to call someone 'bout that roof," Uncle Remy fretted as soon as she pulled away from him. So much for the welcome home. Claire wasn't surprised; Remy lived in the present. He started wringing his hands and shifting from one foot to the other. "Branch went clear through the tar paper, and what if it rains again?"

"Don't worry, Remy," Claire said. "I'll take care of it. Isn't cousin Hog in construction?"

"He's on the shrimpers now," Remy said, grabbing the duffel bag from the back of the truck. Ty brought the heavier suitcases in through the front door, bade them farewell, and hurried back to work.

"They're all on the shrimpers these days," Remy continued. "Them that's not on the rigs."

"I'll call someone else, then. Don't worry."

"Jessica'll know what to do. She knows everything."

"Good idea. Let me say hello to Mammaw, and then we'll figure it out. Okay?"

"Okay." He nodded and seemed to physically relax. "Glad you're home, Chance. Sure enough glad you're home."

As always when stepping through Mammaw's yellow door, Claire was filled with an overwhelming sense of nostalgia mixed with a panicky urge to flee, to run back to her urban life of overpriced drinks and refined beauty and people who followed the international news.

Mammaw had quit smoking a decade ago, but still the house smelled of stale cigarette smoke, old books, and Dr Pepper. An ancient window-mounted air-conditioning unit rattled and spewed out enough cool to take the edge off the heat, but nonetheless the small living room, crowded with furniture and bookshelves, was stuffy. Beyond the front room was the kitchen, and to one side were two bedrooms and a bath. That was it. After Chance had come to live here, she had slept on the couch or, sometimes, with Mammaw in her bed.

"She's awake and waitin' on you," said Remy. "She's only speakin' Cajun, so it's good you come. You want a pop?"

"No, thanks. I'm okay for now."

Claire was struck with a vivid memory of the first time she had walked into this house, age six, knowing she would be staying. That she wouldn't have to go back to her father's. That she was safe. Mammaw had been making salmon croquettes; she met Chance at the door while wiping her hands on a towel, then escorted her into the kitchen, lifted her onto the counter, and poured her a Dixie cup of sweet tea.

She'd declared to Chance that, starting the next day, they would speak only Cajun in her home.

"But . . . I don't speak Cajun," protested Chance, nervous at the thought.

"You'll learn, just like I learned English. When *I* was little we spoke Cajun at home, and when I went to school they wanted me to speak English, 'cept I didn't speak no English. If the teachers heard me speakin' my language they'd make me kneel on rice."

"Kneel on rice?"

"Yup," she said, her gnarled, capable hands mixing canned fish, chopped onions, bread crumbs, egg, and spices for salmon croquettes in a huge periwinkle blue ceramic bowl. Chance watched as the pink goo squeezed through her grandmother's fingers like lumpy Play-Doh. "Go on now and wash your hands. He'p me make these patties."

"But . . . isn't rice soft?" Chance had asked, jumping off the counter and pulling the step stool to the old porcelain farmer's sink, reaching up to turn on the ancient brass tap, wetting her hands. She picked up the huge bar of strong lye soap Mammaw bought down at the Piggly Wiggly and rubbed it between her hands while she sang the entire song of "Happy Birthday to You" in her mind, the way she'd been taught.

Chance was always careful to do as she'd been taught.

She rinsed her hands, then dried them on a faded towel, stiff from line-drying. It chafed, and the strong soap made her hands feel dry and raw. Clean, through and through.

"I'm not talkin' 'bout kneelin' in no cooked rice like in jambalaya, *sha*," Mammaw said with a laugh. "That'd be like a pillow. This was raw, hard grains. They dig into your skin, feel like they goin' right up on under your kneecap. You try it, see how you like it."

"No, thank you, ma'am."

Mammaw laughed again and scooped out a ball of the salmon mixture, slapping it in the palm of her hands to form the croquette.

"You a good girl, Chance. Yup, the good Lord's got somethin' special in mind for you, *sha*, mark my words. That's how come he spared you, helped your mama to speak from beyond the veil."

Claire reached into the bowl, took a handful of the goo, and concentrated on forming it into a patty. She tried as hard as she could, but when she set it on the platter, it looked like a raggedy-edged lump next to her grandmother's smooth disks. Her eyes flew to Mammaw's.

"Now, you hadn't ought to be so skeered all the time, *sha*," Mammaw said, picking up the misshapen wad and smoothing the sides with a quick, practiced movement. "Everybody clumsy when they little. No shame in that. Takes time to learn to do things. Time and practice."

Chance tried harder with the second patty, her tongue planted firmly at the corner of her mouth.

" 'Sides," Mammaw continued. "I don't 'spect the Lord saved you to make you good at cookin'. There's the rest of us for that. He had 'nother purpose for you. 'Nother purpose entirely."

"What is it?"

"Don't rightly know, *sha*. None my business, when it come right down to it. But it's somethin' special. Mark my words."

Claire stepped into Mammaw's sky blue room. It was so small, it barely fit the double bed with its chunky bedstead, *World's Best Mammaw* in childish needlepoint covering one garishly colored pillow.

And Mammaw. Jessica had warned Claire that Mammaw wasn't eating much, but nonetheless it was a shock to see her so tiny, as though she were shrinking in on herself, would continue dissipating until she disappeared into her smooth white sheets. She always used to be stout, her chubby arms and generous bosom a welcome refuge for a scared little girl. Still, Mammaw's light sherry brown eyes were sharp as always, her smile unwavering.

"Ain't you a sight for sore eyes, *sha*?"

Claire perched on the edge of the bed and hugged her grandmother, afraid to squeeze too tight. She could feel Mammaw's bones and the rapid thudding of her pulse through the thin pink cotton of her nightgown.

Once, in the third grade, Claire had found an

31

injured bird on the way home from school. It felt like this in the palm of her hand: tiny, fragile, heart beating wildly. Remy had helped her build a little nest out of newspaper and leaves; they dug up some earthworms but the poor frightened creature ignored their offerings. It hadn't lasted the day. They buried it in a shoe box behind the old Ford, which had sat, rusting and useless, next to the garage for as long as she could remember. Remy marked the spot with a crude wooden cross that still stood.

Mammaw pulled away, and Claire felt the sting of tears in her eyes.

"Don't you dare be sad for me now, *sha*," said Mammaw in Cajun, waving a finger. "I'm 'bout ready to go. All I need is two things: to finish up a few letters, and make the plans for my funeral. And I want to die here at home, ya hear? Don't take me to no hospital. Promise me."

Claire nodded, unable to speak.

Mammaw had never spent much time on sentiment. She took care of business; this was as much a part of her as her quick laugh, the way she ate with her mouth open and believed (and repeated and expounded upon) everything she read in the tabloid newspapers and—as she got older and had trouble moving around—how she would roll across the kitchen linoleum in an office chair, pushing herself off from the table to the counter and back again.

"I got some specifications for my funeral," Mammaw continued. "But first, go help Remy with that tree what fell on the roof so he'll stop talkin' about it. I swear that boy could worry the birds out the trees. Move any of my treasures that might be in the way up there, will you, *sha*?"

"Of course I will," Claire said. "I'll get right on it. But can't I get you something first, though? Something to eat, maybe?"

"I've got a hankerin' for some gumbo. Maybe you could get the fixin's for it for tomorrow supper."

"I will. Nothing right now?"

She shook her head. "I'm gonna take me a nap. You go on now."

Claire kissed her grandmother's soft cheek—it smelled almondy, a mix of Jergens lotion and baby powder—and did as she was told. First she called a roofing company that agreed to come out the next day. Then she changed into old jeans and pulled on a T-shirt.

Claire met Remy in his bedroom and asked for his help. She stepped into his closet, shoved her way past the musty army uniforms and the dark blue suit Mammaw insisted he keep for weddings and funerals, and, using her fingertips, pushed gently on one of the panels at the back of the closet until it popped open, revealing a wooden ladder bolted to the rear wall.

Claire wondered how she had managed to spend

33

time up in this attic when she was young. It was sweltering. Sweat beaded on her forehead within minutes; it was so hot and close, it was hard to breathe as she started moving boxes to the undamaged section of the attic. A few—the ones with correspondence and photographs—she handed down to Remy to stack in a corner of his bedroom. She worked as fast as she could, driven to escape the heat.

But when Claire got to a crate shoved up under the eaves, she slowed her frenetic pace.

"What's this old wooden crate from Paris, Remy? Do you know?" she called down the ladder.

His head popped up through the trapdoor. "I don't rightly know. I don't come up here much. You should ask Mammaw."

As soon as Claire approached the crate, the memories came flooding back.

3

It was August, and as hot as an iron skillet under the eaves.

At ten years old, Chance didn't care. In the attic she had found a refuge.

It was the one place she could hide from her cousin Jessica, four years her senior, and Jessica's ragtag entourage: younger cousins and hangers-on from town who did whatever Jessica said because she had long, shiny platinum blond hair (tinged green from chlorine; Jessica was captain of the swim team) and because she was whip-smart. She lived with her parents in a first-class double-wide complete with an outdoor Jacuzzi and cable TV, including the premium channels. If they played their cards right, Jessica's minions knew, they might just get invited over for pizza-and-pop movie night.

Chance was invited to these social occasions only when Mammaw made a federal case about it, insisting she be included. But Chance didn't care. She didn't want to go anyway.

Probably Jessica didn't even realize Mammaw's little house *had* an attic. If she did, she would have wheedled the location of the secret entrance out of Uncle Remy. "Where's that Chance hiding?" she'd ask with a smile. "We have something special for her!"

And even though Chance was Remy's favorite and he wouldn't mean to tell, he still would. Jessica was that good.

The oppressive heat drenched her in perspiration within moments, but Chance cherished the privacy, the thrill of having a secret lair. She'd passed lazy, stifling summer afternoons up there with a big jar of sweet tea, safe from Jessica and her gang, pawing through what Mammaw called the "treasures of a lifetime," even though it was mostly junk: old albums full of curling photos and faded snapshots—she always searched for photos of her mother—and mildew-scented baby clothes, boxes containing bowling trophies and military papers, and an old pink crib missing two spindles.

But then she spied the wooden crate.

It was shoved up under the eaves, way back behind cardboard boxes that once had held dog food or laundry detergent but were now crammed with school papers and yellowed doilies and handmade Christmas ornaments.

Attention—Fragile was stamped in red ink on the top and sides. *Manipuler avec attention.* A return address read: *Moulage Lombardi, 17 rue de la Huchette, Paris, France.*

Paris. Excitement surged through her.

She tried prying the crate open with her bare hands, ignoring the pinch of splinters. No luck. Then she rummaged around until she unearthed a metal wreath holder in the box of Christmas supplies. Shoved it into a tiny gap under the top of the crate and used all her weight to push. With a loud screech the rusty old nails gave way.

Chance lifted the plank.

Inside was a mix of sawdust and newspapers and crumpled-up scrap paper. She swept them aside and caught her breath at what was revealed: asleep right there in the box was the life-sized face of a lady. Her eyes were closed but she smiled, just barely, as though she knew a secret.

She probably used to be beautiful, Chance thought.

But the sculpture had been broken into half a dozen pieces, ugly jagged fissures running across her otherwise smooth white forehead and round cheeks.

What a shame. She would have looked pretty hanging on the wall. Maybe over the TV so they could look at her during commercials. Right next to the free calendar from the bakery in town, Remy's old army photo, and a blue, black, and green finger painting of a spider in its web Claire had made in second grade and Mammaw had framed and hung with pride.

Chance stroked the mask's fragments, feeling their curves and contours under her fingers. The pieces were heavy, made of thick plaster. On top they were slick with a satiny sheen, as though sealed with varnish. But when she ran the pads of her fingers along the edges of the broken bits, they felt gritty and raw, putting her in mind of the rough gray rocks that scraped at her bare feet when she climbed over them at the beach.

Chalky dust coated her hands when she pulled away. Chance rubbed the white powder between her thumb and fingers, wondering who the lady was and how she came to be in her Mammaw's attic, all the way from Paris.

Chance hesitated, then glanced over her shoulder to be sure she was alone. Of course she was; no one but her ever came up here. But still.

She squeezed her eyes shut, blew out a long breath to help her relax, then reached out both hands and laid them on the lady's broken face, waiting to see if the figure would talk to her.

This was exactly the sort of thing that made Chance weird, a misfit, and invited the wrath of Jessica—*No wonder your mommy killed herself and tried to take you with her!*

Chance *knew* that, but sometimes it worked. Sometimes when she had been hiding from her father in the little triangle formed by the couch shoved up against the wall, she would hold one of her mother's old handmade clay figurines—a little pig, an elephant, a harbor seal—close her eyes and hold her breath, and she could feel them move, come alive just for her. Right there in the palm of her hand.

And they would whisper to her: *You will be all right. You're not alone. You are a miracle.*

So now Chance closed her eyes, laid her hands upon the face, and concentrated. Chance was patient; she waited a long time. But the lady refused to speak. Maybe it only worked when it was something her mother had made, Chance thought. Maybe this was her mother's way of speaking to her from beyond the grave.

Quiet or no, Claire liked the face in the box. The lady looked so kind, so gentle. And she sure did look like she had something to say, but that she would take her own sweet time to say it. Chance wondered . . . maybe she remained mute because she was broken. What if she brought up some of the glue from her craft box? She could piece her back together.

Chance turned her attention to the papers surrounding the sculpture. One after the other, she smoothed them out against her thigh, sticky with sweat. She tried to make out the words, but although Mammaw insisted on speaking Cajun at home, Chance was still learning to read and write in French. But she sounded the words out as best she could. One paper seemed to be an old grocery list—she recognized a few words: *haricots verts, poireaux, pommes de terre.* A handful of scraps appeared to be phone messages, receipts, rough sketches of faces and hands. A list of measurements.

And then she spied the letter.

It wasn't much of a letter, as far as letters go. It had been torn in two, but Chance rifled through the box and found the second part; the halves were easy enough to match.

The calligraphy set it apart from the other scraps. The writing was slanted and dramatic, hard to read. The ink had faded to an earthy sepia tone, the paper yellowed, as though over the years the two hues had reached out to each another, trying to merge.

The heavy paper had been folded once and dated *26 février.* No year. No context, no address on the letter. Written in French, it said:

My love, my dearest,
Olivier has agreed to help. We can wait no longer. We must act. I will be waiting. Take nothing with you.

In a different handwriting—less sure, with ink splotches, as though written by someone unaccustomed to holding a pen—were the words:

He will never let me go alive.

Chance turned the paper over, then emptied the wooden crate searching for more. But that was all there was. Her hands shook as she reread the letter, sounding out the words. It was something special, she was sure.

Maybe this was it, Chance thought. Maybe this was the secret, the special purpose for which she had cheated death.

Tell me again, Mammaw. Tell me about my mama, when the car went off the road. Why didn't I die too?

The Lord's got something special planned for you, Chance. You mark my words. You're a miracle, sha—*don't you forget it.*

4

Claire handed the heavy wooden crate down to Remy. He set it on the floor at the foot of his bed.

"You don't have any idea where this is from?" Claire asked again, kneeling next to it.

Remy shook his head, wrinkled his nose. "Looks awful old to me."

"Hand me your letter opener, will you?" It was sitting on his desk, along with a half-finished model airplane. Remy didn't write letters, but he loved to receive them. Mammaw was big on old-fashioned letter writing, and her three sisters, numerous friends, and fellow church members made a point of sending Remy letters and postcards.

Claire used the brass knife to open the crate, lifting off the wooden plank. Excitement and nostalgia coursed through her in equal parts. She pushed aside the sawdust and random papers used as packing material.

The face was nestled there, just as she remembered. Broken. Gobs of yellowing glue and some old Scotch tape held a few of the shards together, highlighting rather than lessening the effect of her cruel disfigurement.

Still, she was beautiful in her own way. Forever asleep.

"Who is that?" Remy asked.

Claire shook her head. "I have no idea."

She picked up the strange old note.

He will never let me go alive.

Where in the world had this crate come from? Her family wasn't the type to receive packages from Paris.

Claire had never asked Mammaw about it as a girl. For one thing, she thought she might get in trouble for being up in the attic at all, let alone poking her nose into other people's packages. Mammaw didn't cotton to nosy. Chance knew very few things with certainty, but she knew this: she had to be a Good Girl or she would have to go back and live with her father. She could still hear Jessica's singsong voice as she taunted, "Your days here are numbered, Chance. Your mama tried to kill you, and your daddy gonna *whup* you."

For another thing, the sculpture had felt . . . private. Special. Chance had gotten in the habit of slipping up to the attic to speak to the face when feelings of loneliness threatened to inundate her. The mask became her imaginary friend, a confidante for a friendless little girl, and though it remained stubbornly mute, Chance told her about her problems, her worries—and her dreams. The face listened even in those miserable days of adolescence when myriad nameless fears and insecurities pulled her down into the mire and Chance came close to wishing she *had* died in that car accident.

But when Claire went off to college and reinvented herself in Chicago, she had pushed the sculpture to the dusty recesses of her memory.

"You want me to fry up some fish and hush puppies for supper tonight?" Remy asked.

"Oh, sure. Thanks, Remy. I'll help you with supper when it's time."

After closing up the crate again, she drank two full glasses of water and stepped under a cold spray in the shower, scrubbing herself with a bar of nice lemon verbena soap she'd brought with her from Chicago; the strong lye soap Mammaw insisted on buying stripped her skin raw.

Freshly showered and dressed in her coolest summer shift, she joined Mammaw in her bedroom. Remy sat beside her, watching in silence as Mammaw painstakingly scribbled final notes to friends and relatives, her skeletal hand moving slowly and shakily—but determinedly—across the thick white pages.

"Mammaw," Claire asked after her grandmother had addressed an envelope, sealed it, and handed it to Remy to apply stamps and mail. "Up in the attic I found a crate from Paris with a broken sculpture inside. Do you remember it? Where is it from?"

" 'Course I remember. My father sent that back

from Paris when he was there in World War II. I told you: he went there to kick the Nazis out."

"It's a beautiful sculpture. It's sort of . . . haunting."

Mammaw nodded. "My mama said it about brought her to tears when she opened that package and found it broke. But she kept it anyway, said as long as her Jerry come back from the war in one piece, that was good enough for her. Maybe you can get it fixed, you like it so much."

"I could look into it," Claire said, though it was clear the mask was too far gone; there was no way to repair it without the scars showing. Her clumsy childish attempts at repairing it had only made the situation worse. "What about the strange note that was with it, something saying, 'He will never let me go alive'?"

"I don't know nothin' 'bout no note," said Mammaw. "But let me tell you, your mama liked that mask too. She used to ask about it. She always wanted to be an artist, makin' things like that. Oooh, she had some dreams, that girl."

"I remember the little animals she made. Too bad we don't have them anymore."

Claire's father had smashed the clay figures in a rage one day not long before Child Protective Services placed Chance with Mammaw and Remy. She remembered walking into her room and feeling the crunch of dried clay under foot, only then realizing they were her mother's creations, destroyed. She had knelt right there and sobbed, the shards digging into her knees and the palms of her hands, making them bleed. Those little animals were all she had from her mother.

"So you have no idea who the woman is? Who the model was for that mask?"

Mammaw shook her head. " 'Fraid not . . . If you want to know that, maybe you should go to Paris and find where she comes from."

Claire laughed.

"I'm serious." Mammaw's eyes lit up, her hand, the tissue-thin skin stretched taut over her bones, squeezing Claire's with surprising strength. "*Do it, sha.* Find that face, and you will find a secret!"

Claire smiled again, wondering whether Mammaw had "gone 'round the bend" just a tad, as Jessica had suggested over the phone. What was she going on about?

"I'm not about to run off to *Paris,* Mammaw. I just got here so I could take care of *you,* remember? Besides, since when do we travel in this family?"

"We don't go off to fancy Chicago colleges in this family either, but that didn't stop you."

"True."

And the truth was, from time to time when working late at night in her office in Chicago, Claire would find herself scrolling through travel Web sites. She imagined herself lounging on the beach in Bali, sitting in a trattoria in Italy, hiking along the coast of Scotland. But mostly she fantasized about flying to Paris, the famous City of Light. It was a romantic notion that embarrassed her. Claire had worked doggedly to escape her hometown, then studied hard at college, and then landed a good job. Those things were useful.

Going to Paris wasn't useful.

Sometimes she would go so far as to book flights only to cancel them the next day. As far as she could remember, Claire's people left the country only in uniform: two cousins had served in Iraq, another in the Gulf War, Uncle Remy had gone to Vietnam, and her great-grandfather had fought in World War II.

Don't get too big for your britches, Chance Broussard.

Her sensible side always won out over any imaginary vacations to Paris.

Besides, inevitably she would get a call: Uncle Remy was sick and the hospital was demanding payment; her father needed bail money and to hire a decent lawyer; cousin Jimmy's truck had broken down again. So Claire kept her head down and worked long hours and saved her money. Family had supported her all her life. She might have abandoned them for college and city life, but the least she could do was to come through for them when times were hard.

Remy was playing a video game on the TV in the main room while Mammaw continued writing her letters in bed.

Claire curled up on the couch alongside Remy. Mammaw had been talking nonsense; Claire wasn't going to fly to Paris. Of *all* the things to contemplate. She needed direction in her life, not a wild-goose chase. Still . . . it wouldn't hurt to do a little digging.

The house didn't have Internet, so she used her phone to search for the address she'd taken off the crate: *Moulage Lombardi, 17 rue de la Huchette, Paris, France.*

Their name popped up at the top of the list. Disbelief and excitement coursed through her. How were they still in business after all this time?

Their Web site was simple and amateurish; several of the links didn't work. And Claire disliked doing research on her phone's tiny screen. But she read: *The Lombardi family has surpassed in the mold-making and casting business since 1871. Also at our location we include extensive inventory of traditional death masks, friezes, busts, full-sized statues, and other reproductions. Commissioned work available upon request.*

She pulled up a map of Paris and found rue de la Huchette in the Latin Quarter, Left Bank, fifth arrondissement, not far from the famous Cathedral of Notre Dame.

Scrolling through their extensive inventory of famous historical figures and mythological creatures, Claire finally found the photograph she was looking for: the porcelain white face of a young woman with closed eyes, apple cheeks, hair in twists at either side of her head, a secret smile on her face.

It was a shock to see her whole, unbroken. She was beautiful.

According to the attribution on the Web site, the piece was known as *L'Inconnue de la Seine*— the Unknown Woman of the Seine.

That was it. There was nothing more about who she was or where she came from. Intrigued, Claire searched the Internet for *"L'Inconnue de la Seine."* She found several references to an unknown woman who was found, drowned, near the quai du Louvre on the banks of the Seine sometime in the late 1890s. But no one seemed to know who she was.

Of all the ways to kill oneself. Claire shivered. She would take just about any form of death over drowning.

"Chance?" Mammaw called out.

"Coming." Claire went to the bedroom to see what Mammaw needed.

"I want you to write something down," Mammaw said, passing her a pad of paper and pen.

"All set," said Claire, perching on the side of the bed, pen at the ready, like a secretary.

"Gumbo, catfish court buillon, oyster po'boys, alligator chili, hush puppies, collard greens, fried pickles and okra, and the finest sweet tea and plenty of diet Dr Pepper and beer."

"Remy's frying fish tonight, but . . . I take it you're hungry?"

Mammaw laughed. "No, 'course not. This is for my memorial service. Cream cheese pecan pound cake and yammy cake and pralines for dessert. I want there to be food for *days*." Mammaw had grown up dirt-poor; she always worried about there being enough to eat. "Hank Williams and zydeco on the sound track. Only modern music I want is Garth Brooks singing 'Friends in Low Places.' I do like that song—and I surely do have me some friends in low places, don't I, *sha*?"

"Yes, Mammaw," Claire said, her voice tight. "You surely do."

"And don't cry—you hear me, *sha*? I'm ready."

"Yes, ma'am." Claire said.

But her disobedient mind replied, silently: *Don't leave me, Mammaw. What will I do without you? Who will I be?*

5

The next week passed quickly. Roofers took care of the hole in the roof, Remy cooked Mammaw's favorite foods, and Claire sat with her grandmother for hours on end, listening to her long, convoluted stories—which, Claire knew from experience, were half fiction, often inspired by family legends or tabloid news stories she'd filed away in her mind. Mammaw spoke of being a teenager in the 1950s, of sock hops and cruising down their tiny Main Street in a convertible; she claimed her great-uncle was an FBI agent who rounded up stills during Prohibition and wound up arresting his own brother to the dismay of their mother; and she said that she had once waited on Lucille Ball at a diner, that the star had left a twenty-dollar tip and a personal invitation to visit her in Hollywood.

Mammaw's sisters, extended relatives, friends and neighbors and church members streamed in and out of the small bungalow, bringing noodle casseroles and fresh-caught fish and paper plates folding under the weight of homemade pecan pie and pralines.

Claire had made gumbo the day after she'd arrived, but Mammaw requested it again. She bought fresh okra down at the Piggly Wiggly and got a pound of shrimp from Uncle Rudy. Mammaw kept a big mason jar of ground sassafras leaves on the shelf to use for the traditional gumbo filé spice; she didn't trust store-bought seasonings.

The homey aroma of Cajun spices wafted through the small house as the gumbo simmered on the stove. Another round of visitors had just left, leaving behind a green bean casserole and lemon pound cake. If she'd had an appetite, Claire thought, she would have put on five pounds by now. But, strangely for her, she didn't seem to have much interest in food lately.

"What's wrong with you, *sha*?" Mammaw asked, her still-keen eyes fixing on Claire. "You tellin' me you gave up your man and your fancy job in Chicago? What you gonna do now?"

"I don't know. I honestly don't know."

"Even as a child you were always so intent on doin' the right thing, not making mistakes." Mammaw patted her hand. "I reckon that's on account o' your pa, and losin' your mama so early. But listen to me: you hadn't ought to be so skeered all the time, *sha*."

Claire gave her a sad smile. "I'm not scared so much as . . . *lost*, Mammaw."

"You should go to Paris—that's what. Try to find where that mask come from. Your mama always wondered about that sculpture too. Must run in the family."

Claire smiled and shook her head. "So you're

saying I should track down the source of the sculpture in Paris, and then what?"

"*Oooh,* maybe you find a secret."

"What kind of secret?"

"Go to Paris, *sha,*" her grandmother encouraged. "This is important. Go and find the face. Promise me this."

"Mammaw, seriously, what are you talking about?"

There was a long pause. Finally, Mammaw replied, "I'll tell you one thing: that gumbo smells just about ready for my homemade filé." She coughed and fell back into the pillows. A bleak look came into her eyes. "You go tend to the gumbo, and then when you come back, maybe I tell you something important."

"Mammaw, are you all right?"

"Just go on now, *sha.*"

Claire went to check the stew bubbling on the stove, added several shakes of sassafras leaves, stirred thoroughly to keep it from sticking, and by the time she returned to the bedroom it was only to discover that Mammaw had slipped away.

She was gone.

Just like that.

Claire sank to the side of the bed. Broken-hearted. Bereft. She felt like an orphan standing barefoot on a frigid stone street, which was as absurd as it was untrue: she was an adult, after all. And she still had her father, however lacking he was as a parental figure. Still. Mammaw had been her touchstone, her teacher, her refuge, and her friend.

What now?

First there were things to attend to: the memorial service, helping Remy to figure out his situation, cleaning out Mammaw's things. Cousin Jessica had been named as executor of the will, since she was local and was a bookkeeper, good with numbers. But then what?

The thought of returning to Chicago filled Claire with a tight knot in her gut; she didn't want to go back to Sean and pretend she was happy, or try to explain to him—or to everyone else, much less *herself*—why her perfect life didn't feel perfect.

Staying in Plaquemines Parish, especially now without Mammaw, was untenable. Sean had been right: she had fought too long and hard to get out, and Claire no longer belonged here. But where *did* she belong?

Promise me you'll go to Paris, sha. *Go and find that face—she'll tell you a secret!*

Paris.

The idea seized Claire's imagination in a way that proved tough to shake. While she cleaned out, gave away, and packaged up Mammaw's belongings—attending to the grim, quotidian details of death—Claire alternated between sobbing over Mammaw's irrevocable loss, commiserating with Remy, and daydreaming about escaping to Paris. Maybe rediscovering the mask in the attic had been some sort of sign meant to point her in the right direction.

It was a fanciful notion, but . . . what if?

Once things were settled here, what if Claire went to Paris to find the origin of *L'Inconnue*? What if she were to stroll the cobblestone streets and eat croissants and sip wine and be serenaded by strolling musicians? Or whatever the Parisian equivalent of that was—perhaps she had seen that photo when looking at Spain or Italy. But still.

Paris sounded like an awfully good idea.

So why did it make her want to cry?

6

SABINE

1897

Paris leaves Sabine breathless. Within an hour of her arrival at the train station, Gare Montparnasse, she has several close calls with the enormous streetcars clattering down the tracks, and when she pauses to gawk at the unbelievably tall buildings—look at the Eiffel Tower!—she is plowed into by the hordes of people crowding the sidewalks, lucky souls with jobs and families and places to go, striding along with confidence.

She feels like a foreigner in this great capital city, though she is as French as the Parisians. The thought consoles her.

Sabine left her home in the countryside with the clothes on her back and a very few personal items packed in her pillowcase; her provisions have been reduced to a hunk of bread, a wedge of hard cheese, and three slightly bruised apples. And most important of all: the address of her cousin Toinette Morant, who rents a basement room at 27 rue des Trois Portes.

Only through the kind intervention of an old woman standing outside a dress shop does Sabine locate the apartment. When she bangs on the door, no one answers, so she sits on the stoop and waits, falling asleep slumped up against the stone wall. She is roused by the raucous voices of two young women: Toinette and her roommate, Honorine. They are wearing wet aprons, their hair damp with sweat and ringlets hanging down about their collars. Sabine knows they are laundresses, that they work at La Blanchisserie Camboise across the Seine.

They are excited to welcome her.

"Come on in to the palace," says Toinette, and Honorine laughs.

Their room is just that: a single room, with one bed, a small trunk that doubles as a side table for an oil lamp, a pitcher and a bowl, along with a slop bucket and a small chest. Clothes hang from hooks on the wall. The only natural light comes from small rectangular windows near the ceiling, through which they can see the legs and skirts of passersby.

Toinette and Honorine plop down on the bed, breathing long sighs of exhaustion. Sabine worries their wet clothes will dampen the bed, but they don't seem to care, so she holds her tongue, sitting erect on a small wooden stool.

"So, tell me everything!" says Toinette. "How is Tante Thérèse?"

Sabine tells her cousin the family gossip and news from the village, then hands her letters from her little sister and her aunt, along with a package containing a small pear tart, which elicits cries of delight.

"You can sleep on our floor for a few nights," says Toinette, "but you must take care the land-lord does not see you, or he'll charge us extra. He is a short, bald man with a red nose and a huge belly. You can't miss him."

Honorine has fallen asleep and is snoring softly until Toinette nudges her. "Come, let's go get some soup for dinner. And then we'll have tart for dessert!"

Honorine grunts but sits up, stretching her arms over her head and letting out a great yawn like a lion.

"I don't have—" Sabine begins, blushing. She has almost no coin left, having spent most of her money on the train ride.

"I will treat," says Toinette. "You are my little cousin, so I treat! You will pay me back when you start to make money. Do you have any prospects? Where do you hope to work?"

"I thought perhaps I could find employment in a nice house," says Sabine as they leave the little apartment and walk down the street.

"I don't think you'll have much luck finding a position as a housemaid," says Toinette, her voice matter-of-fact but kind. "You have no references."

"And not with that face," says Honorine with a husky chuckle. "The gentlemen would be all over you. Their ladies don't like that."

Sabine isn't sure what Honorine means by "with that face." She has a small mirror, no bigger than the palm of her hand, and has studied the planes and hollows of her countenance. She is a girl, nothing more. Back in her village, the horse trainer once told her she was beautiful. But that was because he was hoping for a kiss.

A shiny black carriage rushes by and Sabine rears back.

Honorine chuckles and nudges her lightly on the arm. "I was the same as you, scared of my own shadow when I first came to Paris. But you'll get used to it. The fiacres are carriages for hire; if you have money they will take you anywhere you want to go."

"Who wastes money on a carriage ride?" scoffs Toinette.

"I would, if I had it," says Honorine, letting out a long sigh. "I do *tire* so of walking."

"I am happy to work, but I have no skills," Sabine says. "Could I be a laundress with you?"

"The proprietor isn't hiring at the moment—I already asked," says Toinette.

On the sidewalk, they approach a small cart that holds two steaming vats tended by an old man. He serves them cabbage soup in wooden bowls, and they sit on a nearby stoop to eat. Toinette is dainty, even with the clumsy wooden spoon, but Honorine slurps her soup with gusto, drinking straight from the bowl and wiping her mouth on her sleeve.

Sabine copies Toinette's manners.

"Can you sew?" asks Honorine. "I hear they're looking for seamstresses at La Maison de Louise."

"Not very well," says Sabine.

"What did you do before?"

"My stepfather had a small farm and a wood-working studio. I helped him with the wood sometimes, but mostly I tended the animals. But after my mother died we had to sell everything."

"Sounds like you've got two choices," says Honorine. "Spread your legs or be an artist's model. Both, more like."

Sabine tries not to let the shock show on her face.

Toinette elbows Honorine. "Stop it—you're scaring her."

Honorine shrugs, collects their bowls and spoons, and brings them back to the old man. She says something to make him laugh. He doles out a half ladle more of soup, which she downs in a single gulp. Then he dunks their bowls in a barrel of wash water, swishes some suds around, rinses them, and sets them on stacks to dry.

"It's not such a bad idea, actually," says Toinette. "You're thin, but with that face you might get a commission as a *modèle de profession*."

"What does an artist's model do?" Sabine asks.

"It's easy," says Honorine with a sigh as she rejoins them on the stoop. "All you have to do is lie there on a divan while people sketch you. Sometimes you have to be naked, though, and let them see *everything*."

Another elbow from Toinette, eliciting another chuckle from Honorine.

Sabine can feel her cheeks redden. It's not as though she knows nothing of such things; the horse trainer taught her more than her mother would have approved of. He had the gentlest voice Sabine had ever heard, and when he held out his hand, she took it and walked with him into the woods. He said sweet things and made her feel safe; his hands left a trail of heat the length of her body.

59

"How would I become an artist's model?" she asks.

"There is a square in Pigalle where the artists go to select their models," says Toinette. "I'll draw you a map."

"It is a long walk," says Honorine, shaking her head. "Too bad you don't have coin for the fiacre!"

That night, they light the lamp and wash their armpits and between their legs, then lie down, and Honorine and Toinette tell stories of their adventures in Paris: of the soldier who took Honorine to see the Lumière brothers' moving-picture show, and Toinette's special friend who once met her outside the washhouse with a beautiful rose made of marzipan. They spoke of the city's wonders: the zoological gardens and kaleidoscopes and a giant mechanical elephant that walked right down the Champs-Élysées.

The tile floor is cold and hard. Toinette hands her a scratchy wool blanket, and Sabine is so exhausted she sleeps without dreaming, her head propped on a pillow of her own bunched skirts.

The next day Toinette and Honorine rise early and rush off to work, and Sabine breaks her fast with an apple and the last bit of cheese wrapped in burlap from her pillowcase.

She must find employment, but first she goes to light candles for her mother and brother at the great Cathédrale de Notre Dame de Paris. She dips her fingers in the basin of cool holy water, crosses herself and genuflects, then enters. Great round windows look like huge flowers made of brilliant colored glass; they are so dazzling, she forgets herself for a moment, forgets her hunger and her fear.

Heaven must look like this, she thinks. A paradise of sparkling color.

Sabine approaches a small side altar with a statue of the Virgin and child, dedicated to Notre Dame de Paris—Our Lady of Paris. The Virgin is surrounded by fresh bouquets of snowy-white flowers, symbols of her purity, but Sabine is drawn to the expression on her face. It is a study in conflicting emotions: tranquil yet fearful, as though the young mother is overjoyed to hold her son but troubled by the ordeal she knows will come.

Sabine drops one of her few remaining coins in the wooden offerings box and lights two white candles, whispering her prayers.

Back when her mother and brother were alive, Sabine had a family, a home. Now she is adrift. She knows it is wrong to question God's plan, but many times she wonders why she was not taken along with them. She ought not allow herself to think this way, but in her heart Sabine wishes she had sickened and died alongside the two people she loved most in this world.

In the privacy of the confessional she admits this to the priest, begs for penance, for forgiveness.

And then she tells him of her plans. He is young and idealistic, and warns Sabine that to remain a decent woman she must beware of the artists flooding the city of Paris.

"The artistic temperament is licentious and unstable, *ma fille*. To protect your virtue, you must stay far away from their world. Especially be wary of the bohemian lifestyle. Trust in the *Seigneur, ma fille*. The Lord will provide."

So instead of heading to the square in Pigalle, Sabine wanders the hard stone streets in hopes of finding a different kind of job. Decent employment.

She speaks to a tired, apron-clad woman outside the Gaullier Frères workshop. But though they are seeking *brunisseuses*—silver burnishers— each woman must supply her own tools to grind the silver into the metal. And unless she has experience, there is a three-month trial period with no pay to learn the trade. Sabine thanks the woman and leaves. How could she survive for three months with no pay?

She inquires at a tavern, but the women are coarse and loud and half dressed; they laugh great guffaws with their painted mouths wide. They remind her of Honorine but lack her kindness, and they shoo her away, telling her to go back to the countryside and marry a nice widower.

Sabine attended school until the sixth grade and

worked hard to learn her letters. But she has no tools, no training, no skills. There seems to be nothing for her.

Her bread and cheese long gone, hunger begins to claw at her belly. She rests on a bench in the Jardin du Luxembourg, watching two well-dressed little boys playing with sailboats in a large shallow pool. The aroma of crêpes from a nearby cart wafts over to her, making her feel faint. She had tried one once, at a Christmas party in her village. The memory tortures her; she closes her eyes, practically tasting the strawberries and sweet cream, the melted chocolate or fruit confiture wrapped in a luscious, paper-thin pancake.

"May I treat you to a crêpe, mademoiselle?"

Sabine opens her eyes. The man is older than her stepfather, dressed in a nice suit, with a trim gray beard and a tall hat and a cane with a silver handle hanging on his forearm.

With a face like that, she remembers Honorine saying.

"*Non, merci, monsieur,*" she says with a quick shake of her head. Pulling her knitted shawl more closely around her shoulders, she scuttles off toward the relative safety of Toinette's apartment.

7

Paris

Claire climbed the narrow stairwell. Aged wooden treads, worn smooth and shiny by the soles of countless feet over the years, emitted a creaking protest with each tentative step.

She felt like an intruder. It didn't help that she was being watched by dozens of unseeing eyes.

One stairwell wall was crowded with smooth white faces, bas-relief sculptures of Roman gods, Renaissance princesses, Napoléon and Beethoven and Baudelaire. Some appeared to be sleeping while others stared out at the world, their expressions blank.

Claire's gaze slipped from one impassive mask to the next, but she didn't find the face she was searching for.

She knew she was in the right place: 17 rue de la Huchette, a narrow street on the Left Bank, just a short walk from the Cathedral of Notre Dame. An elaborately carved corbel above the door declared: *Moulage de la Famille Lombardi, depuis 1871.*

Lombardi Family Mold-Makers, since 1871. Life-sized statues flanked the entrance like hushed sentinels: a few made of poured white plaster, others of resin or concrete, some treated with glazes and colored patinas.

There they stood, out on the street. Unsecured and unattended.

Back home, Claire thought, some good old boy would long since have lifted one into his truck, perhaps wrapped it in a football jersey (*Ragin' Cajuns!*), and taken it for a joyride. And how long would such statues have lasted out on the street like that in Chicago? At the very least, they would by now be sporting spray-painted mustaches or . . . worse.

Dear Uncle Remy, she composed in her head. She had promised Remy two letters a week, plus postcards, and though Claire was rarely at a loss for words, fulfilling her promise to write to him every few days was a challenge. Between the jet lag and the strange foreign ways, it had taken her the better part of a day just to figure out where to buy stamps—*timbres*—not to mention how many to affix to the envelopes (letters versus postcards; should she use the thin, old-fashioned blue airmail paper or write on the thick parchment paper she'd nabbed from Mammaw's stash?) to persuade the French postal authorities to fly her correspondence all the way back to Plaquemines Parish.

Dear Uncle Remy,
Remember that time Wade Penning stole the plastic statue of Hank's Howdy Hippo

from the roof of Hank's Diner, then hoisted it to the top of the water tower? Here in Paris, he'd have to settle for a casting of a Greek goddess. And they look to be a dang sight heavier, I tell you what.

A hand-lettered sign on the front door of the Lombardi atelier stated:

Bienvenue,
S'il vous plait montez au premier étage.
Please to rise to first floor.

Claire was pretty sure it meant visitors should climb to what Americans think of as the *second* floor. Claire had noted that in the travel guide she'd read on the plane. It had been a long flight, during which she'd committed to memory numerous helpful hints: In France the first floor is the *rez-de-chaussée*, and up one flight is *le premier étage*. Always greet strangers as "Monsieur" and "Madame." Buy a metro pass; it's cheaper and easier to get around the city that way. Watch out for pickpockets. Many stores are closed on Sundays and in the middle of the day for lunch or *la sieste*.

Also: *Don't go to Paris in August.* She'd already flouted that one.

Claire paused halfway up the stairs, next to a mask of Frédéric Chopin.

Should I continue?

But Chopin wasn't talking.

Because I'm just saying, I could probably find something else to do in Paris. I've got my list of must-sees burning a hole in my pocket.

Chopin remained poker-faced.

Claire wasn't easily intimidated. It was just that . . . she didn't want to be disappointed. What if she had come to Paris at the urging of an old woman who was no longer entirely in touch with reality? What if there *was* no secret to discover, no delicious narrative to unfurl? Nothing at all remarkable about a seemingly mysterious note and a sculpture hidden in a dusty old wooden crate in the attic? What if, as Sean had told her, she was acting irrationally due to grief over her *pauvre* Mammaw?

Still, it wasn't as though she was intent on losing herself in a haze of alcohol or drugs. Claire had gone to Paris for a vacation, like millions of other tourists. She deserved a little rest, a little adventure, didn't she? What was so crazy about that?

Her thoughts were interrupted by a commotion at the top of the steps.

Two men arguing: one in an American accent, the other in strongly French-inflected English. An occasional piping contribution of an American woman. Then a middle-aged couple—the man in cargo shorts, a baseball cap, and a Yankees T-shirt;

the woman in a cardigan and capris—stormed down the narrow stairwell.

Claire flattened herself against the sculpture-free wall to let them pass.

"Hope you speak French," the man grumbled to Claire. "Otherwise, don't bother."

"I do, actually. Why?" asked Claire. "Everything okay?"

"So rude!" the woman said with a shrug. "I was told everyone in Paris spoke English."

Claire opened her mouth to reply, but the man beat her to it.

"The travel agent only said that so you'd buy the tickets," the man said, then nodded toward the top of the stairs. "Wouldn't want to give that ass—pardon my French, that *jerk*—my hard-earned money anyway. Don't care how historic his business is. A little high and mighty, considering he's not even an actual sculptor. He lifts molds from things—how hard can that be?"

"Maybe you'll have better luck since you speak French," the woman said. "Do you happen to know how to get to the catacombs? I hear they're not to be missed."

Claire looked up the location on her phone, then pointed it out on the couple's tourist map and watched as they continued down the stairs and out the front door. Wondering one more time: should she follow?

More voices overhead. The argument now was

in rapid-fire French, between a man and a woman.

"Keep these tourists out of my studio!" said the man.

"You want to make money or not?" responded the woman, sounding so bored Claire could picture her Gallic shrug. "Make up your mind, Armand. You want to stay in business, then you need to speak English with the customers or hire someone else to do it. And stop scaring the tourists."

Claire made her decision and continued up the staircase.

This is for you, Mammaw.

The stairs opened directly onto the second-floor showroom. Bright afternoon sunshine pooled on the landing, streaming in from skylights overhead.

Claire blinked, feeling like a stage actress stepping into a spotlight.

The man and woman wore white smocks and stood beside a large worktable. Engrossed in their argument, they didn't seem to notice Claire. She took the opportunity to assess her surroundings.

A bank of interior windows overlooked a workshop, separating it from the showroom. The walls were jammed with hanging sculptures or lined with deep, crude wooden shelves on which rested urns, friezes, corbels, and decorative plates. Suspended from the ceiling were busts of beautiful young women and bearded old men, of Roman-looking warriors and grandes dames.

Life-sized statues filled the corners and stood in the center of the room.

Everything—the sculptures, the shelves, the windowsills—was covered in a thick veil of plaster dust. Footsteps on the wide-plank wood floors formed a loop around the showroom, like a path in a snowy wood. Several large buckets of milky water sat by a back door near a broom and dustpan that seemed not to get much use.

Claire searched the walls for the sculpture she sought. The face she had found in Mammaw's attic, the face she had entrusted with her childish dreams and burdened with her adolescent fears. But there were too many: an army of pristine white masks.

The argument was ratcheting up. The man's large, plaster-covered hands gestured as he ranted, white doves swooping and diving.

The woman leaned against the worktable, arms crossed over her chest, watching him with one eyebrow raised, as impassive as the sculptures surrounding them. She was slim, fortyish, with a pleasant round face and honey-colored hair cut short in a chic yet practical bob. A rather incongruous tattoo peeked out from under the collar of her smock—some sort of barbed vine.

The man—Armand?—could have been any-where from his early thirties to late forties. His dark, wild hair was liberally sprinkled with plaster dust, reminding Claire of the powdered wigs aristocrats wore to the court of Louis XVI and Marie Antoinette.

The guidebook had also explained that in France there is no slipping into shops unseen, no browsing unannounced. Patron and shopkeeper trade *bonjours*, no matter how busy they are, no matter how much one might wish to fly under the radar and find a particular item, a certain sculpture, all by her lonesome.

So when another minute passed and the couple still failed to notice her, Claire spoke up:

"*Bonjour messieurs, dames.*"

The couple, startled, looked up from their intense discussion.

"*Bonjour, madame,*" the woman said with a nod.

"I apologize for interrupting," Claire continued in French.

They studied her, intrigued by her Cajun accent, Claire thought.

That is, the *woman* seemed intrigued. The man looked irritated. Claire decided it was his typical demeanor. Intense blue eyes were nestled in a slightly off-kilter face whose broad planes appeared, somehow, to have been broken and rearranged. The effect was intriguing but unsettling.

"May we help you?" the woman asked, unsmiling but not unfriendly.

"I hope so," said Claire. She reached into her leather bag, fumbled for a moment, then fished out her phone and called up the digital photo she had taken in Remy's bedroom last week. "I'm researching a specific piece, the mask of a young woman that I believe came from this atelier. Do you recognize this sculpture?"

They glanced at the photo.

The man rolled his eyes, threw up his hands, muttered something in French—Claire assumed he was swearing, though she did not recognize the words—and retreated to the workshop behind the windowed wall.

He slammed the door. A sign read: *Défense d'entrer. Privé.*

Private, no admittance.

"*Je suis désolée,*" the woman apologized. "Pay him no attention. My cousin is always like this. But I don't speak English, so he is stuck dealing with the tourists. Can you imagine? But you speak French very well, *n'est-ce pas?*"

"A little," said Claire, though she in fact was nearly fluent. But no matter how much she attempted to mimic the formal French she had studied in school, the inflections and vocabulary of the Cajun dialect she had learned as a girl stuck to her like white on rice.

"Over there," said the woman, gesturing toward the wall on the opposite side of the shop. "The mask you are looking for is over there, right under Beethoven."

"Over here?"

Claire had been hoping (against hope) her mask was special, something rare and fascinating.

But now, in a studio that smelled of plaster dust and milky water, old wood and sunshine—after enduring the death of her grandmother and the excruciating memorial service, the explanations to friends and family and the tedious flight to Paris and the unsuitable rental apartment—after all of that, the face of her childhood confidante could be found hanging "over there, right under Beethoven."

Claire approached the wall. And spotted her.

Eyes closed as though sleeping. Her lips curled in a slight but knowing smile, at odds with the innocence of her young countenance. Her hair worn in twists on either side of her apple cheeks, an old-fashioned style even for the time.

A neatly lettered label next to the mask read: *L'Inconnue de la Seine, 1898.* The Unknown Woman of the Seine, 1898.

Claire waited. Willing the visage to speak to her, offer comfort in some way she couldn't verbalize.

But *L'Inconnue* remained as cold and mute as Chopin's mask on the stairs, as uncommunicative as Beethoven and the horde of goddesses and warriors crowding the Lombardi atelier.

She remained *inconnue*. Unknown. She revealed no secrets.

So what in the Sam Hill am I doing here, Mammaw?

8

Y ou want it or not?"
Claire jumped at the man's voice.

She turned to find Armand covered in even more powder, a sculpture come to life. Standing close behind her, almost too close, and staring at her as though trying to figure her out. He spoke in English, but she responded in French.

"Oh! *Non, non, merci.* I . . . I already own one."

"*Déjà*? Already? Then what do you want?"

More tourists appeared at the top of the stairs. They were speaking in British accents, chuckling and chattering excitedly. A look of barely restrained impatience registered on Armand's face, and he swore again under his breath.

The tourists paused at the top of the stairs, looking around, falling silent, as if preparing to flee at the sight of his scowling countenance.

They must be feeling what she had, Claire thought: that they were intruders in an artist's studio. An artist's studio in *Paris*. She thought about what the woman shopkeeper had said: the Famille Lombardi needed the tourist business to keep the place going.

Claire smiled at the newcomers and said in English, "Please come on in—feel free to look around."

The visitors looked relieved, thanked her, and began to peruse the shelves jammed with historical figures, the masks of artists and poets and composers.

In a low voice, Claire said to Armand, "You do realize you need a salesperson who speaks English if you want those tourist dollars."

He shrugged. "We had an American, but she quit."

"I can't imagine why."

"So sorry. I was on a phone call," said the other shopkeeper as she joined them, wiping her hands on a towel. She laughed softly, a husky, attractive sound. "What trouble are you causing now, Armand?"

"Buy the piece or not, it doesn't matter," he said with a shrug, and walked away.

The woman muttered something about Armand. Claire didn't quite catch what she said, but the meaning was obvious from her tone.

"Please let me introduce myself. I'm Giselle Bouvay. Don't mind Armand. He's always like this. Which is why we'll have to leave soon. The neighborhood has become so expensive; it's a tourist mecca."

"Shouldn't that be a good thing?"

"It would be if my cousin did not run them off, yes. But as it is, I think we cannot afford to stay."

"I'm sorry to hear that," said Claire. Across the room, the British tourists were oohing and aahing over a grouping of classical Roman friezes, seemingly engrossed in the inventory. "About this mask, I was wondering: can you tell me anything about the young woman who modeled for it?"

"Only that she is *L'Inconnue de la Seine*."

"The Unknown Woman of the Seine." Claire nodded. "I read that she drowned. But is there any more or . . . is that the extent of the story? Do you know who she was?"

"No one knows," Giselle said, letting out a weary sigh. "Many people come in here asking about her. No one knows anything about her, not really. Not even her name. Just that she drowned herself in the late 1890s."

"It's so sad."

"According to the legend, when she was brought to the morgue, a worker there thought she was so beautiful that he asked my great-grandfather, Jean-Baptiste Lombardi, to make a mask of her before she was buried."

"Is that a true story?"

She shrugged. "What is truth? It is the story that is told."

Claire nodded and studied the face hanging on the wall.

"We still have the original mold, and we pour dozens of faces every month. She is a bestseller, this *Inconnue*," Giselle continued. "It was a long time ago, but still . . . I do not understand why

76

anyone would want the face of a suicide on their wall. I suppose some people find it romantic. But in any case . . ." She trailed off as she glanced at the visitors, who were murmuring about the prices. "Whatever the tourists want, right?"

"Giselle, I don't mean to be presumptuous, but I'd be happy to help translate while I'm here, if you like."

"Really?" Giselle seemed startled but pleased. She glanced again at her cousin, hunched over a bust he was sanding in his workshop. *"C'est super.* That would be great, thank you. I am working on the books, so if anyone wants to buy anything, you can bring it to me and translate. Wonderful. We have one employee who can speak English well enough, but she is on maternity leave. And the other one quit two days ago. Obviously we'll need to hire someone new, but it is a serious business to hire an employee in France. Once you have them, you can't get rid of them."

"Why not?"

"There are laws that protect employees. It is very difficult to fire a worker, so you must be very sure before you hire anyone. Unless they quit, of course—which isn't that unusual with my cousin Armand . . . but, well, it isn't easy."

Claire smiled. "I'm happy to help."

Before heading over to chat with the tourists, she paused for another moment to take in the serene, barely smiling countenance of *L'Inconnue de la Seine*.

Her childhood confidante.

Claire helped the British tourists with their purchases—one couple bought two friezes for either side of their fireplace; another chose a bust of Beethoven; another a mask of a Renaissance-era woman who looked like a princess—and translated for Giselle as they worked out the details of shipping.

"I can't thank you enough for your help," Giselle said as the happy customers departed. "It really is an impossible situation."

"It's no problem. I was happy to help."

"Could I offer you something in exchange? Perhaps you would like to take *L'Inconnue* for a discount? I could give her to you for cost as a thank-you for your help."

"That's a lovely offer, but . . ." What would Claire do with a heavy plaster cast? She was traveling and had nowhere to mail it. Mammaw's house was the closest thing Claire had to a home address, but with Mammaw gone, her connection to Louisiana already seemed to be evaporating as surely as the morning mist over the delta. Uncle Remy was still there, of course, but even before she left, family members had begun to quarrel over how to divide the meager remains of Mammaw's humble life.

Claire loved them, but the family fights over money were depressingly predictable.

"But?" Giselle urged, bringing Claire back to the here and now.

"Sorry. It's just that I'm traveling and I don't exactly have a place to ship it. And I do have one already, though it's broken. I was just hoping to learn the story behind it."

"As I said, no one really knows the true story. In fact, the reason she sells so well may be because of the mystery, don't you think? After all, if we knew the truth, she would not be *inconnue*."

"I suppose that's true," said Claire.

Giselle hesitated, then added, "I could ask my cousin when he is in a better mood if he knows anything more about her. He has been working on the family estate, so he knows more about the history. And frankly he's a better listener—I tend to tune out when the old folks start talking."

"I would appreciate that," said Claire, though she wasn't particularly hopeful. She pulled out her business card, an old one from No-Miss Systems in Chicago, crossed out the old information, and wrote her cell phone number on the back.

"You are in computers?" Giselle asked.

"I used to be. I'm unemployed at the moment." She gestured to a rotating wire postcard holder displaying cards with images of the atelier and the crowded shelves of the Moulage Lombardi. "I wouldn't mind a few postcards, if I may."

"Mais bien sûr. Of course!"

Claire selected several and Giselle slipped them into a robin's egg blue paper bag emblazoned with the ornate Lombardi coat of arms: a roaring lion in the top left quadrant of a shield and a mermaidlike creature in the bottom right.

"Well . . . it was lovely to meet you, Giselle." Claire glanced at the interior windows that overlooked the work studio. Armand was busy working on a bust on the workbench, using what looked like dental tools to detail the facial features. The movement of the muscles in his back showed through his lab coat. "And please say good-bye from me to your cousin too. It was a pleasure."

Giselle laughed. "He's rarely a pleasure, but he is interesting. And talented. And he's family, so what can I say?"

"I know that feeling."

As Claire headed down the stairs, she fought the sting of tears at the back of her eyes.

It doesn't matter, she scolded herself. It had been foolish to think she could discover the story of the woman behind the mask by visiting this Parisian studio, let alone to imagine *L'Inconnue*'s life would somehow give direction to her own.

She turned down a narrow medieval-era stone street, filled with Greek and Middle Eastern restaurants, small cafés, and tacky souvenir shops.

Shake it off.

The idea that the strange old letter she had

found had anything to do with the mask, and that either the letter *or* the mask had anything to say about her future—or her past—was a child's fancy. Fed by an overactive imagination and the belief that Mammaw had a secret to tell. Stoked by too many hours alone with the broken mask in the sweltering attic, imagining it listening to her.

The harsh truth was that the face that had meant so much to her was a mass-produced plaster cast. And the letter was antique litter used as packing material, nothing more.

Here was another truth: Unearthing the mask in her grandmother's attic was not a sign. It was just one more souvenir, one more relic of a life long since passed. There was nothing magical about it, no more so than the pink nighties that reeked of mothballs or her grandfather's bowling trophies or any other random item that had been stuck up in the attic and forgotten.

So . . . where did she go from here?

9

SABINE

Sabine must find work.

Hunger gnaws at her belly, a pang so deep it cuts like a knife, making her double over at night. Still, it isn't the pain that bothers her as

81

much as the weakness, the inability to concentrate.

Toinette and Honorine have been generous, and the last thing Sabine ate—a boiled potato Toinette brought her yesterday—was thanks to them. But they work hard to feed themselves and allow her to sleep on their floor. Sabine cannot bring herself to take more from them. So she tells them she has already eaten, that another friend bought her dinner last night and shared breakfast with her this morning.

As she walks, she remembers what the young priest said: "You must help yourself, child. Beware the licentiousness of the artistic temperament."

But she is starving.

So she makes her way up rue de la Rochefoucauld to rue Pigalle. The streets are icy; every surface in the city seems frozen and unyielding, from the cobblestone streets to the limestone buildings, the metal railings and the cold stone park benches. It is so different from the softness of the countryside—pine needles and dirt paths and haylofts—that Sabine feels a longing for home, despite the unwelcome advances of her stepfather and the specter of death that swept cruelly through the village, a raging fever as its scythe.

As she nears the square, it looks like a street festival, or perhaps a crowded market. But no one comes to buy melons or birds. They are here to choose people. Women, mostly. But there are children too, and a few handsome broad-shouldered young men.

Sabine passes by a black-haired family whom she assumes is Italian, a pair of Gypsies bedecked in bright scarves and silver bangles, two young women in mantillas speaking a language that sounds vaguely familiar but that Sabine does not understand. They seem to be lounging but are also preening, smiling, and standing with their shoulders back; the women lift their chins and push out their chests as smartly dressed men slowly stroll by, looking them up and down.

Those must be the artists, Sabine realizes. They wear suits of varying quality, and many carry sketchbooks. A few seem as desperate as the motley assortment of would-be models, while others wear fine shiny shoes and appear well fed, their plump bellies encased in ornate brocade vests.

Some of the self-possessed, beautiful young women—and a few men—seem to know the artists; they call out to them by name, teasing and flirting, and are chosen immediately. Sabine watches and listens while they haggle over pay; the sums would buy a good dinner and a soft bed for the night.

Honorine and Toinette have assured Sabine she is beautiful, that an artist will be sure to choose her. Still, Sabine is too shy to strut in front of these men, to coax and entice. She is hungry, so very hungry, but the spectacle makes her feel like a heifer on display, like a horse at the fair. Will they ask to inspect her teeth?

Weariness settles over her; she sways on her feet and leans back against a stone wall. Closes her eyes. Imagines food she has seen in the windows as she walks the streets of Paris: pyramids of pastel *macarons*, cream puffs and éclairs and glistening butter croissants, savory quiche made of eggs and cheese. Before the window of the Chocolatière Élise she stood for several minutes studying a tiny Eiffel Tower entirely constructed of delicate strands of chocolate, studded with candied cherries and marzipan. Sabine thinks about the roast pigeon her mother used to make for special dinners, and her succulent stew of leeks and carrots and rabbit.

Her mouth waters. Is there anything in this world more luscious, more perfect than the scent of roasting meat or a stew bubbling on the stove?

"*Bonjour, mademoiselle.* Are you quite all right?"

She opens her eyes. A tall, stocky, bearded man with sandy hair stands in front of her. His features are too coarse to be considered handsome, but he is smiling, and his suit appears to be a fine, soft wool. He wears a silk scarf around his neck and carries an aroma of tobacco and something sweet, like fruit and cloves.

"*Mademoiselle?*"

Sabine realizes she is staring. Remembers she has a job to do. Rouses herself.

"*Bonjour, monsieur*," she says as she straightens and thrusts her shoulders back, allowing her hair to stream down her back, the way Honorine has shown her. "Please forgive me. I was daydreaming."

"What is your name, mademoiselle?"

"Sabine Moreau."

"I am Monsieur Maurice Desmarais. And pray tell, what dreams prompted such a delicious smile upon your lips?"

Shall she tell him the truth? That she was dreaming of a pyramid of *macarons*, of roast squab?

Mustn't seem desperate.

"I was thinking of the Seine." She says the first thing she thinks of. It is true that the river bisecting Paris is often on her mind. The city's warren of streets is disorienting, but the river is a constant, helping her find her way around. Sabine likes to stand on its many bridges, to gaze into its dark waters, wondering where they come from—and where they are going.

"Of the Seine?" One eyebrow goes up.

"It is a lovely river, the Seine, don't you think?" she asks, feeling the stain of a blush upon her cheeks. She is no coquette, never has been. Teasing and flirting do not come naturally to her.

"I'd say its waters are far more *aromatic* than lovely," says a second man, who flings an arm around Desmarais's bulky shoulders. This man's eyes are a light sherry brown, but despite their warm color his gaze sends a shiver through Sabine. His eyes roam boldly, assessing her face, her body.

Sabine pulls her shawl more tightly around her chest and looks away.

A whore or an artist's model—sometimes they're one and the same, Honorine said. Sabine understands the truth of her words now.

"A pretty little bird, this one, eh, Maurice? Very . . . unusual."

"Back off, Clément," says Desmarais. "I saw her first."

Sabine wills Monsieur Desmarais to choose her; though his hazel eyes study her just as closely as the other man, his manner is courteous, gentlemanly.

"She is *le rat des champs*—the little country mouse. Beware the country mouse who dreams of the Seine, Desmarais," says Clément. "You know what they say about drowning women."

The sandy-haired man fixes Clément with a cold glare. "It is barely nine in the morning, and already you are in your cups?"

Clément shrugs. "It's allowed—even expected. I, after all," he says with an exaggerated bow to Sabine, "am an artist."

"You are a drunk," Desmarais responds. "*I* am an artist."

Clément makes a dismissive snort. "You are a rich man. How can a rich man be an artist, if he does not suffer? In any case, mademoiselle," he says, turning to Sabine, "I would like to offer you a commission."

Sabine's stomach clenches, but not from hunger. Her eyes fly to the sandy-haired man, beseeching him. If he does not speak for her, she will have to acquiesce to the mean little man. It is that or starve.

Desmarais hesitates, then appears to make a decision.

"She is already spoken for," he says. Sabine lets out the breath she has been holding in a rush. "And it will be an exclusive arrangement."

Clément presses his lips together, puffs out his chest. "You think you can buy anything you want, don't you?"

Desmarais appears unperturbed. "Run along home and sleep it off, my tipsy friend."

With a final glare at Desmarais and another at Sabine, Clément storms off.

"You do have modeling experience, I trust?" Desmarais asks.

"*Oui, monsieur*," she lies without compunction.

"I am a sculptor as well as a painter. I shall need to work in three dimensions. Is that acceptable?"

"*Oui, monsieur*," she repeats, not sure what he

means but not caring. It is work, and she will be paid, and she will eat tonight.

"Shall we?" he asks, gesturing with his hand. She walks beside him, grateful he has not asked for references. Toinette taught her a couple of artists' names, but if he were to check, she would be revealed as a fraud.

He weaves nimbly through the crowd, calling out greetings from time to time, then striding down the rue Pigalle, away from the busy square full of searching artists and hopeful models.

Sabine tries to keep up but soon stumbles.

"Have you broken your fast this morning?" Desmarais asks, reaching out for her arm to steady her.

She shakes her head. She hasn't eaten anything since her last apple and the boiled potato yesterday.

"You're a scrawny thing, aren't you?" He says, his big fingers feeling her knobby elbow through the thin muslin of her blouse. "Let us stop for coffee and croissants first. We'll have to start fattening you up. And afterward we will get to work."

Coffee and croissants. And all she has to do is sit still while he sculpts her likeness? That seems a small price to pay.

Perhaps there is more, says a small nagging voice in her head. Still, her stomach clenches at the thought of sustenance, her mouth waters, and nausea besets her. For a meal, there is a great deal to which she would agree at the moment. A very great deal.

So she holds her head high, smiles her little smile, and walks beside the sandy-haired, bearded man who carries the scent of sweet fruit and the spice of cloves.

10

The apartment Claire had rented was a good walk down the Seine, not far from the Hôtel de Ville, and she used the river as a landmark to keep her bearings.

But even so, she gave the Seine a wide berth.

Not that she expected it to surge up without warning. Claire was an engineer, trained in logic. She knew better.

Still. She glanced up at the gray clouds overhead. Did it look like rain?

In 1910, she knew from her research, the Seine had overflowed its banks, inundating the city. That was a long time ago, but still . . . Claire had seen old photographs of Parisians in Edwardian dress walking on wooden planks over the flooded streets and canoeing down the wide boulevards. She couldn't get the images out of her mind.

She shuddered at the thought of that young woman, now known only as "the Unknown One," stepping to the edge of the quai du Louvre and tumbling into the dark, frigid waters below.

Claire blew out a long, frustrated breath. She had known the mask was not unique, yet a part of her had expected—*hoped*—to find something different, something extraordinary. Maybe even some of the magic she had sensed from various sculptures when she was a little girl: the sensuality of the curves, the rough and smooth feel of the earth and metal and stone in her palms. The little rounded animals her mother had made of clay, like little balls stuck together, used to speak to her. Back when she would hide behind the couch, her father raging, and she would squeeze her eyes shut and become one of the sculpture people, feeling the figurines as if she were blind. She would curl up in back of the couch and listen for the crunch of her grandmother's tires coming down the gravel road, coming to rescue her.

Because her mother hadn't abandoned her in death. She had called out for the rescuers to save her little girl, and then spoken to Chance through those little animals.

Now Claire sat on a stone bench in a little square a good stretch from the river, chose a postcard featuring the crowded Lombardi atelier, and wrote a note to her uncle Remy:

Found our mystery face! In the Moulage d'Art of the Lombardi family. Remember I

90

showed you the Web site? She is in very good company, hanging on the wall alongside famous composers like Beethoven and Chopin. I wish you could see her unbroken!

Claire now carried stamps with her, so she attached one and dropped the postcard in a little yellow mailbox attached to the side of a building marked *Postes*.

Afterward she meandered a bit, picking up orange and red leaves from the sidewalk and tucking them in the small address book she kept in her bag. She flipped through some old books and maps, lithographs and key chains in the green boxes used by the street vendors—the *bouquinistes*—on the quais along the Seine. Nearby an old man was selling crêpes from a cart, sending a delicious scent wafting through the air. The streets were jammed with thick traffic and half the drivers seemed to be honking. Beautiful women on Vespas, far too chic to wear helmets, scooted between the cars, and several bicyclists braved the traffic.

Cafés and bistros, crowded with Parisians and visitors alike, occupied virtually every corner, their little iron tables and spindly chairs spilling out onto sidewalks and sometimes even into small side streets. A-frame chalkboard signs sat outside each restaurant touting that day's *menu du jour*, usually a three- or four-course meal at a reasonable price. She passed a tall, thin accordion player wearing a red-and-white-striped shirt and a beret, pandering to the touristy image of a bygone Paris.

Claire had worked hard to unlearn her Southern manners when she lived in Chicago, so she didn't try to make eye contact or smile and say hello to passersby. Parisians, like city dwellers anywhere, were urbanites going about their business.

She paused in front of a patisserie's bowed display window, amazed by the pyramids of pastel *macarons*—little sandwich cookies—and the towering *croquembouches*: stacks of decorated caramelized cream puffs. Next door was a chocolatier whose elaborate sculptural confections were worlds away from the sweet shops back home; they seemed to hold nothing in common even with the expensive Godiva chocolates Sean used to buy for her in Chicago.

Speaking of food—it was nearly suppertime. Claire knew it was common to dine alone in Parisian bistros, and she could always bring a book to read. But so far she hadn't worked up her courage; it felt awkward to linger over a solo dinner while the restaurants were filled with couples and small groups. And she still hadn't regained her normal appetite, or much interest in food.

Grief, she thought. It slammed into her from time to time: a full-body tackle. Claire kept thinking she was "over it," but then sorrow would overwhelm her at the sight of a shawl that reminded her of Mammaw, or a turn of phrase, or the scent of the White Shoulders perfume she wore on special occasions.

Claire blew out a long breath. She felt . . . adrift.

She supposed she should pick up some groceries, then go back to her rented apartment and cook something. Claire greeted this thought with a decided lack of enthusiasm. The "lovely kitchenette" touted in the rental advertisement was, in actuality, a tiny refrigerator that kept food barely cool to the touch and a gas stove with a leaky supply line that required her to turn it off at the wall when not in use. Claire wasn't much of a cook anyway. Mammaw had insisted she learn to make gumbo, which was her one signature dish, and she had a fair hand with salmon croquettes since she had helped Mammaw make them too many times to count. But who made gumbo or salmon croquettes for one person?

So far she had survived primarily on sandwiches from the *boulangeries*—freshly baked baguettes with salty cured ham and butter. Twice she had taken her sandwich to the little park behind the Cathedral of Notre Dame, Square Jean XXIII, where she could study those most impressive feats of medieval engineering: flying buttresses. The plaza in front of the cathedral was thronged with visitors, but only a handful seemed to find the serene little park to its rear. Even though it was close to the river, Claire liked the feel of the place.

But despite the beautiful architecture and the picturesque cafés and the stunning pastries and the beckoning parks, Claire had to admit the truth: she didn't care all that much for Paris.

After all those years of daydreaming, of yearning, it wasn't what she'd hoped for.

The streets seemed cold, rushed. Foreign. A little scary. And yet in some ways—the lilt of the language, the taste of the food—France reminded her of Louisiana, which, in turn, made her feel nostalgic. She felt . . . *homesick*. But for what? She didn't want to go back to Plaquemines Parish *or* Chicago.

A few months earlier Claire and Sean had gone to Scrabble night at a friend's house, which was mostly an excuse to drink wine and chat while waging a friendly competition. In a game-winning coup, Sean had played a word Claire had never heard before—*hiraeth*—for the seven-letter bonus. He explained it was a Welsh word that meant a yearning for a place that no longer existed, or that had *never* existed.

The word kept coming back to Claire. *Hiraeth*. And now that she was in Paris, home to existentialist icons like Sartre, it seemed even more apropos. Perhaps she was simply suffering from that oh-so-French affliction: ennui.

Claire wrapped her arms around herself and

checked the level of water in the Seine. Did it look higher than it had been?

One thing was certain. She was a mess.

Claire's stomach growled. In spite of her misery, it made her smile. Mammaw's voice sounded in her head: *At least this is a problem you can deal with,* sha. *A good meal will help set your mind straight.*

But most of the *boulangeries* were closed by now or had only sad dried-out sandwiches left over, and she'd eaten a lot of Middle Eastern street food lately. She needed to mix it up a little.

She started walking, hoping inspiration would strike. As she strolled past an art gallery, her mind wandered back to Giselle and Armand of the Moulage Lombardi. What must it be like to live a legacy? To have your ancestors hand you down their precious customs, to train you from child-hood in the special skills passed along through generations throughout history?

From the outside the tradition of a family business seemed charming. But when Claire applied the concept to her own circumstances, the thought lost its romantic sheen. Then again, toiling in factories or on oil rigs or fishing boats for low hourly wages didn't have quite the same glamour. How would she feel if her kin had owned something historic and valuable, like a successful business or even a family manor? Would she have been more inclined to have remained in her hometown, to have become a caretaker of tradition? Or would she have itched just as badly to get out, to run away?

Maybe Mammaw recognized Claire wouldn't be happy in Louisiana, and that was why she had urged her to go to Paris, assuming she'd enjoy herself. Maybe it was just that simple.

But it seemed like something more.

Promise me you'll go to Paris, sha, Mammaw had said. *You will find a secret!*

Still, her family was prone to telling tall tales. Not lies exactly, but stories that were exaggerated and embellished to the point of being misleading. Uncle Charles swore he had come across a *rougarou*—a sort of Louisiana werewolf—in a field in Saint Landry Parish. Cousin Richard always insisted he had stumbled across a mafia execution-style killing and barely escaped with his life. Cousin Sheila claimed she had proof she'd been adopted and had royal blood. And they all, to a person (except perhaps for Jessica), insisted Claire's mother's voice had called out from beyond the grave the night of the car accident, and that Claire's life was a miracle.

So far as Claire could see, there had been no evidence of that.

Enough, Claire chided herself. If she wasn't going to find some special secret, some magic involving that old mask or the mysterious note, the least she could do was enjoy the City of Light.

After all, what sort of person didn't like Paris? Clearly, she just had to try harder.

She pulled out her list of must-sees and headed to the metro to take the train to the Champs-Élysées. There should be plenty of food options there.

The guidebook called the Avenue des Champs-Élysées "a Paris place-to-go," as iconic as the Eiffel Tower. It was the setting for the annual Bastille Day military parade, the arrival of the Tour de France, and the annual festival of Christmas lights. *La plus belle avenue du monde*—the world's most beautiful avenue—was one of Paris's most elegant addresses. The president of France himself lived there, at the Élysée Palace.

But when Claire emerged from the underground at metro stop Charles de Gaulle–Étoile, she was met not with beauty so much as the blare of car horns as they sped around the Arc de Triomphe. She had read somewhere that once drivers entered the roundabout here, their car insurance was suspended. Perhaps it was apocryphal, but it sure felt apt as she watched the chaotic, seemingly out-of-control movement of traffic around the circle.

She strolled down the broad sidewalks of the Champs-Élysées toward the Place de la Concorde, accompanied by swarms of other visitors looking for signs of the supposedly elegant *belle* avenue.

As she walked, she caught snippets of French,

but it was mostly other languages she heard: English, Spanish, Japanese, German, Mandarin. Buses lined the curbs, belching diesel exhaust and disgorging dozens of tourists. Women in saris and *bindis* clutched Louis Vuitton bags, and young people streamed in and out of Banana Republic, the Gap, and Abercrombie and Fitch. There was a Disney store and even a Hard Rock Café.

Except for the presence of street people begging for change outside the stores, she might as well have been in an American shopping mall.

Claire tried to look past the disoriented tourists and garish commercialism, but it wasn't easy. *I should have come after dark,* she thought. A lot of places looked better then, with twinkle lights.

Her mind wandered: what had these streets seen? In 1940, German troops had marched down the Champs-Élysées in celebration of France's fall at the beginning of World War II. Four years later, Claire's own great-grandfather had been among the American troops who drove the Nazis out of Paris. The war would continue to rage in the Pacific theater and beyond, but running the Germans out of Paris was a symbolic victory, a turning point in the war.

The City of Light had emerged from the war bowed, but far from defeated.

Claire's stomach growled again. And knock her over with a feather: there was a McDonald's. Right there on the Champs-Élysées.

If that wasn't a sign, she didn't know what was. Claire ducked into the fast-food restaurant.

It was a two-story affair teeming with customers. Most were tourists, but there were a good number of young French people as well. The familiar aroma of burgers and fries filled the air. Ever since leaving Mammaw's home, Claire had eaten a lot of junk food. In college she had indulged in pizza and burgers and bright orange Chinese food. And then for years, at work, eating take-out lunches (and many times, dinners) over the keyboard of her computer had sustained her.

She was willing to bet the French would find that practice atrocious.

What distinguished this menu from the American version was that it offered several options with blue cheese. Plus, it was expensive: a burger cost the equivalent of more than nine U.S. dollars.

Best of all, though, was the McCafé with *macarons*. The luscious little sandwich cookies were just one euro each.

Claire bought herself a blue cheese burger and took it upstairs to eat while looking down over the wide boulevard. It wasn't the tourist experience she had hoped for or expected, but it was fun, and perhaps it was homesickness, or the hefty price, or simply her appetite returning, but the food tasted much better than she remembered in the States.

She topped her meal off with a *macaron*, because she could.

Stuffed, Claire decided to walk back in the direction of her apartment, which would take her past the Eiffel Tower, the next item on her must-see list.

She'd seen it from afar, of course. The tower was visible from many streets and along parts of the Seine. But up close the iconic tower was massive, much larger than she'd expected. The wait for the elevator to the top was several hours long, and Claire wasn't willing to commit to such a climb, so she settled for wandering around the square at its base, peering up into the web of girders and beams, joists and lintels. According to the guidebook, when the tower was built for the Exposition Universelle of 1889, many Parisians had been outraged, calling it ugly and industrial and a waste of space. It wasn't even a building— didn't actually *house* anything. It was, quite simply, a structure erected to loom over the city, like a toy from a child's erector set, writ very, very large.

Again, Claire felt underwhelmed.

A worry crept up and latched onto her heart.

If Claire felt this way about Paris, of all places, maybe the problem was *her*. She'd dreamed about Paris for years. And now that she was in what the guidebooks called the most romantic city, the most visited city, the most beautiful city in the world, she was disappointed.

Paris felt cold and impersonal, overrun by

tourists—of which she was one, of course—and even the most famous sights left her . . . *unsatisfied*.

On her way home she stopped at a bookstore and perused a few souvenir shops. Maybe it wasn't Paris itself so much as tourism, Claire thought. After so many years of working toward specific goals, it was disorienting to have nowhere to be, nothing to do. Perhaps if she had a friend with her to share the moment it would be different.

It was after ten by the time Claire reached her miserable little apartment. She had thought she'd save money by letting an apartment for a week rather than staying in a hotel, but it had turned out to be a disaster. The building was modern, but not in a good way: it appeared to have been refurbished in the seventies, a challenging era for architecture. Built of cheap materials, it was poorly designed and shoddily put together. The press-board cabinets were peeling, the harvest gold linoleum tiles were lifting at the corners, and the entire studio was permeated with a mildewy, musty smell.

Added to this was a wall shared with a discotheque, which meant Claire was treated to the pounding of bass until the early-morning hours. It was a chic crowd, all lovely and, it seemed, college aged.

Claire sighed as she pushed through the swollen

line waiting to enter the disco, let herself into the apartment building, took the stairs to the second floor and into the apartment. *Everything is fine,* she told herself. Really. Tomorrow she would go to Montmartre to visit the famous hill where, once upon a time, so many artists had thrived, and perhaps make a side trip to Père Lachaise Cemetery to pay homage to the graves of Oscar Wilde and Jim Morrison. Then she could scratch those must-see sights off her list.

And then she would decide about the day after that.

She sat down at the little breakfast table by the kitchenette and set out her writing accoutrements: thick parchment paper, a stick of red wax, matches, and the signet in the form of a *C* that Remy had given her when she was ten and she had a pen pal in Nepal.

Claire spent most of her life on the computer, but the letter-writing tradition was strong in her family. Her grandmother had insisted she write letters to her relatives throughout her childhood, and from college she had written home at least once a week. Her affinity for snail mail was a source of some amusement to her friends, but she didn't care.

Dear Uncle Remy,
I am writing to you late at night, because it is so hard to sleep here! The apartment is

next to a club with thumping music louder than the big truck rallies you used to take me to. Remember?

Today I walked down the Champs-Élysées, a famous boulevard that stretches from the Arc de Triomphe to the Place de la Concorde. Apparently the Nazis marched down it in triumph in 1940, and then the American forces (even Mammaw's father?) marched down it in the summer of 1944. They say the church bells rang out all over Paris to announce the liberation of the city. Now the avenue is mostly full of expensive stores and tourists, and I had a hamburger at a McDonald's. (Can you believe there's a McDonald's in Paris?) This being France, they put blue cheese on it.

I'm enclosing a few leaves I thought you would like. I found them near the banks of the Seine, the river that runs through the city.

Thinking of you. Miss you. Love you.
Your niece,
Chance

She folded the letter and slipped it into an envelope, then lit a match, held it to the stick of wax, and watched as melted red drops fell onto the junction of envelope and flap, the color as deep and rich as blood. Claire pressed her signet into the liquid and held it there until the wax hardened.

As she did so, she imagined Remy opening the letter with his clumsy fingers, pulling out the page, watching the leaves flutter to the floor.

The disco's thumping bass rattled the apartment's thin walls, accompanied by shouts and loud voices from the crowd waiting in line outside. Claire knew from experience this would go on throughout the night. These Parisians could party. If she was going to stay longer in Paris, she needed to find new accommodations. But why stay?

Had she found the secret? She didn't know anything more now than she had before coming, not really. Only that *L'Inconnue*'s mask was a bestseller at the Moulage Lombardi. She still hadn't figured out what the strange letter she had found among the packing materials meant, but surely it had nothing to do with the face itself?

There was nothing for her in Paris, just as there was nothing for her in Chicago or in Plaquemines Parish. Just plain nothing.

How depressing.

Mammaw had often repeated to her: *Never make a decision in the middle of the night. The cold light of day is the time to think things through,* sha. *Whatever it is, it'll wait until morning.*

Tomorrow, then. Tomorrow Claire would decide her next step.

As she lay in bed, her mind's eye tripped back to the door of the Lombardi atelier. Guarded by statues that beckoned her to enter. The cold air of the sculptures on her cheek. The whispers from the pure white masks.

And her own beloved silent face from Mammaw's attic hanging on the wall, one mask among many.

11

PIERRE-GUILLAUME

1944
Workshop of the Lombardi Family
Mold-Makers, rue de la Huchette, Paris

The shop boy noticed the American right away. How could he not? The soldier was large and loud, with a booming voice, standing on the sidewalk right outside the shop.

Pierre-Guillaume was seventeen and counted himself lucky to have any job at all, let alone one as apprentice to the famous casters the Famille Lombardi. His master, Marc-Antoine Lombardi, was famous for his Gallic temper; he once threw a bust of Robespierre across the room, right over

105

Pierre-Guillaume's head, missing him by mere inches.

Pierre-Guillaume had not been the intended target, but Monsieur Lombardi had notoriously bad aim, so it was best to remain on guard.

Apart from the occasional outburst, however, Monsieur Lombardi was a good master, a demanding but generous teacher. Marc-Antoine's own father, Jean-Baptiste Lombardi, had retired to the family villa in the Franche-Comté and handed the Paris business to his eldest son some years ago. There was another son in the family, and three daughters, but it was Marc-Antoine Lombardi who had inherited the artistic skill. And the Lombardi temper. It was said they went together.

Pierre-Guillaume sometimes wondered whether his own even temperament would be detrimental to his development as an artist. But he kept his doubts to himself.

Monsieur Lombardi had two children, a boy and a girl. The boy was far too young to inherit the business, and much to his father's dismay he seemed more interested in playing soccer and hanging out with his friends than in learning the arts of casting and mold-making. The daughter, Delphine, was a handful, and at the tender age of ten years old would follow Pierre around the studio, peppering him with questions: *What are the strips of gauze used for? Why do you tap the box like that after pouring? Why does the shellac smell so funny?*

Pierre-Guillaume liked to pretend he was next in line to inherit the great house of *moulage* of the Famille Lombardi. He would never dare voice such an absurd ambition, but he had noticed that in the list of masters by the front door, there was one name that was not Lombardi. A man named Olivier Delen had run the shop while Jean-Baptiste Lombardi spent most of his time in the countryside before his son Marc-Antoine was old enough to take over. So perhaps. Perhaps, even though he was not a Lombardi, Pierre-Guillaume might be able to step in if he worked very hard and proved himself worthy. Perhaps one day.

His own family had been devastated during the war: his father shot by a German soldier; his mother, malnourished by the wartime shortages that prompted her to give what little food was available to her children, succumbed to pneumonia, too weak to fight off what had started as a simple cold. His older brother had died early in the war, in a tractor accident, trying to coax food out of the stubborn ground. Food the Germans would have confiscated in any case.

So now Pierre-Guillaume's only family was a younger sister who lived in the countryside with their aunt and uncle. It was up to Pierre-Guillaume to provide for her, to send money to his aunt and uncle, and to do his part to rebuild Paris. And he was ready, filled with a fierce nationalism and commitment to the postwar renaissance of the greatest city in the world.

Paris was much more than buildings and businesses; it was a world capital for art and artisans, and Pierre-Guillaume vowed he would help restore it to its rightful place.

Sometimes Monsieur Jean-Baptiste Lombardi would visit from the countryside and, if plied with enough cognac, would tell tales of the old days: the Belle Epoque, when life was beautiful and Paris was home to the world's greatest writers and artists and philosophers.

Pierre-Guillaume wanted to be part of the *new* Belle Epoque. He wanted that very, very much.

When he first encountered the American outside the shop, Pierre-Guillaume had been carrying a heavy bucket of murky water in each hand. He froze, unsure what to say. Like every Parisian who had heard about the American soldiers marching into France and down the Champs-Élysées into Paris, Pierre-Guillaume felt his heart swell at the sight of the American uniform. Two of his cousins had been active with the resistance, and he himself had removed and changed road signs to confuse the despised German invaders. The resistance had accomplished miracles, but it was when the Americans joined the fight that the tide had turned.

"Hello, sir. How are you?" Pierre-Guillaume finally managed to utter in English, practicing one of the few phrases his father had taught him before he was shot, back when they would sit around playing music in their warm little farmhouse. Before the war, before death stalked his family, stole his happiness.

"Why, hello there, young man," the man boomed. "*Je parle français si tu préfères.*"

"Thank you. I do prefer," said Pierre-Guillaume, reverting to French with relief. When attempting to secure his job, he might have implied that he spoke more English than he really did. "If I may ask, where are you from, monsieur?"

"Louisiana," said the man.

Then how is it you speak my language? the boy thought to himself, but refrained from asking. He had never before met an American who spoke more than a few words in French.

Delphine—all pigtails and knobby knees—suddenly appeared at the bottom of the stairs and demanded: "How do you speak French, monsieur?"

Pierre-Guillaume shushed her and shooed her back into the building, shutting the door.

"Some of us speak French in Louisiana," said the man with a chuckle. "We call it Cajun. Not quite the same, but good enough to be understood—am I right? Name's Jerry, by the way. Jerry Duval."

Pierre-Guillaume smiled and ducked his head. He hadn't met all that many Americans close up, but the ones he had were like this: smiley and talkative, exuding friendliness and good health. He found it disconcerting and charming at the same time.

"You and I, we'll make ourselves understood. Don't let me keep you there, son, if you want to dump that water? It looks heavy."

Pierre-Guillaume nodded and went to empty the buckets into the street drain. As always when watching the milky water splash down into the sewers that ran beneath the city, he thought of something his master had told him: that, during the war, resistance fighters used those sewers and subterranean tunnels to get around after curfew. His master said there were hundreds of kilometers of tunnels beneath the streets of Paris—several levels of them, in fact—and that some were filled with the bones of their ancestors. His master said many such things, and Pierre-Guillaume was never sure which ones to believe. But about the sewers he did believe.

Paris was a city of miracles. It was not too much to imagine an underground web, subterranean layers of history and ingenuity offering even more magic.

"My master is out of the studio at lunch, but may I help you with something, sir?" Pierre-Guillaume asked, picking up the empty buckets.

"Yes, please. I was curious about this mask," said the American, gesturing to the mask of a young woman hanging to one side of the door.

Pierre-Guillaume nodded. "She is very beautiful, is she not?"

"Yes, she is. Is she famous?"

"Oh, no, not really. Except—in a way she is now. Her identity is unknown."

"Unknown?"

"Yes, this is what they call her: the Unknown One of the Seine. *L'Inconnue de la Seine.* She was found in the river."

"Found?"

"Drowned."

"What a tragedy."

Pierre-Guillaume nodded. "But you know what they say: *Ce n'est rien; c'est une femme qui se noie.*"

" 'It's nothing, just a woman drowning'?" the man translated the phrase, a troubled expression on his face. "And what is that supposed to mean?"

"I . . . I just . . ." Pierre-Guillaume felt his cheeks burning. He had no idea what the phrase meant, only that he'd heard someone say it and thought it sounded urbane. But now that the American repeated it, he realized . . . it was a terrible quote. Crass and unfeeling.

The American smiled. "Probably something from a fable—am I right? I only ask because I thought all your masks were of famous people."

"*Oui, monsieur*, most of them are famous. We have Napoléon, and Beethoven, and Pascal."

111

Pierre-Guillaume wished Monsieur Lombardi would return from his lunch engagement to talk with the American. It was exhausting.

"Then why is *L'Inconnue* here?"

Pierre-Guillaume finally set down his buckets, pulled himself up to his full height (which wasn't much; he was dwarfed by the towering American) and launched into the story his master had told him:

"It is said she was a simple girl from the countryside, but that her heart was broken by an evil man, so she threw herself into the cold, dark Seine to join the water spirits there. When her body was fished from the river and brought to the morgue, one of the workers decided she was too beautiful to be forgotten. So he sent for my master's father, Monsieur Jean-Baptiste Lombardi, who was the head of the atelier at the time. He cast her mask even though she was not famous."

"Because she was beautiful?"

He nodded. "Because she was beautiful, and because she smiles as if she knows."

"Knows what?"

Pierre-Guillaume shrugged. "I think she must know what *La Joconde* knows."

"*La Joconde*? Isn't that what we Americans call the *Mona Lisa*?"

"*Oui, monsieur*. She knows what only a woman might know."

12

The next morning, Claire treated herself to something called an "American breakfast" at a café that clearly catered to tourists: in addition to café au lait and croissants, the menu offered a breakfast of ham and eggs, home fries, toast, and "American coffee," which was made by watering down shots of espresso.

The waiter was dismissive to the point of being rude, so Claire did her best to ignore him in return. Despite the familiar food, she couldn't bring herself to eat much. Maybe she was still full from McDonald's, she thought, remembering the hamburger sitting heavily in her stomach.

When the waiter took her plate, she asked for a refill of coffee, spread out a tourist map, consulted her guidebook, and planned her day.

She checked off items on her sightseeing list:

The Champs-Élysées.

The Eiffel Tower.

She had already visited the Louvre and the Impressionist museum, the Musée d'Orsay, and yesterday she'd gone to the Cathédrale de Notre Dame de Paris and the Luxembourg Gardens before looking up the Moulage Lombardi in the Latin Quarter.

It was a full-time job, being a tourist in a city like Paris.

Thumbing through her guidebook, she noted a special little box that read: *Americans sometimes find Parisian shopkeepers and waiters to be rude, but they don't mean to be.*

Claire glanced at the waiter lounging near the shiny brass cappuccino machine. She was pretty sure *he* meant to be rude.

She continued to read: *They are consummate professionals, and they respect patrons who know what they want. They expect to be treated with imperiousness, and they respond in kind.*

"What do you want?" Armand, grumpy mold-maker of the Moulage Lombardi, had demanded of Claire yesterday.

If only she knew. Mammaw had asked her that very question when she announced her plan to go away to college. Sean had asked her that when she told him she was quitting her job and leaving Chicago—and him. Her relatives asked her that when she decided to fly to Paris on the whim of a dying grandmother.

How did anyone know what they wanted?

No reason to entertain that line of thinking. There was too much to do.

Today she would take the metro to Pigalle, the neighborhood that was home to the famous Moulin Rouge. Then she would climb Montmartre, the hill that was once the outskirts of the city, where so many now famous artists lived in squalor as they searched for new ways to see the world. Edgar Degas, Toulouse-Lautrec, Pablo Picasso . . . Maybe she would try to make it to the Rodin Museum too, though that was in a different part of town.

Claire entered the addresses into her phone's GPS just in case, but she liked looking at the paper map because it allowed her to remain oriented. In addition to her phone and the big map, she carried a pocket-sized green book with detailed maps of the city's many neighborhoods with their tangle of streets and alleys.

Claire did her homework; she liked to be prepared.

Her phone rang, startling her. She checked the screen: it was a French number.

The waiter gave her a dirty look. She held up a finger to indicate she would be right back—trying for imperiousness, as the guidebook had suggested—and slipped outside to take the call.

"*Allo?*"

"Claire? This is Giselle, with the *moulage* of the Famille Lombardi."

"Of course! How nice to hear from you."

"My cousin Armand would like to know why you came to his shop."

"I was just curious about the mask. *L'Inconnue.*"

"He says— Wait a minute . . ." During a lengthy pause, Claire could hear Giselle and Armand discussing something.

"Giselle?" ventured Claire. "Perhaps I could speak with him directly?"

There was more muffled discussion. From what Claire could gather, Armand was refusing to take the phone. She imagined him with his hands full of plaster mud, frowning, irritated. Imperious.

After a moment Giselle came back to the phone.

"I'm sorry—he says he can't talk right now. But here is the thing: we are expecting two busloads of Americans today after lunch. You can come and talk to them."

"Excuse me?"

"I thought perhaps you could come and help us this afternoon. You mentioned you were unemployed?"

"Yes, but that's in the United States. Not here. Here I'm on vacation. In *Paris*."

"I know, but would it be possible for you to please come and help us? I cannot be here this afternoon, so Armand will be alone. You can imagine how that will go. Also, of course, I don't speak English."

"I was going to do some sightseeing today . . ." Claire trailed off, thinking an afternoon working in a Parisian atelier actually sounded kind of fun.

"We will pay you, of course. An informal arrangement, just temporary. It would be a great help."

Claire heard Armand shouting something in the

116

background, and once again wished she could talk to him directly.

"Also," said Giselle. "There is a box."

"A box?"

"Yes. Armand says to tell you there is a box with clippings and stories about *L'Inconnue*, along with some family papers. If you could do us this favor, he will let you look through it if you wish."

Claire wondered why Giselle—or Armand—hadn't mentioned the box yesterday. But then, that was their prerogative. She was a stranger off the street; why would they offer to show her private family papers?

"Please, I know it is unusual, but it would be a great favor," Giselle persisted.

Why not? Claire decided. Her plans were flexible. "Yes, of course. I would be happy to. What time?"

Giselle told her they were closed for lunch from twelve to two, and the first bus was scheduled to arrive at two thirty, though they sometimes ran late. Claire agreed to arrive by two at the latest so Giselle could give her an orientation before leaving.

Smiling at this unexpected turn of events, Claire hung up and went back into the restaurant to her table.

The waiter came over, looking down his nose at her, apparently eager to demonstrate his displeasure.

"Is everything quite all right, madame?"

For some reason she felt compelled to respond to his coldness with a little dose of Southern hospitality. She gave him a huge smile. "Just wonderful, thank you. That was my new job calling. Can you imagine? *Me,* working in Paris? *C'est magnifique!*"

13

SABINE

T he work of an artist's model is more strange than difficult.

Compared with laboring on the farm, hauling water, trying to lure vegetables out of the tired earth, tending to the animals, or even using the tools in her stepfather's woodshop, this is simple: Sabine must stand or sit or lie as still as humanly possible, sometimes in awkward positions that make her muscles ache and her arms fall asleep. Even breathing and blinking must be kept to a minimum, or she earns a reprimand. *As still as the dead,* Maurice says.

An itch needing scratching and a gnat buzzing her eyes are her enemies.

Since she lied about her experience, she has to pretend she is not shocked when Desmarais tells his sister Isabelle, a scowling wren of a woman, to help Sabine disrobe. Sabine has always undressed herself, but Isabelle insists on doing as her brother says, following Sabine behind the screen and pulling and pinching as she undoes the laces, clucking at the age and threadbare state of her clothing.

Once Sabine is undressed, Isabelle hands her a silk robe that slides across her limbs; it is old and has a tear, and probably belonged to the last model who sat for the artist. But Sabine catches her breath at the sensation of the fabric as it slips along her skin: it feels like bliss.

Monsieur Desmarais leads her to a dais in the middle of the room. Sunshine pours through skylights overhead, lighting up everything.

She can feel the heat in her cheeks when he demands she drop the robe. He strokes his beard as he walks around the dais, inspecting her naked body from all angles. Every "Hmm" he utters is a torture.

Will he send her away? Toinette and Honorine assured her she had a beautiful face, but what of her body? She has a bosom, and she knows men like that. But what of the rest of her? She hasn't had much to eat for many months, but hers is a healthy vessel: her legs and arms are strong from years of work and exercise; her back is straight. She has never thought much beyond that.

"She's a skinny thing," says Isabelle, eyes narrowed. "Why, I can see her bones!"

"You're right," says her brother. "We'll have

to fatten her up. More croissants, *eh,* my little country mouse?"

"And her hands are so rough," continued Isabelle. "Like a man's hands."

Sabine squeezes her hands closed.

"Of course they are," says the sculptor. "She's been using those hands to work. We'll treat her with some of your lavender salve."

Instead of sending her away, he positions her on the divan. He tells her to lean back, her top leg crooked over the bottom one, her left arm lifted over her head, the other resting across her stomach.

And there she lies for hours, until her arm falls asleep, her hip aches. At least the discomfort helps her to keep from nodding off. Monsieur Desmarais is absorbed with his mound of clay atop a big worktable. He slaps on great hunks here, takes away chunks there. He uses his bare hands at first, working feverishly, spattering the counter and himself with brownish red drops of wet clay. After a time he slows down, using metal tools and wires and brushes as the work becomes more detailed.

Isabelle sits in a corner reading a book, scowling at Sabine whenever she looks over.

Sabine tries to keep her mind occupied. She thinks of the croissant and coffee Monsieur Desmarais bought her at the brasserie: it was served with a square of succulent chocolate, and she took such pleasure in it that Desmarais laughed and handed her his as well. She thinks of her brother's smile, how the two of them used to capture polliwogs in the pond in the summer, and the burning, unnatural sensation of his fevered brow under her hand not long before he died. She thinks of the horse trainer, their walk in the woods, the feeling of his mouth on hers, the pain in the old stable owner's eyes when he told Sabine the young man had passed in the night.

She tries not to think of the way Isabelle frowns at her from her chair in the corner, as though Sabine were a whore; or the warnings of the young priest; or how cold Monsieur Desmarais's eyes seem when they study her, as though he is trying to encapsulate her soul in the lump of clay.

Sabine tries not to think of what he will expect later, where she will sleep tonight.

If she will have a job tomorrow, or when she will eat again.

She tries not to think.

14

Claire arrived at the Lombardi studio barely half an hour before the tour buses were scheduled to arrive. The sculptures still stood outside, unmolested, guarding the entrance.

The front door was locked. A sign read:

FERMÉ 12–2. REVENEZ, S'IL VOUS PLAÎT.
CLOSED 12–2. PLEASE COME BACK.

She banged on the old wood, which was weathered gray with age.

After a few moments she heard footsteps descending and Armand threw open the door.

Claire was again struck by his distinctive face. If she were a sculptor, his would be a visage to capture. There were stories behind that facade, she felt sure. Would they emerge from the stone if she were talented enough to coax his likeness from a lump of clay or a block of marble?

Then again, obsidian might be the more appropriate medium, given his character.

"Monsieur," she said.

"Mademoiselle," he replied with a slight inclination of his head, waving her in.

No *Thank you for spending a day of your vacation with us* or *Thank you for saving our asses* or even *Thank you for coming.* She couldn't help but notice.

Claire headed up the creaky stairs, Armand behind her.

"I'm not really sure what you'd like me to do today, beyond speaking English . . ."

"It is enough. Giselle will show you the basics. And I will be here to take the orders and make the shipping arrangements."

Just as they reached the top of the stairs, Giselle

burst in through the back door smelling of cigarettes.

"Thank you so much for coming!" she gushed, kissing Claire once on each cheek in greeting, enveloping her in a cloud of tobacco and perfume. "I am so sorry about this. It is too much at once, to have our English speaker quit and the other one out on maternity leave during tourist season. And my children are out of school, so I must be with them. *C'est fou!*"

It's crazy, and Claire thought to herself that this was indeed the right word: it was no doubt crazy-making. And the glowering Armand wasn't helping matters. Claire's eyes slewed over to him; he made her nervous, jumpy.

"I'll give you a tour and then I must leave if I am to get home in time; I live on the other side of town, in Fontainebleau—do you know it? But I'll be back this evening."

"I can stay as long as you need," said Claire. The thought of having a job to do—being *useful* after days of dawdling—felt right. And it was exciting, if a little daunting, to think of managing a Parisian atelier, if only for the day.

"Wonderful! Come, I will show you around. Let's start downstairs."

They went through the back door and down a set of exterior stairs that led to a charming patio and small walled garden.

The furniture, greenery, and planters were well

weathered but inviting, like a photo from an article in a garden magazine: *Secret Parisian Gardens!* Brick and stone walls were flanked by tall bushes; a small tree stood in each corner; flowers and vines spilled out from lush planter boxes. A tiered fountain tinkled. One raised *potager* held caged tomato plants and green bean vines reaching up tall poles; another had several kinds of herbs. Several metal garden chairs and two wicker love seats formed a horseshoe around a table, and a brick barbecue was built into one side wall. Full-sized sculptures stood here and there about the garden and along the graveled path, and masks entwined with vines peered down from the garden walls and the exterior of the building.

Unlike the immaculate castings in the show-room, these masks were marked with bright green moss, their crevices mellowed by bits of dirt and dust.

"We leave some of our castings outside to give them a natural patina," Giselle explained. "Some people like them to be weathered, not perfectly white and clean. Did you know Michelangelo used to bury new sculptures for a year or two, then dig them up and sell them as antiquities?"

"Is that true?"

Giselle shrugged. "It is the story that is told."

"You're saying Michelangelo was involved in art fraud?"

"Some say fraud; others say the clever use of copies," she said as she rolled open a huge barn door to lead the way into a second-floor workshop. "And you know, you are speaking to someone in the business of making copies, so be careful what you say."

Claire smiled, unsure if she was serious.

"After all," Giselle continued, "if they are equally beautiful, who is to say what is the more valuable—the original or a gifted copy?"

"Museum curators and art appraisers would be my guess."

Giselle laughed and offered Claire a cigarette. She declined.

Giselle lit up and inhaled deeply, then let out a long stream of smoke. "Armand does not like cigarettes, so I am forced to smoke outside or down here, like a child sneaking behind the backs of her parents. Anyway, these barn doors are nice, you see? This building was a stable many years ago. This way we can open them and work half outside when the weather permits."

Aside from an open work area in front, the rest of the huge room was even more jammed than the upstairs showroom, with only narrow trails allowing access through the statues.

"This is where we cast the large pieces, and at the back we have storage closets and a few other cubbyholes. Some of the more valuable or irreplaceable items had to be hidden during the war, during the Nazi occupation—occasionally we still find things under floorboards or in the walls." She gestured to the workbench near the doors. "And here is where we mix glazes and sealants—that sort of thing. I'm sure you know raw plaster will melt if it is left out in the rain. It must be properly sealed to preserve it."

Numerous cans lined the shelves behind a long workbench. Old pickle jars held brushes, from the fine to the ratty, and wire baskets were full of rags and synthetic and natural sponges.

"We don't have time to let all the statuary age naturally," Giselle continued, "so we also apply various patinas with tinted shellacs, glues, and polyurethanes."

"What are the feathers for?" asked Claire, noting a ceramic jar holding several large goose plumes.

"We use them to make wobbly lines, like the veins you see in marble or other stone. They create the kind of random squiggle that is hard to achieve with a regular brush."

"And this one?" asked Claire, running her fingertips along a soft brush.

"*Blaireau* hair. The best for blending."

"This is fascinating. It's a whole world unto itself, isn't it?"

Giselle nodded and blew out more smoke, apparently unimpressed. "Anyway, we keep the tourists upstairs, mostly, unless they arrange for a special tour of these back rooms."

"For a price?"

"A very reasonable price," said Giselle with a conspiratorial smile as she led the way to the garden, stubbed her cigarette out in a flowerpot, and headed back up the stairs to the second floor. "When the tour buses stop by, their customers almost always buy enough to make it worth our while. If sales don't reach a certain level, the tour company pays the difference. It works well for all—their customers feel like they're getting to visit a historic Parisian atelier, and we sell our products. Everyone is happy. Except perhaps for my cousin, who is never happy."

Upstairs, Giselle gestured through the windows at Armand, who was applying bright blue glop to something atop the counter in the studio.

"We keep the visitors out of the work areas," said Giselle. "But they can watch the castings being done through the windows. This was the compromise we came to, since Armand does not like tourists to bother him while he is working."

"But he doesn't mind them staring at him through the windows?"

"He doesn't like it, but he accepts it is necessary. Most of the actual mold-making takes place downstairs. Up here is for the finer work on the smaller pieces, such as the busts and masks."

"What kind of fine work?"

"The sanding and filling and finishing. One does not simply pour a mold or make a casting and that's the end of it. It's just the beginning. The name Lombardi has been synonymous with quality for nearly two centuries; Armand would not let us slip now, even if we wanted to."

"I can imagine."

"And behind here"—Giselle opened a large solid wood door—"is the kitchen. Not for the tourists, of course, but if you would like to make yourself a cup of tea or anything at all, please make yourself at home. But do keep the door closed to keep the dust out."

It was an old-fashioned kitchen with a painted tile backsplash and a countertop of chipped Carrara marble, pots and pans hanging from an overhead iron rack, and a large copper kettle atop a burner on an old gas stove. Three casement windows looked down onto the garden, bathing the kitchen with sunlight. Here, as elsewhere, faces lined the walls. Fine white plaster powder fanned out from the doorway onto the floor, no doubt drifting in through the cracks.

Back in the showroom, Giselle showed her the main desk, topped with a desktop computer and an old-fashioned landline phone, then handed Claire the extensive price list.

"The prices are fixed," Giselle explained. "We do not haggle chez Lombardi, though the tourists sometimes try. When a customer is ready to make a purchase, call Armand. He will take the money and arrange for shipping; you do not need to worry about that. All you need to do is be charming and convince them to buy!"

Outside, they heard a commotion.

Giselle and Claire went down the stairs and out to the street. The giant tour bus could barely make it down the narrow medieval-era street—built centuries ago to accommodate horses and carriages—and had nearly clipped a tiny car parked too near the corner. The bus driver stopped in the middle of the street and got out to assess the situation. A waiter from the café on the corner offered his loud opinion, a pair of teenage girls stopped to watch the scene, and an old man joined them, making suggestions.

More neighbors and passersby gathered until there were enough strong arms to lift the tiny car and move it onto the sidewalk.

The bus inched by, slowly, until it stood in front of the Moulage Lombardi.

"I've never seen such a thing in my life," Claire said, laughing. She looked over her shoulder at Giselle and saw that even Armand had come down to watch the action. "They lifted the whole car up!"

Armand held her gaze for a moment but did not respond.

Claire shrugged. "It seems like something the boys would do back home."

"They pick up cars like that?" Giselle asked. "Is that necessary?"

"Not really, no. Our streets are pretty wide usually. I'm just saying—it's the kind of problem solving I grew up with. Brute force over technology every time."

Giselle smiled. "Okay, I have to run. Will you be all right, do you think?"

"I'll be fine. Enjoy your day with your children."

Giselle kissed her on both cheeks and hurried off.

Armand had retreated upstairs and, Claire imagined, was already ensconced in his workshop. Claire was just as glad not to have his scowling presence watching her and judging.

She stood by the front door and greeted the tourists as they came off the bus, inviting them to mount the stairs to the showroom.

The first group was from Iowa, the next from Texas. The Texans especially captured her heart; their accents were like a soothing balm to her soul. As she interacted with them, she was struck by how distinct the Americans were from the French. Claire had been in Paris only a few days, but already she could see the differences. The Americans were dressed for comfort and practicality in athletic shoes, oversized T-shirts, and cargo shorts. They were animated and quick to laugh, smiling and ingratiating. Large and boisterous and friendly.

They seemed to bewilder the Parisians, but then the feeling was mutual.

One elderly Texan brought tears to Claire's eyes, the woman reminded her so of Mammaw. Still, there was something so serene, so comforting about the sculptures that crowded the studio. Claire ran her hands along their contours, letting the tiny hills and valleys of the plaster tickle her palms, reveling in the sensations, until she was able to pull herself together.

The afternoon flew by. Not once did she hunch over a keyboard—when customers decided on their purchases, Armand wrote everything out by hand, ignoring the computer. He asked customers to fill out their own mailing labels and recorded the transactions in an old-fashioned ledger. He even wrote paper receipts in a book that made carbon copies. He spoke in his thickly accented English to the tourists but in French the few times he addressed Claire directly; once he completed the orders, he ducked back into his workshop.

Dear Uncle Remy, Claire composed in her head. *You'll never guess what I did today: I worked at a sculpture studio, selling reproductions of statues and famous faces, including Our Special Face. The lovely lady watched me all day long. Or she would have, if only she would open her eyes!*

For the first time since she'd landed in France, Claire realized she was thoroughly enjoying herself.

15

Giselle returned in the evening just as Armand informed Claire the business was closed for the day and she should lock the door.

Giselle had two kids in tow, a six-year-old boy she introduced as David and a four-year-old girl named Victorine.

Each child kissed Claire on both cheeks and murmured a polite *"Enchanté, madame"* before flinging themselves into their uncle's arms.

Claire steeled herself for a belligerent outburst from Armand, but instead he dropped to his knees and hugged the children tight. He whispered that he had something special to show them in his workshop and escorted them in, his big hands on their shoulders.

Claire felt Giselle's gaze upon her.

"He loves children," Giselle said softly. "He is never harsh with them."

Claire nodded.

Upstairs, Giselle went through the day's receipts as Claire straightened a few busts she had pushed aside to extract the last copy of Robespierre for a man from Galveston who proclaimed he adored French history.

"We made a lot of money today," said Giselle as she gathered paperwork and put away the books.

"I'm glad. It was really fun. I enjoyed myself thoroughly."

"Even with Armand?"

"He was fine, since he mostly worked in his studio. In fact, I think we made a good pair."

Giselle handed Claire an envelope containing a small stack of euros.

"Thank you," Claire said, hesitating. Should she offer to come back? Or just leave? "I'll see you another time, then?"

"Won't you stay for *apéro*?" Giselle asked.

"*Apéro*?"

"A glass of wine and a snack before dinner. Join us, please. It's a warm evening; we'll sit outside."

The walled garden was even more charming in the fading light of the early evening. Giselle had dressed the little table with a checkered cloth and switched on the strings of white lights that decorated the garden walls and tree branches. The soft orangey tinge of sunset cast a glow on the Greek chorus of faces studding the walls and trees, bringing them to life.

Armand opened a bottle of rosé and poured three glasses. Plates had been laid out with thin-cut salami, sliced apples, rosemary crackers, and salted almonds in olive oil. Giselle placed a bottle of Pellegrino on the table.

"What's this?" Armand said, picking up the bottle. "Where's the Badoit?"

"They didn't have any, so I bought the

Pellegrino. Anyway, what's the difference?" asked Giselle. "They're both sparkling water."

"One is French; the other is Italian," Armand said, as though explaining something to a child.

"You have something against Italy?" Claire asked.

"Italians," he scoffed but did not elaborate.

The children snacked on a few almonds and apple slices, then retreated to a corner of the garden where they played in the fountain and poked through the flower boxes.

Giselle held up her wineglass: "Let us toast to a lovely day of art and business."

They touched glasses and Claire took a sip, pleased to note the chilled wine wasn't sweet, but dry and crisp and luscious. Perfect for the sultry summer evening.

"So tell us," said Giselle, "where are you from, Claire?"

"Louisiana, originally. My family is Cajun."

"That explains why you speak French with that accent," said Armand.

"Better than nothing," she said with a shrug. "Especially since you don't want to speak English."

"I say quite enough in English," he said, in English.

He kept his deep blue eyes on her. After a moment of ignoring him, she stared back.

His face reminded Claire of a Chinese puzzle

she sometimes played with while hiding from her father; *quiet, quiet, don't make noise.* Slide one tile to the right, another to the left. One up, one down. If you did it correctly, a picture emerged.

"And you learned about us how?" asked Giselle, lighting a cigarette.

"Must you?" said Armand to his cousin, in reference to her smoking.

"*Oui*, I must," said Giselle. "I'm outside; it's allowed. Anyway, go on, Claire."

"I found a copy of the mask of *L'Inconnue* in my grandmother's attic when I was a little girl. I guess I always wondered where it came from. So I read about her on the Internet, and that led me to you."

Armand waved his hand dismissively.

"What did I say?" Claire asked.

"My cousin does not enjoy the Internet," explained Giselle with a smile. "I insisted we have a Web site for the business—in fact, my oldest boy, Luc, created it. He's in college now. You are in computers, so I'm sure you noticed it needs work. But it's better than nothing."

"Well, it led me to you, so it did its job," said Claire. It was true that she had found the Web site amateurish. But it was definitely better than nothing. "It's funny. I haven't gone online for days. Back home I practically live on the Net."

"Then why bother coming to Paris at all?" asked Armand. "Why not just stay in your box of an office and stare into the box of the computer and do your boxed-in research?"

"Because the food's better here," she answered, doing her best to imitate a Gallic shrug. "Not to mention the wine."

Armand pushed out his chin, nodding as though conceding her point. "Now this, this is true."

Giselle laughed. "So, Claire, have you been enjoying your visit in Paris?"

"Yes," Claire said, to be polite. "Yesterday I went to the Champs-Élysées and the Eiffel Tower."

A loud dismissive sound from Armand.

"What did I say this time?" Claire asked.

"The Champs-Élysées is famous for being famous, nothing more. And the Eiffel Tower? This is not Paris. There is a reason no French people visit these places. They are tourist traps. Corporate nonsense."

"Oh, I don't know, it seems to me I heard French being spoken on the Champs-Élysées. Even in McDonald's."

Giselle's eyes widened and she cast a wary look at her cousin.

"MacDonald's?" he demanded, pronouncing it *Mac*Donald's, in the French way.

"They have *macarons*, did you know?"

"Typical." He snorted. "Americans come to Paris and eat 'Big Macs.' "

"I think it was a *bleu* burger. It was really quite good. Also, *macarons*. Did I mention that?" Claire hoped her words sounded sure and confident, but inside, her heart was pounding. What was it about this grumpy sculptor? She felt exhilarated but jittery; her nerve endings hummed. And it wasn't just the wine talking.

"The only decent *macarons* come from Pierre Hermé," said Armand. "Everyone knows this. And if you heard French accents they were from the countryside. Not Parisians."

"That brings up a good question: are you as disdainful of French tourists as you are of other tourists?"

Armand frowned, as though not understanding her question.

"It seems to me," she continued, "that everyone everywhere looks down on tourists, but what is the alternative? Should they stay home and watch the travel channels but never travel? Weren't you just complaining about people sitting in front of their computers?"

"I can see why you two did so well together today," Giselle said with a chuckle. "I think you are well matched!"

Armand ignored his cousin and changed the subject, asking Claire, "Why are you so interested in this mask of *L'Inconnue*?"

"I told you—my great-grandfather bought one from this very shop at the end of World War II and had it sent to Louisiana. I found it in my grandmother's attic."

"That explains how you knew about her, but not why you came all the way to Paris to find her."

Because I used to talk to it. I thought it was a sign. And . . . I didn't know what else to do with myself.

"It seemed as good a reason as any."

"Huh." He stood. "We have another bottle of rosé in the fridge," he said, glancing at Claire's glass. "I see you like it."

Was she drinking too much? Claire wondered, feeling her cheeks burning. She hadn't drunk any more than they had, had she? She watched as Armand climbed the exterior stairs that led back to the main floor.

"So you and Armand are cousins?"

Giselle nodded. "His grandmother is my aunt, so I'm not sure exactly how we're connected, but we're family. Two Lombardi brothers came to France from Italy in the 1870s. One brother made his home in the Franche-Comté, in eastern France, and the other came to Paris and founded this studio. Ever since then, the talent—and the business—has been passed down through the family, and the family members share our time between the family estate and this atelier."

"That's fantastic. It's rare to find that kind of continuity where I come from. So is a Lombardi still in charge of Lombardi's?"

"Officially, Armand is a Fontaine. It was his grandmother who carried the Lombardi blood.

But we make an exception for him because he inherited the talent, eh, Armand?"

He grunted as he came back to join them, setting a chilled bottle of rosé on the table.

"I hope my oldest boy will take an interest in the business eventually," continued Giselle. "When he finishes his studies at L'École des Beaux-Arts."

"He would do better to work here as an apprentice," said Armand.

"He has broader interests, and he is still young," said Giselle. "Let him explore a little and perhaps he'll come back to the family business. Among other things, he'd like to learn more about computers."

Armand remained silent and brooding, watching the children play. Their piping voices carried across the garden and mingled with muffled street noises from the other side of the building, the occasional horn or shout.

"Perhaps you can convince Luc to work with you while we are in the countryside," Giselle said. To Claire, she explained, "We will take our August break in two weeks. Our family has a big event coming up. A wedding party in the countryside."

"How lovely."

"A wedding of two people who have been together for sixty-five years," said Armand, sounding unimpressed.

"Which only makes it more romantic," said Giselle.

Claire smiled. "They've been together for sixty-five years?"

"They are Armand's grandparents," said Giselle. "Delphine was only seventeen when they married and eighteen when she had her first child, Armand's father."

"So is it a recommitment ceremony?"

"What's that?"

"Where a couple takes vows again," Claire explained as best she could, though she didn't know the right words in French. "To refresh their marriage."

"No, nothing like that. I can't imagine they need to renew their vows after all this time! No, my uncle—Armand's grandfather—is a romantic, and he and Delphine weren't able to have a party when they married. Life was so difficult during the war and for some time afterward; the studio barely survived. In France, you know, everyone is married at the courthouse. They make a party if they can afford it, but many can't."

"So they've waited sixty-five years to have their wedding party? I agree with you, Giselle—it *is* very romantic." Claire tried to stifle a yawn. "Excuse me—I'm sorry. I haven't been sleeping well."

Giselle used a phrase Claire didn't know—*décalage horaire*—but after a short discussion she realized Giselle was asking if she was suffering from jet lag.

"No, it's not that," said Claire. "It's the place I'm renting—a tiny apartment not too far from the Hôtel de Ville, in a great location, but it shares a wall with a club called Le Ciel Bleu. Do you know it?"

"I have two small children at home. I never go out," said Giselle. She looked at Armand. "How about you?"

He nodded. "I know it. So you are up all night dancing?"

Claire laughed. "Hardly. More like trying desperately to cover my ears—but there's no escaping the vibrations coming through the wall. I really need to find another place to stay, but as you know Paris is expensive and it's the height of the tourist season. I don't know how long I'll be staying in any case."

"You don't have a ticket back?" Giselle asked.

"Not yet. I wasn't sure what I'd find here, so I left it open-ended. As I told you, I'm currently unemployed, so I'm a bit of a free bird."

Giselle cast a glance at her cousin, who shook his head. And then they began a heated discussion, lowering their voices. They were only on the other side of the table, so although Claire heard most of it—*But I can't be here more than a few hours a day, Armand*—they spoke quickly and used a lot of unfamiliar slang. She couldn't make sense of it all.

In an effort to be polite, Claire got up and joined

the children, who had discovered something in one of the raised beds.

"*Escargots*!" Victorine yelled, showing Claire a snail. She held it high in the air and called to her mother, "Shall we eat them, *Maman*?"

"Gather them in a bucket if you want, and we will take them home and feed them cornmeal," said Giselle, who then resumed her discussion with her cousin. Victorine fetched a bucket from a shed and gathered the snails, picking them up carefully by their shells.

"I don't like *escargots*," said David. "Do you, madame?"

"I'm not sure, actually," responded Claire. "I've never in my life tried one."

"Never?"

"Never."

"It isn't your custom to eat them?" asked David.

"Where I come from, people eat them sometimes, but we call them *bigarno*."

"Bigarno? Why?"

Claire laughed. "I really don't know. It's just the word we use. But my grandma didn't like them, so we never ate them at home."

Victorine looked at her with huge eyes. "One time we had a disaster with a whole bucket of snails at home and—"

She was cut off when Armand threw up his hands and shouted, "*Fine*—do what you want."

"Claire," Giselle called out, "we have a proposal for you."

Claire returned to the table and took her seat. "A proposal?"

"Yes," said Giselle. "Would you like to stay here and work for us for a little while?"

"Excuse me?" Claire wasn't sure she'd heard right. Though she was usually able to understand the Parisian French, she lost the occasional word here and there. Perhaps she hadn't understood her meaning. "You're suggesting I *live* here?"

Giselle nodded. "There is a small bedroom off the kitchen."

"Very small," said Armand. "I do not think it will suit you. Americans like enormous houses."

"Believe me, size is not the issue." Claire hadn't had a bed of her own until she went off to college. It would take more than a small room to faze her.

"We cannot handle the work, Armand and I. Our shop assistant is expected to return after the August vacation," Giselle said. "But we need someone until then, or we will have to hire someone permanent."

"Am I allowed to work in France as a foreign national?" Claire asked.

"*Non*," said Armand.

"Not officially," said Giselle. "But we will pay you in cash, and the government will be none the wiser. It is only for two weeks. I think it's a brilliant plan—you will have a decent place to get a good night's sleep and we will have someone to handle our English-speaking tourists. Best of all, Armand doesn't scare you!" Giselle sat back with a satisfied smile and lit another cigarette, clearly convinced she'd found the perfect solution.

"I really don't know, Giselle," Claire said. The truth was, Armand *did* scare her. She felt on edge and hyperaware around him—could practically feel his energy buzzing from across the table.

"Also," Armand said, "Giselle tells me you are looking for more information on *L'Inconnue*. There is a box with clippings and stories. If you agree to help us, you may look through it."

"Giselle told me I could look in the box if I came to help *today,*" Claire pointed out. "Besides, I thought *you* didn't want me here. Weren't you just arguing with Giselle about it? What changed your mind?"

He shrugged.

"I tell you what, Monsieur Armand Lombardi Fontaine," Claire said in English. "Back home we would say you're as contrary as a mule."

"*Une mule? C'est vrai!*" said Giselle. Apparently some things did not need translation.

"Yes, I suppose I am," said Armand after a long pause. "So, will you stay and help us? Surely it would be more interesting than the Champs-Élysées. At the very least, more of a genuine

Parisian experience than *Mac*Donald's. You can impress your friends upon your return, tell them you worked in a genuine Parisian atelier."

Claire smiled, not sure who she would tell these stories to. Her Chicago friends had regaled her with more tales of Paris than she ever could—most of them had made several trips to Europe by the time they'd graduated college. And her family wasn't impressed by travel, wondering instead why she spent her money on such a silly endeavor.

Still, he had a point. She'd enjoyed herself more today than any day since her feet had touched French soil.

"Think about it and let us know. If you'll excuse me," said Armand, getting up from the table, "I have a few things to attend to before dinner."

He joined the children for a moment, tickling them and inspecting the snails. They gave him big hugs, and then he disappeared up the stairs.

"He's not a bad man," said Giselle in a low voice. "He's a little . . . *overwhelmed*. In addition to trying to keep this place afloat, he's been working on the old family château—not that it's worth saving. It was virtually destroyed in the war."

"What a shame. But if it's that far gone, why is he trying to save it?"

She shrugged. "One must. It is his duty. Just as running this studio is his duty. *C'est la coutume*"—it's the custom. "Try to be patient with him; he has suffered a great personal tragedy, and he is still trying to come to terms with it."

"I'm sorry to hear that," said Claire. "My grandmother used to say that time heals all wounds."

"I think you Americans are very optimistic. There are some things . . ." Giselle seemed to consider her words, then shrugged. "Some things, one never gets over."

Claire could feel her stomach clench. How many times had people told her over the years, *You need to get over it. Move on*?

And she had. Or at least, she had tried. She didn't remember what had happened that night in the car when they veered off the road, not really. Only in her dreams, her imagination reconstructing the scene from her family's stories. Still, there were times the legacy of her mother's accident seemed to drag her down into the depths of that bayou.

"Come," said Giselle. "I will show you the room where you will stay, and you can see if it's acceptable."

The chamber off the kitchen was more like an oversized closet or former larder than a bedroom. A single iron bed, smaller than the American version, hardly more than a cot, was tucked against one gray stone wall; a petit escritoire and small armoire occupied the opposite side. A single oversized casement window looked out over the patio and walled garden below. It was covered with curved decorative wrought-iron bars, giving Claire the impression of being in a birdcage. Or maybe a nunnery.

The room was small and dim but still charming; it was something her child's mind would have dreamed up for a princess being held in a tower.

"Is this all right?" Giselle asked, worry in her eyes. "I know it isn't fancy. I wish I could invite you to stay in my home, but my in-laws are with us at the moment. Also, this way you have no commute to worry about, of course. I'm all the way over in the Arrondissement de Fontainebleau."

"No, no, it's fine," Claire said. "It's charming, truly, in a historic Parisian way."

Armand approached with a pile of folded sheets and blankets. He handed them to Claire without a word. They smelled of lavender and fresh air. The scent reminded Claire of Mammaw's penchant for saying, *Line drying is free, and don't it make things smell like heaven?*

"There is a small bath over here, with a shower," said Giselle, gesturing to the other side of the kitchen. "The towels are clean. And the toilet is over there."

"Thank you. This all looks fine. I'm looking forward to actually sleeping tonight."

"You will have full use of the kitchen, of

course," said Armand. "I ask only that you stay out of my quarters. *Je vous souhaite une bonne soirée.*" He wished her good night, stalked into his workroom, and shut the door.

"Wait. Armand lives here?" Claire asked Giselle. "As in *here* here?"

"Of course," Giselle said. "He has a room behind his workshop. Claire, thank you so much for doing this. I believe you are saving our business! Here is a key to the front door. Just for two weeks, that's all."

She held up a huge old-fashioned skeleton key that reminded Claire of something she might have seen in a movie.

"I . . . of course," Claire said as she took the key.

Two weeks selling plaster casts and living with Monsieur Grumpy. What was she thinking?

On the other hand . . . it was two weeks selling plaster casts and living with Monsieur Grumpy in *Paris*.

If nothing else, it was going to make great fodder for a story. Too bad she didn't have anyone to tell it to.

16

SABINE

Monsieur Desmarais likes to study her face, even when she is sleeping. She has awoken many times to find him staring. Is he searching for the secret to his artistic success?

It is a success that has eluded him so far, Sabine soon realizes. Maurice—as he insists she call him—has family money, though his father despises his artistic ambitions and threatens to disown him. But Maurice received an inheritance from his maternal grandmother, and this is what pays his rent. Still, it earns him the disdain of his fellow artists, many of whom live hand to mouth.

"It is as if you came to me from another time, my little country mouse," Maurice says. "I do believe the gods have sent me a muse."

He dresses her in antique clothing, has Isabelle arrange her hair in old-fashioned twists that frame her face. He is convinced that art must return to its classical heyday and wishes he had been born a century earlier so that his style would be appreciated.

Sabine finds Maurice to be a strange man. One moment he is kind, the next he is preoccupied, and the next he snaps at her. His temper is unpredictable, volatile. He once threw a maquette at his sister, Isabelle, when she suggested they visit their father.

Isabelle is no less pressured than Maurice to marry and conform to the family's expectations—more so, in fact. But her brother supports her, and she respects his rebellion, his railing against their parents and insistence upon creating his art. Unfortunately for Isabelle, she has no such talent, no fire in her belly to pursue anything in particular other than to do as her brother says. She adores him, the light shining in her dark eyes as she watches him.

She is like his little wife, Sabine thinks. *Or at least, some secret part of her would like to be.*

Perhaps the priest at the Cathédrale de Notre Dame had been right when he warned Sabine to be wary of the artistic life. She understands now that it is a seductive idea: the challenge to reinterpret the world through one's own eyes, one's own imaginings. Perhaps it is blasphemous. Should the world be seen only through the eyes of God? But what of religious art, then? Before she had come to Paris, only in church had Sabine seen sculptures and paintings and stained-glass windows so beautiful they humbled mere humans.

These are some of the things she wonders when she stands (or sits or lies) perfectly still for hours on end while Maurice creates.

His attentions, while unwelcome, are not

abhorrent. His bed is made of down; it is so soft, it is like sleeping on a cloud of silk. Sabine never knew such softness existed in this world. She thinks of other things, allows him to do as he wants. At least he is not her stepfather.

Also, he ensures he will not get her with child— his life is dedicated to his art, Maurice repeats often; he has no time for children.

He pays her little, since he provides her with room and board. But the coins are enough for her to repay Toinette and Honorine for their kindness. On a free day, when Maurice does not feel like working, Sabine meets them outside their workplace and buys them bowls of soup. They gossip about the artists she has met but do not ask about her arrangement with Monsieur Desmarais. They guess, but they do not judge.

Sabine has not returned to the cathedral, has not confessed her sins.

But she is not hungry.

Every morning there is food. It is miraculous. In the mornings she drinks coffee with sugar and cream, eats croissants slathered with rich butter and cherry preserves. For lunch, crusty bread and ham and fruit. For dinner, there is meat and salad. For dessert, a raspberry tart or poached pears or strawberries in sweet cream. He even buys her chocolate from time to time.

Sometimes at night they stop work early and go to a brasserie where Maurice smokes and drinks absinthe and talks with his friends. He likes to order the plat du jour, and they eat escargots or rillettes followed by *moules frites* or *steak au poivre* or *lapin à la moutarde* with a sauce so rich, Sabine wishes she could lick the plate. She adores chocolate mousse and once tasted a new dessert sensation that is soaked in orange liqueur and set afire before it is served: crêpes Suzette.

For many days, for weeks, for a very long time, this is all that matters. She is not hungry.

Sometimes Maurice does not want her with him. On those nights, and sometimes for days at a time, she has the studio to herself. He allows her to play with a small hunk of discarded clay, to sketch with her charcoal, to use his old dried paints and ruined brushes. She shows him what she makes; it amuses him. Also, in the studio there are three books: two on sculpture, one on painting. Sabine has never owned a book. The words are long and difficult, but she makes her way through the sentences painstakingly. And she studies the pictures: lithographs of famous works by artists with names like Michelangelo and Caravaggio, Gérôme and Falconet.

Whereas before Sabine saw only crowds and carriages in the streets of Paris, she now sees paintings and sculptures everywhere, from the monuments in the parks to the groundbreaking paintings of the Impressionists and those who came afterward, who call themselves Nabis.

When Maurice's friends and colleagues converse, she listens: they speak of color and shape and the world of the mind. It is exhilarating.

One night Maurice promises to take her to the Palais du Louvre. Sabine wonders aloud if she'll be allowed into a *palace*, but he laughs, calls her his little country mouse, and says since the Revolution even the poor are welcomed within its hallowed halls.

At night, Sabine lets herself drift off, knowing there will be coffee with rich cream in the morning, and perhaps chocolate.

17

Claire took the metro to the musty little rented apartment and called her landlady to tell her she would be vacating. She'd haggle over a refund later. She went online and caught up on her e-mails and ate the now soggy half of yesterday's sandwich, washing it down with the last of the wine.

Then she packed her toiletries and clothes, gathered her letter-writing kit, her laptop, and the novel she was currently reading, and bade farewell to the nightclub and the mildew.

She didn't want to return to the Lombardi studio too soon. Making awkward conversation with Armand or hiding in her tiny cubby all night was not an appealing prospect. So she rolled her small travel bag along the quai, keeping one eye on the Seine and taking in Paris at night: lovers strolling arm in arm, of course; a young woman in a long silk gown playing the violin on the corner; a trio of impossibly old men at an outdoor café table sharing a bottle of wine, smoking cigarillos, and debating loudly.

She crossed the ornate Pont Neuf, walked the width of the Île de la Cité—the Cathedral of Notre Dame looming large—and turned onto the quai de Conti, passing outdoor cafés, souvenir shops, and ethnic restaurants touting souvlaki and couscous and panini.

Reaching at last the front door of the Moulage Lombardi, she paused to wonder whether she should knock. No, she *lived* here now, she thought—for two weeks, anyway. Feeling like Alice in Wonderland about to plunge down the rabbit hole, she took the massive iron key from her shoulder bag, inserted it into the ancient lock, and let herself in.

Locking the door behind her, she lugged her suitcase up the stairs, nodding at the army of masks as she passed, and paused on the landing at the top. The scent of plaster seemed to welcome her, the chalky aroma signaling a sense of belonging: she had a role to play, a purpose in life, however temporary.

She started toward the tiny cubby off the kitchen,

then hesitated. Through the wall of windows the lights blazed in the studio, and Armand sat with his back to her, working on something—not a mask or a bust, but something else; she couldn't quite see what. When she tapped lightly on the workshop window, Armand yanked a cloth over whatever he was working on and came to the door.

"I thought you understood French," he said in English. "I asked you not to bother me."

"*Oui, je parle français,*" she replied. "And I apologize for bothering you, but I'd like to see the box with the information on *L'Inconnue*. I forgot to ask Giselle before she left."

He let out a sigh. "Really? You are truly obsessed with this poor dead woman?"

"*I'm* obsessed? All your subjects are dead, aren't they? And you live among them here in the atelier of the dead."

"You have a flair for the dramatic, I see. As you wish. It is downstairs."

She followed him down the back stairs and through the barn door, the two of them winding their way through the crowd of sculptures to a rear storage closet, which Armand opened with a small key. On one side was a well-stocked wine cellar, on the other a stack of file boxes. He reached up and grabbed one that looked older than the rest: a cardboard box stamped with a design that appeared to be from the 1960s: *Bas Couture*. Women's stockings.

"That's it?" she asked.

He nodded and brought the box back upstairs, passing through the kitchen and into her room. He placed the box on her little desk and looked around the tiny chamber.

"This is . . ." He seemed to be searching for words. "This isn't a very nice space."

"It's fine. Really."

"It is where the apprentice slept, years ago when an apprentice wasn't treated particularly well. The last one to stay here was my grandfather."

"He was?"

He nodded. "My *grand-père* Pierre-Guillaume Fontaine married Delphine Lombardi, the daughter of my great-grandfather Marc-Antoine Lombardi, son of Jean-Baptiste Lombardi, who was son of the man who founded the *moulage* in Paris."

"I'll need a spreadsheet to keep all the names straight."

"Ancient history. Anyway, the only other bedroom is mine."

"I'll be fine, truly. You should see where I grew up."

He looked at her for a long moment.

"Well," she said softly, "thank you for sharing the box with me. And for letting me stay here."

He scoffed. "Such as it is. Tomorrow—maybe you can fix the room up a little. There are some things in the basement you could use."

"Clean sheets are all I need."

He nodded. "All right, then. Good night."

"Good night."

He hesitated for another moment before turning on his heel and striding back to his workshop.

Claire surveyed her little cubby and smiled. If only her family could see her now. What would they make of a "fancy college-educated city gal" living in this tiny chamber off an artist's atelier?

Other than the muted murmur of street noises, it was blessedly quiet. The evening was warm, so she left the window open and a soft breeze blew in from the garden, filling the room with a subtle floral perfume. She made the bed, hung up her clothes, and set out her stationery to write a letter to Uncle Remy.

But first . . . she sat on the bed and opened the box.

A thick manila envelope held newspaper clippings—some brittle and yellowed with age, others fairly recent. There were photocopies of short stories and handwritten notes referencing literary quotes about *L'Inconnue de la Seine*. And two slim leather-bound volumes.

She brought out her French-English dictionary. She would need assistance to make her way through some of the denser newspaper articles.

Most of what she read seemed to agree with what she had dug up on the Internet while sitting in Mammaw's living room. *L'Inconnue* had lived during the late 1800s, though the exact year of her death was in dispute because at the time the Paris morgue did not keep careful records of all the unknown bodies fished out of the Seine.

Just as Giselle had said, the articles agreed that Jean-Baptiste Lombardi had been summoned by a worker at the morgue to make a death mask of the young woman because she was so beautiful.

During the Belle Epoque, *L'Inconnue*'s face had become the toast of Europe's bohemian scene and her visage was said to grace the walls of virtually every writer and artist in the city and throughout Europe. Greta Garbo and German actress Elisabeth Bergner were both said to have modeled their looks—and their attitudes—on *L'Inconnue*. When a book publisher asked novelist Louis-Ferdinand Céline for a photo in 1933, he sent one of *L'Inconnue* instead.

One story claimed *L'Inconnue* was a naïf from the countryside who had become pregnant by a wealthy married man. Another said she was a young British woman who had been abandoned by her lover after he married a titled debutante and moved to Egypt. Rilke wrote a meditation on her fate, supposing she had been seduced and abandoned; several reporters asserted she was German or Russian. One author described her as "a delicate butterfly who—winged and light-heartedly—had her wings prematurely singed."

As she delved deeper into the box's contents,

Claire learned that *L'Inconnue* was also variously referred to as Ophelia from *Hamlet*, the *Mona Lisa* of the river, or the *Bewitching Beauty*. Anaïs Nin and Vladimir Nabokov wrote stories about her as a spirit of the river. And Austrian playwright Ödön von Horváth called *L'Inconnue* a descendent of Mélusine, the mermaid known to lure men to their deaths.

But no matter the author, each of the tales ended in *L'Inconnue* meeting her watery death in the Seine at a brutally young age. Yet no one knew who she really was. How could so many have written about her, obsessed over her—including some of the greatest minds in Europe—and yet she remained *inconnue*?

Claire kept reading, working her way through the papers stored in the box until the words swam in front of her eyes. It was slow going because she had to stop and look up a word every line or two.

She rifled through the rest of the box, half hoping she'd find a letter similar to the one she'd found in Mammaw's attic, or some other correspondence. Something that wasn't obviously fiction.

But that would be expecting too much. The note she'd found had come with the sculpture, sent from Paris in 1945, forty or fifty years after *L'Inconnue*'s mask had been cast. It probably had nothing whatsoever to do with that poor woman. It was a joke, maybe, or perhaps a relic of someone else's tragic story.

He will never let me go alive.

Claire laid her head on the surprisingly soft lavender-scented pillow—grateful for the lack of frenetic disco music thumping through the walls—and closed her eyes.

One thing she had learned when she was very young: there was no shortage of tragic stories.

18

C laire awoke to the rich aroma of coffee brewing.

She had slept in a T-shirt and shorts, but was still flustered to encounter Armand in the kitchen when she stumbled out of her little room to go to the toilet.

" 'Morning," she mumbled.

"*Bonjour*," Armand replied, not even looking at her. He stood at the counter cutting strawberries. A bag from a *boulangerie* sat on the counter.

She hurried to wash up, then—figuring her T-shirt and shorts were sufficiently modest—rejoined Armand in the kitchen, where he had just finished loading a tray with plates and food.

It seemed oddly domestic for one so driven.

And strangely intimate. Breaking up with Sean had been the right thing to do, Claire knew, but she missed this part of being a couple, when she would sleep over at his place or vice versa:

moving about the kitchen in the early mornings, saying little, their movements orchestrated, the silent companionship before the daily barrage of words and demands of work drowned out their thoughts.

"Grab the newspaper and the fruit," Armand said as he lifted the tray laden with croissants and jam, coffee and cream. "And . . . you might want a sweater. We'll be in the garden."

"Great. Do you mind if I charge my cell phone here?" she said, gesturing to an outlet over the kitchen counter. "I couldn't find an outlet in my room."

He grunted. She was going to take that as a yes.

Claire pulled on a sweatshirt and shoes, plugged in her phone, then picked up the newspaper and the bowl of strawberries and went downstairs to the garden.

A chill hung in the air; the sky overhead was gray. The birds, the mist, the sounds of the traffic and someone calling for Antoine surrounded her. They were in the middle of Paris, but if not for the traffic and horns they could be anywhere in France, in a walled garden somewhere out in the countryside.

One thing Claire could say for Armand: he set a pretty table. She had made the assumption that the *apéro* last night had been laid out by Giselle, but perhaps it had been Armand. Or maybe it

161

was just that she was in France and everything involving food seemed to be reason for celebration.

She took a croissant from the stack and placed it on a yellow plate dotted with blue flowers. Armand pushed a small dish of butter toward her, despite the fact the bread already glistened, its tissue-thin layers held together with artery-clogging deliciousness. She watched as he dunked his croissant in his coffee, liberally splashed with cream.

"So, what time do we open?" Claire ventured.

"We?"

"The shop. What time do you open your doors?"

"When I feel like it."

She laughed.

Armand disappeared behind his newspaper, *Le Monde*. No Internet news for this artist. Claire hadn't worked up the nerve yet to ask about Internet service and, truth to tell, there was something rather appealing in not having to think about it.

So she resolved to relax and drink her coffee.

After several minutes, she tried again: "I just wanted to be sure to be ready. It's my first day on the job after all."

"You started yesterday."

"Sort of."

"Mmm," he replied, still hiding behind the newspaper.

"It's just that I'd like to take a shower, show my best face, and all that." She bit into the pastry and let out a little moan. "This croissant is incredible."

"It's a good *boulangerie*."

"We have croissants in the States, of course, but they don't taste like this." She hadn't felt hungry, but the croissant was changing her mind. "It's strange—even the butter is different here. Tastier, somehow. Who knew different *butters* would taste different?"

Armand lowered his newspaper. "Do all Americans talk this much in the morning?"

"I really can't say; I don't know all Americans." Her heart fluttered, but she quipped: "Are all French this rude?"

He snorted. "Just relax, enjoy your coffee. It is bad for the digestion to move too quickly through meals."

"Yes, boss. Whatever you say."

In French, the word for "boss" was *chef*. For some reason it amused her to say, *Oui, chef*! As though she were working as his sous-chef in a professional kitchen.

The newspaper rattled as he raised it again, and Claire made an effort to enjoy the quiet of the morning, the calm before the storm.

As a matter of fact, Claire had been raised in this tradition. Though the Cajuns had their own unique culture, they shared much with the French: sitting down to beignets and strong chicory-laced coffee for breakfast, lingering over long, drawn-out family dinners. Claire thought about the picnic table covered in newspapers upon which the huge pots of crawfish and shrimp were dumped, the fragrance of the steam of the crab boil, the huge loaves of bread and the spicy sauce that accompanied everything. She had changed when she went off to school and adopted what her family called "Yankee ways": living according to a tight schedule, with only half an hour for lunch, crackers and cheese and fruit for dinner. Grabbing something quick, whatever was handy, eating last night's Chinese takeout in front of the computer. Rushing through meals.

Though Paris could not have had much less in common with Plaquemines Parish, Claire again felt a nostalgic familiarity. Mostly it was an attitude: a slightly grumpy embrace of the day, fatalistic, irritated, but determined to enjoy things to the fullest. As though the knowledge that the world was out to get you—that bad things would happen—made a person stop and enjoy the simple things, like family and food and wine.

After breakfast Claire washed up in the teeny shower and then stood in front of her armoire, trying to decide what to wear. She traveled light and hadn't packed much that was appropriate for her current situation. How did one dress to work in a mold-maker's studio?

Something white, probably, she thought as she

eyed the determined dust that sifted under even closed doors. Most of what she owned was black and semiformal: clothes meant for working at a computer in an office. Finally, she settled on a clean pair of jeans and a light blue blouse.

Once dressed, she wandered the showroom floor, wondering whether Armand would join her and tell her what exactly she was supposed to be doing. Behind the desk a white lab coat was draped over the back of the chair. She pulled it on, unsure whether it was Armand's or Giselle's or whether it had been laid out for her.

She found she liked it. It made her feel dressed for the role she was playing.

With still no sign from Armand, Claire decided to rewrite the sign on the front door in English, telling visitors they were welcome and they should come on up to the *second* floor. She found pens and paper in the desk drawers, wrote out a note, and descended the creaky stairs to open the front door.

She noticed a plaque that she had overlooked before:

Moulage de la Famille Lombardi, est. 1871
Maîtres Propriétaires:
Giuseppe Lombardi, 1871–1891
Jean-Baptiste Lombardi, 1891–1924
(Olivier Delen, 1898–1924)
Marc-Antoine Lombardi, 1924–1957

Pierre-Guillaume Fontaine, 1957–1981
Loic Lombardi Fontaine, 1981–2010
Armand Lombardi Fontaine, 2010–

Again Claire wondered what it would be like to be part of such a lineage. Was there comfort in knowing exactly what was expected of you? Or was it stifling, having no choice but to follow in the footsteps of others? Could this be one reason (among many) that Armand seemed so unhappy?

Across the street a white-haired woman in a chic pantsuit was opening a small shop that sold tchotchkes: kitchen towels, small purses, music boxes printed with the Eiffel Tower and the Chat Noir, the famous Parisian nightspot named for a black cat. If Armand didn't want to be inundated with tourists, Claire thought to herself, he would have to move the studio out from the shadow of the Cathedral of Notre Dame—and that was a long shadow indeed, stretching across all of the fourth arrondissement and much of the fifth.

Claire waved to the neighbor: "*Bonjour, madame!*"

The woman looked startled and not particularly pleased, but uttered a quick *bonjour* before scuttling back into her crowded shop.

A tall, thin man emerged from the neighboring building: classically handsome, his long honey brown hair pulled into a ponytail, a worn leather satchel in one hand. He nodded in Claire's direction.

"*Bonjour*," Claire said.

"*Bonjour*," he responded, then paused. "Are you new to the neighborhood?"

"I am."

He pushed out his chin, as though surprised. It was a very French move. "I did not think Armand would find a new girl so soon."

"*C'est moi.* That's me. I'm Claire Broussard. It's my first real day."

"I'm Quentin. The neighbor. It's a pleasure."

"*Enchantée*," Claire responded. Literally this translated as "Enchanted." It sounded so much nicer than a simple "Hello."

"*Est-ce que vous êtes Américaine?*" he asked.

"Yes, I'm from Louisiana."

"I love America. I was there one time, many years ago. I did a school exchange in high school, to Milwaukee."

"Really? I've never been there," Claire said, wondering how in the world a Parisian had landed in Milwaukee. Then again, that city had probably offered him a more representative view of America than New York or Los Angeles.

"I suppose I'll see you soon, then," said Quentin. "Perhaps this evening I will drop by for *apéro*."

Claire nodded, not at all convinced that her new boss would appreciate her inviting neighbors over. It wasn't her place. And frankly, Armand did not seem like the kind of person to ask folks to drop by. Then again, he did set a pretty table. And he had invited Claire—via Giselle—not only to *apéro* but into his home, such as it was. Still.

No point in worrying about it now. For now, Claire would savor the novelty of being a shop-keeper in Paris. It had never been one of her life's goals, but she was enough of a chameleon to enjoy the exhilarating strangeness of stepping into another person's shoes, trying on a new life. The miracle of make-believe.

As she attached her sign to the door in place of the old one, Claire reminded herself that it was only for a couple of weeks.

She would have to figure out what she was doing with her life in the long term. But just for now, she could give herself this reprieve: a couple of weeks as a Paris shopkeeper.

19

The atelier needed a good cleaning, Claire decided. She found a broom by the back door and a feather duster and some rags in a closet. She gave the showroom area a quick once-over with the broom—just the most egregious corners that showed more than half an inch of plaster, like a miniature snowdrift—and then started wiping down the merchandise.

It would be impossible to keep all the sculptures and friezes dust-free, and besides, the untidiness added to Lombardi's authentic ambience. It seemed more artist's studio than showroom, and that was what the tourists liked and responded to, she imagined. That's what *she* liked, anyway. As the resident foreigner, she was going to go with her gut.

So mostly she used the feather duster to clean the visages of the masks on the walls, the faces of the statues. They should gleam for the atelier's visitors, putting their best feet forward. Even if they had no feet.

"What on earth are you doing?"

Claire had been so caught up in her own thoughts that she squeaked and whirled around in surprise.

Armand stood watching her, a frown on his face.

"*Whoa,* you startled me! I'm just dusting—what does it look like I'm doing?"

"That's not your job."

"Whose job is it?"

"Not yours."

"You hired me to translate, but since there aren't any customers I thought I would make myself useful."

"If you want to be useful, you could haul those buckets of dirty water downstairs and pour them down the drain."

Claire cast a dubious glance at the five-gallon

plastic buckets full of milky water standing by the door that led to the back stairs. They looked awfully heavy.

"I don't want to be *that* useful."

He let out a reluctant chuckle. "You are correct, though—it is not as though there are customers needing translation every minute of the day. In between, you will help me in the workshop."

"I'm allowed in your hallowed studio?" she asked, but since she couldn't think of the word for "hallowed" in French she said *"sanctifié"* and he gave her a strange look.

"Wrong word? Sorry. Never mind," she added, because the truth was, she was dying to see the inside of his workshop.

The scent of wet plaster hit her right away, much stronger than in the showroom. It was a chalky mineral aroma that reminded her of the hot sand of the Gulf of Mexico, minus the smell of fish and seaweed. On a shelf under the workbench, Claire noticed something bulky covered with a towel. That must have been what she saw him working on late last night. Why cover it up?

"Have you ever gotten your hands dirty?" Armand asked.

"I . . ." She shrugged. "I've done a fair amount of housework in my day."

He made an impatient gesture. "Have you ever *sculpted?*"

"Not really . . ." she said. Though as the words

came out of her mouth she recalled the feeling of clay squishing between her fingers, the Play-Doh and the mud pies and sandcastles of her youth. The way she used to enjoy creating figures from anything malleable. The sensations of dimension and heft in her palms as she shaped the material according to her will, her vision.

Until she grew up and realized she needed to get a real job.

"Never?" Armand asked, noting her hesitation.

"Not formally. I mean, as a kid I used to like to make things, but all kids are like that, right? And my mother sculpted . . ." She trailed off, wondering whether the silly little animals her mother had made out of craft clay would count as sculpting in Armand Lombardi Fontaine's book. Claire added, "A little."

"Did you watch her at least?"

"No. She died when I was a baby."

"I'm sorry."

"Thank you."

"Your father raised you, then?"

"For a while, and then I went to live with my grandmother. And I don't think *she* ever sculpted anything but salmon croquettes. They were pretty amazing croquettes, though, I have to say, and always perfectly round. She won a second-place ribbon at the county fair once. And a *blue* ribbon for her Yummy Yammy Cake, two years in a row."

"Huh." He grunted.

"Besides, isn't mold-making different from sculpting, per se?"

"Of course, but they share some of the same sensibility. In order to make a mold properly, you must have a feel for the contours and voids, the form of the object. And then after the casting, we make refinements by hand."

Armand handed her a dust mask.

"Put this on and you can help me mix a batch of plaster to cast these molds."

He gestured to three bright blue mask molds resting in boxes full of raw white rice. A notch at the top held hooks that would extend into the plaster once it was poured so that the finished mask could be hung. It was difficult to recognize the shapes because the molds were "inside out," the reverse of what the plaster casts would look like, but Claire thought one might be Beethoven. His heavy brow was distinctive.

"Is plaster toxic?" Claire asked, donning her mask. Armand did the same.

"Not really, but it's never a good idea to inhale powder or smoke."

He lifted a large bag of plaster and shook some dry powder into a large bucket, filling it one quarter full.

"Take that bucket of water"—he gestured with his head—"and start pouring a very small stream while I mix."

She let a thin stream pour from the bucket, and

he turned on an electric mixer with a long attachment.

"With plaster, you mix the water into the powder," Armand explained. "With some of the other mold-making materials we use today, it's the opposite: the powder must be introduced to water."

Claire nodded, remembering her grandmother saying the same thing about making cookies. She wondered why it would make a difference whether you poured liquid into dry ingredients or dry ingredients into liquid, then pondered whether she would be around long enough for this training to be necessary. Still, it was interesting to learn about the techniques, something so totally different from what she knew.

Watching Armand work, she realized this was where he got his brawny muscles: it took upper-arm strength to lift buckets full of wet plaster. The manual nature of the work, the mixing and lifting and hauling, its sheer *physicality,* struck Claire, who had always worked with her mind. Hold the bucket this way, the tool that way. *Get your hands dirty.*

She thought about her cousins working the oil rigs and the shrimp boats, their lives dictated by the strength of their backs or shoulders, the whims of weather and circumstance—would the well peter out? Had the shrimp disappeared? Could an oil slick put you out of work for years?

Would a hurricane barrel through, flooding and devastating everything in its path?

Claire often wondered whether leaving manual labor to work in an office was really a step up. It certainly paid better, but wasn't sitting hunched over a computer ten to twelve hours a day a physical challenge as well?

When the wet plaster achieved the consistency of a yogurt smoothie, Armand shut off the mixer, dropped the mixing attachment into a nearby bucket of rinse water, and hoisted the heavy pail onto the counter.

"The rice holds the molds so they don't rock while we fill them." Armand lifted the bucket high and started to pour a narrow stream of plaster, a little at a time, watching carefully as it filled the nooks and crannies of the molds. "Adding water to plaster ignites a chemical reaction, so you must pour in a steady stream. If you stop and start, you will create lines. Fill to the very top—you see?"

Claire nodded. "What's the bright blue stuff?"

"That's called alginate. It's the same product the dentist might use to create a mold of your teeth. It's an algae derivative and is easier to use than plaster for making molds. But we always cast the positive figure in plaster or resin."

After filling the molds to the brim, Armand handed Claire the bucket, grasped the sides of the boxes with his white-powdered hands and jiggled them, then tapped and knocked firmly on the exterior of the boxes.

"The molds must be agitated to get rid of bubbles," he explained. "If air is trapped, it creates a bubble void, which will mar the face."

Claire nodded. She'd watched Mammaw do the same thing when making her famous lime Jell-O mold.

"Once the plaster begins to set, we will scoop some out to relieve it of some weight. Now, while those are hardening, you can start to sand the edges of the ones that I poured yesterday."

He showed her a series of raw plaster masks, their backs hollowed out, and explained how he refined and shaped the features.

"Dentists' tools are the best for this work; anything else will bend. But I will do this part. You stick to sanding these rough edges—you see?"

Claire held a mask in her left hand and wielded the sandpaper with her right. It felt awkward at first, but once she figured out how to hold the mask securely she started to get the hang of it. She could feel Armand's gaze on her hands, but he didn't criticize.

"Have you ever done any actual sculpting?" she asked him.

"You think mold-making is not the same as sculpture?"

"It doesn't seem quite the same."

He shrugged. "Casting is simple, straight-forward. Mold-making, that's another beast altogether. That is where the skill is."

"Are you going to teach me mold-making?"

"I thought you were complaining about having to help me cast. Now you want to learn mold-making?"

"I *am* sleeping in the apprentice's room after all."

"For two weeks only."

"I'm a quick study. But here's what I'm not entirely clear on: why make molds at all?"

"The molds and castings of the Famille Lombardi keep the past alive. They allow others to enjoy the genius of the first artist by making copies, you see? Not everyone can travel to the Louvre or the Uffizi in Florence, much less Egypt and beyond. This way thousands can appreciate the genius that created these sculptures. In the old days, we also provided art and medical schools with sculptures they could use as sort of three-dimensional textbooks, more informative than a flat painting or drawing. Art students use these pieces to learn perspective, shadow, and modeling. Photography has made the molds less necessary, but cannot replace the three-dimensionality of our castings."

"Wouldn't holographs do that?"

"They might, one day." He nodded. "But we've been around for hundreds of years. We'll endure a few more."

"Also, you cater to the tourist trade."

He grunted. "Now, since you are so fond of cleaning, you get to deal with this. The tools must be cleaned before the plaster hardens on them."

"I never said I was *fond* of cleaning . . ." Claire protested. Still, she began sloughing the plaster from the metal tools before being saved by the sound of footsteps climbing the stairs. She dropped her task to greet the new arrivals, wiping her hands on a rag.

A large family from Seattle—grandparents, adult children, cousins, grandchildren—was excited to see an artist's lair. Most of them lined up at the workshop windows to watch Armand.

"Uncle Fred passed away and left us a little money," explained one woman to Claire. "It wasn't enough to do anything major with, like buy a house or pay for college, but it was enough for a family vacation! We're renting a house in the Loire Valley. Do you know it?"

"Not very well. I'm new in Paris myself."

"Oh, well, how lovely!"

Claire could read the question in the woman's eyes: how did an American woman come to be working in a caster's studio in Paris? Claire began to prepare a story in her mind just for fun: she had come here to join her fiancé, but he had abandoned her for a Parisian and fled to Saint-Tropez, leaving Claire to beg for a job to earn enough money for the plane ticket home.

But the woman was too polite to inquire further and turned her attention to a series of friezes taken from a villa in the Loire Valley not far from where they were staying.

Claire helped the family select a few pieces and called to Armand to complete the sales. Claire had wiped down an area of a tall worktable so the family could fill out their address on the postal delivery forms. Business transacted, they went happily on their way, headed to the Cathedral of Notre Dame.

Claire straightened up the counter, gathering the extra postal forms and scattered pens. The ancient counter's wood grain was filled with plaster dust; the bright white stood in stark contrast to the dark brown wood, creating a tapestry of snowy veins. As she watched, they seemed to come alive, flowing into one another like the waters of the Louisiana bayou.

She reached out and traced them with her fingertips, feeling the slightest raised area, like reading braille.

"Everything all right?" Armand asked.

"Just looking at the veins of the wood," Claire said. "They're very . . . interesting."

"Are you a Da Vinci fan?"

"Is a person even *allowed* not to be a Leonardo da Vinci fan?

"He was fascinated by veins, and wrote a good deal about them."

"Veins? Really?"

"Da Vinci was a scientist as well as an artist. He compared the veins in wood to those in the human body—he referred to the body's 'tree of veins'—and the branching of the trees, and the coming together of streams and creeks to form rivers. They all take a similar form, like a fractal."

"A fractal?"

"A pattern that repeats itself on different scales. Like scaling down or up a sculpture, for instance."

"Huh," said Claire, turning to greet a new group of tourists clomping up the stairs. "Pretty smart guy, it sounds like."

Armand gave her a reluctant half smile. Their gaze held a fraction of a second too long.

20

SABINE

It is a beautiful, sunny day, rare for Paris, the first time Maurice strikes her.

The sweet and the bitter, Sabine reflects, so often go together. Great happiness means great grief. She had loved her baby brother with a devotion surpassing understanding; he died before dawn after a terrible night, felled by the same fever that had claimed her mother three days prior. Sabine should have—*would* have gladly—

died in his stead but she did not. Despite the hunger and the fevers that swept through the town, taking one life after another—even the horse trainer with the gentle voice—Sabine had endured.

So the day is sunny and beautiful and begins with art and chocolate. Maurice has decided to take Sabine to the Louvre. He is feeling indulgent; on the way, he allows her to pause and peek into shopwindows.

Sabine is fascinated by the chocolate shops. They are like museums, full of the sweetest creations imaginable. The bouquet of cocoa and sugar hangs in the air, tantalizing, almost cloying. The chocolatière offers Sabine a square of chocolate that nestles in the little hollow in the palm of her hand and starts to melt before she can bring it to her mouth. It tastes the way velvet would if it had a flavor—so soft and rich and luxurious, she thinks she might faint right there on the mosaic floor, whose tiles spell out *Chocolatière Élise*.

If only she had known, back when she was starving, that she might have ducked into the shop for a free taste of chocolate. But no, that would not have been possible. The proprietor would have shooed her from the minute she appeared in her worn country clothes. Now she wears a fine dress of royal blue wool, nothing like what a proper lady would wear, but appropriate for a salesgirl, at least. And now she is in the company of Monsieur Maurice Desmarais, who is well-off—something he likes to make obvious so as not to blur the lines between the classes.

The Palais du Louvre is magnificent, overwhelming. The vast stone courtyard is pristine, and Sabine imagines it filled with kings and queens and their sumptuously costumed entourages. For a moment she is afraid. Surely the haughty attendants will know she doesn't belong in a palace, that she is a simple country girl?

But as soon as Maurice ushers her inside, she forgets her doubts, forgets everything, she is so utterly captivated by the colors, the beauty, the glimpses into worlds unknown to her. Images of places where women wear nothing but gauze scarves, or frolic naked with a swan, or run from satyrs on the banks of a pond. Her cheeks burn at the paintings of women lounging naked on chaises longues, even though Sabine is now one of them. Until this moment she hasn't allowed herself to imagine others standing and staring at a portrait of her naked body.

But she puts this out of her mind, focusing instead on the exquisite beauty of a bouquet of flowers painted by an Italian named Caravaggio.

Maurice enjoys being her tour guide and tutor, pointing out the works by the Old Masters, explaining what she should appreciate, training her to look for brushstrokes—or the lack thereof— and cross-hatching, the way painters used light and dark, which he called "chiaroscuro," and how, if one looked closely, painted-over figures were sometimes still visible, which he referred to as "pentimento."

She has learned many of these terms from the books in the studio, but she remains mute, lets him talk. Sabine watches the way his mustache twitches and sees the first signs of displeasure. Maurice is angry that his work does not hang on these walls, that his chiseled pieces do not grace the hall of sculptures.

She suggests they go, but he insists she see one more painting.

"This is the pièce de résistance," he says, leading her to a painting of a fully dressed woman, her hands demurely crossed in front of her and a slight smile on her face. "She is known as *La Joconde*, from the Italian *La Gioconda*. But the English call it the *Mona Lisa*."

"Why?"

He laughs. "You are a curious little mouse, aren't you?"

She doesn't think it is such a strange question— after all, since the artist called his painting *La Gioconda*, why would anyone change the name? But Sabine knows better than to pursue the topic with Maurice. He does not enjoy her inquisitive nature, finds it challenging rather than charming.

So instead she gives him a little smile.

"Your smile is like hers—you see?" he says, pointing to the lady in the painting. To Sabine she appears mysterious but perhaps also a little tired or wary. Sabine wonders whether *La Joconde* feared the artist might be stealing a bit of her soul.

Sabine feels that way often. It is a creeping anxiety that seizes her imagination in the hours she holds absolutely still, trying not even to blink. Sometimes Maurice allows her to close her eyes, but that is worse: she prefers to see the world around her, to remain anchored to reality.

Maurice often grumbles and rips up his sketches, paints over his old canvases, smashes his dried clay models. Sabine does not know what he wants from her, but she fears that he will not be satisfied until he has captured her soul.

"You are full of mysteries," he says as they walk back to the studio. "You are like *La Gioconda, la belle Italienne.*"

Sabine concentrates on the beauty she has seen today, and the sensation of chocolate melting on her tongue, the warm sunshine on her cheeks.

When they arrive at the studio, a letter is waiting for Maurice. From the expression on his face, she fears it is from his father. This always puts him in a bad mood. Usually she is able to placate him; she is accustomed to her stepfather's rages.

But this time he begins to drink and accuses her

of frowning, of forgetting to smile, and what was she worth without that smile?

"Life is not all about smiling," she ventures. She is about to say more, to add that one can be happy without smiling, but he cuts her off.

"You smiled for the man in the chocolate shop—I saw you."

Sabine senses danger, tries to backpedal. "I didn't, not really. I was trying to be polite, to be a fitting companion for you."

"Whore."

And just like that, he backhands her.

The force of the blow sends her careening into the wall; she knocks over a work in progress as she falls. It crashes to the floor, the dried clay splitting into a pile of dust and chunks.

"You see what you made me do?" he yells, then kicks her.

The kick is not hard—more annoyance than rage—and is directed to her thigh, for which she is grateful. Sabine knows from experience with her stepfather that a blow to the gut is the worst: the mixed sensations of nausea and spasm and the failure to breathe for so long one begins to wonder whether the ability will ever come back. Physically it is painful, horrible. But the emotional pain is worse: someone who is supposed to protect you is hurting you, and your body, which has always known how to breathe by itself, suddenly forgets the skills of a lifetime. The sense of betrayal, of perfidy, lingers long after the bruises have turned from blue to purple to green to yellow.

Sabine cringes when Maurice reaches for her, but through the fog of pain and the throbbing of her head she realizes he is helping her up, brushing the dust from her skirts, apologizing.

"Look what you made me do. Look what happened to my little mouse. Are you hurt?"

He says this last in a soft voice, the one he used when he hired her. In the square in rue Pigalle, when Sabine was starving and she thought her prayers had been answered by the bearded man who smelled of fruit and cloves.

Now she knows his scent comes from the flavored tobacco he smokes in his pipe. Now when she smells it, she feels nauseated.

The priest had tried to warn her. The artistic life is dangerous for women.

"Smile for me now," Maurice says, smoothing her hair. "Please, smile like the *Mona Lisa*, my *belle Italienne*."

21

A little before noon Giselle arrived at the studio, bringing lunch with her and hanging the sign:

FERMÉ 12–2. REVENEZ, S'IL VOUS PLAÎT.
CLOSED 12–2. PLEASE COME BACK.

"I'm so sorry I could not be here this morning!" Giselle said as Claire helped her lay out a lunch of quiche and salad on the table in the garden. "This is why we need our employees, because my schedule does not allow me to be here every day. Was Armand nice to you?"

Armand arrived in time to hear this last comment and made a rude noise.

"He was a perfect gentleman," said Claire. "He showed me how to pour plaster and sand the molds."

"You're making her work in the shop?" Giselle demanded of her cousin. "I thought we hired her to translate?"

"English-speaking tourists are not standing around every minute of the day waiting for a translator. And even as a translator she is lacking—she doesn't speak Japanese or German."

"But you do, so it's not a problem."

"You do?" Claire asked Armand.

"A little," he said.

"He speaks Italian as well," said Giselle. "So many languages for a man who prefers not to speak. But for now, *bon appétit*!"

Claire was enough of an American to wonder about the need for a two-hour lunch. Wouldn't an hour be more than sufficient? Still, she tried to sit back and enjoy the relaxed schedule. Perhaps this was part of a healthy European lifestyle: they worked hard while they were working, but took frequent breaks.

"Claire, the *moulage* is closed on Sundays and Mondays," said Giselle. "Do you have more sightseeing you'd like to do?"

"I'd like to go to Montmartre, and maybe back to the Impressionist museum. But I especially wanted to see the Rodin Museum. That's not too far from here, is it?"

"Not far at all," said Giselle. "I love Rodin."

Armand scoffed.

"You disagree?" Claire asked. Despite her childhood fascination with such things, she didn't know much about sculpture. In college Claire had been so focused on preparing for a good job that she hadn't allowed herself to study art history, much less art.

"Rodin was a man of his time, obviously," said Armand. "But others were more innovative. And even then . . . it was his 'student,' Camille

Claudel, who sculpted the famous hands in *The Burghers of Calais*."

"I'm sorry, the burgers of . . . ?" Surely he didn't mean hamburgers.

"*The Burghers of Calais*—they were citizens of the town. The city of Calais commissioned Rodin to make the sculpture, and he gained many accolades for it. But much of the work was actually done by Claudel."

"Camille Claudel was Rodin's muse," explained Giselle.

"Muse, yes—but she was a sculptor in her own right," said Armand. "And in my opinion, she was more innovative and talented than Rodin."

"Why isn't she more well-known?" Claire asked.

"She was a woman," said Giselle, blowing a long stream of cigarette smoke out of the side of her mouth. "Also, she went crazy."

"Crazy?"

"Her family put her in a mental hospital," explained Armand. "She and Rodin had a dramatic breakup, and she accused him of trying to sabotage her career. Whether she was 'crazy' or not is hard to say. I imagine after a few years of being an inmate in an asylum she was less than stable, certainly."

"She smashed much of her work," added Giselle.

"That is unfortunately true. But some of what was left is featured at the Rodin Museum," said

Armand. "If you go, you should pay special attention to that section."

"Why would her work be displayed at Rodin's museum if they broke up?"

"Rodin requested it. He was an established sculptor by then, recognized by the formal Academy. Whether it was a sign of his enduring love or because he felt guilty, I suppose there's no way to know for sure."

"You said she sculpted the hands for *The Burghers of Calais*. Why is that such a big deal?"

"The hands are everything," said Armand. "Second only to the face."

"I wondered about the casts of Chopin's hands hanging in the showroom."

He nodded. "Chopin had extraordinary hands, very long fingers, the secret to his success as a composer and pianist. In the past, if it was impossible to take a death mask of a famous person, the hands would be cast instead. The lines of the hand are unique, as individual as the face."

"Enough talk of Rodin," Giselle said. "Claire, after lunch I will show you how to transact the sales so that you will not have to bother Armand, our resident genius."

Several customers came by in the afternoon, some simply browsing but others eager to make a purchase. A woman from Southern California explained she was looking for a series of statues to grace her pool. Claire felt like she was channeling Mammaw as she spun a story about the mermaids of the Seine and pointed out the mermaidlike creature in the Lombardi coat of arms. By the time the woman left she had ordered six statues to be shipped to her Los Angeles mansion to flank her pool house, with a sculpture of a mermaid to have pride of place at the head of the pool.

"You are amazing, Claire," said Giselle to Claire after the customer left.

Claire smiled. "I don't think I can take much credit for that sale; it was the art that spoke to her."

"But I have noticed—you smile so much. All the time!"

"It's the way we do it in America," Claire replied. "We're a service-oriented people."

"But you let them wander around on their own, without assistance."

"True. I suppose it's more accurate to say we're a *welcoming* people. But then we're used to helping ourselves."

Giselle uttered something that sounded like "*Bof*!" and returned to the desk to finish up some paperwork, announcing that she had to leave by five.

Claire took advantage of a lull in business to make a phone call home to her cousin Jessica. She had been avoiding it, but it was time.

Claire felt guilty for not helping more with the aftermath of Mammaw's death. She had stuck

190

around Plaquemines Parish for the memorial service and burial but had left the rest of her grandmother's affairs in Jessica's hands since Mammaw had named Jessica executor of her will, which shouldn't have been overly complicated since Mammaw had not owned much. But of course, these things were often more involved than one might expect.

Claire and her cousin traded a few pleasantries when she answered; then Claire inquired about Remy and the rest of the family, and Jessica asked about Paris and when Claire was coming home and getting back to work. Claire tried to distract her cousin with talk of cheese and chocolate and plats du jour.

But then she told Jessica her new address and mentioned she'd be staying a while longer.

"Let me get this straight," Jessica said. "You're a shopgirl?"

"Sort of."

"I don't understand. If you wanted to work as a shopgirl, you could do that right here at home. What'd you go off and get that fancy college diploma for if you're just gonna work in a store?"

"It's a little hard to explain. It just came up and I jumped at it. Because, yes, I'm a shopgirl, but I'm a shopgirl in *Paris*."

"Why go to college, then? And how long are you planning to stay?"

"I'm really not sure. I'm sort of playing it by ear."

"I tell you what, Chance Broussard: you are getting weirder all the time."

"Maybe so." Claire's tone was light, but inside, her emotions were a different story. Amazing how her cousin's cutting voice could make her feel like a child again, hiding in Mammaw's sweltering attic. *Your days here are numbered, Chance. Your daddy gonna whup you, and your mama tried to* kill *you.*

When Claire hung up, she saw Armand had been watching her.

"May I help you?" she asked.

"Are you quite finished?"

"Yes."

"Do you like duck?"

"Excuse me?

He repeated, slowly, in English: "Is it that you like duck?"

"Sorry, I understood what you were saying. I was just surprised. I . . . yes, I do like duck. But I don't expect you to cook for me."

"Do you have plans for dinner?"

"I figured I'd pick something up or eat out."

"Eat out where? The *Mac*Donald's?"

She smiled. "No, as much as I enjoyed it, once was enough. But just between you and me, I've heard there are some excellent restaurants in this town."

"You are rich? Eating in a restaurant is not cheap. They are very expensive."

"I just . . . I don't expect you to cook for me—that's all I mean."

"You will cook tomorrow."

"Me? I don't really cook."

"What do you mean, you don't really cook?"

"Um . . . I mean: I don't really cook."

Armand frowned. "You make these . . . 'salmon croquettes,' I believe you said."

"What's all this about salmon croquettes?" Giselle asked, gathering her things to leave.

"She tells a lot of stories," said Armand. "And this one was about her grandmother making salmon croquettes."

"I don't tell 'a lot of stories,' " Claire protested. "Anyway, I mentioned salmon croquettes in the context of sculpting, not cooking."

Giselle laughed. "Don't bother arguing with Armand, Claire. We French take our meals very seriously, and my cousin is more serious than most."

"All right," Claire said, throwing in the towel. "I give up. If my apprentice's room is contingent upon making dinner, I will figure something out."

"Tonight I will do the shopping and cook the meal," Armand said. "You stay here and watch the store."

"*Oui, chef.*" She saluted him. "I shall not fail you or this grand enterprise."

Giselle laughed. "You are doing so very well, Claire," she said, giving her a smoky kiss on each cheek. "*On y va, Armand?*"

Armand grabbed a couple of woven shopping bags. Then he and Giselle descended the steps, leaving Claire alone in the shop for the first time.

In her solitude, she felt even more the almost palpable sense of history of the atelier—not just from the art itself but from the traces of all those who had spent time here: the masters, the apprentices, the soldiers and students and tourists who had visited over the years, including Mammaw's father—Claire's great-grandfather. Mammaw had been a child during World War II, probably no older than Giselle's daughter, Victorine. Claire smiled to herself when she realized that Mammaw must have been only in her fifties when Claire first went to live with her. In her child's mind, Mammaw had always seemed *old*.

Grief gripped her heart. Now that the acute sadness at losing her grandmother had dissipated, Claire kept trying to convince herself she was fine. But then a wave would hit her again, out of the blue, plunging her into sorrow and emptiness.

Claire found herself staring blankly through the windows overlooking Armand's workshop.

She shouldn't. Really shouldn't. She had no business snooping around his workshop. She should respect Armand's privacy, just as she expected him to respect hers. But . . . maybe just a quick peek?

She reached out, turned the knob. Opened the door.

22

Claire perused the works in progress sitting atop the workbench: images of poets and artists and political figures awaiting Armand's talented hands to detail, sand, and seal them. The plaster casts she had helped to pour were now set, and she itched to turn them over, to rid them of their molds and see who they were, how they had turned out.

But she would have to wait for the master for that.

Beyond the work area a single door stood slightly ajar. She pushed it open a few inches to peer inside. It was Armand's bedroom, with an attached bath partially visible through an open door.

It was a spare space, with tall beamed ceilings, old plaster walls a patchy shade of yellow with an earthy red peeking out here and there, and the wispy remnants of a painted frieze, faded and chipped, near the ceiling. The neatly made bed stood high off the ground; its heavy frame featured carved, twisty posts at each corner. It must have been very old, and was so massive Claire couldn't imagine how it had been brought up the narrow stairs and passed through the doorways. Perhaps it had been built here, in this very room.

On a bedside table sat a reading lamp and a thick novel; to one side of the room were a chest of drawers, a crowded bookshelf, and a small desk. Other than the lamps and books, there was nothing on any surface in the room, and it took Claire a moment to realize what it was that seemed odd about the place: there was very little plaster dust. Did Armand wipe down the surfaces each night before going to bed?

Another thought occurred to her: there was no television anywhere. Other than the computer in the showroom, Armand could have been living in the Paris of fifty years ago, with the old-fashioned phone and the lack of modern conveniences.

It was jarring, but strangely appealing. Even relaxing, not to feel compelled to stay on top of e-mail and social media and world events.

Still, Armand had such a melancholy, brooding disposition that Claire wondered whether it might not be good for him to lighten up a little with a sitcom or two, or perhaps a movie. A lighthearted comedy, not the bleak, depressing kind of film that came to mind when she thought of French cinema.

Or perhaps his mood was a matter of nationality. After all, *ennui* was a French word.

Claire was sorely tempted to slide open a drawer or two to see what lay within. But she resisted the impulse, not only because she had invaded his privacy enough, but also because there was no way she could enter the room without leaving a trail of plaster dust in her wake, Pig-Pen style.

She left the door slightly ajar, just as she'd found it.

She was about to leave the workshop when her gaze alighted on the shrouded object on the shelf under the workbench. This was the object he had been working on late at night, the one he'd covered up when she came in. Why was he so secretive about it?

One corner of the towel was hitched up, revealing what looked like a tiny stone wall. Claire crouched down and lifted the towel to peek.

It was a miniature castle.

Giving in to temptation, she lifted the tray on top of the table to examine the castle.

The building was symmetrical, with a grand central entrance and a spire on either side. A castle—a château—fit for a queen. The roof lifted off in sections, displaying an elaborately carved central stairway with a decorative balustrade, stone fireplaces with acanthus leaf details, and several bedrooms with miniature armoires and dressing tables made of wood. Only a few of the rooms were furnished, and though the left wing of the château was finished on the outside, the interior was lacking in detailing.

Perhaps it was a commissioned piece, an ornate dollhouse for some enormously spoiled child.

But then why cover it up, as though not wanting anyone to see it?

Now she felt bad. If the poor man played with dollhouses at night, that was his business. *Enough with the snooping, Claire.*

She heard footsteps on the stairs and put the tray back as she'd found it. Then she hurried out to the showroom to greet a newlywed couple from Albany, New York, searching for the perfect souvenir of their honeymoon in Paris.

"You've come to the right place," said Claire, showing them around.

They weren't particularly interested in famous historical figures, so Claire showed them *L'Inconnue*, the unknown woman of the Seine. She told them how Jean-Baptiste Lombardi had been called to the morgue to make her death mask because she was so very beautiful and smiled her mysterious smile, despite her death.

They fell in love with her sweet visage, as had so many before them, and Claire arranged to have her shipped to them in New York.

"Another name for your mystery woman is *La Belle Italienne*," Armand said later that afternoon, over *apéro* in the garden, surrounded by fairy lights. Tonight they sipped champagne and snacked on *pâté de campagne*, water crackers, and fat walnut halves seasoned with cinnamon and black pepper. "She is known as 'the Italian Beauty.'"

"And was she Italian?" Claire asked, reaching for a walnut. She seemed to have gotten her appetite back and couldn't get enough of the food her host kept offering her. "I started reading through the papers in the box last night. Some authors claim she was German, others Russian or English."

"No one knows for sure. Over the years I believe every nation of the European Community has claimed her for itself. No, she is called *La Belle Italienne* because back in the day the Italians were considered the most beautiful artist's models."

"Just as it should be," said a new voice. "But then, I am Italian."

Claire turned to see the ponytailed man she had met that morning, Quentin, emerging from the narrow alley that ran along the side of the building. He carried a little lilac-colored box in one large hand.

"*Salut*," he said, leaning down to kiss Claire first on one cheek, then the other.

Though the greeting was perfectly conventional in France, having a man lean over and kiss her felt intimate: the scratch of his whiskers, the musky aroma of his cologne. And was that . . . the scent of cocoa? She felt herself blush and hoped the evening light was too dim for either man to notice.

Armand acknowledged his neighbor with a reluctant nod and a subdued, "*Salut, ça va?*"

"*Ça va bien, merci*," Quentin replied, taking a seat.

"I take it you've already met Claire?" Armand asked, retrieving another glass from the sideboard and pouring Quentin some champagne. Claire realized this was the first time she had heard Armand speak her name. She liked the sound of it.

"*Oui*, this morning we said hello in the street," said Quentin. "I must say, my friend, I am impressed that you found someone so quickly. And such a charming native English speaker. Much more so than your last."

"I've been meaning to ask," Claire said. "What happened with your last translator?"

Armand shrugged. "She had some talent, but was very difficult."

"Unlike you," said Claire.

Quentin chuckled.

"She wanted to be sculpting her own pieces, not making copies. She was dissatisfied."

"With life in general, it seemed to me," said Quentin.

"Where was she from?"

Armand shrugged. "She did not tell stories like you do."

"So you think I talk about myself too much?"

"I did not say you talk too much," Armand said quietly, his blue eyes on her. "Only that you tell many stories."

Unsure how to interpret his words, Claire

changed the subject: "Why were the Italians considered the best artist's models?"

"It is handed down to us through classical history: we admire the Romans for their culture, which established the standards of beauty that were later upheld in art schools and by the Academy."

"Seems a bit limiting," Claire said. "Is there only one form of beauty?"

"Yes, in a way. Today we have fashion magazines to tell you what you should look like, with digital alterations, no less. At the time, the Academy kept the ideal defined, and casters like my grandfathers did so as well, by providing the models that would influence generations of artists."

Just then a black cat jumped onto the ivy-covered garden wall, a sleek silhouette against the gray dusk.

In a rush, Claire thought, *This is more like it. This is the Paris I was seeking, hoping for.* Sitting in a beautiful little garden under the twinkle lights, two interesting men—one a grump, but no matter—and now a *chat noir*, a black cat, which was practically a symbol of the city. If only the Eiffel Tower loomed overhead, it would be the ideal setting for a Hollywood movie.

"How perfect," she said, giving voice to her thoughts. "A black cat, a beautiful night, and *apéro* with two handsome men."

Quentin smiled warmly.

"So, you are Italian?" Claire asked.

"You don't hear my accent? The Parisians never let me forget."

"Since I have my own strange accent, I guess I'm less sensitive to it."

Claire told him about Louisiana, the parishes, and the French-speaking people there. They chatted about the cultural differences and over-laps between Cajun and Creole. Armand remained silent, sipping his wine and glowering. Claire felt bad about leaving him out of the conversa-tion, but when she tried to include him she met the stone wall of his features.

At a lull in the conversation, Armand asked, "And Odile?"

Quentin's easy smile faded; the flirtation left his voice. "She is well. She enjoys Provence. It is quiet there."

Armand nodded and returned his attention to his wine. The tension between the men was as thick as the crowds swarming the sidewalks on the Champs-Élysées.

"Anyway," said Quentin, opening the box and holding it out to Claire, "I came to give you this little present. I am a chocolatier; I made you a little Statue of Liberty—you see?"

"Oh, that's incredible! Thank you, Quentin. It's beautiful."

"This is the symbol, is it not, of our countries'

mutual love and respect? The French made it, you know."

"Yes, I know that. But I thought you were Italian."

"But I am French now," he said with a shrug. "Tell me: how does she look in person?"

"Actually, I've never seen her. I haven't been to New York."

"Never?"

She shook her head.

"But why wouldn't you go to New York? This is a very famous city, perhaps almost as famous as Paris."

"It's on my list. I changed planes in New York on my way here, but I've never visited the city itself. I haven't seen that much of my own country, I suppose. You're right—I should travel more."

"This is a shame, I think. Many people in France haven't been to Paris—can you imagine?"

"They're missing out," said Claire. "So, Quentin, if you are a chocolatier, how do you stay so thin?"

Claire was of average size for an American woman, but she felt like a heifer in Paris, where many women were not just thin but as petite as a typical American fifth-grader. The men were similarly small; Armand was larger than average, by far. He had the broad shoulders and bearish physique of an athlete.

Quentin laughed. "I never eat my own product. It is enough that I smell of chocolate all the time, don't you think? You should come by the shop sometime, near the corner of rue de Rivoli and rue Saint-Paul."

The cat had joined them and was winding itself around Armand's legs. A sinuous shadow come to life.

"Tell me, Claire," Quentin continued. "How did you come to work at the Moulage Lombardi?"

"It's a long story," she said with a sidelong glance at Armand. "But the short version is that I found a copy of *L'Inconnue* in my grandmother's attic, and I wanted to know where she came from. Have you heard of her?"

"Yes, yes, of course I know her. One of my uncles had that mask hanging in his front room; I remember wondering about her when I was a boy. Did you know she became the CPR mannequin?"

"Excuse me?" Claire wasn't sure whether she'd understood properly. "The CPR mannequin?"

"Oh, yes—you don't know this story?"

She shook her head.

"In the 1950s, a physician was working on the technique for cardiopulmonary resuscitation and needed a mannequin to train others. He consulted with a famous Belgian doll maker. To make the mannequin lifelike it needed a face, of course. The doctor decided it should be a beautiful woman so people would not be afraid to put their mouth on hers."

"Is this true?" Claire asked, looking at Armand. Armand nodded.

"Why didn't you tell me this?"

"I thought you enjoyed the mystery. Besides, there's an article in the box about it—you probably haven't gotten to it yet."

"The doll maker had the mask of *L'Inconnue* hanging in his living room," Quentin continued. "So he said, '*L'Inconnue* shall be the face of our doll.'"

Claire thought back to a CPR course she had taken in high school as part of disaster-preparedness training in case of a hurricane. She had only a vague recollection of the practice dummy, but she certainly hadn't thought of it as beautiful.

As though reading her thoughts, Armand said, "It is her smile that makes *L'Inconnue* so intriguing. But because of the requirements of CPR, they had to change her mouth, make it open, so she looks quite different. I find it all a bit . . . macabre."

"I think it is a beautiful story," said Quentin. "This poor girl drowned in the river, abandoned and alone, but in the end thousands of people— perhaps millions of people—have tried to save her, to resuscitate her."

It was a striking image, yes. But beautiful? That wasn't the word Claire would have used.

"You must admit it is very romantic," Quentin said.

"I admit only that it is tragic. There is nothing 'romantic' about it. No one would choose to invite such tragedy into their life if they understood it. Excuse me," Armand said, pushing back his chair with a screech and standing. "I have to begin preparing dinner. *Bonsoir, Quentin.*"

Armand went to the grill and lit a pile of charcoal, snipped a few sprigs of herbs from the *potager*, then headed up the stairs. After a moment a light appeared in the kitchen windows overlooking the garden and cast a yellow glow onto the courtyard.

Claire felt she should go with Armand, but it would be rude to abandon Quentin. A moment of awkward silence reigned.

The black cat jumped into her lap.

"Oh!" Claire exclaimed in surprise.

Quentin reached out to scratch under the cat's chin. "She's a flirt."

"She's not the only one."

He laughed.

"Hello, *mee-noo, mee-noo,*" Claire said. She stroked the cat's velvet fur, felt her purring. After a moment the cat started to knead Claire's thighs, her sharp claws digging into the fabric of her jeans and pricking her skin.

"Leonardo da Vinci once said, 'The smallest feline is a masterpiece,'" said Quentin.

"The man was full of opinions, apparently. Armand told me he had a few thoughts about veins too. Whose cat is she?"

"No one's. Armand found her, starving and pregnant, and started feeding her. He got her medical care, found homes for her babies, had her spayed."

"Sounds like she's his cat, then."

"He does not claim her." After a pause he added, "You do not know Armand well."

"I don't know him at all."

"Nor are you likely to."

"That sounds like a warning."

"I do not mean it that way. It's only . . . he is a difficult sort. But there is good reason for it."

"What might that be?" Claire asked, her voice low. She wondered whether Armand was watching from the kitchen windows, whether the evening breeze would carry her words to him.

Quentin seemed about to say something, but then simply smiled again.

His smile was lovely. He looked almost model perfect, with high cheekbones and a classic Roman profile. He was slender but strong looking, with shiny hair that reflected the string of lights.

Claire thought of Armand's strangely crooked face, how the broad planes didn't seem to quite meet up. His nose was bent, his brow lopsided. It made his countenance not handsome so much as intriguing. And then she thought of his mien of intense concentration when he worked, his hands tapping the boxes to force the bubbles from the castings, the way he smiled ever so slightly when she managed to amuse him.

"I'm sure Armand will tell you if he would like you to know," said Quentin. "For now it is enough to say that he is a man who will take in a stray, feed it, pay its vet bills, and yet refuse to claim it."

"So she has no name?"

"Not as far as I know."

The cat was now rubbing her face on Claire's shoulders, leaving a trail of fine black hairs. Claire scratched the cat's neck and the purring began again in earnest, a deep rumbling in her chest.

Claire's family had always been dog people; she remembered Mammaw saying: *A dog'll let you know a stranger's at the door. They'll run a person off and round up sheep if you got 'em. They're useful. Cat won't do nothin' for you but kill mice if it's hungry enough, and even then not all are good at that.*

Mammaw had been big on "useful."

Maybe it was the evening air, or perhaps simply that she was in Paris, but as Claire looked into the glowing green eyes of this black cat, she understood the appeal of the feline.

"Well, now that I've run off our host, I suppose I should go," said Quentin. "I am remaining in

Paris all month, so let me know if you need anything when Giselle and Armand are out of town. And please, enjoy the chocolate. Eat it— do not save it because it is beautiful. There are some things in life meant to be ephemeral, short-lived. This is why I sculpt in chocolate, not stone. Or plaster, for that matter."

Claire stood, and the cat leapt to the ground, landing silently and slinking off to a dark corner of the garden.

"*Bonne soirée*," she said. They kissed cheeks, and Claire watched as he brushed by the watching faces, disappearing down the dark walkway to the side of the building.

23

SABINE

A tall pink box sits upon the nightstand; it is the first thing Sabine sees when she awakens with a jolt, startled from a dream.

Her head throbs. Her ribs ache. She is beset by nausea.

Sabine remains absolutely still, waiting. Listening. *Is he here?*

It has been several months since he hit her the first time, after their trip to the Palais du Louvre to see *La Joconde*. These days she often wears the signs of Maurice's frustrations: the black eyes, the reddened cheeks, the split lips. Ugly bruises that begin purple before fading to blue, green, yellow.

Maurice has always called her his little country mouse and now she feels that way, like a preyed-upon animal that must keep attuned to constant threat. She had practice: at home when her stepfather would start drinking, he would rage at her, demand she take care of the children, the cooking, the wash. She learned how to tiptoe past him to the sleeping loft or to tell which nights it was better by far to stay in the barn if it wasn't too cold, wrapped in a horse blanket.

Still. There are times when Sabine wonders whether living in fear is all there is. She passes women in the street and wonders: are they afraid? Do they return home to the unpredictable, the volatile and capricious, never knowing whether some innocent glance, some wrong word might elicit a fierce slap, a chuck on the chin? Should she flee to Toinette and beg her for help finding
a job in a factory or workshop where she could avoid men altogether? Is there such a place?

And if she leaves . . . would Maurice come after her, track her down, drag her back—or worse?

He believes she is his muse, that she will help him attain the success he so desperately wants.

After several minutes she is sure he is gone.

He is a loud man, and he makes his presence known. Harrumphing, banging, pushing things out of his way. Talking to himself while he works, his frustrations and dissatisfaction given voice freely.

In fact, she welcomes the noise. It is when he falls quiet that he is most dangerous.

But it is possible he has left his sister, Isabelle, here to look after her. Isabelle is hushed, shuffles through life as though hoping no one notices her. She wears clothes in shades of gray and brown and Sabine can't help but think of her as a hapless little wren, unassuming but alert, hopping about ineffectually, unable to find her own worms. But she is a mean little bird, the kind that would peck you to death if it could.

The country mouse and the ill-tempered wren. They are quite the pair.

Sabine sits up slowly. Feels that her lip is swollen, finds the metallic taste of blood when she explores with her tongue. Wonders how bad it looks, if Maurice will insist she remain indoors.

She reaches out for the pink box.

He brings her presents often. Flowers, pastries, lace. After one terrible night he brought her a fine gold armband.

Sabine pushes back the flaps on the box to reveal an intricate Eiffel Tower entirely made of chocolate. Fragile brown strings stretch from one cocoa girder to the next. At the points of joinery are candied cherries and at the very top sits a marzipan rose.

It is an interesting choice because Maurice likes to rail against Monsieur Eiffel's project built for the Exposition Universelle, calling it ugly, atrocious. It is an opinion shared by many in the artistic community; she hears them talk about it in cafés and bars while sitting at Maurice's side.

Sabine would never voice her opinion but the truth is: she likes *la tour*. She likes to stand underneath the massive structure, to tilt her head back and peer into its belly, to see the sun and blue sky peeking through its webbed iron. It isn't even a building, not useful at all. Simply a tower soaring so far into the sky it joins the birds and the clouds. As though thrusting itself into the heavens for no other reason than to set itself free.

She takes the chocolate Eiffel Tower out of the box, gazes at it. Dry eyed and empty.

Sabine remembers seeing something just like this in the window of Chocolatière Élise, on her way to the square in Pigalle. Back when she was starving, when she was willing to ignore the priest's warning in order to find work. When she was willing to do just about anything in order to eat.

Back when she had been disposed to make a deal with the devil.

24

Claire followed the scent of frying onions, carrots, and celery root and found Armand clad in a striped apron sautéing vegetables in a pan on the stove, seemingly as engrossed in his cooking as he was when working on his sculptures.

"May I help?" she offered.

"Did Quentin leave?"

She nodded. "Are you . . . are you two friends?"

"Not exactly."

Do you have *any friends?* was the next question on her lips begging to be asked. But of course she kept her mouth shut. It was none of her business, none of her concern.

Armand placed a wooden cutting board in front of her and handed her a knife. "That's very sharp," he warned, watching for a moment to see how she gripped the handle. He took it back from her, demonstrating the proper usage on a stalk of celery.

"Like this. Would you like a glass of wine? I have a Sancerre open."

"Sounds great," she said, then tried chopping the way he had shown her, keeping the tip of the knife on the board rather than lifting the entire blade. He was right: it was easier his way.

"What are we making?" she asked.

"*I* am making. You are helping."

"*Oui, chef.* So what are *you* making?"

"*Magret de canard*, potatoes, beans. We will make the sauce and vegetables here, then go down and grill the duck outside. It cooks very quickly."

Strains of French music played on the sound system: a man singing soulfully with a deep, resonant voice. Claire was relieved; the disco had played nothing but the worst pop music from the U.S., put to an incessant house beat. This music was a little soupy, but at least it sounded authentically French.

"Who is this singing?" she asked.

"Serge Lama."

At her distracted nod, he tilted his head and said, "You don't know him?"

She shook her head.

"Serge *La-ma,*" he repeated, enunciating very clearly.

She shook her head again.

"He is incredibly famous."

"I don't know much about French music, sorry to say."

"How about Lara Fabian, or Julien Clerc?"

"I hate to break it to you, but we Americans don't really listen to European music. Some Brits, maybe, but other than ABBA in the seventies and the very occasional Icelandic breakthrough, I'd say we're pretty chauvinistic about our music.

214

Édith Piaf is who comes to mind when it comes to France, or maybe Jacques Brel."

"Serge Lama is a national treasure," he muttered, whisking finely chopped herbs into his sauce. "I believe he is as famous as your Frank Sinatra."

"Again with the Italians."

He gave her a ghost of a smile.

"Hey, speaking of Italians, Quentin introduced me to your cat."

"She is not my cat."

"Have you told *her* that?"

Silence. Armand's head was bent slightly over the stove, doing that thing that good cooks—her grandmother, people she'd seen on TV, Sean's brother the professional chef—did: pulling out packages from the refrigerator, turning back to stir the pan on the stove, cleaning vegetables at the sink, slicing on the cutting board. Fine chefs, it seemed to her, were the ultimate multitaskers.

"I always heard that if you fed an animal and named it, it was yours," said Claire.

"That's a rather simplistic view of the world."

She shrugged and sipped her wine. "I'm a simple woman."

He had poured cognac into the pan and now set it afire. The flames rose from the pan in a *whoosh*.

Sauce flambée. For a simple dinner at home. *How Parisian,* Claire thought.

"I didn't name her," Armand said, holding the

pan aloft and swirling its contents until the flames calmed, sputtered, and finally died out.

"I'm sorry?"

"The cat. She has no name. So by your estimation she isn't mine."

"I always thought Gertrude would be a nice name for a cat."

Armand let out an impatient sigh and set the pan down with a clatter. "I didn't refuse to name the cat because I couldn't think of the right name, Claire. And even if I had, why on earth would I name her *Gertrude?*"

"After Gertrude Stein? She loved Paris; it was her adopted city. Her apartment wasn't far from here, I don't think. She once said, 'America is my country, but Paris is my hometown.' Anyway, I think Gertrude fits. Or you could go with Alice B. Toklas, but that seems too obvious, somehow."

Another snort and Armand muttered to himself about naming cats after crazy expat Americans.

They finished the rest of the preparations in silence. It was on the tip of Claire's tongue to ask whether someone else was joining them for dinner; again, it occurred to her that this sort of elaborate preparation was more suited to a formal dinner party than a casual weeknight supper. But she remained silent, preferring to observe how smoothly he moved around the kitchen, the look of concentration on his face, his broad hands—callused and rough from his plasterwork—for once not covered in white dust but instead cradling radishes and wielding knives and grasping panhandles.

For a brief—very brief—moment her mind wondered how skilled those hands might be at other things.

When he finished, they carried everything down to the garden, where he grilled the duck breast on the barbecue. When done, he sliced the meat into delicate strips, placed a portion on each plate, and drizzled sauce over the meat and the already arranged beans and potatoes. Finally, he opened a bottle of red wine and served them both.

"*Bon appétit.*"

Had Armand been a different man, or this a very different situation, Claire might have suspected him of trying to impress her. But given the circumstances, Claire knew this was simply the way he was. As Giselle had said, the French took dinner very seriously.

For several minutes, Claire lost herself in the food: the duck breast was tender and succulent and the sauce was amazing. The tiny roasted potatoes were crispy on the outside, tender on the inside, and sprinkled with herbs. The green beans had been cooked to the perfect consistency, bathed in butter, and lightly salted.

It was a hearty step up from a *boulangerie* sandwich.

"Is it good?" he asked.

"I want to lie right down on this plate and roll around in the sauce," Claire said in English.

"And that's a good thing?" he asked, a slight smile on his face.

"A very good thing. It's amazing, Armand. Thank you."

The evening was warm and sultry, with a soft breeze that carried the subtle scent of jasmine and roses. As she ate, Claire considered the stone walls and ivy and flowers and the water trickling in the fountain. It was all so charming, it made Claire wonder whether there had been a woman in Armand's life who had decorated this courtyard and then broken his heart, leaving him a bitter shell of a man with a lovely garden. A woman who had eaten his sumptuous meals and shared his big bed and been witness to the private side of himself that he kept so well hidden.

Could that be the tragedy Giselle and Quentin had alluded to? Was this the pain that Armand carried around like a yoke?

In that moment she recognized the sense of kinship she felt with others borne out of tragic circumstances: her college roommate, Zoey, who had lived in terror of her abusive father. The colleague at work who had lost a baby to SIDS. The neighbor whose grown son suffered from uncontrolled manic depression and now wandered the streets homeless. Countless adult children of alcoholics.

The walking wounded seemed to gravitate to one another in work situations, neighborhoods, even at parties. It was as if Claire had a sixth sense for misfortune. Put her in a room of a hundred people and she could sort out the dozen with a tragic personal background in fifteen minutes tops. She was surprised it had taken her so long with Armand.

Still, a breakup could be heartbreaking and difficult, but . . . tragic? Then again, this was France. Probably they took their romance as seriously as dinner.

After a while, it felt awkward to sit together through an entire meal without speaking, though Armand seemed content to do so.

Claire tried a conversation starter: "Giselle mentioned you are working on a family estate in the Franche-Comté."

He nodded, apparently happy to let the statement stand for itself.

"What is it like there?" she tried again.

"What do you mean, what is it like?"

"I just . . . I've never been to that region."

"It's quiet. A lot of cows and fields, dotted with small villages. It's in the Département de Doubs, which is primarily agricultural. The Loue runs through it; it is a beautiful river."

"Sounds lovely."

"Very few tourists," he added, as though as an accusation.

"Yes, I imagine. I don't know about people from other countries, but I don't think many Americans know much about that area. We're mostly focused on Paris and Bordeaux, and maybe the South of France, Provence and Cannes. But not the Franche-Comté area."

He nodded and kept eating.

So much for that conversational gambit. Next Claire considered asking about Giselle, or her children or husband. Or perhaps French history.

What she really wanted to ask about was the dollhouse she had found.

She took a deep sip of wine and felt his eyes upon her. Expectant.

"What?" she asked.

"Did you even taste it?"

"Pardon?"

"The wine. It is Négrette, from the Frontonnais region. It is dry and dark, strong, but it is subtle, not like your American wines."

"What are my American wines like?"

"Too jammy, too bold, too alcoholic. Too eager to please."

"And the French wines are less eager to please?" She smiled. "Are you saying wine reflects national character?"

"To some extent, yes."

"How do you mean?"

"The wines of my country are known for their delicacy. They are meant to reveal themselves not

220

only on the tip of one's tongue upon the first sip, but to develop as they travel to the back of the mouth, and then linger on the tongue after swallowing."

She laughed.

"I'm serious. Take another taste, a large sip, and concentrate as it moves across your palate."

To humor him, she took a large gulp, holding it in her mouth for a moment before swallowing.

She really hated to admit it, but he was right. The taste changed and developed as it passed over different parts of her tongue. After she swallowed, the flavor filled her palate and nose with subtle but lingering sensations.

His blue eyes were still on her, intent. As though willing her to taste, to understand what he was saying. "You see'?"

"I do see."

He stood suddenly and grabbed their empty plates.

"I cooked, so you will do the dishes."

"*Oui, chef.*"

25

Despite his declaration, Armand helped Claire clean the kitchen, though he did so in silence. He turned the music up and they worked in concert, she washing, he drying and putting away the dishes.

Afterward, he went into his workshop and closed the door.

Back in her tiny apprentice's cubby, Claire noticed someone—Giselle, or Armand?—had made a couple of additions to the décor: a small oval rug by the bed, a mirror (so old the silver was flaking off in sections) hanging over the desk.

Claire felt the softness of the rug under her feet and ran her hand along the old gilt frame of the mirror. There was one loose stone below it, right behind the desk, making Claire wonder how long these walls had stood and what they had endured.

Funny how at home she felt in her little room. She immediately sat down to write another letter to her uncle.

Dear Uncle Remy,

Today we had duck for dinner! It was an elaborate meal cooked for me by a very grumpy boss who doesn't like me very much. Still, the way they treat dinner here reminds me of Mammaw and her sisters, how they would chop and mix and cook all afternoon for a meal that was gone in an hour.

Also, an Italian chocolatier brought me a Statue of Liberty made of chocolate! Quentin (the chocolate man) calls it ephemeral art, which means it's not meant to last. I have just eaten her torch and can attest: *c'est magnifique, le chocolat français!*

Now I will say good night, because I am reading through the many articles and books about *L'Inconnue* gathered in a box at this atelier. Perhaps I will find her identity eventually, if I keep looking. What do you think?
With love, your niece,
Chance

After addressing the envelope and sealing it with wax, Claire wrote chatty postcards to Jessica, a few Chicago friends, and Sean. Then she got ready for bed, sat down, and began to rummage through the box.

She was hoping to find some reference to the CPR doll—that story seemed so strange and macabre, it was hard to believe it was true—but then she picked up a slim novella, entitled *The Worshipper of the Image* by Richard Le Gallienne.

She let out a quick sigh of relief when she realized the book was in English. Though she felt comfortable in French, Claire still had to stay on her toes. The way she had explained it to friends in Chicago was this: When she heard English being spoken around her, she couldn't help but understand. But when she heard French, she had to make an effort to decipher the words; it was easy to tune out. It was tiring after a while.

And reading was simultaneously easier—she could see the words written—and more difficult—it was harder to maintain her concentration, and there was no body language to assist in her comprehension.

She snuggled into bed—the sheets *still* smelled like lavender; how was that even possible?—pulling the bedding around her more for comfort than for warmth. The studio had no air-conditioning, but the evening air was refreshing, and scents of the garden wafted in through the open window along with the sounds of the city. She began to read.

In the story, a man was wandering the streets of Paris when he passed by an atelier that sounded remarkably similar to that of the Lombardi family mold-makers. Le Gallienne had written:

Through white corridors of faces he passed, with the cold breath of classic art upon his cheek, and in the company of the dead who live forever he was conscious of a contagion of immortality.

And then his gaze settled upon the mask of a young woman.

Soon . . . he grew conscious of a presence. Someone was smiling near him. He turned, and, almost with a start, found that—as he then thought—it was no living thing, but just a plaster cast among the others, that was thus shining, like a star among the dead. A face not ancient, not modern; but a face of yesterday, today, and forever.

He called her *Silencieux*, but despite her name, she began to speak to him. As the story continued, the man became so enamored of the mask that he neglected his daughter and wife in order to be with her and only her; in the end he forfeited everything for *Silencieux*.

Claire read the entire novella, then turned out the light and lay awake for quite some time pondering *L'Inconnue*. In most of the other fictional accounts, she was conceived of as a victim of circumstance, of predatory men and a heartless society. In Le Gallienne's tale, in contrast, the seemingly innocent face was powerful and intent on orchestrating men's demise.

In one sense, Claire agreed: the face of her silent companion from childhood had been powerful enough to get her to travel to Paris. But in every account of her, *L'Inconnue* remained elusive; it was not her in the stories, but others' reactions to her. She was an object, not a true subject.

Who had this young woman been? And why did it matter so much to Claire to figure it out?

Claire put the novella back into the box, fell into a fitful sleep, and dreamed.

Chance—eighteen months old, with her daddy's dark eyes and ringlets—gazes at her mother's face, willing her to open her eyes.

Open open open.

Her mother's expression is serene yet distant. A Mona Lisa–*like smile plays upon full lips. Long, dark hair floats about her: a halo of silk drifting in graceful slow motion, a laconic modern dance. A chocolate corona.*

Chance strapped securely into her car seat in the back of the ten-year-old Ford; her mother behind the wheel. So how can Chance see her mother's eyes?

But there they are in front of her, closed tight, refusing to open.

The moment when the car careens off the road, flipping and landing on its roof.

The face of her mother with eyes closed.

The strange quiet of the bayou waters that slip into the car with a rush, inundating and surrounding them, muffling her infant cries.

Chance upside down in her car seat, suspended in a pocket of air.

The stench of the brackish water. The hot, stifling air. The fear. The thirst. The rage.

Chance's whimpers dissolve into sobs. She calls out: "Mama! Mama!"

Her mother's eyes do not open.

They never open.

26

All day long, Claire chatted with tourists. A small group from Cleveland, another from Berlin, a family from Seville. A mother and daughter from Chicago filled Claire in on local politics. Claire found herself spinning tales about the masks and statues and busts, about the process of mold-making, the secret techniques and talents of the casters. Explaining that the master—Armand hunched over his projects behind the windows—must not be disturbed from his work.

She smiled to herself, thinking of how Armand had accused her of telling "a lot of" stories.

He was right, she realized. In college and even more so later, as a professional in Chicago, she had told long, often exaggerated tales about her childhood in Plaquemines Parish. Even though part of her would always love the place, it was an easy target, especially for Northern city dwellers who didn't know a hush puppy from a crawfish. And at least she came by it honestly: Claire had grown up with storytellers. And wasn't it funda-mentally human to want a narrative, a chronicle that gave meaning to life, and to death?

After selling two masks, matching friezes, and one small bust of a Roman soldier, preparing the paperwork for shipping, and sending the tourists happily on their way, things fell quiet.

Claire knocked softly on the workshop door.

"May I help you with anything?"

"Not here." Armand looked up from a series of friezes he was detailing. He straightened and wiped his hands on a towel. "But the woman who quit, she took a set of keys with her. I'd like you to go to her apartment and get them from her."

He handed Claire a piece of paper with an address written on it.

"Also, bring her mail to her. And remind her she should change her mailing address—she used this address because she was in her apartment temporarily, but it won't work for her to continue."

Claire gave him a look.

"You are thinking this isn't in your job description," he suggested.

"It really isn't."

He let out a sigh. "I guess it's good you are only here for two weeks."

"Hey, you and Giselle begged me to come help you, remember? Also, Quentin says I am a very charming English translator. Better than your last."

"Are you going to get the keys from her or not?"

"I'll go, I'll go," said Claire with a quiet chuckle. "I'm just giving you a hard time. Do you have a phone number so I could call first, make sure she's home?"

"She doesn't have a phone."

"She doesn't have a phone?"

"Would you rather speak in English?" he asked in English.

"No, I understand what you're saying. I'm just surprised that anyone doesn't have a phone in this day and age."

"This is Paris," he said, as though that explained everything. "Perhaps we do not all want to have one attached to our ear like you."

"I thought there were more cell phones in Europe than in America."

He shrugged. "Perhaps you can have this fascinating discussion with her when you see her."

"Perhaps I will."

"All I am saying is, someone needs to go to her apartment to get the keys from this woman. And since you have several more decades of training to go before you become a master molder, and there is a good deal of casting work to do here, I nominate you to go instead of me."

"All right, no problem. Are you sure you can handle the hordes of tourists?" she asked, inputting the address into her phone.

He rolled his eyes when he realized what she was doing.

"You could simply ask me directions. Take the metro to Buttes Chaumont—you will have to change trains once. From there, you walk along rue Botzaris until you reach rue Fessart, then take a left. It is an apartment building."

"All right. Anything else while I'm out?"

"You can buy the groceries for dinner. I like the Marché Couvert de Saint-Quentin in the tenth arrondissement; it is not far from there." He handed her a list of dinner supplies, along with two woven shopping bags.

"Nice bags."

"You must bring your own to the store here."

"But I thought you wanted *me* to cook tonight," she said, glancing at the list. Still, she was teasing. She knew how to make only one thing, and where would she find gumbo filé— much less okra—in Paris?

"Do you *want* to cook tonight?"

"I do good takeout," she offered in English. At his questioning look, she explained in French, "I'd be happy to pick something up. Do you like falafel?"

He waved his hand dismissively. "I will cook. We will have lamb chops and *tomates provençales*."

Claire grabbed her purse—if he was going to cook, the least she could do was buy the groceries—and then descended the stairs with a bag over each shoulder, saying hello in her mind to the faces lining the wall and emerging on the bustling narrow street.

Now that she had a purpose, a role—a Parisian shopgirl on a mission to collect a set of keys, and then to buy a few groceries—she found she thoroughly enjoyed walking the streets of Paris, woven bags slung over her shoulders, head held high. She felt as much a part of the bustle of the city as the delivery trucks and the pushcarts, the trash collectors and the government bureaucrats.

Useful, as Mammaw used to say.

One overriding worry hadn't left her: what would she do when the shop closed for August vacation? She could visit more of the must-sees on her list, she supposed. But Claire decided she wasn't cut out to be a tourist, meandering from one historic site to the next, lounging and lingering. Even as she defended tourism to Armand, Claire had disliked being part of the visiting throng standing in line for the Louvre or pushing through the crowded sidewalks of the Champs-Élysées.

But right now, in this moment, she was happy.

She made her way to the Saint-Michel metro station, dropped a few coins for a Gypsy family playing music there, found Buttes Chaumont on the metro map, and figured out where to change trains. Twenty-five minutes later she emerged from the underground in a relatively modern neighborhood with recent structures mixed with a few traditional gray stone apartment buildings, their only embellishment little black wrought-iron balconies.

Claire followed Armand's instructions, walked a few blocks to the apartment building at the address on the paper. She found the name, Lisette Villeneuve, on a panel by the front door and rang the buzzer once, then twice.

No answer.

A tattooed young woman with bright blue hair and big black boots that looked too large for her petite frame arrived and used her key on the front door.

"Excuse me," Claire said. "Do you know a woman named Lisette Villeneuve? Apartment 110?"

"Yes, I do. She never answers her bell, but she's almost always here. You want to come in?"

She let Claire into the lobby and led the way down the hall to apartment 110.

The young woman raised her arm and banged loudly on the door. No answer. She banged again. "*Madame*?"

"Thank you for your help," said Claire.

"She should come eventually," she said. "Give her a minute."

The young woman continued down the hall, disappearing into an apartment at the end of the corridor.

Claire remained at the door, listening. She thought she heard some shuffling sounds, but still no one answered. Claire considered leaving, but she had come all this way and hated the idea of not completing her errand. So, following the young neighbor's example, she raised her arm and banged her fist on the door.

"*Madame?*"

"*J'arrive!*" came a muffled voice—I'm coming!

At long last the door opened to reveal a woman in her late forties or early fifties, neatly coiffed and dressed in that way of Parisian women of a certain age: svelte and put-together and classy.

"*Comment?*"

"Madame Villeneuve? I was sent by Armand Fontaine, from the Lombardi studio, to get the keys to the shop."

"Armand sent you?" She breathed. She looked pale, as though startled by the inquiry. Her eyes shifted down the hall to the front door.

"Yes. I'm sorry to disturb you. I just need to get the keys for the studio."

The woman stared for another moment, then asked, "You're American?"

Claire nodded. "You too, right?"

"Of course. Of course. All right. Just . . . just give me one moment."

She closed the door. Claire stood there, feeling awkward. She checked e-mail on her phone, looked up and down the uninspired hallway.

After several minutes the woman returned with a key ring from which hung three huge, ancient-looking keys, along with several smaller ones that appeared to fit padlocks or lockers.

They clanked as she held them out to Claire.

"Oh, I almost forgot," Claire said, digging in her bag for the mail. "These came to the studio for you. Armand mentioned that you should change your address with the postal service."

"You are my replacement at the atelier?"

Claire smiled and nodded. "Just temporarily. I—"

"And what is your name?" Villeneuve interrupted.

"Claire. Claire Broussard. Nice to—"

The woman slammed the door in her face.

Claire raised her eyebrows, blew out a breath. No wonder Quentin had described Claire as an upgrade from the Lombardi studio's last English speaker. The bar didn't appear to be set very high. Perhaps Villeneuve had been able to turn on the charm with the tourists, or maybe her haughty air fit in with the Parisian approach to shop-keeping. Still, it didn't seem like sales would be her strong suit.

As Claire was leaving the building, she met the same tattooed woman coming back down the hall.

"Did she ever open the door?" she asked Claire.

"She did, yes."

"Is she your friend?"

"Not really. More a . . . business associate."

"She's a little bizarre, *n'est-ce pas*?"

"Yes, I noticed."

"She is an artist," she said with a shrug. "I think sometimes artists are tortured by things others cannot understand."

Claire again thanked the young woman for her help and they left the building together but headed in different directions down the street. Claire consulted her phone to get her bearings on her next destination—the farmers' market that Armand had mentioned—and then headed north.

As she walked, she enjoyed the street scenes of a nontouristy neighborhood: normal people living life. A pair of teenagers clattered by on the bicycles—called Vélib—available for rent throughout much of the city. A stooped old woman shuffled by; she wore all black and carried three baguettes in a basket. Two young women, one wearing a hijab, chatted as they pushed baby strollers. Four men who looked to be in their sixties were seated at an outdoor café table, gesticulating as they indulged in an animated discussion, espressos in front of them. A bored-looking, apron-clad waiter leaned against the wall, tapping his fingers as though he wished he could smoke.

But soon Claire's mind started to wander. It was clear Villeneuve was, as her neighbor had so astutely mentioned, *un peu bizarre*. But could there be something more? Could she and Armand have had a romantic relationship? Was this the heartbreak Giselle (and Quentin) had hinted at?

Villeneuve was clearly a good deal older than Armand, but she was attractive, chic, refined. And wasn't Paris famous for the older woman/ younger man relationship?

It was none of Claire's business. *None.*

Still . . . she glanced down at her jeans and blouse, the handmade silver jewelry she had bought from street vendors in Chicago, and her well-worn black leather boots. Claire liked to think she had her own style, a certain je ne sais quoi, but she was no fashion plate. Certainly nothing compared to Parisian women. Not particularly chic *or* refined.

And so what if Armand and his last assistant had been involved? Actually, it was sort of sweet to imagine two such grumpy misfits finding each other and making a connection.

But for some reason, Claire was bothered by the idea.

27

The farmers' market was located in a covered arcade made of wrought iron and glass, like a massive gazebo with sides open to the air.

She stood in the entry for a moment to appreciate the scene.

Claire had been prepared—perhaps overly so— for the wonder of famous Parisian sights like the

Eiffel Tower and the Louvre. But what truly impressed her were the incredibly beautiful historic buildings that were used for everyday affairs in Paris, such as pharmacies and hair salons, automotive repair and farmers' markets. In her hometown most of the historic structures had been destroyed or damaged by hurricanes over the years, replaced with the cheapest possible structures for a less-than-well-off populace. In nearby New Orleans some beauties had survived, of course, and tourists thronged to the French Quarter for good reason.

But it was the nonchalance, the insouciance with which the Parisians treated their historic architecture, that most impressed her.

Claire glanced down at the list Armand had handed her. He wrote in a bold, slanted script.

Côtelettes d'agneau
Tomates, oignons, ail
Herbes de Provence
Paté de campagne
Fromages—Petit Basque, Comté, Epoisses
Salade
Yaourt
Oeufs bio
Lait bio
Melon, pommes, poires

The hall was jammed with stalls and crowded with shoppers. In addition to fruit and vegetables and meat and fish and cheese, there were small stands that offered café fare, sandwiches and pastries and coffee. Immediately apparent was that the crowded booths where people fought for the attention of the sellers must have the best meat and produce—or the best prices. Others were quiet, with flies buzzing the goods as workers lazily shooed them away.

Claire watched little old women bringing melons—only slightly bigger than a softball—up to their noses to sniff the ends. They clucked and fussed and argued with the vendors. As Claire lingered and watched, she realized: customers and sellers were blunt and sometimes insulting, but it was a game they were playing. They sparred, teased, coaxed, and eventually bought and sold.

She remembered her grandmother at Old Man Patterson's farm stand, complaining and haggling over prices. But Mr. Patterson was the only vendor, so if his collard greens were studded with aphids or his potatoes were tinged with green, you were out of luck.

Claire took a deep breath and dove in. But this sort of thing wasn't her strong suit. As much as she was enjoying her stint as a Parisian shop-keeper, part of her was starting to miss being *good* at her job. Armand's critical attitude certainly didn't help. She was almost to the point of longing for some computer code glitches to work out, just so she could enjoy mastery over something.

She followed one particularly choosy woman around for a while, buying what she bought. But after a while Claire ran out of patience, purchased the remaining items on her list from a vendor with no line, and took the metro back to the fifth arrondissement, walking past students and tourists, locals and foreigners, to the Moulage Lombardi on rue de la Huchette.

She hauled the heavy bags up the stairs and set them on the kitchen counter, happy to be relieved of her burden. Her arms ached.

Armand emerged from his workshop and started pulling things out of the bags. At first Claire thought he was being uncharacteristically helpful but soon realized he was inspecting the produce and meat as he pulled it out, muttering under his breath, *"Ooh la la"* or *"Putain."*

Some of the groceries—the items she'd bought with the old woman as guide—Armand seemed happy with, but as he scrutinized the rest he started to cluck and exclaim. He threw up his hands and flew around the kitchen for a moment, grumbling about Americans who didn't even know how to shop.

"In Chicago—heck, even in my hometown—we have these places called 'grocery stores,'" said Claire, leaning back against the counter, arms crossed over her chest. "And you just go in and buy what they have. It's very convenient."

"We have those in France too. Here they are

called Casino or Monoprix. They are well-known to have inferior meat and produce. And the seafood . . ." He trailed off, shaking his head as though it wasn't even necessary to explain the state of the seafood.

"Mmm." Claire made a noncommittal reply, finding it hard to get worked up about it.

"Anyway," he said with a shrug, calming down, "it is fine. At least the lamb looks decent. We will make do."

Dinner was delicious.

Dear Uncle Remy,

You will never guess who has become a chef's assistant. No, not really. But here in the studio where I am staying my boss insists on cooking a grand meal every night, and now I am his assistant, washing vegetables and chopping and stirring.

It reminds me of Mammaw, but it is all accomplished without talking. No stories here, unless I tell them, and they make him impatient. So he turns on his French music and cooks in silence, and I am forced to enjoy the sumptuous dinner in the garden.

Also, I help do the dishes!

Love you and miss you,

your niece,

Chance

· · ·

It was late, after midnight. Claire read through more items in the box, but she didn't feel sleepy. In her old apartment she had assumed the night-club kept her up, but now she realized: she had other reasons for not sleeping. Maybe it was the constant doubt about her future buzzing in her brain.

She perused the ancient stone walls, the big window overlooking the neighbors' garden, the gilt-clad mirror over the desk.

There was no denying she had landed in an awfully interesting situation here in Paris at the Moulage Lombardi. But it was temporary. And she couldn't keep the disappointment from rising from time to time during the day whenever she looked over at *L'Inconnue*. Claire had no clearer idea who the young woman was, whether she was related to the mysterious note, and why any of it mattered at this point.

Most likely was that Mammaw had sent Claire to Paris because she knew, in her Mammaw way, that Claire desperately needed a direction, a quest, an adventure.

But where did she go from here? What did she do?

Finally, she gave up trying to sleep, kicked off the covers, and headed to the kitchen for a glass of water.

The light was still on in the workroom. Armand

was hunched over a project on the tall bench. Claire approached the windows as quietly as she could; he was working on the little plaster château. A man with his dollhouse.

Armand suddenly looked up, pulling a cloth over the *petit château* in one smooth move. He came to the door and opened it.

"Did you need something?"

"No, thank you. I'm sorry to disturb you."

He said nothing further, but held her gaze.

Finally she shook her head. "I just noticed the light on and wondered if you were all right."

"I'm fine. Good night."

"*Bonne nuit.*"

Instead of going back to her cubby, Claire sat down at the business desk and logged on to the Internet. She answered a couple of e-mails, paid her credit card bill, checked her bank balance, and then called up a search engine.

She did another, more thorough search of *L'Inconnue*, but she didn't find anything more in-depth than the information contained in the articles in the box, some of which she still hadn't read. She did find an article noting the frequency of suicide in the Seine in the late nineteenth century, however; some days they pulled dozens of bodies out of the frigid river. So *L'Inconnue* was one among many. If not for her youthful beauty and intriguing smile, she would be as forgotten as all the rest.

She found three articles confirming the story that *L'Inconnue* had been the model for the CPR doll, from reputable sources—*Le Petit Journal*, *The Guardian*, and *Smithsonian*—so she supposed it really was true.

Then Claire began a new search: "Leonardo da Vinci, veins."

Multiple references popped up right away. As she read, she learned more about Da Vinci and his philosophies connecting different aspects of the natural world—the branches of trees, the tributaries of rivers, the veins beneath our skin—to the networks of society and humanity.

Humans connected to the natural world, branching out with growth and time and experience. It was all connected.

Claire glanced again at the lit windows of Armand's workshop. Feeling dissatisfied but unable to pinpoint why, Claire logged off, poured herself a glass of wine, and savored it as she read in bed.

28
SABINE

Maurice is spending less time in the studio and more time in cafés and bars. When Sabine is not too bruised, he brings her with him. She sits by his side, a glass of Lillet in front of her. He prefers absinthe himself, but does not find it ladylike, so he orders her the sweet wine.

Though she remains quiet, Sabine cherishes these times. She loves to hear the people—men, mostly, but the occasional woman too—talk of philosophy and politics, of art and craft. Their words swirl in a confusing mélange over her head, but they hint at other worlds, other lands, other ways of thinking. She tries to remember the things they say, to keep the tidbits for when she is modeling and must remain still as the dead for hours at a time. She uses the time to consider the novel concepts, turning them over in her mind, inspecting, weighing them.

Often Maurice introduces her to famous or influential writers and artists: Edgar Degas, Émile Zola. Zola speaks very animatedly about something called the Dreyfus affair. The names flow over her; she has not heard of them. Maurice teases her for this, but the men seem unfazed, laughing at her naïveté. Sometimes they ask if she will model for them. Mostly, they ignore her.

One night a man named Jean-Baptiste Lombardi joins them. He smokes strong Gauloises cigarillos, and compared with the other men—content to talk over one another, shouting and proclaiming—he is subdued.

He startles Sabine by speaking to her directly, instead of through Maurice. Monsieur Lombardi smiles and tells her that he is free from the angst of the artist, because he is a mold-maker.

"He is a *death* mask maker," booms Maurice.

Sabine's eyes grow large at the idea. Still, she once saw Napoléon's death mask in one of the museums Maurice took her to. She remembers thinking that this was a true representation of the emperor's likeness, rather than the interpretation through the eyes of an artist. It felt closer to the truth, to the person he was.

As the men talk, Sabine studies the mask-maker under her lashes. His callused hands gesticulate as he talks. The nail beds are white with embedded plaster, the wrists thick. An ugly scar runs across his brow and continues onto his cheek. Sabine decides it is a miracle the blade did not pluck out his eye. His eyes . . . they are a beautiful blue, deep and cool as the lake in the woods outside her village.

"What about you, mademoiselle?" asks Monsieur Lombardi. His gaze is intent, focused on her. Making her blush.

"Me?" she responds, losing her breath.

"Yes, what do you think of the Impressionists? Has their time already gone? Shall they stand aside and make room for the Nabis?"

"I don't . . . I don't know anything," Sabine whispers.

"She is my little country mouse!" Maurice declares, in his cups. *"La rate des champs!"*

"But a country mouse knows many things," says Jean-Baptiste. "Not the least is how to survive in the city, off the crumbs cast from the tables of the wealthy."

Maurice glares at him. He does not like to be reminded. At any time, he could ask his parents for money; the temptation is forever there, taunting him. He knows, as does everyone else, that he is not hungry enough.

Sabine notes the danger signs: the twitch of his mustache, the way he falls suddenly silent. She remains mute; anything she says will make the situation worse.

One hand, heavy and hot, lands on the back of her neck. Maurice puts his other hand under her chin, to raise it. Sabine forces herself to smile.

"You see what I am telling you, Jean-Baptiste?" says Maurice. "She has a *Mona Lisa* smile. *Le sourire de* La Joconde. Why can I not capture it? I ask you."

Her face burns.

But then she realizes: the mask-maker does not

stare at her, but at Maurice. First at his face, and then at his big hands, which handle her so roughly.

This shames her even more. She looks away, drops her smile.

"Perhaps I should commission you to make her mask, eh, Jean-Baptiste? A life mask I could study at my leisure. Perhaps then I could capture what I seek."

When it is time to go, Maurice tosses a fistful of coins on the table; he cannot be bothered to count them out. Sabine's gaze falls on them; it is more than he pays her for a full week of work.

When he leaves the table, he does not bother to push his chair back in. That is what servants are for.

29

As the days passed, Armand and Claire fell into a pattern. He would awaken early and put on coffee, and Claire would run to the *boulangerie*—Le Boulanger de Monge, 123 rue Monge—for croissants, as well as baguettes for later in the day. The bread had to come from the best *boulangerie*, of course.

"Otherwise," Armand said, upon specifying the bakery, "why bother to eat bread at all? Life is too short."

During the day Claire would tend to customers,

though not all of them spoke English. She was able to help with the French speakers and stumble through with a little Spanish, and most of the Germans spoke English, but occasionally Armand would have to emerge from his lair to speak with the Japanese.

Claire enjoyed telling tales, repeating what Armand had told her about the history and process of mold-making, embellishing and extending the story. When there was a lull, she would work with Armand and occasionally Giselle, sanding and sealing the plaster casts.

During the long lunch breaks, Claire got in the habit of walking and exploring the tangle of narrow boulevards and alleys that made up the Latin Quarter. No matter the day or the hour, it felt akin to a street festival. Small hotels and bed-and-breakfasts hung out shingles. Most buildings were the traditional cream limestone, but wooden facades were painted in bright hues of turquoise, red, yellow, and orange.

The tiniest passages were pedestrian-only and were crowded with both tourists and locals; bicycles, motorcycles, and scooters vied with automobiles in the narrow streets that allowed vehicles. Street musicians played accordions or guitars for spare change; a Peruvian band drew a crowd in the Place Saint-André-des-Arts. There were covered outdoor cafés and eateries, poster shops, wine cellars, and kiosks selling key chains, aprons, and silk scarves. A bar called The Gentleman offered happy hour, which the hawker standing outside pronounced " 'appy hower."

Moulage Lombardi wasn't far from the Sorbonne, the famous university founded in the thirteenth century. Somber-faced students and artists still haunted the neighborhood, and it wasn't hard to imagine bohemians scribbling away in attic apartments and corner cafés down through the centuries. Claire wondered whether this academic presence accounted for the numerous bookstores, card and magazine shops, and stationery and art supply establishments in the area.

She passed a Starbucks but resolutely ignored it. A coffee to go appealed to her, but she wasn't sure she could handle Armand's derision were she to show up at the *moulage* with the telltale cardboard cup in hand.

On one of her walks, Claire came across an odd little alley called rue du Chat-qui-Pêche—literally, "Street of the Cat That Fishes." And later that same day she found herself in front of Shakespeare and Company, the famous English-language bookstore. She took time to meander through its crowded stacks and made two selections, both set in Paris: Ernest Hemingway's *A Moveable Feast*, which she'd never read, and a contemporary romance about an American woman finding a second chance at love in the City of Light.

After closing their doors to business at the Moulage Lombardi, they would break for *apéro*—sometimes with Giselle, sometimes with Quentin, sometimes just the two of them. Claire would caress the cat; then Armand would cook and she would act as sous-chef. At night she read more about *L'Inconnue*, every scrap in the box and everything she could dig up on the Internet.

One day a more comfortable chair appeared at the little desk in her apprentice's cubby; another time a drawing was hung near the armoire. It was a charming charcoal sketch of a man leaning over a sculpture on a workbench. At first glance Claire thought the figure might be Armand, but then she realized it was a different man, with a jagged scar running from his brow to his cheek but a sweet expression in his clear eyes.

When she mentioned these additions to her comfort, Armand shrugged off her thanks.

Sometimes, late at night, she was able to coax Armand away from his workbench for a glass of cognac. They would sit in the dark garden and Claire would tell him family stories. About her great-grandfather Jerry Duval, who had come to Paris—to this very store—in World War II looking for a gift for his wife; the alligators that stalked the bayous; the devastation of the hurricanes; the dance and music and food of the Cajun people. The time Uncle Charles had come face-to-face with the *rougarou* or when Uncle Bill got his finger stuck in a cannon in Galveston and they had to cut it off to free him.

"He lost his finger in the cannon? I don't believe you."

"You believe the *rougarou* but draw the line at the cannon story?" she said with a smile.

"We both know the *rougarou* is mythology. But I think you believe the finger story."

"Well, actually, it was just the tip of it. He had no fingernail, and he used to wiggle it at me. I was fascinated. Hey! Here's a question for you: I found a little alley called rue du Chat—"

"—Qui-Pêche," he finished with a nod. "Everyone is curious about that name."

"Where does it come from—do you know?"

"It sounds like one of your stories."

"I can't wait to hear it."

He gave her a small smile. "According to legend, in the fifteenth century an alchemist lived on that street with his loyal black cat. It was said this cat could grab a fish out of the Seine with a single swipe of his powerful paw. Some students from the Sorbonne got it into their heads that the man was a dangerous sorcerer and that the cat was his familiar. So—"

"Don't tell me—"

"They killed the cat."

"*Non*," Claire said.

"I'm afraid so. And after that, no one could find the alchemist."

"What happened to him?"

"It is said he turned up years later, so he was still alive. But his life was so entwined with his cat that he lost his life force for a while."

Claire stared at him for a long moment. "You believe that?"

He shrugged. "Who knows the truth? It is the story that is told."

But as Claire knew too well, the stories told could just as soon be fiction as fact.

"I want to learn how to do mold-making," Claire announced one morning over coffee.

"Mold-making is much harder than casting. Anyone can cast, as long as you mix well and learn how to avoid bubbles. Mold-making is . . ." Armand trailed off with a shrug.

"An art."

"Exactly." He nodded. "A very old art."

"How old?"

"Cennino Cennini's *Il Libro dell'Arte*, from the year 1392, referred to life casting as a skill passed down from 'the Ancients.'"

"Which Ancients would those be?"

"Good question. The Egyptian artisans dipped gauze into plaster to make their casts upon death so that the Pharaohs' sarcophagi would fit snugly as they cradled them on their trip to the afterlife. They also made what is referred to as death masks, but they're much more actual idealized sculptured masks than ours. Think of Tutankhamun's painted burial mask, for example."

"They had plaster back then?"

"In this, we haven't advanced all that much over thousands of years," he said with a nod. "They used plasters, wax, and clay. And the Egyptians used gold, of course."

"So your ancestors learned it from . . . ?"

"That's hard to say exactly. You know how these family stories are. Some survive, some are simply made-up legends, but most are forgotten. I know the family came to France from Italy in the nineteenth century. But Madame Tussaud had long since established the death mask business here in Paris."

"Madame Tussaud? As in the wax museum?"

"*Oui.*" He nodded and poured himself more coffee.

"You mean the wax museum woman was a Parisian death mask artist?"

He nodded again.

"And here I thought she was all about cheesy wax museums." Claire didn't know how to say cheesy in French so she just used the word in English.

Predictably, Armand asked her, "Excuse me, *what* is made of cheese?"

"Not *made* of cheese exactly. In English 'cheesy' means sort of 'corny.' " As she said this she realized they were both food references and

253

neither applied in French. "It's just that I think of wax museums as being kind of . . . silly. *Bête*. Not serious museums. They're very touristy, more so than the Champs-Élysées."

He raised his eyebrows, stuck out his chin, and nodded as though considering her words. "I don't think I've ever been in a modern wax museum, but I do know that Madame Tussaud was a gifted artist."

"And she was French?"

"Of course she was French."

Claire smiled. "Not everyone who's talented is French, you know."

He made a snorting sound. "This shows what you know—or more to the point what you don't." He gathered several of the breakfast items, filled the tray, then carried it up the stairs. Claire grabbed the rest of their dishes and followed behind. "At a very young age Tussaud was apprenticed to Dr. Philippe Curtius, a famous wax artist. He recognized her artistic skill and trained her well. At the age of seventeen she went to live in the Palace of Versailles as art tutor to the sister of Louis XVI."

"Louis XVI? Wasn't he the guy whose head was chopped off?"

"Yes." Armand rinsed their dishes while Claire put away the bread and returned the butter and jam to the refrigerator. "When the Revolution came, many aristocrats lost their heads, literally.

Tussaud was forced to make death masks of several of the most famous victims, including her former friends Marie Antoinette and King Louis."

"Wow. I had no idea. And to think that after that she went on to open horrible tourist trap museums."

"I think sometimes you purposely misunderstand me."

Claire laughed and was gratified to note a small smile on Armand's face. He led the way into the workshop.

"Since the Renaissance both death and life casts have been popular in Europe. But mold-making from the live human body was once considered heresy by the Holy See. Even Michelangelo was accused of it."

"Of heresy?"

"Italians." He made a snorting sound. "But it wasn't just the Church. Later, Auguste Rodin was accused of taking a life mold and passing it off as freehand sculpture—it was quite a scandal. After that, he never made another sculpture true-to-life size; it was always smaller or bigger."

"I'll look for that when I visit his museum."

"You should. Anyway, it was natural for the art of casting to become big here in Paris, because of the huge natural deposits—called gypsum—under the city. This is why they call it plaster of Paris."

"I guess I never thought about that name. So it's a natural mineral?"

"It begins that way. It is ground into a powder and cooked at high temperature so it loses water. Adding water back allows it to reconstitute—there is an actual chemical reaction. Because it does not contract upon drying, the casting loses no details. Plaster is a marvelous material; it can be carved, drilled, sanded, cut . . ."

"That's quite a love letter to a mineral."

He shrugged.

"But now you use something else in your molds, right? What's the blue stuff again?"

"Alginate. It's made of algae and seaweed. Plaster has an exothermic reaction and can become quite hot when it is setting. It's also time-consuming; in the old days, people might have to sit for forty-five minutes to have their cast done."

"Which might explain why it was primarily done on dead people."

"Exactly. If you time it just right and make sure to put the correct release on—such as Vaseline or grease—it can be done safely by a profes-sional. But a lot of people have suffered serious burns from plaster applied directly to the skin."

"Plus, the alginate is a nifty blue color."

"The bright color is helpful, actually, in dis-tinguishing it from the plaster. Because even though we use this directly against the skin, we still place plaster gauze on top to create a hard shell. The alginate stays pliable within the stiff plaster. I'll show you when we get to that point."

Armand filled a deep plastic bucket one quarter full of water. "With alginate, we add the powder to water, like this, rather than the other way around."

He sprinkled powder into the water and mixed with his hand until it formed a goopy consistency.

"Would you like to volunteer to be the model?" he asked Claire.

"What, *me?*"

"You seem very interested. How can you be a mold-maker if you've never had your face cast?"

"I . . ." The idea made her heart flutter. All that stuff on her face . . . ? "No, thank you."

He chuckled. It was a deep, rich sound.

"I grew up with this, you know. I must have had my first mask made when I was eight or so. There are several generations' worth of family face molds in storage downstairs. It's a way of life for the Lombardi family; it has always been this way. It's hard to become accustomed to it otherwise, I realize."

He scooped out a handful of bright blue goop and plopped it onto the face of a bust of a young woman with a headdress. The material sagged and slumped; Armand kept calmly scooping it back up and pressing it into the voids of the eye sockets, the form of the mouth.

"Obviously, when you do this on a live person, you must take extra care to avoid the nostrils."

"Yes, I would imagine breathing would be a priority. Do you put straws in the nostrils?"

He shook his head. "It is better simply to be careful not to place the alginate under the nose at all at first. I leave it to the very end, then very carefully place just a thin film around and between the nostrils with a single finger, *comme ça*." He demonstrated, deftly leaving a bright blue trail of alginate around the nostrils and across the narrow bridge in between.

Airholes or no, Claire thought she would panic if she were encased by wet material like that, dependent upon the skill of the mask-maker not to suffocate her. It was too close to drowning for her taste.

Claire changed the subject. "I've noticed you often scoff at Italians, but isn't Lombardi an Italian name?"

He shrugged, even as he continued to scoop up the sagging alginate and place it back on top of the face. His movements were smooth, practiced, and he didn't make much of a mess, all things considered. She could only imagine that if she were let loose with the sticky, goopy material there would be bright blue trails all over the workshop and probably throughout the show-room floor and the kitchen and her bedroom, like so many neon snails on the loose. "My ancestors came to this country many years ago. We have been here so long, we are now French."

"I see," Claire said. Quentin had said something similar, but it seemed to her an awfully convenient excuse. On the other hand, the United States was a country full of immigrants and she had never found that fact extraordinary: apparently, France had similarly embraced other peoples over the centuries.

"In the nineteenth century, the rise in cheap and easy photography made cast models less popular. Also, romantic authors started writing about castings as specters, which made them suspect."

"How do you mean, as specters?"

"Many stories featured castings as characters that came to life; it is no surprise, as I'm sure you have imagined these casts becoming real from time to time. Like your favorite, *L'Inconnue*."

Claire thought back to the novella she had read in which the mask of *Silencieux* began to speak to the narrator of the tale, demanding more and more of his soul.

"And do you sometimes imagine these casts coming alive at night, all alone here with the images of the dead?" she asked.

He gave a humorless chuckle. "I don't need plaster casts to see ghosts. I'm quite haunted enough, thank you very much."

30
PIERRE-GUILLAUME

1944

P ierre-Guillaume packed the mask as carefully as he could.

The American soldier was excited to send this beautiful face to his wife in Louisiana. Jerry Duval himself wouldn't ship out for several more months, so he wanted the gift to arrive so she would know he was thinking of her all the way from France. Duval said he had imagined sending her perfume or silk stockings, but if such items were to be had in the war-torn city, he certainly didn't know where to find them.

Pierre-Guillaume didn't know either. Besides, this mask would endure long after the last drop of perfume had been sprayed or the silk had run.

Pierre-Guillaume's only concern was that *L'Inconnue* would crack before arriving in such a faraway land. He tried to imagine it. Would she travel by plane or by ship? Would she hang in a beautiful hall or perhaps a lady's bedchamber? What did American homes even *look* like?

He pictured strong, fine brick houses as hale and hearty as the American soldiers themselves.

Someplace sturdy enough to contain their energy, with friendly porches and a swinging bench. But then, that image was probably based on an American movie he had seen before the war: *Bringing Up Baby* with Katharine Hepburn and Cary Grant.

Pierre-Guillaume thought about all this as he tucked papers and sawdust, anything he could find, around the serene countenance.

He stood back and gazed at her. Like most men who saw her, he was half in love with *L'Inconnue*. What was behind that very slight, very mysterious smile? What could she have been thinking in the final moments of her death?

Last month, on his single day off, his master had insisted on taking him to the Louvre and showing him *La Joconde* by Leonardo da Vinci. The painting had recently been returned to her perch on those revered walls.

"She was taken away from Paris for safe-keeping while the German invaders were here," explained Monsieur Lombardi. "They would have stolen her, had they been able to find her."

"Where was she hidden?"

"They say she was sent to Château d'Amboise first, then to the Loc-Dieu Abbey, and finally to Château de Chambord. But no one knows for sure."

"Why not?" Pierre-Guillaume asked. He tried to be patient and let his master tell his stories at his own pace, but Monsieur Lombardi sometimes fell silent, tumbling into the catacombs of his own thoughts, and it left Pierre-Guillaume on the outside, wishing for more, a child's face pressed to the window of a patisserie. Sometimes Pierre-Guillaume had an image of himself crawling into his master's brain, learning everything his master knew. He felt that way about his master's father, Jean-Baptiste Lombardi too. Both men fascinated him.

"The actual painting that went on that journey might have been a decoy. A fake."

"A decoy?"

"This is why I wanted so badly for you to see her, Pierre-Guillaume," said Monsieur Lombardi as they ceded their spot in front of *La Joconde* to other excited visitors.

They walked toward the little courtyard for a cup of tea. These were moments Pierre-Guillaume cherished, when he was not simply following work orders but his master took time to explain things to him, to help him understand the ways of art, the ways of the world.

"Sometimes a copy can play the part of an original. There are people who see the Moulage Lombardi as a house of mold-makers and casters, and they don't believe we are true artists. But though we make reproductions, they are things of great beauty, souvenirs of past genius, and saviors of artistic sensibilities. We are caretakers of history, Pierre-Guillaume. Never forget that."

And now, as Pierre-Guillaume looked at the mask of *L'Inconnue*, he thought she was as mysterious and enigmatic—and as worthy of saving—as *La Joconde*.

But why would such a lovely woman drown herself?

Pierre-Guillaume could only suppose it was part of the great mystery that was woman.

"What packing material did you find?" asked Monsieur Lombardi. He was harried because of a recent commission to help rebuild some of the Louvre's historic collections lost to the Nazis. The city was abuzz with activity; the rebuilding could not wait. They would all do their part.

"I used newspaper—old copies of *Le Petit Journal*—and also some sawdust from the construction next door," Pierre-Guillaume said, pleased with himself for thinking of it. Now that the war was over, anyone who could find lumber and tools was making repairs or starting over. The neighbor's house had been ransacked, even set afire at one point. But they had family abroad who had sent money and they were already rebuilding.

"Very good. Was there enough?"

"I used some scrap paper as well, but it's not quite sufficient."

Monsieur Lombardi went into the workshop and returned with an old tin box. It was covered in a blue-and-brown picture of a mother feeding her daughter cookies, in the outmoded Art Nouveau style of long ago. It was a style Pierre-Guillaume associated with his grandparents, of Paris during the Belle Epoque.

"There are some papers in here you can use. This old paper stock was very thick, made of linen. It should work well."

Pierre-Guillaume pried off the top of the tin and found a pile of yellowing parchment notepapers written upon in old ink.

He picked one up. It read: *Thank you.* And below it in a different script: *Thank you for what?* And then: *For sharing a glimpse of the beauty of your soul.*

"What are they?" Pierre-Guillaume asked.

"Nothing—a bunch of old correspondence of my father's. He has no use for them anymore."

"Aren't they important, monsieur? They're . . ." What was it about them? "They're pretty."

Monsieur Lombardi laughed. "You are a sweet boy, Pierre-Guillaume. You're right; I suppose the old writing is pretty. But it's useless, and we want *L'Inconnue* to arrive safely, don't we?"

His master grabbed a note on the top of the pile, tore it in two, crumpled each piece, and dropped it in the crate. "It might take quite a few, but it should do."

Monsieur Lombardi went back into the workshop, his head bending over a bust of Robespierre.

Pierre finished tucking in *L'Inconnue* using

two more newspapers, three grocery lists, the pages of an old book left out in the rain, sawdust from the building next door—but not one single more of the notes from the old tin box.

Instead, he snuck them into his little room off the kitchen and read through them at night; they read like a love story.

31

Quite predictably, that night Claire eschewed Hemingway's classic memoir and dove right into the romance instead. It was a fast read; half-way through she decided to save the rest for the next day and went to the desk to write to Remy.

But she didn't feel inspired. In part it was because she felt out of touch with him, given their one-way correspondence. Remy never answered the phone, much less wrote letters, so he was starting to feel far away. She thought about telling him the story of Le Chat-qui-Pêche, but it was too sad.

Her attention wandered and her eyes fell on a loose stone.

It was larger than a brick, not a perfect rectangle, but with rather irregular edges. She glanced around at the other stones: how many would have to be loose for the whole wall to teeter? But then, these buildings had withstood centuries and war. They would hold a few more.

She poked at it. It was definitely loose.

She thought about what Giselle had said, about people hiding things from the Nazis. That would be a good place to hide things, wouldn't it? Could it be . . . ?

The tricky part was getting to the sides to pull it out. Her fingers didn't fit. She used her letter opener, slipping it in on one side, wiggling it a little. Once the stone protruded from the wall face a fraction of an inch, she was able to get a grip.

The stone was heavy, her grip awkward. It scraped along as she pulled it out, a soft spray of powdery mortar marring the top of the desk.

Finally, she managed to pull the stone all the way out. She peered into the void.

There was a metal box.

It was rusted, but markings in robin's egg blue and chocolate brown were still evident, showing an illustration of a mother with her child, with the swooping curvy lines of the Art Nouveau style. It was an old cookie tin.

Claire placed it on the desk and stared at it for a long moment. Armand said his grandfather Pierre-Guillaume had been the last apprentice—and the last person to occupy this room.

Could it be his?

He had been a teenager when he first moved in

at the tail end of the war. If the box belonged to him, it would probably contain—what, old hair cream and a dirty magazine, maybe? A photograph of a girlfriend, or letters from his family?

Claire was tempted to open it, but she should probably hand it over to Armand. She still felt guilty for having snooped around and discovered Armand's dollhouse. She couldn't bring herself now to open an ancient box that belonged to his family.

She brought the box to the workshop and stood outside the window for a moment. As usual, Armand was working; after a moment he looked up.

"Excuse me for interrupting, but may I come in?"

"What is it?"

"I found this box," she said, stepping into the studio and setting it on the workbench.

Armand looked at her, a question in his eyes.

"It was in the apprentice's room."

"So?"

"It was hidden behind a loose stone in the wall. I think it must have belonged to your grandfather."

"*Huh.* All right. I'll bring it to him when I go to the Franche-Comté." He turned back to the frieze he was sealing with pungent, brown-tinted shellac.

Claire lingered. "Aren't you curious about what's inside?"

"I take it you are."

"It's a box *hidden behind a stone in the wall*."

"It wasn't uncommon to hide valuables, especially during the occupation."

"So you think it's something valuable?"

"No, I think it's a girlie magazine. Or it could be something as simple as a few old francs or an heirloom watch. I'll take it to my grandfather, see if he remembers it."

"You're probably right," Claire said, wishing she had opened it when she had the chance; no one would have been the wiser.

"You look disappointed. The box of papers I gave you about *L'Inconnue* isn't enough for you? My grandfather Pierre-Guillaume lived decades after that poor woman's demise. He had nothing to do with her."

"I know. I was just curious."

"You are always curious."

"So I've been told."

On Sunday the shop was closed. Giselle offered to take Claire to the Rodin Museum, if she didn't mind the children coming along. Claire happily agreed.

On the way, they walked past a restaurant called Café Le Procope.

"This is said to be the oldest café in Paris," said Giselle. "Voltaire and Robespierre and Marat ate here. And some of yours too—Benjamin Franklin and Thomas Jefferson."

"Seriously?" Claire paused to read the sign. Café Le Procope had been open since 1686. "That's amazing. More than three hundred years? That makes the Moulage Lombardi seem like a newcomer."

Giselle nodded. "We French like tradition. We can stop in later for a coffee, if you like. They serve a wonderful baba au rhum."

"I want one!" said Victorine.

"Me too," said David.

"Later, if you behave yourselves in the museum," said Giselle.

The Rodin Museum was at 70 rue de Varenne in the Hôtel Biron. The building itself was a beautiful structure, originally called Hôtel Peyrenc de Moras, built in the eighteenth century.

As lovely as the building was, the museum's gardens—in which a multitude of Rodin's sculptures, mostly bronzes, were displayed—appeared to be just as popular, at least on this warm, sunny summer day. There were several groups studying the sculptures, and more than one person with a picnic lunch, reveling in the shade and the art.

As the children ran and chased each other around the garden, Claire felt the urge to grill Giselle about her cousin—what *was* Armand's story?—but of course it wasn't appropriate. It was the strange intimacy of their living situation that made her forget she had only known the Lombardi family for a few days, and would be leaving soon.

After twenty minutes they corralled the children and entered the museum building. They strolled through several halls devoted to Rodin's development as a sculptor, pausing to assess one of his most enduring sculptures, *The Kiss.*

Giselle tilted her head. "Yes, I think this is what passion looks like. Don't you?"

Claire nodded. The piece was lovely, sensual, vibrant, the white marble grouping appearing both sedate and supple, majestic and intimate.

"I think this one is even more passionate," said Claire, studying a bronze of *L'Éternel Printemps*, showing a man and woman embracing with less overt tenderness and more blatant physicality. She read the nearby plaque. "It says this was inspired by his love affair with Camille Claudel, twenty-five years his junior. Like *The Kiss*, it was originally meant to be included in his *La Porte de l'Enfer*, or *Gates of Hell*, but was too joyous."

Giselle glanced over at her children, who were giggling over a small bronze version of Rodin's famous *The Thinker.* Giselle asked, "How about your love life, Claire? You have never been married?"

She shook her head.

"Never close to it?"

"I had a boyfriend when I lived in Chicago. He didn't propose exactly, but I know he was interested in starting a family."

"You don't want children?"

"I do. At least, I think I do. But . . ."

"Not with him," Giselle said with a nod. "This is a big decision. Better not to have children if you are not sure or you are not with the right partner. Children are difficult."

"You make it look easy."

Giselle burst out laughing. "Oh, I'm so glad you think so! But it's not true. I struggle. My tattoo reminds me—" She pulled down the neck of her T-shirt to show a barbed vine with three roses and several knots. "One rose for each child, but the barbs and the knots are a reminder of the difficulties of life."

"I like it."

Giselle looked down her own shirt, then let the neckline fall and shrugged. "I think I was feeling very dramatic in that moment. Perhaps I was a little drunk—I don't remember. My husband doesn't like it! Let's go see the Camille Claudel section. Want to?"

Upon entering the room, they read a plaque with a phrase Rodin had written about Camille Claudel: "I showed her where she would find gold, but the gold she finds is her very own."

"Well, that's sweet, right?" said Giselle with a sigh. "I think perhaps Rodin really did genuinely care for Claudel. Armand is harsher about such things. I suppose I'm a romantic. I want to believe that he truly loved her. What do you think?"

"My grandmother always said there are as many ways to love as there are to cook possum." She didn't know the word for the animal in French, so she used the English.

Giselle stared at her. "What is 'possum'?"

"Actually, it's *o*-possum. That's my accent coming out. Or"—she noted that Giselle still looked confused—"do you even have those here? Maybe they're a New World animal. They're . . . they're not very attractive. Sort of like a big albino rat."

Giselle grimaced. "And you eat these?"

Claire laughed. "No, not really—not in my family anyway. But Mammaw liked to reference them a lot." The smile lingered on her lips and Claire realized that she had thought of Mammaw without the stab of pain she'd come to expect. Sadness, of course, but the feeling was tolerable, and tempered with a glow of nostalgia. "Besides, if you're hungry enough you'll eat anything. Most Americans cringe at the idea of eating snails."

Giselle laughed and conceded her point. "Shall we?"

They continued into the section that housed several pieces of Camille Claudel's work. The signs described Claudel as being most famous for being Rodin's muse but noted she was a talented and lauded sculptor in her own right, blazing a trail for early female artists.

Claudel was only twenty-two when she embarked on one of her most famous pieces, called *Sakountala* or *L'Abandon*, sometimes also known as *The Kiss*. But unlike Rodin's grouping of the same name, Claudel's sculpture seems electric with passion but also fraught, edgy. In it, lovers are reunited after a separation. The man is on his knees, the woman standing over him, leaning back slightly. His arms are wrapped around the woman's waist and she is tilting her head to him but not quite returning his embrace, as though holding herself back. The sculpture captures a moment of tenderness and passion, desire and trepidation.

L'Age Mûr, or *The Age of Maturity*, was said to portray Claudel's torturous love for Auguste Rodin. Here a young woman is on her knees and reaching out to a man who is turning away from her into the embrace of another. It was an anguished, rawly emotional piece. Claire recognized it from the Musée d'Orsay; here at the Rodin Museum they had a plaster copy.

Claire could almost sense the artist's pieces whispering, reaching out to her; her palm itched to touch the sculptures, to feel their contours under her palm.

Giselle seemed to be watching Claire more than the sculptures.

"What do you think?" she asked.

"I think I agree with Armand, that her works

have an energy, an urgency, that appears lacking in some of Rodin's sculptures."

"I suppose it makes sense: Rodin was anxious to be accepted by the people in power at the time, the Academy, and to receive commissions, of course. Claudel was already an outcast by virtue of her gender, so perhaps she was more willing to push the boundaries."

"You think the outsiders more easily find the special energy in their art?"

"Some say this," said Giselle. "Maybe true artists have to suffer for their art. Our former employee Lisette, for example, used to say she had a special genius that could not be recognized by the Academy. A lot of artists think that, of course, but only a few are true artists, in my opinion."

"I don't really know anything about art," murmured Claire. "But . . . the price Camille Claudel paid for her bravery was madness? Doesn't that seem unfair?"

"Perhaps it is the artistic temperament. Take Van Gogh, for instance, and so many other artists who seem to find life difficult, or impossible. Even my cousin, as you've seen."

"Has Armand always been unhappy?"

"Unhappy? No. He's always been difficult, driven to perfection, strong-willed. *Soucieux.* But he was happy enough before."

"What happened?"

Giselle hesitated. "I'm sorry, Claire. He is

private to an extreme. If he hasn't told you himself, I just don't feel comfortable—"

"I totally understand," Claire said with a shake of her head. "Please forget I asked."

The children ran up to them, whining about being hungry.

"What do you say, Claire?" Giselle asked. "Going to museums is hard work. I think it is time for a treat. Don't you?"

David and Victorine fixed Claire with eager expressions.

"Actually," said Claire with a smile, "I was just thinking how I could use a baba au rhum. Whatever that is."

32

SABINE

Occasionally Maurice lends Sabine out to other artists. Usually Isabelle accompanies Sabine, but today Sabine is to pose for a woman. So Isabelle only walks her as far as the bridge, then goes off to look through a new dress shop on the Rive Droite, the right side of the river, where the businesses and banks and wealthy people reside. The students and artists populate the Rive Gauche, the Left Bank.

Sabine arrives at the address written on the little

note she holds in her gloved hand: 117 rue Notre-Dame-des-Champs. On the blue door is a big brass knocker in the shape of a curved fish.

It is the address of Mademoiselle Camille Claudel.

Sabine reaches up, bangs the knocker. Soon enough Mademoiselle Claudel herself comes to the door. There is no maid to answer.

Sabine stands there, staring.

Mademoiselle Claudel laughs and says, "Won't you come in, mademoiselle? You're not afraid of me, are you?"

They met in the café a few nights ago. Sabine had never seen Mademoiselle Claudel there before, though other women came to debate with the artists and writers from time to time, some of whom wore the nice clothes of a lady while others seemed no better off than Sabine herself.

But Mademoiselle Claudel is different; that is apparent from the start. Sabine admires what Claudel said that night about the role of art in society and her insistence that *women* could contribute to the conversation.

Sabine was flattered and excited when Mademoiselle Claudel's note asking Sabine to sit for her came. Maurice was in a good mood and acquiesced with the proviso that Sabine learn all she could about Claudel's relationship with Rodin. He loved gossip, especially those tidbits that might come in handy to use as leverage someday.

After all these months of stripping for men, Sabine is not embarrassed to be nude in front of Mademoiselle Claudel. She takes her clothes off behind the screen, then walks naked to the divan on the pedestal in the middle of the room under the skylight. It is a familiar setup by now; Sabine has been in and out of so many ateliers.

"I like to work in clay first," explains Claudel as she circles Sabine, inspecting her body. "And only when I am happy with my composition do I move on to stone. There are some in the new wave who carve directly into stone, but while I admire innovation in most things, in this I am a traditionalist."

She stands behind a large worktable, a mound of red-brown clay in front of her.

"Do you ever sculpt or draw, Sabine?"

Sabine is shocked she is being spoken to. Maurice hates it when she moves while modeling, and talking requires moving the lips. "I draw a little. I enjoy it."

"What of that mold-maker—what's his name, Monsieur Lombardi? Jean-Baptiste Lombardi? Wouldn't you like to draw him?"

"Um, yes. I believe I met him in the café."

"I saw him talking to you the other night. Surely you've noticed his hands," said Mademoiselle Claudel knowingly as she worked the clay, her own hands covered in wet earth. "And that look in his eye. I am convinced this is why the fates allowed him to keep his eyes when he received that scar."

"What look in his eye?"

"As though he's really seeing you. It is rare among men."

The conversation ends quickly as Mademoiselle Claudel's mind escapes into whatever vision she is seeing in the unformed clay. Sabine stares at the sculptress as she loses herself in her creation, watching her work the clay with furious intent. What is she thinking? Where has she gone? How has she managed to escape while remaining right there?

Mademoiselle Camille Claudel is the most remarkable woman Sabine has ever met. She does not appear to care what men think of her.

Sabine has heard the gossip: Claudel has turned her beloved Rodin away because he refuses to leave Rose Beuret, the mother of his child. Claudel is bitter, but she does not change herself for him. She does not run to him. She is true to herself.

As Sabine sits, trying to be still as a statue, she ponders Mademoiselle Claudel's words about Monsieur Lombardi. Maurice stares at her all the time—not only when she is posing for him, but many times she would awake to find him poised above her, up on his elbow, studying her face. Or when she was dressing or, worse, trying to bathe or use the chamber pot. He watched her, studied her, deliberated on her. And yet . . . did he ever truly see her?

But Jean-Baptiste Lombardi saw her that first evening in the crowded café. His eyes alit upon her and the world went away but for the two of them. He saw past the honey-colored hair, past the apple cheeks that other men commented on. Past the dark eyes that might cloud one day with cataracts, like her grandparents' eyes had, nestled in a web of wrinkles. A beauty no more.

And somehow she knew in that moment that, clouded by cataracts or no, a man like Jean-Baptiste Lombardi would see her still.

It is a revelation to be truly seen.

Sabine decides she likes sitting for Mademoiselle Claudel. She does not feel like the sculptress is trying to capture her soul. Instead . . . it feels as if she is trying to amplify whatever it is she sees, to share it with the world.

Claudel works. Her damp skirts grow heavy and wet with clay, the apron soaked through, her hair escaping its pins. She doesn't seem to notice.

When they take a break, Mademoiselle Claudel serves Sabine a glass of wine, puts out plates of pâté and bread.

"*Merci, mademoiselle*," says Sabine. Most of the artists don't provide her with snacks, and she must ask even for water. They think of her as an object, as blank as their canvases.

"Please call me Camille," she says. "Oh! Look

279

how prettily you blush at my suggestion! Listen to me, Sabine: women are not necessarily inferior to men, and the poor are not necessarily inferior to the rich. Education and experience are important, of course, but in here"—she taps her head—"and here"—she pats her chest over her heart—"is what matters. You, Sabine, are not my inferior."

Sabine can feel the heat in her cheeks and knows she is blushing even more. The things Mademoiselle Claudel—*Camille*—says are startling, almost frightening.

"Have you heard of Berthe Morisot?" she asks, slathering lotion on her hands and arms to combat the dryness; clay sucks the moisture out of one's skin. "How about Marie Bracquemond, or the American called Mary Cassatt?"

Sabine shakes her head.

"Three incredibly talented women—'*les trois grandes dames*' of Impressionism."

"Maurice told me Pierre-Auguste Renoir was the father of Impressionism. And Monsieur Degas, and Monsieur Pissarro." Sabine is eager to show Camille that she is not entirely uneducated. She reads. She listens when Maurice speaks, and he speaks often, dispensing his opinions about art and artists, politics and food and architecture.

It is the best part, by far, of being with him. She met Monsieur Degas at the café, and he sketched her right there in a few seconds. Sabine likes to sketch, even brought her charcoal and some paper with her in her pillowcase. But to watch Degas's hand move across the paper was like being a witness to a miracle.

Camille smiles. "I see you have been learning! Very good. But my point is, remember that women can be artists too. A woman can see the world, Sabine, just like a man can. We can filter it through our eyes and express it through our art just like men can."

Sabine nods, sips her wine, and savors the creamy pâté on a crusty bit of bread.

"Better, perhaps, for we understand suffering in a way that men cannot," says Camille. "Listen to me, my little friend: A muse cannot be held captive. A muse must be free. It is the *muse* who chooses her artist, not the other way around. Do you understand?"

"I think so," says Sabine, though in truth she does not.

"And sometimes," adds Camille in a quiet voice, her tone wistful, "the artist you choose is yourself."

33

How long is the drive to your family estate?" Claire asked Armand over coffee the next morning.

"I don't drive," Armand said, holding the news-paper up in front of him.

"Really? I could teach you, if you like."

"I know *how* to drive. I choose not to drive. I take the train."

"Oh. What about Gertrude?"

"Who?"

"Your cat. Who will feed her while you're gone?"

After a pause, he shrugged and said, "She is a stray. She will find her own way."

Claire was bothered by the thought, but again she reminded herself: none of this was her concern. This wasn't her life, in a few days the Lombardi relatives would take off for their family gathering in the countryside, and chances were great Claire would never see them again. Her two weeks in a Parisian atelier would be an interesting footnote in the story of her life, an entertaining cocktail party story. She could hear it now: *Death masks! I've never heard of such a thing!*

Short of adopting the cat herself—which would be a neat trick since she would be going back to the U.S. soon, where there were plenty of local strays looking for homes—Claire would have to let it work itself out.

Still, after unlocking the shop door and putting out the *Open* sign, Claire went next door to Quentin's apartment building, found his name on a list by the stairs, and rang the bell.

A moment later he came to the door with a leather satchel under his arm.

"Claire, what a lovely surprise! I was just leaving for work, but would you like to come in for a minute? Coffee, maybe?"

"No, thank you. I have to get back to the shop. I just wanted to ask you a quick question. Could you feed the black cat next week?"

"The cat?"

"You mentioned you weren't leaving the city in August. Armand seems to think the cat will be fine, and I suppose she will—after all, she's independent. But I still feel bad. Armand puts food out for her every night, and I thought maybe you could—"

"He already asked me to."

"He did?"

Quentin nodded.

"Why didn't he tell me that?" Claire wondered.

"He adores that cat—he would never abandon her. But I think he enjoys goading you. And I believe the feeling is mutual."

She returned his smile. "You might be right. Thank you. Oh—and thank you so much for the chocolate. I did as I was told and ate the whole thing. I started with her torch but then couldn't stop. It was beyond amazing."

"Wait—" He brought a box of bonbons out of his satchel. "Here—have some more."

"You just walk around with chocolate in your bag?"

"I try," he said with a shrug. "As I said, I never

eat the stuff myself. It is enough that I smell like cocoa at all times."

"Most people would consider that a good thing."

He gave her a slow smile. "I hope so."

That night, Claire brought out the chocolates after a delicious meal of *truite meunière*—a trout dish—served alongside leeks in vinaigrette and a bacon-and-onion *tartine*.

"These are from Quentin?" Armand asked.

"Yes—"

"When did you see Quentin?"

"Briefly, this morning. I actually went over to ask him about the cat."

"What about the cat?"

"I was worried she wouldn't be fed when you left for August break, and since Quentin mentioned he wasn't leaving the city, I thought—"

He threw up his hands. "Why are you obsessing about this cat?"

"It's not obsession. I like animals and I was worried about her, that's all. But I should have known you had already taken care of it."

He blew out a breath and gazed into his cognac.

Claire watched him for a long moment, thinking about the adjective Giselle had used for him at the Rodin Museum: *soucieux*. Its meaning was close to the English word "brooding."

They had extinguished the garden lights so they could fully appreciate the brilliance of the stars and the gibbous moon; it was a mild, cloudless night. Muted sounds from the street—snatches of conversation, the clanging of security shutters, the honk of a car horn—provided a pleasant sound track to the evening. The air was fragrant with roses mingling with scents of grilled onions and roasting meat from nearby restaurants.

"Anyway," Claire said, "the chocolate's pretty amazing with the cognac. I think if you allow yourself to truly taste, to sense the flavors as they roll across your palate . . ."

Armand gave her a reluctant smile.

"I made you smile!" she teased. "Every time it happens, it feels like a little miracle."

"I don't believe in miracles," Armand said with a curt shake of his head.

"No? We had a miracle in my hometown once."

"I am beginning to worry about your hometown. People lose fingers. They are chased by *rougarous* . . ."

"Do you want to hear the story or not?"

"Sure, go ahead."

"Late one night, a young woman was driving and she veered off the road and into a bayou. Her baby was in a car seat in the back. The car flipped onto its roof, and there they hung, upside down, for hours. When the rescue workers arrived, they heard the woman calling for help. *'Help us! Help my baby!'*

" *'We're coming!'* they yelled in return. *'Hang on!'* "

Though Claire had no actual memory of that night, she knew the story by heart, right down to the words that were shouted. How many times had she heard Mammaw repeat the tale to friends and relatives?

"The woman's voice, faint but clear as day, spurred them on," Claire continued. " *'Help! Help us, please!'* They yelled back, reassuring her they were on their way. Later, when they told the story in the firehouse, they would speak of the special adrenaline, the surge of strength and single-mindedness of purpose. The smashing of the passenger's-side window and finding the woman hanging upside down, submerged, long brown hair floating around her in the murky water. Dark eyes wide open."

"She had passed?" Armand asked.

Claire nodded. "But then they saw the car seat. A baby, hanging upside down like her mother but too short to reach the water. Suspended in a pocket of air. Was she alive? Jimmy Romero used his knife, easily cut through the heavy canvas strap. Released her, feeling her heaviness in his arms, praying *'Our father, who art in heaven . . .'* over and over again because, even though he hadn't been to confession in about twenty years, the words came back to him in times like these, in those moments when reason fled and he reverted to instinct: smash the window, *pray,* cut the strap, *pray,* apply breathing apparatus, *pray,* swim to shore, *pray,* administer mouth-to-mouth resuscitation and CPR. *Pray.*"

"So the baby survived."

"Yes. She didn't need CPR; all she needed was to be released from her upside-down chair, to be upright and in the fresh air. Her eyes fluttered open, her pudgy fists lashed out. Once she came to, the emergency workers looked at one another and asked, 'Who was that who called out to us? It sounded like her mother . . .'"

"But her mother was dead," said Armand. "And yet she called out for help."

"And yet."

"So that was the miracle."

"Everyone said her mother's voice—her mother's *love*—reached out clear across the veil that separates the living from the dead, just to save her baby."

Claire sat back and took a sip of her cognac. The summer night was warm, she was full from a wonderful dinner and chocolate, and the liquor made her feel relaxed and ever so slightly fuzzy.

"Why do you tell the story in the third person?" Armand asked in a quiet voice.

"Pardon?"

"I think the story is about you, isn't it?"

"How did you know that?"

"Isn't it?"

She nodded.

"And yet you tell it like a made-up story, as if it happened to someone else. Do you not live your own life, Claire Broussard?"

She didn't know how to respond. Usually people enjoyed her stories, responded to them with gasps and chuckles and a slack-jawed fascination that only grew when she informed them the outlandish tales were true.

Silence reigned for a long moment.

Ne vis-tu pas ta propre vie, Claire Broussard? Armand had asked. She knew she'd translated it properly, knew she understood what he meant to say. And did she live her own life?

When she failed to answer, he continued. "I am very sorry to hear your story, Claire. Do you have any actual memory of it, or is this a story gleaned from others?"

"I've grown up hearing the story, but no, no actual memory."

"Still, it must have been profoundly traumatic."

"More for everyone else than for me. I wish I could have known my mother, of course, but I guess everything turned out all right in the end. After all, I'm a shopkeeper in Paris now—beat *that* with a stick."

He ignored her weak attempt at humor, took a sip of his drink, ate another chocolate.

"The first day you came here to the studio," Armand said, "when you appeared at the top of

288

the stairs like some sort of apparition, you took a moment to look around, standing in the sunshine like a star stepping onto the stage. Do you remember?"

"Yes. I thought you didn't notice me."

"I noticed you."

"You didn't say anything."

"But later I asked you, 'What do you want?' "

"What about it?"

"You never answered me."

"That's not true. I said I was looking for the mask of *L'Inconnue.*"

He snorted. "The mask of a long-ago dead woman? Why would you search for this? And you did not even want it—you already had one."

"I told you- it's broken."

"And yet you did not want a replacement."

"I like the one I have, broken or not."

"Have you ever heard of the Japanese art form called *kintsugi*?"

"I think it's safe to assume I'm not up on my Japanese art forms. In fact, I learned only two days ago that Paul Gauguin is considered a *Post*-impressionist, that there was a big scandal about him breaking ranks with the Impressionists. Who knew?"

"Yes, Gauguin and some others called themselves Nabis, which means 'prophet.' I suppose they thought pretty highly of themselves. But I don't believe the title has caught on, so most people lump them in with the Impressionists. But then, I'm no art historian."

"You know a lot more than I do. Anyway, what's *kintsugi*?"

"Literally it means 'golden joinery.' When a valuable piece of pottery is broken, artisans mix gold dust into lacquer and use it as a glue to put the pieces back together. Rather than hiding the damage, the gold lines make a *feature* of the breaks."

Claire took a moment to imagine the fractured face of *L'Inconnue* repaired with jagged lines of gold. The image lingered, heartbreaking yet beautiful, in her mind's eye.

"If only the scars of life could be mended with lines of gold," she said softly.

"Exactly. *Kintsugi* is connected to the philosophy of *wabi-sabi*."

"I'm guessing that's not what we eat with sushi?"

"*Wabi-sabi* has to do with embracing the flawed or imperfect. It teaches that the scars of history are an integral and even beautiful part of our experience, rather than something to disguise or feel shame about."

It was on the tip of Claire's tongue to ask Armand about his own scars. They were as apparent as shiny gold fracture lines. But she refrained. The pain was too palpable, the effort it took him to hold himself together too great.

Instead, she said, "I want to show you something. I'll be right back."

She returned to her room and unearthed the torn note—the one she had found in the crate with the broken face of *L'Inconnue* in Mammaw's attic—and then brought it back to the garden. Clouds were rolling in and the wind was picking up. Claire flicked on the outdoor lights so Armand would be able to see.

"You're right. One of the reasons I came here was because I found the face of *L'Inconnue* and wondered about her. But that wasn't the only reason."

She handed Armand the torn note.

"'He will never let me go alive'?" he read. "What is this?"

"It was in the crate with the mask of *L'Inconnue* I found in my grandmother's attic, along with some old newspapers and receipts, that sort of thing. I think it was tossed in there when the mask was first packed up, right here at the Moulage Lombardi."

"It was the tail end of the war," said Armand with a shrug. "They were using whatever they had at hand to try to make sure she'd be safe. They probably couldn't afford proper packing materials."

She nodded. "That's what I assumed."

"But the model for *L'Inconnue* lived decades before World War II, in the 1890s. There's no reason to believe this note had anything to do with

291

her. It could be anything—a bit of teenage melo-drama, an overreaction to something. In any case, whatever it's referring to happened ages ago."

"I know."

"Perhaps you are swayed by the drama of *L'Inconnue*'s story, the things you read from the box I gave you about her life. Why does it matter?"

"It's hard not to wonder what happened to her."

"I beg your pardon, but it is *easy* to imagine what happened: she was a poor girl from the countryside who found herself pregnant and abandoned and threw herself into the Seine." The sound of thunder punctuated his words, and Armand calmly stood up, gathered an armful of dishes, and headed up the stairs. Claire followed his example and did the same.

"It was a popular way to kill oneself back then," Armand continued as they put things away in the kitchen. Already fat raindrops were falling outside, unleashing the delicious scent of warm rain on the garden. The summer storms here were as heavy and unexpected as they were in Plaquemines Parish.

"I read about that."

He nodded. "Officials pulled hundreds of people a year from the Seine. Afterward, they were put on display at the morgue, and the ones who weren't claimed were buried in a pauper's grave in Père Lachaise Cemetery."

"How do you mean, they put them on display at the morgue?"

"The old Paris morgue sat right behind the Cathédrale de Notre Dame. It served as a tourist attraction; it was even listed in the guidebooks of the day. People would go in one door, file past the room where the unknown dead were laid out behind glass, and then go out the other side."

"Why would they do such a thing?"

"Ostensibly the bodies were displayed so their relatives could identify them, but it became a macabre spectacle. Very popular. Especially if there was a beautiful woman to see, or a particularly gruesome death."

"That's . . . awful."

"It was a different time."

"Death was considered entertainment?"

"I don't watch a lot of television," Armand said with a shrug, "but I think it still is, is it not?"

34

SABINE

Maurice has gone to visit with his parents, and every time he comes back even more frustrated, feeling less appreciated as an artist.

Sabine is sure part of his yearning for the acclaim from the Academy is to prove himself to his father. Somehow his dissatisfaction has become attached to her, to Sabine. It drives him crazy that he cannot capture her essence in either media: clay or paint.

"Where do you go when I try to capture you?" he demands, his face very close to hers. She can smell cognac on his breath. He squeezes her face in his big hand, callused and rough from carving hard stone. "Why do you elude me?"

Sabine remains mute. It is best not to respond. If she ventures an answer, he will pause and consider her words, trying to make sense of what she is saying. And then his voice will become very quiet and deliberate, and he will ask her a question.

And no matter her answer, the rage will grow.

This is how it goes. It is better by far to take a cuff early on before he manages to work up a good temper.

Often he feels contrite afterward and he begs her pardon and leaves, or he starts to drink in earnest and she slips out the studio door that leads to the little brick alley. Many times she has gone into the cold without her coat, not even the meager shawl her mother had knitted for her sixteenth Christmas.

One day Sabine is posing on the divan, uncomfortable, her arms crisscrossed in an unnatural position that makes her think of all those models in the paintings in the Louvre. By now she is good at making her mind go elsewhere, especially when in a difficult position. The cramps and stiffness make her feel connected to the women in those museum paintings: they are the mute objects of the artists' attention, forever hushed, speaking only through their expressions and the falseness of painted or sculpted flesh.

Sabine ponders the connection of *art* to *artifice*. Is it all falseness?

Her nose itches. She twitches, then takes a deep breath, lets it out slowly. Sabine tried to commit to memory the paintings and sculptures she had seen in the Louvre. She likes to let her mind wander over both the deep hues and the expressions on their faces.

Maurice tells Sabine most artists' models are whores. He laughs and says the beatific, holy Madonnas everyone prays to in church are actually women of the streets, even Da Vinci's *Virgin and Child with Saint Anne*.

This is why everyone loves the *Mona Lisa*, he says. Because she is not a whore, but a lady, Lisa Gherardini del Giocondo. An upstanding woman of decent reputation but nonetheless enticing, knowing.

Sabine holds her tongue when he says such things. But she does wonder whether he says these things to hurt her, or whether he truly forgets that she is no better than a prostitute—that if he hadn't hired her that day in the square she might well have started to work the streets herself. To be a *modèle de profession* does not, in fact, feel so removed from prostitution. In some ways it is simply one step above. Her nude image is already hanging on more than one rich man's wall, and she joins Maurice in his bed when he asks.

Sabine thinks back on a sculpture she saw at the Louvre, by Étienne-Maurice Falconet, called *Pygmalion aux pieds de sa statue qui s'anime* (Pygmalion at the feet of his statue that comes to life). In it, a sculptor kneels at a woman's feet, except she actually *has* no feet—she is emerging from the stone.

She had read about the myth of Pygmalion and Galatea in one of the books at the studio. Pygmalion was sculpting the most beautiful woman he could imagine, and, naturally, he fell in love with her. But no human female could compare to her beauty and grace. So the goddess Aphrodite took pity on the poor man and brought the statue to life.

In that moment Sabine realizes Maurice sees himself as freeing *her*. But he is doing the opposite: trying to make a living woman into a statue.

Sabine is calcifying, turning to stone.

She goes back to the Cathédrale de Notre Dame, enters the confessional, and again the young priest tells her: "Art is dangerous. You must find another way. You must not give in to the temptations of the flesh."

She almost laughs when he says that, right there

in the confessional. As though the temptations of the flesh had brought her to Maurice. The only seduction she has experienced is that of food; the desire to eat overwhelmed her.

And try as she might, Sabine will not be ashamed of herself when her belly is full, when she knows that every day she will break her fast and look forward to bed without being kept awake by the gnawing pain of hunger.

As she poses for Maurice, she considers his contemptuous remarks, the condemnation of the priest, the disdain of Isabelle. She turns their harsh words over in her mind, burnishing them like the wooden pieces in her stepfather's workshop. Sabine sands them and smoothes them until their sharp edges no longer pinch, until their splinters no longer lodge in her ticklish core, no longer pierce the tender flesh of her heart.

She will wear down their edges. Her soul will grow as tough with calluses as her hands once were.

35

"Come," said Armand the next afternoon. "We will go to the market together so I can show you how to shop."

"And here I've been doing my own shopping since puberty."

"But not in Paris."

"No," Claire conceded with a chuckle. "Not in Paris."

The truth was that Armand was in such a good mood—for him, which is to say that he hadn't complained even once today about their customers—that Claire was happy to accompany him to the market. Eager, even, to see him in a new environment, one not bounded by the ancient stone walls of 17 rue de la Huchette.

The afternoon was beautiful and the streets freshly washed by last night's rain, so they walked along the Seine rather than taking the metro. Without thinking, Claire checked the level of the river and moved to the other side of Armand.

"What's wrong?" he asked.

"Nothing's wrong."

His eyes slewed over to her, eyebrows raised. He didn't believe her.

Claire shrugged. "It rained a lot last night."

"It rains in Paris. You are afraid of rain?"

"No, not really. Of course not. It's just that the river could flood."

"The Seine?"

She nodded.

Armand was quiet, but when she glanced at him, she realized he was silently laughing, a rare grin on his face.

"You mean to tell me you are afraid the Seine will flood because of a little rain?"

"It's not out of the realm of possibility. There was a massive flood in 1910—did you know that? And others not quite so severe in 1924 and 1955. And I'm sure before that as well."

"You've memorized all the flood years?"

"I'm just saying that I'm not sure Paris is prepared for the worst. It's a very flat city after all. Except for the Butte de Montmartre . . ." She shrugged.

He chuckled. "I suppose it's lucky that we sleep on the *premier étage*, then, right?"

He was more right than he knew. She had selected a second-floor apartment for a reason. She always preferred to sleep high above the ground, just in case.

"But don't be afraid," he added. "Even if it floods, we can always swim."

"Not all of us."

"You can't swim?"

She shook her head. Perhaps a little too vehemently.

"You mean not well, or not at all?"

"First of all, it's important to know when a river floods it's not just nice river water," said Claire, in the tone of a teacher. How could he not be aware of the danger of flooding? "There's mud and gasoline and sewage and all sorts of nasty stuff in the water. That's what makes it so dangerous, not just the water itself."

"I think you are changing the subject. How do

you mean, you don't swim? Isn't this something all adults should know how to do in a civilized society? Is there no water where you grew up?"

"*Yes,* everywhere. Plaquemines Parish is criss-crossed with bayous, and it's a delta. It's been devastated in hurricanes many times."

"Claire, I'm so sorry," Armand said, stopping suddenly and swinging around to face her. "I just realized—are you afraid of the water because of the accident with your mother?"

"No." In this, at least, she was truthful. "It was . . . my father gave me 'swimming lessons' once. It didn't go well."

"Is this one of your stories?"

She shook her head. This one wasn't worth repeating.

Five years old. Chance and Daddy and four six-packs at the beach. Usually they traveled with family; she liked it better when there were other cousins to play with (or, in the case of Jessica, to run away from) and aunties and uncles and Mammaw to pack sandwiches and potato chips and noodle salad. Daddy forgot to pack anything but the beer. There was an old leftover bottle half full of water in the car, so she sipped that, but it was hot and tasted like plastic.

Chance busied herself making a sand castle. She liked building things out of sand, like the little animal sculptures Mommy had left behind.

Sometimes Chance thought if she could just build something nice enough, her mommy might speak to her through it.

"Go on now—don't be afraid of the water," her father said. "Go on in."

"I'm all right. Thank you, sir," she said.

Sometimes Chance liked to walk in the surf just so it splashed on her toes, to make a slapping sound with her bare feet and feel the tickling suck of the sand under her soles, or looking down and watching the water recede so fast that it made her feel dizzy and giggly.

But she was afraid of the deep water. She couldn't swim and felt a sense of panic every time her cousin or auntie tried to take her in and teach her. They put it down to some deep, all-but-forgotten memory of that night in the car, and let her be.

"Go on now," her father said. "Get in the water and swim. I wanna see you swim."

With a sick feeling in the pit of her stomach, Chance realized he hadn't even taken off his boots, just unbuttoned his shirt, put on his sunglasses, and plopped himself down in the low beach chair. There were at least half a dozen cans crumpled and half buried in the hot sand. Whenever he made his way through the next six-pack was the danger zone. Time to disappear for a while. He would become sad, sometimes even cry, and then he would start to rage.

Why do I never catch a break? Why does everything that could happen happen to me? How did I end up all by myself with a brat but no wife?

Chance calculated her opportunities. There weren't many other people on the beach. Families with mommies were the best ones to approach. Usually she would join those groups and Daddy would eventually fall asleep for a while. She would be hungry and thirsty, but at least he was sleeping, and when he woke up he would drive them home and maybe she could talk him into dropping her off at Mammaw's house, where things smelled like rice and spices and there was not one but *two* refrigerators full of food, one out in the garage for on-sale groceries and the vegetables and fruit from the garden Mammaw chopped up and put into special plastic baggies and froze. Chance liked to help; there was even a little machine that melted the edges together.

But this time there were only teenagers on the beach. They didn't want a kid around, wouldn't provide the kind of shield Chance needed. Maybe if she just went to play behind the bush, he'd stay where he was—he didn't like to get up once he was settled in with his beer—and she could wait it out.

A shadow fell over her sand castle. Daddy's big foot landed on the tallest turret, the one she had worked so hard to get to stand. The tower squashed easily under his heavy boot.

He grabbed her by the arm, started pulling her. Toward the ocean.

"No!" Chance yelled. "No, Daddy, *no!*"

The teenagers looked over when she started screaming, but then realized she was with her father. Assumed, therefore, that she was safe.

"No!" she yelled, and flailed. She tried dropping down like deadweight, but she was no contest for him. John Broussard was a powerful man. He worked in the oil fields, sometimes on fishing boats, and had the muscles to prove it. "Please, Daddy, sir! Please, no!"

He waded out into the ocean, letting the water pour into his work boots and wet his jeans. When he was about waist-high, he threw his daughter as far as he could into the surf.

Chance was hyperventilating before she even hit the water. She went under.

Panic. It was sheer, raw, enveloping terror. Underwater she screamed, but her cries were silenced by the water. The roiling ocean tossed her, seemed to suck her down. She opened her eyes but everything was a murky green, the light sparkling overhead but so far away.

In movies people who were drowning splashed about, bobbing up out of the water long enough to shout for help. But Claire had simply sunk. She tried to hold her breath the way her auntie had taught her, but she didn't really have any breath to hold. She took a deep gulp of ocean water, then vomited it back out. Her muscles cramped and convulsed. Blackness crept in at the edges of her vision.

She saw her mother's face hovering in front of her, her dark hair drifting in the water like silk.

Strong hands grasped her arm, pulled her up.

At first she thought her daddy had relented and rescued her. But the hands belonged to a high school boy who had been training for a summer job as a lifeguard. He put his arm around her shoulders and dragged her onto the beach and even tried to perform mouth-to-mouth resuscitation, until he realized she was breathing on her own. She doubled over, convulsing, coughing up water and then vomiting all over the hot sand and the ruined remnants of her sand castle.

A circle of teens stood around her, staring and snickering out of nervousness. Kids saying, *Eww, she threw up!*

Chance heard an odd, raspy, snorting sound and thought again that perhaps her father was sorry for what he had done. But then she realized: he was laughing so hard, he cried.

Finally, a grown-up pushed through the crowd, praising the teenager for his quick thinking. Glaring at Chance's father, escorting her to the outdoor shower, helping her to wash up. Chance's chest ached from coughing; nausea enveloped her. She looked up, focusing on the spigot that came right out of the wall, the heat of spring sunshine on her back, the sensation of rough concrete under her feet.

Anything but what had just happened. And if it would happen again.

Someone called the police, and Chance spent the night in a foster home, and after that went to live with Mammaw and Remy.

So no, Claire did not swim.

36

Before starting shopping in earnest—an endeavor Armand took so seriously that he declared they needed sustenance beforehand— they sat and had coffee and shared a pastry. The marketplace bustled around them.

"When I went shopping before, I followed an older woman around for a while," said Claire. "That was how I guessed the good butcher."

"This is the best way to learn, in fact."

"Who did you learn from?"

"My mother and my aunts. I always enjoyed going with them to the market."

"Is your mother still alive?"

"Yes. She lives in the countryside."

It was on the tip of her tongue to ask him about the dollhouse, but Claire decided against it. There was something secret there, something private. And she had known grown women who enjoyed miniatures, setting up elaborate dollhouses with Oriental rugs and tiny cups and saucers and itty-bitty telephones. One of her colleagues at No-Miss Systems, a real power broker, built dollhouses in her spare time and donated them to fund-raisers. Miniature Victorian fantasies complete with tiny doilies on the backs of velvet chairs, itty-bitty tea sets, and thumbnail-sized gilt mirrors. Claire had asked her about it once; the woman said building a minuscule world gave a person a godlike sensation and made one see the world in|a different way, just like *Gulliver's Travels*.

Why couldn't a man do the same?

It just seemed at odds with the rest of Armand. He was so gruff, so easily frustrated. Claire could imagine Armand playing sports, perhaps wielding a sword or driving too fast, to vent his frustrations with tourists and the business and Giselle and Claire herself. Playing with a dollhouse seemed meditative, out of step with his character.

But, as Quentin had pointed out, she did not know him.

They finished their coffee and started to shop.

"The fruit here, they are smaller than in your country, I think," Armand said, picking up a cantaloupe the size of a large orange.

"I think you're right." But even from several feet away, she could smell the melon. The aroma wrapped around her: the scent of summer.

They visited Armand's favorite fish man, then the cheese man. Each vendor knew Armand well, and as he approached their stands he insulted their wares and they asked how he managed to be in the company of a good-looking American.

At the cheese stand, the man behind the counter kept giving Claire tastes of cheese. Every time she said she liked one, he would say, "Wait. That's not a good one. Try this one instead."

It was an education. Armand told the cheese man to "leave the American alone" and bought hefty wedges of Roquefort, Petit Basque, and a small wheel of fresh goat cheese.

"From my region, we have Comté cheese," Armand said. "Do you know it?"

"I think so, yes," Claire said. Upon moving to Chicago and shedding her small-town habits, she had learned there were more cheeses in the world than American singles and mild cheddar. Her colleagues had held cocktail parties with baked Brie surrounded by tiny champagne grapes, goat cheeses drizzled with honey, and Spanish Manchego accompanied by almonds. Even the array of olives available had been a surprise: she had grown up with basic black out of cans (they had them on special occasions and she liked to put them on the ends of her fingers, eating them off one by one; first she would lick each one so Jessica wouldn't try to steal them from her) and green pimento-stuffed ones her father used for martinis.

"If you tasted good Comté, you would know for sure. It is a wonderful cheese. There are 287 official cheeses in France. Every region has its specialties."

"Those are the *official* cheeses? What are the unofficial ones?"

He shrugged. "The homemade varieties, that sort of thing. I suppose it's countless, actually, the forms the cheese can take. Farmhouse versus industrial, or those made by co-ops. Cow, sheep, goat, unpasteurized. Fresh, *bleu*, washed rind, blooming rind . . ."

She started to laugh.

"What's funny?"

"I'm just . . . overwhelmed. In a good way. You French are really something. It's like the patisseries. Have you ever looked in the window of a patisserie?"

"Of course I have. I live here after all." They stopped in front of a vegetable stand and Armand bought a fat bundle of fragrant basil, along with broccoli rabe and shiitake mushrooms.

"It's not even like I want to *eat* everything," said Claire. "I just can't stop looking at the towers of perfect little pink-and-white confections; it's breathtaking."

"You do have bakeries in the United States, don't you?"

"Not like these." It occurred to her to ask, "Have you ever been to the U.S.?"

308

He nodded and put the greens into Claire's basket. "I have been to San Francisco and New York. *I* visited the Statue of Liberty. She seemed much smaller than I thought she would be. I think I expected the Eiffel Tower."

"Well, that's on you guys. You made her for us after all."

"But you made the inscription," he said, quoting in English, " 'Give us your tired, your poor . . .' "

" 'Your huddled masses yearning to breathe free.' " Claire nodded. "A beautiful sentiment, don't you think?"

"I think most people think so. That's why she looms at least as large as the Eiffel Tower in our collective imagination, even though the tower is three times as tall."

"That much?"

"I think so, or very close."

Claire smiled as Armand perused, then rejected, the apples at two different produce stands. "It was so sweet of Quentin to bring me a little Statue of Liberty the other evening. I confess I ate the whole thing. Is his shop nearby?"

"No, he's over off of rue de Rivoli." As usual when the subject of Quentin came up, Armand's voice tightened. "Let's go get some eggs from the woman in the corner, and then I think we're done here."

"What's going on between you and Quentin?"

"It is very complicated." Armand appeared to be

on the verge of saying something more but was searching for the words. "I—"

Just then a man with a laden pushcart backed into Claire, knocking her off balance. She stumbled and dropped her basket.

"*Pardonnez-moi, madame!*" the man apologized.

Armand reached out to steady her, pulling her to his chest.

The embrace should have felt awkward, but it did not. Instead, everywhere they touched felt electric, alive, overheated.

"*Ça va?* Are you all right, Claire?" Armand asked. His tone was formal, but Claire was gratified to hear a slight edge of huskiness to his voice. "Yes, I'm fine," said Claire. "Thank you."

He did not let go. Not for a very long moment. Their bags on the ground, the bustle of vendors and shoppers and the marketplace surrounding them. But for Claire and Armand there was nothing but this: their eyes locked together, arms and legs entangled, the heat of their bodies pressed close.

Their breath mingling.

37

SABINE

The market is bustling.

Though Sabine has grown more accustomed to city life, the pace still threatens to overwhelm her, especially in the crowded marketplace. She must watch herself on all sides, and above all be sure her purse is safe; the small leather bag is tied to the belt at her waist. She clutches a half-full basket in one hand, a grocery list in the other.

Sabine steps back to let a fish cart pass, and two boys run by, knocking the basket out of her hand, yelling, "*Pardon, désolé!*"—Pardon, sorry!—but not stopping. She loses her footing and trips on the curb.

Someone grasps her arm, helps to steady her.

It is the mask-maker. Jean-Baptiste Lombardi.

Her breath leaves her.

"Are you hurt?" he asks as he releases her arm, rights her basket, and starts to gather the leeks and potatoes, carrots and mushrooms from the grimy cobblestones, rank with the muck of the food stalls. "Did you twist your ankle?"

Sabine shakes her head, though her ankle throbs. She swallows hard, not knowing what to say, casting a glance behind her, as though Maurice might be following her, watching. But of course he isn't. She left him asleep in his bed; he doesn't like to rise before noon after a night of drinking.

Jean-Baptiste follows her lead, looking around the crowded hall. "Are you looking for someone?"

She shakes her head. Begins to walk, thinking only that she needs not to be seen with him, or with any man. But her ankle feels weak, and it twinges as though not able to support her weight.

"Wait, *wait,* mademoiselle," the man says, gently holding her arm. "Please. Let me see you to a table—rest your ankle, just for a moment. I'll buy you a coffee."

"I don't think . . ." She pulls away and he lets go of her arm.

A look of anger comes over Jean-Baptiste's face as his gaze fixes on the small split in her lip. She can see the muscles in his jaw clench. She prepares her answer: she fell off the dais after her leg fell asleep in a difficult pose.

But when he asks his question, it is not about her lip.

"Does he watch you? Maurice? Is he here?"

She shakes her head.

When next he speaks, his voice is impossibly gentle. It is the tone of voice she has heard from a man only once in her life: the young man who trained the horses.

"Then let me take care of you, mademoiselle. Just for a few moments. Give your ankle a chance to recover."

Within the covered marketplace a stout, nearly toothless old woman has set up a little café consisting of a few barrels for tables and small wooden stools. She makes coffee in an elaborate brass pot. Jean-Baptiste leads Sabine to a stool, orders coffee and cake.

When she sits, weariness washes over her. She is tired not from the day, but from the burden of making excuses.

But Jean-Baptiste does not force her to speak. Instead, he tells Sabine how his father and uncle came from Florence years ago as young men, bringing with them the skills of mold-making and casting. The extended family now divides its time between Paris and the Franche-Comté, where his uncle's family keeps a château (he married well). His own parents retired there when they grew tired of the city, passing the *moulage*, the mold-making business, on to Jean-Baptiste. Sabine listens, rapt, as he describes the mask-making skills honed and passed down through the family since the days of the Renaissance. He recounts the number of times sculptors have tried to bribe him to take molds of human models so they could claim they had sculpted them perfectly.

Sabine, revived by the coffee and Jean-Baptiste's stories, says, "*No*, truly?"

"Truly," he says with a smile.

"But why? If they are artists, why would they attempt to perpetrate fraud?"

Now he laughs outright. "An excellent question." He shakes his head, stirs a hunk of raw sugar
into his coffee. "I consider myself more artisan than
an artist per se; my work is more technical than
creative. But of course I have spent a lot of time
with artists, and all I can say is the frustration is
sometimes insupportable. Imagine trying to *create*
beauty out of nothing: a lump of clay or stone."

"Or *re*-create it," says Sabine, then blushes at
her boldness. The blush intensifies as he studies
her, as though suddenly intrigued.

"Indeed, or *re*-create it. For instance, I imagine
Maurice has repeatedly tried, and failed, to
capture your face on canvas or in clay? And this
drives him mad?"

She nods, savors her coffee. Thinks how she
couldn't have imagined such a thing only a few
years ago: sitting in the middle of a bustling
Parisian marketplace drinking coffee with a man
she barely knows.

He pushes the little plate toward her.

"Try the cake."

She does not have to be asked twice. She
picks up the small fork, takes a bite of the spongy
white cake with creamy frosting. It is heaven on
her tongue, like melting sugar.

Monsieur Lombardi watches her closely, his
chin cupped in his hand, leaning his elbow on the
table. The way Maurice does, but it doesn't give
her the same feeling, that she is a mouse being

watched by a predatory bird. This is more the way she imagines her own face might look when she gazes at the patisserie window, the vivid colors in the paintings she saw at the Louvre, or the streetlights reflected in the Seine.

"Please, why do you look at me that way?" she asks him.

"What way is that, mademoiselle?"

"Like . . . like I am this piece of cake."

He chuckles again and straightens. "I apologize. It is just . . . you have a fascinating look about you. Especially with your hair worn like that, as though you've walked out of another time."

She licks a bit of sweet cream from her lip. "If you are wanting me to model for you, you must go through Maurice. He lends me out from time to time."

"To Monsieur Rodin."

She nodded.

"And to Camille Claudel, I hear."

"Once or twice. But no more."

"Why not?"

"He believes Mademoiselle Claudel is a bad influence on me."

"Ha! I can easily believe that. Camille is a formidable woman. An impressive artist. She is lucky to be able to pursue her art."

There is another pause in the conversation. Sabine takes the time to savor the coffee, the last bit of cream on the cake.

She considers her words and finally ventures:

"In some ways I agree. But . . . Mademoiselle Claudel does not seem lucky to me."

"No?"

"She is very sad, I think."

He nods slowly. "I imagine you are right about that. I spoke more in general terms: that she has the resources to maintain her studio, to make her art and speak her mind."

"But I do not," Sabine says in a rush, her eyes lifting to his. Wanting him to understand, daring him to interpret what she is saying, to know her heart. "I am not lucky in that way."

Jean-Baptiste holds her gaze for a long moment, nods slowly. "I know that, mademoiselle. I know that very well indeed."

They exchange no more words of substance after that. They finish their coffees in companionable silence. They watch the people around them, the young mothers and children and maids and hawkers of everything from rabbits to mushrooms to spices from the Orient. Sabine wonders whether Monsieur Lombardi is as aware of her presence as she is of his: it is as though he is vibrating across the table from her, making every part of her feel aware and alive.

When they are finished, he counts out coins to pay the bill, stacking them neatly on the table. He smiles his thanks at the proprietress and pushes their stools back in so they won't be in the way.

38

When Claire woke up the next morning, there was no aroma of coffee.

Yesterday, after their embrace in the market, Armand seemed to remember his distaste for interfering Americans. He withdrew, testily demonstrating which butcher he used—Monsieur Faucher, whose meat was *le meilleur*—then bought some *bio* (organic) milk and eggs, and they returned home, walking side by side in silence. Claire tried teasing him a little—asked him about buying a crêpe to eat on the sidewalk alongside the tourists—but he did not take the bait.

Upon returning to the atelier and putting away the groceries, Armand disappeared into his workshop, closing the door behind him. After a few moments of uncertainty, Claire retreated to her small bedroom.

Dear Uncle Remy,
You would hardly recognize me with all the white powder in my hair from the work I am doing at the studio. Do you remember how you always told me you like my mud creations? These are like those, but sturdier. I am including a little plaster dust

in the envelope, just so you can rub it between your fingers and think of me covered in it.

I don't think my boss likes me very much, but since I am only here temporarily I don't suppose it matters. He blusters a lot but it doesn't bother me too much.

Can you imagine shopping at a huge farmers' market every day? My boss insists on buying his groceries there on a daily basis. He says the produce and the meat are fresher and better quality, and after all what is life if not for good food and wine?

Today the shop is closed, so I am going back to the Louvre. I went once already, but it is worth a return trip. It is the biggest museum in Paris, and the *Mona Lisa* lives there. Leonardo da Vinci called her *La Gioconda*, and so the French refer to her as *La Joconde*. Why do you suppose we changed her name? Perhaps it is like the family, where everyone but you and Jessica have nicknames!

═══════════════════════════════

Claire had considered asking Armand to show her a little of what he called the "real" Paris on their day off, but since he was so distant last night she hadn't mentioned it.

So she had the day to herself.

She packed her laptop and notepad into her big tote. Today Claire planned to return to the Louvre to look at some Rodin and Claudel sculptures not included in his museum. She also had a new must-see list, which included the Paris morgue and the National Library of France.

She crossed the Pont de l'Archevêché to the southern tip of the Île de la Cité, behind the Cathedral of Notre Dame. The Square de l'Île de France was simple and open, with views of the Seine on both sides coming together off the point. The rather stark Mémorial des Martyrs de la Déportation paid tribute to the more than two hundred thousand souls sent to Nazi death camps under the Vichy government.

There were no signs of the old Paris morgue that used to occupy this spot, the building that had held the remains of *L'Inconnue* alongside so many other unidentified bodies pulled from the Seine or gathered from the streets and parks. The tourist attraction.

She passed through Square Jean XXIII to appreciate the flying buttresses that encircled the chancel and to peruse the four bells that had been retired when Notre Dame put in new bells to ring beside Emmanuel, the thirteen-ton bourdon bell. According to her guidebook, there was also a beehive kept right behind the roof of the sacristy, but try as she might Claire couldn't see any evidence of happy bees.

The trip to the Louvre, as before, was a bit of an odyssey. Despite the former palace's massive shell, it was not up to the task of gracefully absorbing the thousands who came to visit on a daily basis. Claire had hoped to glimpse the *Mona Lisa*, but while she got into the same room as the iconic painting, it was nearly impossible to see past the crowd huddled around its bullet-proof (and presumably theftproof) glass case.

Instead, Claire lingered in the hall of sculptures. There was something about the three-dimensionality, the sensuality, that made her want to stroke her hands over the bumps and curves. Maybe it all went back to holding those little clay animals her mother had left behind; she could still remember the feel of them in the palm of her hand. Sculpture felt like a palpable link to her mother.

"Your mama always wanted to run off and make her creations," Mammaw had said. "She loved that mask in the attic too, just like you."

After the Louvre Claire stopped in at L'Institut Médico-Légal de Paris, otherwise known as the current Paris morgue. The bored-looking young woman at the front desk was anything but charmed by Claire's tale of trying to hunt down the real identity of *L'Inconnue de la Seine*.

"Do not think you are the first to come looking for her," said the woman, who insisted on speaking English. "And do not imagine you will be the last. But there were not careful records kept in that time. The unknown ones were buried in a pauper's grave in Cemetery Père Lachaise. If you wish to pay her tribute, it is there you should lay the flowers."

The librarian at the National Library of France, located in modern glass-fronted towers that looked like an office building, was kinder but ultimately no more helpful. Though there were numerous fictional accounts speculating about *L'Inconnue*'s life and death, there were no clues as to her true identity.

Finally, Claire stopped into an Internet café, ordered a cappuccino, and opened her laptop. She answered a few e-mails and sent a note to Jessica "just to check in."

Then she started working on the Web site for the Moulage Lombardi. Giselle had put Claire in touch with her teenage son, Luc, who had given her the passwords and account he had used when creating the original site. Claire made place-holders for the images and exact text—she would have to work with Giselle or Armand (if he would be willing) to fill all of that in—but she put together an overall concept and started working through some of the link glitches.

It felt good to contribute in this small way; even after she was gone, a little part of her would live on at Moulage Lombardi through the Web site.

But the truth was . . . her heart sank at the thought of leaving Paris. She was finally finding her groove here. She supposed she could look for another rental, something not too far away—she had fallen in love with the twisty medieval Latin Quarter. It even crossed her mind to look into the possibility of getting a real job—software engineers were always in demand, weren't they? And wasn't English the technical language throughout Europe?

Before closing things down and returning to the studio, she scrolled through some employment services in Paris and tried to familiarize herself with local software companies. Clearly, though, this wasn't the best way to approach job hunting here in France. As an American, she would need a special permit, she imagined, and an extended visa to remain more than a few months. There were a lot of hoops to jump through, but if she could make herself attractive to a company, maybe they would be able to streamline the process for her. She would ask Giselle about it.

When Claire returned to the studio that afternoon, Armand still hadn't returned.

She fixed herself a simple dinner of salad and leftover lamb and took her plate down to the garden, where she turned on the twinkle lights. She poured a glass of wine, tried to savor every bite and sip, and felt very Parisian. But very alone.

Tuesday dawned cool and gray. Armand still

hadn't returned, but Claire decided to go to the *boulangerie* as usual to buy croissants and baguettes. She had fallen into the habit and now craved her daily dose of fine baked goods along with her morning coffee; also, she loved her morning walk through the narrow streets of the Left Bank, the cafés opening up, delivery trucks unloading, and shopkeepers sweeping the sidewalks in front of their stores. It was too early for most tourists, so the feeling was mellow, intimate.

In the big picture, it hadn't been long since Claire had arrived at Charles de Gaulle Airport; still, it was easy to imagine herself living this life.

When she returned to the Moulage Lombardi with the bread in her basket, a customer was already waiting outside the door. Claire grew closer and realized: it wasn't a customer. It was the studio's former English speaker, Lisette Villeneuve.

She wore a trim, well-fitting belted coat and a silk scarf around her neck. Her brown hair was up in a neat chignon. She might have been born in the States, but she had clearly lived long enough in Paris to pass for a native, at least to Claire's American eye.

Claire wondered, again, whether there had been something going on between her and Armand. There was no particular reason to assume so; perhaps it was simply because Villeneuve seemed as taciturn and secretive as he was. Claire could only imagine the atmosphere Armand and she together had created in the Lombardi atelier. Back home, they would have called it "bad gree-gree."

"*Bonjour, madame. Est-ce que je peux vous aider*?" Claire asked in French as the other woman approached, and then repeated in English, "May I help you?"

"Is Armand here?" the woman responded in English.

"Not at the moment, no."

The woman hesitated and appeared to be reaching for words. Something felt *off* about her; she seemed fragile and intense, but also angry. Perhaps she wasn't just *un peu bizarre*, Claire thought to herself. Maybe she was actually unbalanced.

"Have I . . . received any mail?" Villeneuve asked finally.

"I'd be happy to check," Claire said, unlocking the door with the huge old-fashioned key, the other keys clanking loudly against the wood frame. "Why don't I look upstairs, and if I find anything I'll bring it out to you?"

"Are you involved in the casting here, or just the sales?"

"Both. Why do you ask?"

At that moment Giselle rushed up to join them, smelling of fresh cigarettes.

"You have no business here, Lisette," she said. "Go on now."

Lisette glared at Giselle, then looked back at Claire. Then she turned and walked away, her hands deep in her pockets, as though to keep out the cold—or, perhaps, to hold in her emotions.

Giselle raised her eyebrows at Claire and shook her head.

"What was all that about?" Claire asked in a low voice.

Giselle let out a sigh. "She had some talent, but she was frustrated here, from day one really. She wanted to sculpt, not mold and cast. It is a common problem with the artistic temperament—people are not content with being artisans; they want to create something new."

"You make that sound like a fault," Claire said as she led the way up the stairs past the bank of silent faces on the wall.

"It *is* a fault if you work here at the mold-maker's studio. We are copyists. If you cannot believe in the art of imitation, if you cannot respect the skill it takes to create true copies with integrity, you shouldn't be here."

"Well, that makes sense, I suppose."

"And on top of that," Giselle added as she stashed her things behind the desk, "she made a great scene—she became very angry with Armand. Smashed all her creations, somehow afraid that he would steal them. I am still finding shards under the tables in the workshop."

"That reminds me of Camille Claudel," said

Claire. "I walked by where her studio was just yesterday. It's so sad to think that many of her works were lost."

Giselle nodded. "I don't know that I would compare Lisette's work to that of Camille Claudel, but they both had a temper—that much is true."

And perhaps they were both unstable, thought Claire. She wanted to ask Giselle if—also like Claudel—Lisette had been having an affair with the man she worked with. But how did a person ask a question like that?

"It's not that uncommon for sculptors to smash their work," said Giselle. "I have even seen Armand do this from time to time. Artists, they are very dramatic, don't you think? And it must be satisfying to hear the explosion, watch the shards heading everywhere. Perhaps I'll try this next time I am frustrated. What do you think?"

"I think *we* are usually the ones who get stuck cleaning up those shards," said Claire with a laugh. "You're here early today. Would you like a croissant?"

"No, thank you. I already ate cereal and yogurt."

"That doesn't sound very Parisian."

She laughed. "It is my cousin Armand who insists on living the traditional Parisian lifestyle, not me. Anyway, I just stopped by to do some paperwork while my husband is with the children, but I have only an hour to spend."

Claire dropped the baked goods on the kitchen counter, put on a pot of coffee, and then closed the door to discourage the spread of the plaster dust—which sifted in through the cracks anyway, as sure as creeks flowed toward the ocean, as Mammaw would say.

"Speaking of Armand," Claire said to Giselle when she returned to the shop floor, "he's gone."

"Gone where?"

"I don't know. He seemed . . ." It was after the moment in the market, she thought. All through the dinner preparation and the meal he was silent, uncommunicative. That was the last she'd seen him. "He seemed bothered on Sunday evening, and the next day he was gone."

"Sometimes he disappears for a few days. I wouldn't worry about it." Giselle kept her tone light, dismissive, but there was a note of worry in her voice. "Sometimes . . . sometimes he needs some space. In fact, it is probably a vote of confidence—he assumes you can handle things here. And we're closing the studio for August vacation at the end of the week anyway."

"Don't you miss out on a lot of tourist money by closing during such a popular vacation month?"

Giselle shrugged. *"C'est la coutume."*

It is the custom. This seemed to be the answer to many things: Why do you shop here rather than there? Why do you cook the vegetables until they're so soft? Why do you close for two hours in the middle of the day when you could be making a lot of money? *C'est la coutume.* Perhaps Armand was right: maybe this was an issue of national character, and Claire was too American to ever truly understand.

Claire showed Giselle the work she had been doing on the Web site. Giselle was thrilled, especially with the form she was working on so people could place orders directly through the site.

"This is amazing, Claire. This could be wonderful for the business. Thank you so much. I know Armand is impossible with this sort of thing, but it's obviously the wave of the future."

"It's my pleasure. I hope it might help. Speaking of the wave of the future, do you know anything about the demand for software engineers in Paris?"

Giselle reared back, looked at her a long moment, then grinned and hugged her. "You want to stay in Paris! But this is wonderful!"

"Do you think I could make it happen?"

"It is not easy to get a permit to work here as a foreigner. But since the technology industry is so important, if a company needs you they can make a special appeal. I will ask Thiérry, my husband. He works for a large company—he might have some ideas."

"Thank you—that would be great."

It really had been nice to lose herself in the Web for a while, like a duck to water. Still, Claire thought to herself, looking around the dusty atelier: despite the less-than-luxurious accommodations, Claire was loath to give up the smells of plaster and the buckets of milky water and the excited tourists and the grumpy caster and the faces of the dead watching her every move.

Somehow she didn't think a software company would offer such an interesting working environment. Then again, this was Paris.

"So what does everyone do with their August vacations?" Claire asked as she straightened and swept.

"If they have money, they might go to Spain or to the South of France or the seashore. But some of us just go visit our family in the countryside every year, like birds going north."

"I'm sure it's beautiful."

"It is, actually," Giselle said with a rueful smile. "And it's nice to see the aunties while they're still with us. My mother passed away two years ago. I still miss her."

"I'm sorry to hear that. My grandmother died just before I came to France."

"Ah, that explains something."

"What's that?"

"Why you were so willing to come here and become part of the studio. It seemed odd for someone just visiting Paris. Grief explains so many things, doesn't it? Including staying here around Armand."

Claire smiled. "He's not so bad. In fact, we have some interesting talks."

"I'm sure! He's . . . I know he seems strong, but he's really quite sensitive. Claire, I wonder, have you ever been to the Franche-Comté?"

"No. This is my first time to France at all. I haven't been anywhere but Paris."

"You should come."

"Come?"

"To the countryside. There's all kinds of room at the house; we could probably find you some-place a tad more luxurious than the closet you're living in now."

"I thought the family villa was a ruin?"

"It is. But we still have the old farmhouse. It was built to house Jean-Baptiste Lombardi's five children, plus cousins, so while it's not a villa, it's quite large. There must be seven or eight bedrooms, and lots of other cubbies. Made of stone. Very traditional. You'd love it."

"But . . ." *But what?*

The sculptures were not talking to her. She had come no closer to figuring out the "secret" her grandmother had sent her here to discover. And Armand's words filled her head, swirling around like bees:

You have to get your hands dirty.

The Japanese art of kintsugi, *putting pieces together with gold, making a feature of the breaks.*

Do you not live your own life? What do you want, Claire?

"Anyway," Giselle was saying, "it will be my husband and me in the car with the two kids, but there is room in the back if you don't mind sitting with two sticky children. Our oldest is coming separately."

"What about Armand?"

Giselle looked away and flipped through the receipts atop the desk. "He might decide to stay here instead. And in any case, he prefers the train."

Claire barely knew Armand, not really. Quentin had tried to warn her off, as had Giselle. People who knew him. It was just . . . She thought of him hunched over his dollhouse in the middle of the night. The way he'd slipped into her little room when she was absent, bringing her a drawing, a mirror, a rug. The way he hugged Giselle's children and looked after a stray cat. The triumph she felt when she coaxed the slightest smile from him.

The sensation of his arms around her, the scent of him, the electricity she had felt in that crowded marketplace.

But he had gone. And the studio would be closing. And Giselle was offering Claire a free ride to the countryside and family-based accommodations upon arrival.

What do you want, Claire?

"Yes," Claire said. "Yes, Giselle. I would love to go with you."

Dear Uncle Remy,

I am going to the countryside with Giselle (one of my bosses—the nice one) to visit her family. I am excited to see another part of the country. Apparently they have a country estate. What do you think Mammaw would have made of that? Sounds pretty highfalutin, doesn't it?

They are having a big party for a couple that has been together for sixty-five years, but who never had a wedding reception because they didn't have the money. Apparently they are still in love, and the family will celebrate. And your lucky niece will be in attendance!

If only I had something to wear . . . Remember how you teased me that everything I own is black? Now everything I own is black covered in white plaster dust!

Your loving niece,
Chance

39

SABINE

Later that day, a few hours after returning from the marketplace, Sabine receives the first note.

It is unsigned, delivered by a street boy wearing old pants and a cap. She had been sweeping the work space when the knock came on the door.

The boy is small and probably looks younger than he is, with a dirty face and a sweet expression. He reminds Sabine of her little brother.

"I waited until the bearded man left the studio," he says, apparently eager to please. "Just as I was told. Also, the man what gave me the letter says to be sure to tell you that you're not to pay me; he will pay me for both ways."

Sabine searches the street to be sure no one is watching. Her hands shake as she takes the note. It is on heavy sketch paper, folded once. She opens it.

Will you come sit for me?

That was all. The breath leaves her body. Sabine stands right there in the doorway for a long moment, as still as she was when she is posing.

Staring down at the dark ink against the light paper.

These are *his* words, she thinks, running her fingers over the letters. The inky traces of the man with the sweetest voice she's ever heard, even gentler than the horse trainer's. The man with the blue eyes, the one miraculously saved from whatever blade had cut him. Monsieur ean-Baptiste Lombardi.

He was thinking about her.

Just as she was thinking of him: his eyes, his hands, his voice crowding out other thoughts.

She leaves the boy waiting on the stoop while she finds ink and quill, then writes at the bottom of the page. She forms the words with great care, the ink splotching in places—she knows how to read and write, but has not had much practice recently. Her hand shakes. She hopes the ink might carry a little of what she is feeling, that her sentiments will cascade through her heart to her arm, flowing along her hand and into the ink on the page.

But in the end she writes, very simply:

You must ask Maurice.

40

Claire rolled her small bag down to the corner of boulevard Saint-Michel to meet Giselle and her family, since the narrow rue de la Huchette was blocked by a garbage truck.

They pulled up in a red Renault with a good deal of baggage strapped to the roof and a lamp sticking out of the back window: a French version of the Joads. Giselle introduced Claire to her husband, Thiérry, a bespectacled, bookish-looking man in his late forties who greeted Claire in English and strapped her small bag down on the roof along with the others. Claire kept her purse with her, just in case; she had a vision of the luggage tumbling off the roof rack and trying to gather her wallet and personal papers from the median strip of the highway.

Giselle used the break to grab a quick cigarette, standing a few feet down the street so the smoke didn't waft over her children.

Victorine and David each gave Claire the traditional greeting, *"Bonjour, madame,"* with a kiss on each cheek. They smelled like *pain au chocolat.*

"Thiérry is driving, but why don't you sit in front, Claire. It is too crowded in the back," said Giselle.

"No," said Claire. "You're already bringing me with you to a family gathering. I won't take your seat. Besides, I like kids."

"You haven't been stuck in the back with *these* kids," said Thiérry.

"You might not thank me after all," Giselle said with a husky chuckle. "It takes four hours in the car, and only two in the train."

"The train is twice as fast as the car? But isn't there a highway . . . ?"

"Yes, the autoroute. We will go fast. But the train is much faster. We would take it except that, with all of us, it becomes very expensive."

"Besides," said Thiérry, "my lovely wife is incapable of traveling anywhere without bringing the entire house with her."

"It is complicated to travel with children," Giselle said. "When I was young, I lived out of my backpack! No more."

Claire smiled and climbed into the back with the kids. Victorine, the smallest, sat in the middle. It made Claire think back on so many family road trips, where she was always the smallest and given the middle seat or had to sit on an older cousin's lap: to the beach, to visit relatives in Saint Landry Parish, twice to New Orleans.

The autoroutes were vast toll roads, and though there was traffic—a lot of people trying to leave Paris for their August break—the cars moved along at a good clip. Thiérry told Claire a little about the high-tech scene in Paris—which was thriving—and said that if she hung around the city for a few more weeks, he would try to help arrange some introductions for her. As Giselle had mentioned, it was best to approach the French bureaucracy with a job already in place and allow the acquiring company to do a lot of the legwork.

As they continued, the children taught Claire a game similar to bingo in which they had to spy the items on a long list: a cow, a windmill, a trailer. She won the first round, then purposely failed to see the next item on the list.

Instead, she noticed a road sign with a simple graphic of a castle. Claire scanned the wooded horizon but saw nothing but pastures of sheep, a vineyard, a few small stone cottages surrounded by flowers. No massive turrets sticking up out of the greenery. She sat back, disappointed. It was probably hidden from the road, back behind the hill. She decided then and there: she was not going back to America without seeing at least one genuine castle. The Louvre didn't count. Perhaps she should jump on a tourist bus to the Palace of Versailles, which lay less than an hour outside of Paris. She smiled at the thought of what Armand would have to say about that tourist destination.

Ten minutes later, Claire saw *another* sign indicating a castle.

"Is this an area known for castles?" she asked.

"Not particularly," said Giselle. "The Loire and

the Dordogne Valleys have many more. And sometimes what they refer to as a 'castle' might be just a ruined stack of stones. But still, back in the old days it used to be a full day's ride from one castle keep to the next, if you were lucky enough to be on horseback or in a carriage—more on foot. Now we can drive from one to the next in an hour or less on the autoroute."

Claire spied an overpass crowded with greenery. There didn't appear to be a road, just the overpass itself.

"And what is that?" she asked.

"*C'est un pont à faune*," said David.

"A wildlife bridge?" she asked, wondering whether she understood the French correctly. "What's that?"

"Just what it sounds like," said Thiérry from the front seat. "In the fifties, when we were putting in the autoroutes, someone realized it would cut the animals off from their normal migratory patterns. So they created these bridges so the wildlife can cross safely. Now other nations have followed suit, but I believe France was the first."

"Don't you have them where you come from?" asked Victorine.

"I come from a very big country," said Claire, "and we have a lot of autoroutes, so it's possible we have some. But I don't remember ever seeing one."

"How big is your country? Is it bigger than France?"

"Yes, a bit."

"Really?" the boy asked, skepticism in his young gaze. "France is very big."

"That's true," Claire said. "But the U.S. is bigger. There are fifty states, all linked together."

"In France we have many departments," said David. "My grandma lived in Franche-Comté but she died."

"I know; I'm sorry. My grandma died recently too."

Victorine reached out and patted Claire on the arm. "Are you sad?"

Claire nodded and swallowed hard, willing away the sudden sting of tears. She cleared her throat. "In Cajun we say, *'J'ai gros couer.'* It means, 'I feel like crying.'"

The girl nodded sagely, as though she understood. Then she added, "Even though our grandma died, there are still a lot of aunts in the Franche-Comté."

"A *lot* of aunts," seconded David.

Claire smiled. "And what are your aunts like?"

"They are fat and soft and you can sit on their laps while you collect the lavender blossoms," piped up Victorine. "And when you take a walk with them they always point out nice things, like pretty leaves or fuzzy caterpillars. Also there are a lot of cows there. May I tell you a story?" Before

339

Claire had a chance to respond, she jumped in, "One time we brought home a bucket of snails—"

"Victorine," interrupted Giselle, twisting her head to look back at us. "Leave the lady alone. She does not have to hear all your stories."

"I don't mind," Claire said. "In my family, we all tell stories."

"How big is your family?" Thiérry asked.

"I was raised by my grandmother. She was one of seven children and they all had kids, so even though I'm an only child, there were always a lot of cousins running around Plaquemines Parish."

"Plaquemines Parish?"

"It's an area in the state of Louisiana. We're Cajun."

"And what's that?"

"From what I was always told, the word 'Cajun' comes from 'Acadian.' They were French settlers in the United States a long time ago. There's still a lot of French spoken in parts of Louisiana, though it's dying out. My grandmother was pretty insistent about it; they didn't let her speak it in school, so she took it very personally. Since I lived with her, I had to speak Cajun or go hungry."

"Speaking of hungry . . ." Giselle cast a significant glance at her husband.

In Claire's mind, road trips were synonymous with junk food: stops for burgers and milk shakes, passing around a bag of chips. But in Thiérry and Giselle's car there were no Doritos, no sodas. Only a bottle of mineral water.

Thiérry pulled into a rest stop and parked. Giselle took a picnic basket out of the trunk.

Claire offered to buy drinks or something from the nearby refreshment stand to contribute, but they demurred, Thiérry mentioning that Giselle always overpacked lunch in addition to luggage.

Instead, Claire volunteered to take the kids to the restroom located in a large building. Inside, there was the French version of fast food—ready-made ham sandwiches, croissants and pastries, flatbread with caramelized onion and Gruyère cheese. The children lingered over a large display of handmade candies, and Claire was enchanted by an assortment of regional items from pâté to olives to marzipan, all packaged beautifully, like perfect little presents. There was even a small dress boutique and a stand selling local wine.

By the time Claire and the children joined Giselle and Thiérry, the picnic table was dressed with a yellow-and-blue Provençal tablecloth, white china plates, small glasses, a bottle each of wine and mineral water. Giselle had packed sandwiches of crusty bread and ham and salads of shredded carrot and celery root. On a plate in the center was a pyramid of small plums and pears, and there was a beautiful fruit tart for dessert.

"This looks like a spread out of a magazine,"

Claire said as the children fell on the sandwiches like hungry seagulls.

Giselle looked up at Claire, uncomprehending.

"It's beautiful," Claire tried again.

"It is lunch," said Giselle.

"I know that. It's just . . . you set a lovely table."

"Thank you," Giselle said, but she sounded annoyed. Claire had noted that many French disliked being thanked for something they felt to be a normal part of their job, or their life, or their responsibility. Almost as though she was insulting them by pointing it out.

Afterward the kids begged to go buy candy, but their parents refused, telling them the aunties were no doubt preparing cookies and tarts for their arrival. They filled the car with gas and got back on the road.

"May I tell my story now?" Victorine asked her mother, her voice slightly whiny. "Madame says she *likes* stories."

Giselle raised her eyebrows at Claire in question.

"I would love to hear your story, Victorine," said Claire.

"It's a good story, and it's *true*. One time we brought home a bucket of snails to put on the cornmeal, but we didn't have time to tend to them because we were going out to a movie, so we left them in the bucket in the kitchen and we put a heavy screen on them so they could breathe but they had to stay in the bucket. But when we came back from the movie they had *escaped!*"

"No," said Claire.

"Yes," insisted Victorine.

"How did they escape?" asked Claire.

"They worked together," said David, "and lifted the heavy screen!"

"I'm telling the story," said Victorine with a scowl at her brother.

"Let your brother help tell the story," chided Giselle.

"Is this a *true* story?" asked Claire with a smile. "I've heard of ants working together, but snails . . . ?"

Victorine nodded so vigorously, her curls bounced. "It's *true!* When we came home, the snails were all gone from the bucket, leaving shiny trails *all* over the *house!*"

Giselle chuckled and looked over at Thiérry, who was shaking his head and groaning at the memory.

"It was a nightmare," said Thiérry. "Giselle called me at work screaming."

Claire laughed.

"I wasn't *screaming,*" said Giselle, punching her husband playfully in the arm. "I was . . . disturbed."

"That's why I don't like escargots," said David. "Because I found one in my bed!"

"And they were on my toys!" added Victorine.

343

"They really were everywhere," said Giselle, laughing. "On the walls, the ceiling—*everywhere*. Their shiny trails crisscrossed the house. And we couldn't get them all out from under the cabinets, so—"

"*They had* baby *snails!*" shouted Victorine.

The family erupted into gales of laughter, and Claire joined in.

41

Thiérry edged the car along a steep, twisty road through thick forests. Farther below the road Claire could see a river with several small waterfalls and a little town.

"It's Lods!" said Victorine.

"It's what?" asked Claire.

"Lods is the name of the village," explained Giselle. "The river is called the Loue."

"Does the Loue ever flood?" Claire asked.

"I don't remember it being a problem," said Giselle. "Why?"

"Just wondering."

The town had a slight Bavarian flair: the houses were built along the thickly treed slopes, mellow white-and-yellow stone cottages with steep tile roofs; a few showed the open timber construction Claire had always associated with Switzerland. As they grew closer, she noted window boxes with orangey red geraniums and delicate lace curtains blowing in the breeze; cats lazed on windowsills and a smattering of elderly people sat outside, snapping beans or chatting; they stopped to watch as the car rolled by.

"Lods is a very small town, very quiet," explained Giselle. "There are two hotels for the tourists, and an interesting museum about wine and viniculture. A couple of *restos*"—this word, Claire had figured out, was short for "restaurant"—"and the river. That's about it. But during this season the campground is open, and they light up the waterfalls at night in the summer—we should come to town one night to show you. Very pretty."

Many of the houses featured ornate windows or engraved stones embedded in the walls or fountains by the front doors.

"Besides winemaking, this region was famous for its iron forges in the nineteenth century," Thiérry added. "And that is the Church of Saint-Théodule with the steeple, and there's a stone bridge from the sixteenth century."

"And sometimes we can borrow boats to take out onto the water," said Victorine.

"We can *rent* them, you mean," said Giselle. "It isn't free after all."

"It's beautiful," said Claire. "It's so picturesque."

They gave her a strange look, making Claire wonder whether she used the wrong word—it sounded French, but sometimes there were false cognates or words that lulled her into a mistaken notion that they were French because they sounded French—or whether they did not agree that the village was worthy of a postcard.

Perhaps it was because she was American, Claire thought, that she relished these villages, the ancient stone homes and the sense of history. Two world wars and innumerable other momentous events, struggles with the English and the Romans and countless other invading hordes over the centuries. How many of these fields had seen battles, had fallen to conquerors—or, conversely, had played host to tournaments and festivals of art and music over the years?

They continued through the town, turning left onto a main street that followed the river.

Giselle rolled down her window and waved to an old man sitting on a bench outside a white-washed building. He wore a beret and an unbuttoned black vest and leaned with both hands on a cane. *He should definitely be featured on the tourism poster of this town,* Claire thought.

"*Salut, Gabby!*" the whole family shouted as they rolled slowly by, Victorine practically sitting in Claire's lap to reach out the window.

Gabby raised his hand to return their greeting: "*Salut, Famille Lombardi!*"

"Do you go by Lombardi, then?" Claire asked as they continued on. She had a hard time keeping all the names straight; clearly, she needed a spreadsheet on this family.

"No, our last name is Bouvay. But anyone associated with the château and the house is called Lombardi in this town. *C'est la coutume.*"

They rolled slowly through the rest of the village, then rode another several minutes along the river before turning onto a gravel road. Several lines of staked grapevines marched up the hill, surrounding a large stone house.

They stopped at a pair of rusty iron gates. David jumped out, Victorine hot on his heels, to open the gates for the car. Two big dogs—one yellow, one black—ran up to meet them, wagging their tails and barking happily.

Thiérry pulled the car slowly through the gates and into a courtyard. The wheels popped on the gravel drive. Several old women—and a few men and younger people as well—began to pour out of an open set of French doors painted a chalky blue-green.

The dogs barked, the children ran around, and the women exclaimed.

True to the children's description, "the aunts" were plump and smiley, clapping their hands together and laughing. Claire was introduced to Michèle and Loic Fontaine, Armand's parents. His mother, Michèle, was dark haired and pretty with a huge smile and an easygoing way about her; his father, Loic, looked like an older, gray-haired version of Armand, blue eyed and intense. Michèle introduced her sisters, Colette and Pauline and

Louise, and her elderly aunts, Marie and Françoise.

And Giselle introduced her eldest son, Luc, who looked like a younger version of Thiérry, studious and bespectacled. Luc said he was eager to review the changes Claire had made for the *moulage* Web site.

After that, Claire lost count of all the relatives, almost immediately forgetting their names—she imagined this was why everyone seemed to refer to the collection of women as "the aunts." She was introduced to everyone as *"l'Américaine"* and was welcomed into the house.

Claire felt simultaneously disappointed and relieved when she didn't spy Armand among the relatives.

She had known the man for such a short time, but perhaps because of the forced intimacy of their living situation—or this point in her life, or his, or both—their short time together seemed heightened, charged. But he had walked away when things became too intense; she should follow his example. It was hard to forget the electric feeling of his arms around her in the marketplace; but after all, Claire would not be going back to live in the *moulage*, and unless she managed to land a job she would probably be leaving France soon altogether. She might never see Armand or Giselle and her family again; rather, she would always remember these weeks as an interesting detour in her life. Claire began to craft the story in her head. *Did I ever tell you about the time I landed a job in a death mask factory in Paris?*

The relatives urged them into the house; the doors opened directly onto a large but cramped kitchen dominated by a huge farm table surrounded by ten chairs. An oven and a refrigerator were lined up along one wall, a sink and a long butcher block counter on another. A lace-curtained casement window was open and looked out over a verdant vegetable garden; a calico cat sat in the window, taking in the scene with imperiousness. One old woman shooed her out into the garden, grumbling about cats in the kitchen, while another told her not to be so harsh.

Claire moved toward the window to take in the view.

There, on the crest of the hill overlooking the valley, stood Armand's dollhouse.

His dollhouse at full size. Finally, it dawned on her that he had been working on an architectural model.

It was magnificent atop the hill, backlit in an orangey pink light by the setting sun. But, unlike the model, part of one stone spire had tumbled and sections of the roof appeared to be missing. From what she could see at this distance, the rest of the building looked intact, though Claire knew enough about real estate to realize: once a roof was compromised, the building wouldn't last long.

"That's the family château?" Claire asked.

"Yes," said Michèle. "The château used to be beautiful. It has been in the family since the 1870s, when our ancestors came from Italy."

The aunts nodded and clucked and laid out snacks and drinks. They invited Claire to sit at the kitchen table, and then took turns recounting the family history, first one, then the next. The only ones who didn't vie to tell the story were the men, who appeared to be focused on the snacks, and sister Louise, who nodded and smiled and chuckled but remained virtually mute.

"Luigi Lombardi stayed here and married the daughter of an aristocratic family," said Pauline. "The family lost most of their money and power in the Revolution, of course, but were able to keep the château. It was a bit run-down, but it was still a beauty."

"The other brother, Giuseppe, opened the *moulage* in Paris. Ever since then our people have kept the land here and the shop in town," said Colette. "Here they farmed, had their small vineyard, and Giuseppe's son Jean-Baptiste took over the *moulage* when Giuseppe retired. But Jean-Baptiste didn't want to raise his children in the city, so he went back and forth to Paris for many years while his wife raised their children here in the countryside."

"Their firstborn son, Marc-Antoine, went to Paris to take over the shop when he was old enough," added Pauline. "And then it passed to Pierre-Guillaume Fontaine."

"The château looks gorgeous from here," said Claire.

Louise chuckled.

"Looks better the farther away you get," said Michèle with a sigh. "And the less light there is."

"It's sad it's gone to ruin."

"It was still beautiful when the Nazis moved in during World War II; that's when the family moved out for the last time. The Germans used it to house their officers, and when they left they took the art and tapestries, the silver, anything else of value," said Tante Marie.

"They also did some damage," said Colette. "They set one bedroom on fire, and a shell went off and damaged the spire, and falling bricks damaged the roof. Now it is full of nothing but ghosts. No one wants it now."

"I thought Armand hoped to renovate it?" Claire said.

Several significant glances were cast around the table.

"He used to say he would do so, but then . . ." Pauline left off with a shrug.

"Things change," said Michèle in a gentle but distant tone that put an end to the conversation.

Claire studied Michèle for a moment, wondering how hard it must be for her to see her son, Armand, suffering. If his pain was clear to Claire, a virtual stranger, how much more difficult would it be for his family to witness?

After they snacked on seasoned nuts and succulent plums and slices of vegetable tarts, the aunts shooed them out of the kitchen, refusing their offers of help with the dinner preparations. It was a hot summer afternoon, insects buzzing, a fragrant breeze fluttering the leaves. Giselle proposed taking the kids for a walk through the woods that bordered the vineyard. Thiérry declined, but Claire was happy to stretch her legs.

Victorine and David ran ahead, grabbing sticks to pretend sword fight. The well-worn dirt path opened onto a clearing with a large pond.

Their arrival spurred dozens of frogs to jump into the water, their splish-splashing preceding the human visitors as they skirted the edges. Dragonflies hovered over the shallows. The children threw handfuls of small stones into the pond, sending concentric rings rippling out along the glasslike surface of the water.

Claire pretended to find the pond charming for the sake of the children; the last thing they needed was to be saddled with her phobia. When she had children—*if* she had children—Claire thought, she was going to have them taught to swim in infancy, before they were sensible enough to know fear.

As they started to walk back, the château was visible through a clearing in the trees.

"Could we poke around the old château?" Claire asked.

"Yes, please!" piped up Victorine.

"No," said Giselle.

"It's *haunted,*" said David in a timid voice.

"It *isn't,*" said Victorine. "And anyway, *I'm* not afraid."

"It's *not* haunted," said Giselle to her children. "There's no such thing as ghosts. But it is dangerous. It is off-limits—do I make myself understood?"

Claire wondered whether the ruins were off-limits to grown-ups as well, but decided to ask when out of earshot of the children.

They returned to a table set for fifteen—a card table and several mismatched chairs had been dragged in for the occasion—and feasted on onion tart with bacon, celery root rémoulade, roast chicken, and crisp little potatoes with rosemary and *haricots verts*, green salad served after the meal in the French custom, and a cheese plate. The wine flowed easily; Armand's father, Loic— who had scarcely spoken a word, much like his son—poured more into any glass where the level of wine fell below the halfway mark.

Claire savored the meal and let the boisterous conversations flow over her. Family members traded news of Paris and friends and relatives in the village, recounted old memories, and suggested ideas for day trips. It reminded Claire of family dinners in Plaquemines Parish but made her wonder: When she was with her own family, there were undercurrents of old grudges, difficult histories, as between her and Jessica. Was it true for these family members as well? From the outside, it all seemed impossibly loving and charming.

Coffee, tea, and pear crumble were offered for dessert. Dinner lasted nearly two hours, and the cleanup—for which the aunts *did* accept help—another forty-five minutes. It was nearly ten o'clock by the time they were finished, and the children were sent off to get ready for bed.

Giselle showed Claire to a small guest room on the first floor. It was a simple chamber, with a full-sized bed and a small dresser. A single window looked out over the garden and offered a view of the old château, partially obscured by trees.

"You'll have to come upstairs to shower, but at least you have your own toilet under the stairs."

"It's lovely. Thank you."

"Better than your tiny room at the atelier, isn't it?"

Claire smiled. "To tell you the truth, I've grown very fond of my little closet. But this is an amazing house."

"Since it's still early, do you want a quick tour of the place?"

"I'd love one."

There were a sunroom, two sitting rooms, a

huge larder, and, best of all, a small library. Up in the attic was one big open sleeping loft for the children, full of cots and sleeping bags on the floor; shelves held books and old-fashioned board games. It looked like camp. The house featured high-beamed ceilings and low doorways, tiny hallways and nooks crowded with antique furniture; walls and shelves were jammed with family photos and mementos.

Claire paused to remark upon several framed charcoal sketches that reminded her of the one hanging in her "closet" in Paris, and a painting in the same style. It was an intimate scene of two children playing in a bath, in a loose, impressionistic style that reminded Claire of works by Mary Cassatt.

"They were done by a great-great-great-grandmother or something like that. They've hung here forever. Most of the pottery you see was made by a great-uncle—even though not everyone's involved in the *moulage*, there have always been a lot of artists and craftspeople in the family."

"I know it might be overwhelming sometimes," said Claire, "but the sense of family history here—it's really something." She thought of the château, what secrets and family history it must contain. Or had David been right: was it full of nothing but ghosts?

The whole farmhouse was charming, but

Claire's favorite part was the basement. They passed through a narrow door and went down a steep flight of stone steps with no railing. The air was musty, but it was so cool, it felt air-conditioned; it was a refreshing reprieve from the summer heat. At the bottom of the stairs Giselle reached up to pull a string for the overhead light.

There were several rooms. One was full of hunting and fishing gear; another included children's furniture, a crib, and a high chair. Wide shelves held jumbo packs of toilet paper and paper towels and boxes of Badoit mineral water.

The largest room was lined with full corked bottles without labels and four massive barrels. It smelled of wine.

"*Ça, c'est notre cave*," said Giselle.

"Your wine cellar?" asked Claire.

"*Oui*. The barrels are from the family vineyard. It is not a major one, just enough for the family. The old men tend the grapes, make their own wine. You had it at dinner."

"I enjoyed it."

"It's not the best, but it tastes like home. One of my uncles makes something he calls a 'tonic' too, which he claims is good for stomachaches. He uses a mix of local herbs; he goes and gathers them from high in the mountains. I think it's mostly alcohol, but it seems to work. Just so you know—the food can be very rich."

"Thank you. So I know you were warning

the children away from the château, but are grown-ups allowed to go up there? I'd love to look around."

"It's best not to, probably," said Giselle. "It's really falling down. If Armand shows up, you can ask him about it."

"Do you expect him?"

"Maybe," she said with a shrug. "It's hard to say. Claire . . . I wanted to say . . . my cousin cannot afford to be hurt again. He . . . it has been so hard for him. He has come a long way."

"I have no intention of hurting him."

"Sometimes it happens, whether we intend it or not."

"There's nothing going on between us, Giselle," Claire said. "I would like to be his friend, but you know how he is. I just work for him—and even with that, I think as of yesterday I'm unemployed, right?"

Giselle shrugged, apparently unconvinced.

"And anyway," Claire continued, "whatever Armand is dealing with, surely with time he will be able to get past it. My grandmother always used to say: what doesn't kill you makes you stronger."

"You Americans always think people can get over things, but there are some things one never gets over."

"But there are ways to cope, right? Otherwise, we should all throw ourselves into the Seine and have done with it."

Giselle nodded distractedly.

"On the other hand," continued Claire, "my grandmother always said I was a miracle baby, and my life hasn't turned out to be particularly miraculous, so perhaps she wasn't the most reliable source of wisdom."

Giselle gave her a sad smile. "Isn't all life a miracle?"

"I suppose so, in the broader sense. Anyway, since when did you become anti-American? You sound like Armand."

"I'm sorry. Of course I'm not anti-American. It's just that it seems you think everything is possible. We French—we have seen more, perhaps. We understand that tragedy is a part of who we are. Our history is very different from yours."

"What are you doing down there?" came an elderly voice from the top of the stairs. "Is that you, Giselle? Will you bring up two bottles, please? And some paper towels?"

"*Bien sûr, Tante Françoise*," said Giselle, handing Claire a three-pack of paper towels and grabbing two dusty bottles of wine from the rack in the cave.

As they climbed the stone steps, Claire pondered Giselle's words. She thought about the concept of *kintsugi*, making a feature of the breaks, of the scars we attain over the course of a lifetime. After all, even if time healed one's wounds, they still left scars. Perhaps there was no "getting over" tragedy.

In this, Claire thought to herself, she did not feel particularly American. But then, as she had explained to the children, it was an awfully big country.

Claire got ready for bed and turned out the lamp. She stood at the window for a moment, letting the warm night breeze whisper along her bare arms while she gazed up at the ruined château. It loomed dark against a bright night sky.

She froze, squinted. Was that a flickering light in one of the arched stone windows?

When she looked again, it was gone. The trees partially obscured her view; their branches were swaying slightly in the wind, so perhaps she had simply misinterpreted moonlight gleaming off leaves wet with dew.

She kept watching for so long, her vision went fuzzy. Finally, *yes,* there it was again.

A soft golden glow, visible first through one arched window, then the next. As though someone was walking down the hall holding a candle. Was this the haunting the children had talked about?

Claire didn't believe in ghosts any more than Giselle did. Grown-ups were haunted by their past plenty, but a *literal* haunting was something else altogether. In her hometown people told stories of such things, of course; the bayous were riddled with specters and monsters, what her people called *tatailles*. But Claire had learned at a young age that the *tataille* to fear was human, not a ghost.

Maybe there were squatters up at the château; perhaps that was why Giselle considered it dangerous. The light disappeared, and though she watched for several more minutes, she didn't see anything else. Weariness washed over her. It had been a long day.

But as her head hit the pillow, Claire's mind cast back to Armand hunched over his miniature château, sanding and scraping and sculpting its tiny pieces in secret, late into the silent night.

42

SABINE

Y ou remember Monsieur Lombardi, the mold-maker?" Maurice asks Sabine while she is scraping the stubborn clay off his worktable.

She went still, her hands red with the wet earth.

"I remember a mold-maker," she says carefully. "We met him at the brasserie the night Monsieur Degas was there."

"Exactly. The ugly man."

Sabine does not think the mold-maker is ugly. All she can think of is the gentleness of his voice, the cool pools of his eyes. The scar on his cheek and brow does not bother her. Quite the opposite; it reminds her that a person could be handsome yet hide an ugliness deep inside. And certainly the opposite is also true. Don't most people hide their scars within?

She thinks of something her mother told her once: that many things are ugly only to those who cannot see.

At the Louvre, Sabine sees the beauty of the paint, of the technique, of the colors and the sumptuous clothes and furnishings. But the expressions on the faces—especially in the portraits of the aristocracy—sometimes seem ugly, as though the artists have captured feelings of contempt for their fellow men. Much less women.

"Monsieur Lombardi has asked about you modeling for him."

Sabine keeps her eyes cast down. She finishes cleaning the workbench and washes her hands, then applies salve. When she first arrived in Paris, her hands were rough from farmwork; she has tried to soften them with lotions, even sleeps with gloves on at night. Maurice insists upon it.

"Do you think it's a good idea?" Sabine asks. "For me to model for him?"

It is a delicate balance: Maurice is flattered by the attention, enjoys believing that he made a discovery of Sabine back when she was a skinny, inexperienced naïf straight from the countryside.

He likes that others want her to pose for them, that they are then beholden to him and admire him for his perspicacity and magnanimity. But f Maurice were to realize how much Sabine desires to spend time with Jean-Baptiste Lombardi, it would be calamitous.

"I think it is amusing," says Maurice. "I didn't even know he was a sculptor; he tells me it is a new love. Perhaps I should ask him to make some casts of you in return."

Sabine remains silent. She fiddles with the pink ribbon she saved from a box of chocolates. She likes the sleek, slippery feel of the satin as it runs through her fingers; it calms her.

"I see no reason you shouldn't go," he says finally. "I have no use for you this week in any case."

He is sculpting a male figure now, for a new piece he is hoping to present to the Academy. Sabine prays that it will be accepted. It will not go well for her if Maurice is thwarted, once again, by the entrenched artistic powers that be.

"Isabelle will go with you," Maurice adds.

"*Oui, monsieur.*"

43

By the time Claire came out for breakfast the next morning, more relatives had arrived and were crowding the kitchen and courtyard.

Claire couldn't keep the names and relationships straight, so she stopped trying. Instead, she ignored the awkwardness of knowing almost no one and focused on enjoying the action. Adults talked and laughed and put away food; children ran in and out of rooms, playing with the dogs and chasing the cats.

Claire accepted a cup of coffee and a croissant from a young woman in braids she hadn't met before. Then, spying Giselle sitting outside, she carried her breakfast out to the patio, where Giselle sat with "the aunts"—Michèle, Pauline, Colette, and Louise—in a circle around a broad, tightly woven basket. Their hands were in constant motion, scraping the blossoms from stalks of dried lavender.

"We are making small gifts for the party," explained Pauline. She held up a little bag with names embroidered on them—*Pierre-Guillaume* and *Delphine*—and the date. "Afterward we will put the blossoms in little bags—you see?"

"Those are charming. What a great idea for a favor," Claire said, joining the circle. "May I help you?"

"*Bien sûr.*" Of course. "As soon as you finish your breakfast."

There was a rhythm to their work: they would grab a stalk from the piles sitting on cloths on the ground, *shuck shuck shuck,* toss the denuded stalk, grab another.

As they worked, the women gossiped. Many of their subjects were unfamiliar to Claire—names of cousins and nephews and nieces flowed over her—but Claire's ears perked up when they started speaking about a woman named Odile who had gone off with Armand's neighbor, the chocolatier.

"Quentin?" Claire suggested.

"Yes, that's the one."

"And . . . who is Odile?" Claire asked.

They exchanged glances.

"Armand's wife," said Colette.

Michèle shook her head, got up, and left the circle.

"Wife? Armand's *married?*" Claire asked, looking at Giselle.

"*Ex*-wife," said Pauline, answering before Giselle had a chance. "Odile is Armand's *ex*-wife."

"He's lucky to be rid of her," said Colette.

Giselle cast a quelling glance at the old women.

"Quentin is not a bad sort. And Odile deserves to be happy," Giselle said, shutting down the line of talk. "It is complicated."

Complicated? It didn't seem all that complicated to Claire: if Armand's wife ran off with another man, that would explain a lot. Though it seemed strange that Armand would have allowed Quentin into his garden and served him wine. She would have expected a bloody nose at the very least.

Or was that a typically American response? Claire's cousins were prone to rowdy, punch-first-ask-questions-later kinds of interactions, especially when dealing with affairs of the heart. Perhaps here in France things were settled with a slap of a glove and a proper duel—or better yet, an intense discussion over a glass of wine—and then forgotten. She had always heard the French were much more urbane with this sort of thing, that it wasn't unusual for men *and* women to take lovers throughout their lives.

On the one hand, Claire supposed such an arrangement might keep a lot of marriages together that would otherwise crumble. But on the other . . . could she live like that? Remain sanguine in the face of her husband's infidelity, or her own? *No, thanks.*

Giselle seemed remarkably forgiving. Claire made a mental note to ask her about it the next time they were alone.

"So, you are from America, Claire?" asked Michèle as she returned to the group, sat down, and picked up a handful of dried lavender. Her strong-looking hands worked the stalks with a rhythmic pace, sending a generous spray of blossoms into the broad basket.

"From Louisiana," said Claire with a nod.

"This is why you speak French?"

"Yes. My grandmother spoke it at home. As I'm sure you can hear, we use some different vocabulary and my accent is strange. But I'm pleased, to tell the truth, at how well I can understand the language. I wasn't sure how I would do in France."

They chuckled and talked among themselves for a while, comparing the French spoken in parts of Africa, from Quebec, from Haiti, and elsewhere.

Claire was working on her third stalk of lavender while the old women had moved through a dozen each in the same time period. Clearly this was harder than it looked. The skills of a lifetime.

"And tell us, Claire, how did you come to be working with Armand?"

"I needed a place to stay, and I was able to help with the English-speaking customers for a couple of weeks."

"So you are not . . . *with* him?" Pauline asked, her brown eyes keen.

"No, nothing like that."

"Then why are you here in Lods?"

Claire gave a little laugh. "I'm not completely sure, actually. Giselle talked me into it. But the reason I first went to the Moulage Lombardi was because of the mask called *L'Inconnue de la Seine*. Do you know it?"

More glances were exchanged over the rapidly filling basket. Colette nodded very slowly. "A little. That face has made a lot of money for the family over the years."

"So I hear."

"They say it hung in every fashionable house in the 1920s and '30s, and in every artist's atelier. There was even one in the château, if I remember correctly."

"You could ask Pierre-Guillaume," suggested Pauline. "He worked for the family business way back when."

"It wasn't *that* long ago," said Giselle. "He started working at the *moulage* at the end of the war. *L'Inconnue*'s face was cast before the turn of the twentieth century."

"Actually, my great-grandfather bought a cast of *L'Inconnue* when he came to Paris in World War II," said Claire. "I wonder if their paths crossed. Wouldn't that be amazing?"

"Your great-grandfather was in the American army?"

Claire nodded.

"It was a great day when the Americans came," said Tante Marie. "The young people don't want to hear it; they forget. They weren't there. I was just a child, but I remember exactly where I was when the Americans marched through town. That was a great day. Thank you."

"I wish I could take some credit," said Claire, "but it was long before my time."

"Still, it was a wonderful thing."

"We refer to that group as the Greatest Generation for their bravery," said Claire.

She nodded. "I like that."

"Pierre-Guillaume is my father-in-law," Michèle said to Claire. "Perhaps he does know more about *L'Inconnue*."

"No one knows," said Louise, the usually silent aunt. "That's why she is *L'Inconnue*. People love the mystery."

After they finished with the last of the dried lavender stalks, Michèle turned to Claire. "I will take you to meet my father-in-law, Pierre-Guillaume, if you like. He and his wife, Delphine, live just down the way. We can walk."

"They still live on their own?"

"It is a small house built behind the big house, where they raised their family, including my husband, Loic. When the children grew up and married, they gave us the big house and moved into the cottage. That way they are nearby."

"That's a nice tradition."

"Isn't it? I raised my children in that house, and now my daughter, Armand's sister, lives there with her husband and children. And it's a short walk to this old stone farmhouse. We're a very close family."

"So it seems. It's nice you can all be together."

She laughed, a pleasant, throaty sound. "We have our moments. But overall, yes, it's lovely. Loic and I still like to spend time in Paris once or twice a year, but the country is our true home."

It was on the tip of Claire's tongue to ask, *Have you heard from Armand? Do you think he'll be joining us?* But she held back. Clearly there was already gossip, and worry, about the two of them. No need to stoke those speculations.

They walked past a large two-story house that looked like many in the village: white stone with a steep shingled roof, window boxes featuring bright red-orange pops of color, trailing ivy, and lace curtains. A black-and-white cat sunned itself in a bay window, and a dog in the yard wagged its tail and barked. Chickens clucked and scratched in a large coop.

The cottage behind the larger house was a simple one story that looked like it had been built in the fifties or sixties. Michèle rapped smartly on the door but didn't wait for an answer before opening it. She led the way into a small but comfortable home devoid of stairs—which must be a comfort when you are nearly ninety, Claire thought.

An elderly couple was seated at the kitchen table.

"*Ah, salut, Michèle!*" said the woman.

Michèle greeted them with kisses on both cheeks.

"*Papa, Maman*, let me introduce you to Claire, *l'Américaine*," said Michèle in a loud voice. "Claire, this is Pierre-Guillaume and Delphine Fontaine."

They greeted one another and asked Claire to join them, offering her a cup of tea. Claire referred to Pierre-Guillaume as Monsieur Fontaine, and they all laughed.

"Everyone here calls him Grand-père," said Michèle. "Because he is the head of the family."

"For the moment," he said. His voice was weak, but his eyes were sharp as they fixed on Claire. "So you are American? I like the Americans."

"Thank you," said Claire with a smile. Just as she defended her nationality to Armand, she didn't feel as if she could take much credit for it either. It was a chance of birth, nothing more. "I like the French."

He laughed, and Delphine told a story about the Americans marching into Paris, the deafening sound of the bells tolling at the Cathédrale de Notre Dame. She had only been a little girl, but she remembered it well.

"So, what brought you to Paris, Claire?" asked Delphine.

"I guess it all started when I found the mask of *L'Inconnue* in my grandmother's attic when I was just a girl. I . . . I even began to talk to her, as if she could hear me."

"She is very special, *L'Inconnue*," said Pierre-Guillaume. "Perhaps she was speaking to you through this dream."

Delphine laughed and slapped him lightly on the shoulder. "The tales you tell, old man."

"My sweet Delphine does not believe the sculptures can speak. But we do—don't we, *Américaine*?" Pierre-Guillaume gave Claire a conspiratorial wink.

Claire smiled. "As a matter of fact, I did feel as if they could. Not always, of course, but every once in a while."

"You see, Delphine?" said Pierre-Guillaume.

Delphine called him an old fool, in a loving tone, and pushed herself up from the table to put on more hot water. Michèle went to help her.

"What part of America are you from?" asked Pierre-Guillaume.

"Louisiana. A small town in Plaquemines Parish, in the delta south of New Orleans."

"I remember," Pierre-Guillaume said with a nod. "I remember your grandfather."

"I—" Claire was about to argue with him—how could he remember?—but didn't want to be rude. She wondered whether Pierre-Guillaume was mixing things up in his old age.

Michèle brought a plate of cookies to the table and gave voice to Claire's thoughts. "Surely you can't remember that far back, *Papa*? Selling something to an American when you were just a boy?"

He tapped his temple. "I have one of those minds. Also, he was one of the first Americans I met after the war. We were so happy to have them in Paris—you cannot imagine. He was kind to me. He gave me a Hershey's chocolate bar! And he told me one day I would fall in love with my Delphine."

"I can't believe you remember him after all these years," said Claire, astonished.

"I do remember. Because I sent him the mask. This was the first time I had sent something all the way to America. It seemed so far away, so safe to me. The soldier was not going home for some time, so he had me send it to his wife so she would not forget him."

Claire nodded. "I never knew him myself. His name was Jerry Duval. He passed away before I was born."

"You must understand, at that time my Delphine was only a child. So skinny, and how she annoyed me! So when he told me I would fall in love with her, I could not believe him. And then one day I looked at her and realized: she has become a woman—a beautiful, demanding, intelligent woman."

Delphine came back to the table, sat, and beamed at him, and he at her. Then, with a mischievous smile, he added, "And still she annoys me."

She swatted him again. He feigned fear, chuckling.

"Your grandfather told me he wanted to send his wife some perfume or chocolate or silk stockings from Paris, but these were impossible to find at the end of the war. So instead he bought the face of *L'Inconnue*. I packed it and mailed it to Louisiana. Tell me, did it arrive safely? I have always wondered."

"Yes," Claire lied without compunction. "Yes, she did. She's beautiful."

"*Papa*," said Michèle in a loud voice. "Claire was wondering if you had any idea who the young model was? For *L'Inconnue*?"

He considered, but shook his head. "I was in love with her, though, I can tell you that. Right up until I fell in love with my Delphine. They are the only two women I have ever loved."

Delphine scoffed but again smiled lovingly at her husband.

"One time," said Pierre-Guillaume, "I asked Monsieur Jean-Baptiste Lombardi, my master's father, about *L'Inconnue*."

"You did?" Claire said, on high alert. "Wasn't Jean-Baptiste the one who made her death mask?"

"*Exactement*." He nodded. "He was master of the *moulage* back in that time, at the turn of the twentieth century, the Belle Epoque. When the woman was brought to the morgue, the worker there—his name was Olivier Delen, so you see, Michèle, I still have my memory!—he was a friend of Jean-Baptiste's. Later, Olivier came and worked in the *moulage*, when Jean-Baptiste moved part-time to the countryside."

"Did Jean-Baptiste tell you anything else about her?"

"Olivier sent for him, asked Jean-Baptiste to make her mask because she was so very beautiful. Jean-Baptiste said he thought he'd met her once—perhaps he ran into her at the market. He thought she had been an artist's model, he said. Or maybe it was because she was so lovely she *should* have been a model."

"Nothing more? He didn't know anything about how she died, or her name?"

He shook his head, coughed slightly. "He said only that it was a shame she had to die so young."

44

That night Claire borrowed a flashlight from the kitchen and ventured outside and up the hill, across the vineyards, and beyond the trees to the château.

Michèle had assured her they had no problem with squatters; Loic made regular visits to check in on the place. She had, however, warned her that the building was in disrepair and it could be dangerous to walk around.

That was what the flashlight was for. Claire would be careful. Still, the moon was nearly full, so she had no need of the lamp while she walked the path up the hill. Crickets chirped, an owl hooted, and she heard the occasional rustling of an animal in the brush. Otherwise the night was silent, tranquil. The warm evening breeze carried the aroma of dried grasses and herbs crushed underfoot.

The exterior of the château was magnificent.

Gilded with a shimmering silver moonlight, the massive facade seemed like something out of Disneyland, or a dream. As she approached, she noted faces carved over the gothic arch of the front door: seven cherubs. Old stones created thick, fat walls.

The door at the main entrance stood wide open; weeds poking up from between the stones of the threshold indicated it had been that way for a while.

She stepped inside. Claire had always been fascinated by abandoned buildings, though she couldn't put her finger on why exactly. She enjoyed imagining the lives that had been lived here, the souls who had passed through the doors and down the hallways.

How many times had children run up and down stairs, shouting for someone to watch them? How many couples had fallen in love, out of love, gotten married within these walls? Who had moved into this building with a thrill of pride, vowing to die here? Which artisans had brought their skills and talents to the creation of these carvings and moldings? Who or what had stood guard outside, protecting all within from the outside world?

Claire passed the flashlight beam around the entry hall. Straight ahead was a grand stairway with a decorative balustrade; she recognized it from Armand's model. The symmetrical building had one broad corridor leading off to the right, another to the left, leading to opposite wings. The floor of the entry was stone, but it was littered with leaves and dirt, a few bricks here and there. A massive fireplace with a carved lintel that had once warmed visitors now held only twigs and straw; Claire imagined a bird had built a nest in its chimney. One door off the entry was open to reveal shredded curtains hanging at tall windows, whose panes were broken.

Aristocrats had lived here long ago, with their servants and kitchen staff. Standing in this great hall, she found it easy to imagine the excitement and threat of the French Revolution. The Lombardis, who held on to the château tooth and nail, finally ceding to the German occupiers.

If she held very still, would Claire hear the boots of Nazi invaders stomping upon these stairs, these stone floors?

She turned right and made her way carefully down the corridor, peeking into chambers as she went. One held something that looked like smashed old-fashioncd radio equipment on an ancient desk. Another must have been a parlor, with an old red velvet chair, the stuffing spewing out, sitting in front of another broken window.

Continuing down the hall, Claire stopped cold when she saw a golden glow spilling from a doorway into the corridor.

A ghost?

She hesitatcd, trying to decide between fleeing or saying hello.

A man stepped out into the hallway.

She was so frightened, she dropped her flashlight. It clattered on the stone floor, the beam dying.

Her heart leapt to her throat. This had been a supremely stupid idea. What did she think— that because she was in an almost mythically beautiful countryside there was no danger in sneaking around abandoned ruins all alone at night?

"What do you want, Claire?"

"Armand?" Now her heart pounded even more, for other reasons.

They stood for a long moment staring at each other, bathed in the silver light of the moon sifting in through broken windows and holes in the roof. There, in that ruined mansion, sad and crumbling, but no less beautiful for its decay and devastation.

"What are you doing here?" he asked.

"I—uh . . ." She shook her head, shrugged. "I was in the market for a country house, and thought this place might be for sale . . ."

He didn't respond.

Claire cleared her throat. "I gotta say, though, I'm a little worried about the plumbing situation."

"Why do you follow me around incessantly, asking questions, making your jokes, Claire? *Why?*"

"I—I'm sorry, Armand. Truly. I didn't mean to intrude on your privacy. I just saw the light and wondered . . . I apologize. I thought it—" She let out a soft laugh. "Giselle's children insisted there was a ghost, and I suppose I let my imagination run away with me."

"So you came here alone at night because you thought there was a ghost?"

"I never was one for common sense."

He shook his head, let out an exasperated chuckle.

Claire hesitated, overwhelmed with unspoken questions.

Claire wanted to ask Armand why he had allowed the betrayal of his wife to destroy him. Why he was camped out here in this ruin when a beautiful stone house full of family and food and love was right down the hill. Why he could not see all that he had—talent, a successful business, a beautiful tradition, a loving family— and choose to move on, to be happy. But none of it was her business, just as it had been none of her affair when she discovered his dollhouse. The man kept his secrets wrapped around him like a cloak, protecting the pain within; that was his right. It didn't matter what she wanted.

"Anyway," she finally said, "I'll just be going now and leave you to your château. *Bonne soirée*, Armand."

She turned to leave.

Armand placed a strong hand on her shoulder. Gently, he spun her around to face him.

In the silvery light his expression was desperate, searching. The strange planes of his face seemed to coalesce into a mask of need and desire and fear and doubt. And hope.

When he spoke, his voice was low, husky:

"Tell me what you want, Claire Broussard."

"What I really want?"

He nodded.

"This."

She stepped into the circle of his arms and lifted her face to his.

Armand pulled back, frowning. His blue eyes searched her features. Around them, the house shifted and moaned, an ancient well of echoes and dreams.

His mouth came down on hers.

Hours passed, and still they held each other.

Armand had made a little fort in a former sitting

room. He had gathered leaves and moss to make a mattress, topping it with several layers of soft flannel sleeping bags. A few candles sat on a stone hearth, lending the space a golden glow. A stack of old books acted as a bedside table and was topped by a novel he was reading, a small glass, and a bottle of wine. A basket held bread and cheese and fruit.

Overhead the stars twinkled through a hole in the roof, reminding Claire of the little lights in the courtyard of the Moulage Lombardi in Paris. Through an arched window made of gray stones Claire could see the lights from the big farmhouse down the hill. She imagined the aunts and the children sleeping there, tucked in and well fed and safe.

Armand's arms spooned her from behind. Claire could feel his breath on the back of her neck. She was loath to speak, afraid to break the spell.

But finally she whispered, "How long were you planning on staying up here?"

"I was going to go down tomorrow," Armand said. "I just enjoy having a night or two here on my own before facing the crowds."

"It is quite a group down there."

"I love them. It's just . . . a little overwhelming sometimes."

They fell silent. His scent enveloped her, mingling with the aroma of leaves and dampness and the slight smell of must from the old books.

Somewhere far away a dog barked. The summer night was cool but Armand was warm, the sleeping bag soft, here in this ruined mansion. They were two grown-ups playing in their playhouse.

"I dreamed of renovating this château for my daughter," said Armand, his words slightly muffled by her hair.

She stilled. "Daughter?"

"Her name was Léonor. She was my light."

Was.

"She and I would roam through this place," he continued. "Reimagining it. Looking up old papers, putting it back together. We started to build a little plaster model of the place together. She had a very good eye."

After a long pause, Claire felt him move away from her. She rolled over to find him on his back, looking up at the sky through the hole in the roof, unblinking.

"She was only eight, but she showed great talent for one so young. I took her to work with me; she practically grew up in the studio. I imagined training her, leaving the business to her. She was to be the first *mademoiselle* to be mistress of the shop." He cleared his throat. "She was very funny, a little goofy. Smart. She liked to tell stories. Like you.

"We were driving back from Paris. Taking the back roads, making a day of it. She loved getting off the autoroute, checking out all the castles and châteaux along the way, comparing them to ours.

"It was a drunk driver. I didn't even see him coming. I woke up in the hospital."

Claire held her breath. The silence went on for so long, she thought perhaps Armand had fallen asleep. But then she saw the glistening of tears in the moonlight.

She reached out and placed her hand very gently on his chest. Over his heart.

"They say she didn't suffer. That it was instantaneous."

Claire scooted closer, laid her cheek against his shoulder, molding her hip and thigh to his. There were no words.

After a very long moment, he whispered: "I wonder if they always say that."

45

PIERRE-GUILLAUME

Present day

Pierre-Guillaume's heart broke for his grandson.

He saw Armand sometimes. When he was "disappeared," when no one knew where he was. Pierre-Guillaume knew he was up in the ruins of the old château, with a flashlight or candles in hand to light his way. The way he used to explore with Léonor. When they would bend their dark heads together, their hair mingling so it was impossible to know where one ended and the other began, plotting about how to bring the building back from the brink, how to rid it of its Nazi ghosts.

But Armand was not haunted by spirits from World War II. It was the specter of his daughter that would not leave him. Or perhaps *he* would not leave *her,* would not allow her to pass on.

No one could get through to him, not his mother, not his aunties. Not his beloved grandfather Pierre-Guillaume.

Perhaps this American woman would. Could.

The aunts were hopeful, but afraid. Afraid that if Armand fell in love with a foreigner he would be even more lost to them than he was already. But Pierre-Guillaume did not worry. They called him old-fashioned, but he knew this truth: the right woman could open the heart of a man like the finest corkscrew opening a bottle of wine, allowing the goodness out to be savored and enjoyed. If the wine stays too long in the bottle, it will sour, go cloudy, lose its fruit.

And Pierre-Guillaume believed in signs. The moment that soldier showed up on his doorstep and spoke his prophetic words about Delphine, he knew the American soldier would be important in his life.

And when Pierre-Guillaume packed the face of *L'Inconnue* for him, tucking her in as best he could, he imagined her winging her way to some far-off place in America and somehow tying them all together. One person's life overlapping with another's in an endless web of humanity.

The war was over, and Pierre-Guillaume had had faith that France would rise from the ashes, like a phoenix. It was an optimistic outlook that would never leave him: he had married his beloved, raised many children, and they in turn had raised their own sons and daughters. After working for years in the *moulage* under Marc-Antoine Lombardi, Pierre-Guillaume himself had taken over, and then his own son, Loic, had become master, and now his grandson, Armand. It was all as it was meant to be.

Only the tragedy of Léonor hung over the family, a shadow of pain and loss and sorrow.

But Pierre-Guillaume had watched his father die, his brother, his mother, and from that he learned this lesson: Life—and death—could be harsh, devastating. But if you hung on long enough, the bitter would turn to sweet. If you hung on long enough, you might be granted a Delphine, children, a life.

Armand had to hang on just a little bit longer. He was a good boy; he listened more than most. But the old people's insistence on recounting the family tree was tedious, he knew. Whenever they tried to tell the stories of the war, the young people would grow bored, say, *Toi et ta guerre.* You and your war. Perhaps it was because he had lost his parents so early that Pierre-Guillaume had enjoyed listening to his elders when he was young.

Marc-Antoine's father, Jean-Baptiste, had gone to visit Paris from time to time. He would recount stories about the Belle Epoque, the gilded age when Paris was home to some of the world's greatest artists and writers and poets. The teenage Pierre-Guillaume had hung on every word the old man said. Fascinated to hear how Paris had been, to dream of how it could be again.

Pierre-Guillaume had listened to the stories, imagining the young woman of the mask when she walked the streets of Paris. Perhaps she had been an artist's model, Jean-Baptiste Lombardi had said. Perhaps Jean-Baptiste Lombardi himself had met her in the old marketplace.

Sometimes Pierre-Guillaume thought he caught a glimpse of *L'Inconnue*'s smile in Delphine's own sweet countenance. But then he supposed every man felt this way when smiled at by the woman he loved. Had *L'Inconnue* been smiling for the man she had loved in the moment of her death?

For now, Pierre-Guillaume would leave such mysteries to the world. His sight was worsening, his hearing, his memory. Soon he himself would fade into the earth, leaving nothing behind but

385

his own death mask, if he asked his grandson to cast one of him, to place in the collection of family masks. But perhaps it was best to move on without leaving a trace. Centuries from now, who would even know? He would be an unknown face, as *inconnu* as *L'Inconnue* herself.

And perhaps that was for the best.

46

A great deal was made over Armand's arrival at the house the next day. He was a clear favorite of the aunts—and his mother, of course—and spent much of the day talking and teasing and helping to cook a four-course lunch featuring a regional specialty called *tartiflette*, made of bacon, potatoes, and Reblochon cheese.

"It's very rich," Armand explained after lunch as they were cleaning the kitchen. "More appropriate for the winter months, but it's my mother's favorite, so I have to make it every time I visit."

"She adores you," said Claire.

"I'm fortunate to have both my parents."

"And they're fortunate to have you."

Their gazes met and held for a moment. Though the kitchen was bustling, it felt like just the two of them.

Armand gestured with his head. "Want to get out of here? Take a walk?"

"I'd love to."

They headed down the path through the woods that led to the pond.

Along the way, Armand spotted some twisty orange mushrooms. He took a pocketknife from his jeans and collected a handful.

He held them up to her.

"Smell," he said.

She bent her head and inhaled deeply.

"What do you smell?" he asked, studying her face.

"Earth?"

"Yes." He smiled. It was a genuine smile that reached to his eyes, full of excitement like a little boy.

I want to make him smile like that, Claire thought. *Every day.*

He held the mushrooms up to his own nose and breathed. "I love that smell. They can grow overnight—did you know that? Once they find the right conditions—rot and moisture and the spores, of course—they can appear in no time. You come out one day and there's nothing, and the next you discover a bounty. As though the gods themselves reached down and scattered little gifts of gold out here for us poor mortals."

"Aren't you afraid they're poisonous?"

He shook his head. "Chanterelles are so distinct from other mushrooms, you see? There are a lot of other edible mushrooms in these woods, but since I'm not an expert I only go for the obvious ones. My grandfather taught me."

"Pierre-Guillaume?"

Armand nodded. "He lived in the countryside during the war. Like a lot of people, they came close to starving during the Nazi occupation. He learned how to scavenge for food: dandelion leaves and roots, wild birds' eggs, mushrooms. Even today, the man can't take a walk without bringing back a pack of foraged items for dinner." He chuckled. "It drives my grandmother crazy."

He reached out for her hand. His palm, typically caked with plaster dust, was now streaked with mud from the chanterelles.

Claire clasped his hand. He squeezed gently, gazed down at her for a moment, then looked back out to the woods.

"Your grandmother Delphine grew up in the studio, at the Moulage Lombardi in Paris?" Claire asked.

He nodded. "That's how they met. Pierre-Guillaume started working there as an apprentice when he was a teenager—just a boy, really."

"He says he remembers selling the mask of *L'Inconnue* to my great-grandfather and shipping it to Louisiana."

Armand gave her a dubious look. "I'm sorry to say my grandfather is losing it a little. His memories are fuzzy."

"Maybe," Claire said with a smile. "But I like

the idea that he would remember such a thing. And if he's anything like a lot of older folks, he might be fuzzy on the here and now but remember the past with great clarity. The human mind is truly amazing."

"*You* are truly amazing."

He pulled her to him. The kiss started out gentle but deepened, reminding them both of lying in each other's arms the night before.

They continued on to the pond. As they drew near, they heard a series of splashes: *plink, plink, plink.*

"Frogs," Armand says. "They leap in whenever you come near. In the spring we can gather them and have frogs' legs. My mother prepares them very well."

"They eat frogs' legs where I'm from too. But I don't know if I could do it. I like frogs."

"You eat beef. Don't you like cows?"

"Yes, but frogs are a lot cuter than cows."

He pulled her toward the water, but she hung back.

"How can a woman such as you be afraid of the water?"

"What do you mean, 'such as me'?"

"You don't seem to fear anything."

She laughed out loud. "That's not exactly true."

"You arrived alone in Paris and moved in with a strange man."

"It's true—you really are strange."

"And then you confronted me there in the dark in the ruins."

"I thought you were a ghost."

"That's my point. What were you doing, chasing ghosts through the ruins?"

She shrugged. "I couldn't resist."

"But my point is, how are you afraid of water, of all things?"

Claire hesitated. She had never talked about what had happened with her father; Mammaw knew, of course, but they seemed to have made an unspoken pact of secrecy. There was family gossip, but no one else knew the whole story. Even now, Claire's first thought was to make something up, fabricating a tale about a water-skiing accident, perhaps, or something funny involving an inflatable raft.

But Armand had shared his anguish with her. It was only right she do the same.

"I almost drowned once. When I was six, I think. Maybe younger. My father threw me in the ocean, but I didn't know how to swim."

"He threw you in?"

"He's an alcoholic. He was drunk."

"Did he at least go in after you?"

She shook her head. "A teenager on the beach was training to be a lifeguard. So I guess I was good practice for him. When the police arrived, my father said he was just giving me 'swimming lessons.'"

Armand cupped her face in his hands, looked into her eyes. "I'm so very sorry, Claire."

She tried to laugh it off. Usually she was good at this: transforming painful stories into funny anecdotes, shrugging off the implications. But this time she couldn't. In this moment, she felt compelled to tell Armand the truth. The raw, miserable truth.

"Sometimes I wonder—" She cut herself off.

"What? Tell me, Claire."

Finally she blurted out the words and thoughts she had barely let herself entertain in her conscious mind. The fear she'd carried with her since it happened, when Jessica used to taunt her as a child, and all through school; the burden she'd carried with her to Chicago, and now to Paris. The dread so heavy it threatened to drown her.

"I wonder if . . . maybe my mother's car accident was no accident. Maybe she wanted to kill herself, and tried to take me with her."

Armand wrapped his arms around her, and they stood on the side of that pond for a very long time. Birds chirped, the sun glinted off the water, and a bee buzzed by.

"Which would mean," Claire continued, her head resting on his chest, "that *both* my parents tried to kill me: my father by throwing me in the ocean, my mother by driving me into the bayou."

"I'm beginning to understand why you're so afraid of water."

She gave a mirthless laugh. "It reminds me of some story out of Roman mythology about parents intent on killing their child but the child insisting on living anyway. I just . . . I have to wonder sometimes: was I so impossible to love?"

Her voice broke on the last word.

"No, Claire. *No*." Armand held her out in front of him, looking her straight in the eyes. "Listen to me: You were a *child*. Every child is worthy of love. If your parents were cruel or unbalanced, it had nothing to do with you. *Nothing*. It wasn't your responsibility; you were an innocent child."

She nodded and again rested her head on his chest. Claire knew his words were true. She had learned this in college, from books she had read and friends she had opened up to over the years: it was not her fault that her father was an alcoholic, much less that her mother drove into a bayou. Not her responsibility.

And yet.

Armand brushed a lock of hair out of her eyes and gave her a sad smile. "The problem, for me at least, is that you are so very *easy* to love. Hey—" He changed the subject. "Would you like a tour of the château in the daylight?"

"That would be great," she managed, her mind reeling. Had he just said what she thought he said? Had Armand just said that he loved her?

She thought of the grumpy mold-maker smiling

like a little boy over his mushrooms. Talk about easy to love.

Claire couldn't stop casting glances in his direction as they made their way to the château. Unfortunately, as Michèle had pointed out, the once-grand manor really did look worse up close in the light.

Dirt, straw, and leaves had collected in all the corners and vines grew through broken windows. A few newspapers and old chip bags or sandwich wrappings littered the floors; names and swear-words had been etched here and there in the old plaster; a spray-painted smiley face marred one mirrored parlor wall. There were scattered piles of bricks and old lumber, and the occasional incongruous upholstered chair or grand piano sitting in an otherwise empty room.

Some areas were miraculously unaffected—the grand stairway was splendid, undamaged other than a few leaves in the corners—but other rooms had been savaged by the combined forces of weather and neglect, water damage and insects and animals and vandalism.

Still, carved friezes retained their elegance, showcasing high, ornate ceilings edged in gilt moldings; some were painted with blue sky and cherubs. Massive limestone and brick fireplaces dominated most rooms. Arched doors were made of heavy, carved wood that still gleamed. Tile floors underfoot had withstood the years and still boasted mellow tones of ocher, earth red, and sage green, but several of the inlaid wooden floors had buckled and rotted clear through in some areas.

"I know, I know," Armand said as they stepped gingerly over fallen beams and pushed past vines. "It's quite a project. I think Léonor was the only one who didn't think I was crazy to want to bring it back from the brink."

"It's beautiful," Claire said, but she feared this château might already have fallen clear *over* the brink. She knew nothing about construction prices in France, but given the sheer size of this place she would guess it would cost millions to put right. "In a way, it's really quite lovely just the way it is."

"Here's what I wanted to show you," he said, leading her to a double door off the main hallway. He took an old skeleton key from his pocket and opened it.

This room was virtually untouched; an intact roof had protected the inlaid floors and built-in bookshelves, and the windowpanes were unbroken. It was empty of furniture but the shelves were full of old leather books. What most intrigued Claire, however, was one wall decorated with a series of white masks, reminding her of the Paris studio.

"They're masks of the family," said Armand.

"The family?"

"For generations the Lombardi family has made death masks of famous people, but also of each other. My father stopped the tradition; he thinks it is *larmoyant*." Claire translated that as "maudlin," more or less. "So if my grandparents want their masks made, I suppose I will be the one to do it."

"Would you be willing to?"

"Of course." He smiled down at her. "I don't find it *larmoyant*, personally. There's something very intimate about it. It's a way to honor those who have passed."

Claire walked along the wall, studying face after face, each with its eyes closed, as though sleeping. Some displayed a certain family resemblance; they had wrinkles or scars, the signs of long lives. There were a few gaps where masks appeared to be missing.

And then she spotted *L'Inconnue*'s sweet face.

"So you see," said Armand, "you are not the only one obsessed with this young woman. She has hung here as long as I can remember."

"Do you know who every face is?"

"Most of them. In this row are all the masters of the studio: this was Giuseppe Lombardi, the ancestor who came from Italy to establish the Moulage Lombardi, and his wife, Maria. And this was their son Jean-Baptiste—with a rather dramatic scar, as you can see. Here is his son Marc-Antoine with his wife, Anne-Lucille. They were my great-grandparents; Delphine was their daughter. As I said, we will see if Pierre-Guillaume and Delphine wish to be added to their ranks."

"What about Jean-Baptiste's wife?"

He shrugged. "Unfortunately, some of the masks were smashed when the Germans were here. We have all the molds in storage at the studio; I always intended to sort through them, to make new castings to replace the missing ones."

Armand pointed out several of the other faces—a favorite great-aunt, a beloved cousin—but these family members were not directly involved with the *moulage*.

But Claire's attention kept drifting back to *L'Inconnue*.

"Why would *L'Inconnue* be hanging here, if all the others were family?"

He shrugged again. "As I said, she hung on virtually every artist's wall back in the day. I'm sure they thought she was fashionable—and beautiful, of course. And she's always been a top seller after all. Come, I have something else to show you."

"Something *else?* You are full of surprises, Armand Lombardi Fontaine."

"You have no idea," he said with a wink.

He closed and locked the door behind them.

"I'm surprised no one's gotten into that room," Claire said.

"I suppose someone could if they tried hard enough. But there's so much else that's open and easily accessible, it hasn't been a problem so far. My father keeps an eye on the place; we don't get many tourists in this area, so it's mostly just locals who know about it. Other than a few teenagers, there hasn't been much of a problem."

Armand led the way out of the building through a back door. The gardens showed vestiges of a formal design: low stone walls, box hedges gone wild, and old fountains filled with brackish water. Armand directed Claire toward an out-building that looked like an old stable.

"According to family lore, my great-great-grandfather Jean-Baptiste Lombardi had this stable redone as an art studio when he moved out to the countryside."

"He wanted to be an artist?"

"Actually, it was his wife who was the gifted artist. The charcoal sketch I hung in your little room in Paris was one of hers. It was of Jean-Baptiste working, as a matter of fact."

"It was lovely. She had a wonderful eye for expression. What was her name?"

"Mélusine."

"Like the mermaid?"

He gave her a quizzical look.

"Mélusine is a sort of half-fish, half-woman creature who lives in rivers and streams," she explained. "You have one on the family crest."

"I guess I'm not up on my folklore," Armand said. "And I think you notice more about my family than I do at times."

"There was something about her in the box of scraps about *L'Inconnue*—Ödön von something or other suggested *L'Inconnue* became a mermaid."

"I suppose that's nicer than her simply drowning. Anyway, I never knew them, of course—Jean-Baptiste and Mélusine passed away long before I was born—but I always had the sense that Mélusine was the one who loved it here; Jean-Baptiste used to go back and forth, dividing his time between Paris and the countryside."

"I noticed that on the plaque at the studio," Claire said. "It had Jean-Baptiste's name as master, but another man was in parentheses."

"Olivier Delen," Armand said with a nod. "He was a good friend, apparently, and took over much of the day-to-day operations when Jean-Baptiste spent time here."

"How shocking, to have someone in charge who wasn't a member of the family," she teased.

"I suppose Jean-Baptiste was a radical thinker," Armand said, opening the studio door. "And he was waiting for his eldest, Marc-Antoine, to take the reins."

Claire entered. Light streamed in through skylights and big windows; the wooden walls were rustic but inviting. There was a mound of plastic-covered clay on a worktable, and several small maquettes and studies in wire and rebar. A few small blocks of marble and limestone stood along the wall, and hammers and chisels and other tools were laid out neatly on a shelf.

"I didn't know you sculpted." Claire whirled

around to face him. "You were quite cagey about it when I asked you about it at the studio in Paris."

"I don't do it seriously. Just for fun. I enjoy getting my hands dirty, and I believe I did emphasize how important it is for a mold-maker to understand sculpting."

"True, you did at that. How fun," she said, pausing by the worktable. Claire clasped her hands behind her back, as though afraid to touch.

"Feel free," he said, gesturing toward the moist clay.

"I don't really know anything about sculpting . . ."

"What about those salmon croquettes you were going on about?"

She laughed. "I had a fair hand with sand castles when I was a girl too, but somehow I don't think it's the same."

"I've seen the way you run your hands along the sculptures at the studio. I think you might have more inclination for this than you think." He removed the plastic and twisted a hunk of clay off of the main piece, then held it out to her. "Just take some clay in your hands, get a feel for it."

She squeezed it in the palm of her hand.

"Sculpture is an art," said Armand. "And like any art it's much more about passion than technique. Skills can be learned, practiced, honed, but passion is innate. It can't be taught."

"You're saying I have the passion to sculpt?"

"You tell me."

Claire was enjoying the sensation of clay in her hand. "Do you have any finished pieces I could see?"

He snorted. "When it comes to sculpture, I fear I am all good intentions but haven't had the time to do more than these small maquettes— just ideas I've had in passing. Usually I work in the studio in Paris, which as you know is about making copies, not originals."

"And yet that is very worthy work, according to what I've been told."

"That's true," Armand said. "And don't forget it. But one of the interesting things to me about sculpture is that there are two main methods, and in some ways they are diametrically opposed: With clay you add pieces, little by little, building up. With stone you subtract, chipping away little by little, to find the shape within."

"I never thought of it that way."

Claire was suddenly itching to make something. Anything. Thinking of the little animals her mother had made, she started rolling little balls and sticking them together. They didn't quite look like what she remembered, but she enjoyed them nonetheless. Claire picked up a sharp tool that looked like a fingernail pick and made tiny eyes, little smiling mouths.

She looked up to find Armand watching her.

"My mother was a frustrated sculptor, according to my family's stories," said Claire with a shrug. "As I told you, I have no actual memory of her, but she had made some little clay animals for me. They looked a little like this. Sort of. If you squint. Actually, now that I look at them . . ." She squished her little creations. "Hers had a lot more style."

"I liked yours," he said quietly, staring at her with a slight frown.

"What is it?"

"Nothing," he said with a quick shake of his head. "Anyway, they're not bad at all for some-one who has no experience with clay. You seem to enjoy the feel in your hands—you should let yourself play with it."

As she rolled and squished the clay, Armand pushed her hair back.

"Your ear is very unusual," he said. "I noticed it that first day. It is like a seashell, the way it folds like that . . ."

He kissed her earlobe, sending a shiver skittering down her spine.

"I've never in my life thought about the shape of my ears," said Claire with a breathy laugh.

"It is for me to consider, not you," he said with a small smile.

They shared a kiss, and then he grabbed a hunk of clay and they stood side by side shaping and creating, then squishing their creations and starting over. The feeling was meditative, peaceful, almost hypnotic.

Claire found herself telling Armand more about what had happened with her father: Before the "swimming lesson," how she would hide from him behind the couch, her mother's animals in her hands. How they seemed to come alive for her. Her fear in the water, the panic, the pain. How happy she was to go live with Mammaw and Remy but also how she was plagued by guilt, because her father had no one to take care of him. How even now she heard from Papa Broussard only when he needed money.

And she told him that she had spoken to the face of *L'Inconnue* day after day, month after month, up in Mammaw's stifling attic. Confided her fears, her dreams. How she had worked to get out of her hometown but could never quite release the sense of nostalgia, the strange homesickness she felt when she left, and how France seemed somehow familiar, like home, even though it was a foreign country.

And Armand told Claire about waking up in the hospital, no longer a father. How he knew he was in a nightmare, that no just god would have spared his life while taking that of his daughter. How he had begged to trade places with her. How he had raged at the fates and at himself.

He tried to remember the accident. Could he have swerved to avoid the silver Audi? Had a split second of inattention meant that he had missed his chance, that he had failed to keep his Léonor safe? What if they had stopped to visit that last castle? If they had taken one more bathroom break, or if they had taken the train like his wife, Odile, had asked him to?

The moment Odile had arrived at the hospital, anger and rage and wrenching sorrow in her eyes. Unspoken accusation shimmering off of her.

Odile claimed it wasn't true, that she didn't blame Armand. She said she knew it wasn't his fault. But as the days turned to weeks, to months, she kept asking: *Why didn't you take the train like I asked you to? Why?* Why?

Armand abruptly stopped speaking and smashed the clay figure he'd been working on.

"There is no reason," was all Claire could say. It was the best she could do. "Sometimes, there is no reason."

47

SABINE

Maurice sends his sister, Isabelle, to accompany Sabine to the studio of the mold-maker. Isabelle is taciturn and quiet, as is her wont. She brings a book, a serial novel she has checked out from the circulating library. It is a gothic tale of spurned love.

Sabine has the urge to make fun of the story, which she tried to read but found overwrought and melodramatic. But she holds herself back. Isabelle has no sense of humor and would feel attacked; she is such a quiet, stern thing like a worried little bird, it would be like pulling the feathers off a tiny wren.

Still, when Isabelle tells her about the story, it makes her laugh—it is so absurd.

But as soon as Sabine remembers where they are going, she stops laughing. The way Monsieur Lombardi looks at her is frightening. Not in the same way that Maurice scares her; this is deeper, in many ways more disturbing, because it is also alluring. Are the light blue pools of his eyes her salvation, or will she drown in their depths?

"No man will be your salvation, Sabine," Mademoiselle Claudel told her last time they spoke. "You must unlearn that."

"*Unlearn?* Is that a word?"

"Save yourself—that's my point. Do not trust a man to do it for you."

Sabine believes Camille; she knows that men have brought her only misery. Everyone except the horse trainer, but then he abandoned her too.

Still, though Sabine understands Camille's words, she has no idea how to accomplish this: Save herself? How could she do such a thing?

The studio of the Moulage Lombardi is on rue de la Huchette, in the Quartier Latin, on the other side of the Cathédrale de Notre Dame. They go up a flight of narrow stairs and arrive in a cramped space, everything unified with a coat of plaster dust. Not like the artists' lofts she has been in, the ones that smell of linseed oil and turpentine, clay and stone. The *moulage* smells only of plaster; buckets of milky water abound.

And Jean-Baptiste Lombardi, standing there in a coat to greet them, covered in dust, so he looks almost like a statue himself come to life.

But those eyes are very much alive. Very human.

By now she is used to dropping her clothes in front of artists, but because this is Monsieur Lombardi, she blushes at the thought as she moves toward the screen to disrobe.

"Stop." His hand settles atop hers at the button at her throat. "I . . . will sculpt you just as you are."

The heat of his gaze. The unspoken understanding, as though he knows who she is. As though he truly sees her.

Isabelle sits on a chair in the corner and reads.

Jean-Baptiste leads Sabine to a chair, asks her to make herself comfortable.

He goes to stand behind a worktable, atop which is a lump of fresh clay. He starts to work it, looking at her the whole time.

After a very long time, he still has nothing resembling anything lifelike. The clay remains a

405

misshapen lump at the table. Still, he studies her, plays with the clay. But it is clear he has no talent. None at all. Sabine can see this; she has spent the past many months with artists of all kinds. She knows when someone has an eye.

She starts to get nervous. If Isabelle notices, will she report to her brother that Monsieur Lombardi did nothing but stare at Sabine for the entire session?

"I have changed my mind," Monsieur Lombardi says. "Would you permit me to make molds of your hands?"

"Molds?"

"I am much better at making molds than sculpting, I fear."

Sabine glances at Isabelle, but she is absorbed in her story. "Of course, monsieur. As you like."

He prepares the plaster, then applies grease to her skin.

"This is so it will lift off properly," he says in a quiet voice.

Every stroke of his fingers is a caress. Sabine used to feel embarrassed about the roughness of her hands. Maurice had made fun, but then he brought her a salve, and now that all she had to do was stand still as a *modèle de profession*, they had softened. She is glad now. Happy that they are soft for Jean-Baptiste, that she can feel every tingle of sensation as he touches her skin.

Sabine feels hot, flushed, and again thanks the

heavens that Isabelle is not paying attention and, even if she did, that she is obtuse when it comes to personal interactions.

Monsieur Lombardi dips strips of gauze into the wet plaster and lays them on her skin. "You will have to stay as still as you can for half an hour or more. Tell me if the plaster starts to feel very warm, will you? I am usually good at timing, but I wouldn't want to burn you."

"*Oui, monsieur.*"

"We will do the top of the hand first, then the palm. Later I will join the two halves; this is the true skill of the mold-maker."

"What will you use the molds for, monsieur?"

"Life casts are considered essential to art schools, and occasionally to medical schools. Your hands and feet are delicate, mademoiselle, and well proportioned. Hands are the most difficult for an artist to depict, did you know? It is so difficult to follow each crease, each indentation, the scale and taper of the fingers, the raised veins, the lifelines."

"What about feet?"

"They can be depicted wearing shoes. Easy solution." He smiles. "No, it is the hands that are testament to a real artist."

"And faces?"

He inclines his head. "Those, too, of course. Would you like me to make a life cast of your face?"

"How would you cast a face without smothering the person?"

"Very carefully," he says with a wink.

When the plaster has set, he frees her and holds her hand in his for a long moment, ostensibly cleaning off the grease and small bits of plaster. When he places his palm against hers, it tingles.

Her eyes fly to his. They both feel it.

"What are you doing there?" demands Isabelle from the corner.

"My grandmother learned to read palms from a Gypsy queen," says Monsieur Lombardi without missing a beat. "Or at least, that is what she claimed, perhaps it was simply a tale to excite her grandchildren." He traces a finger along Sabine's lifeline. The shiver shoots straight to her belly. "This means you will have many children, and live a long life."

Now Isabelle is interested. She sets her book down and comes to join them in the middle of the room. "Let me see. Where do you see that?"

Monsieur Lombardi smiles, asks if he may see Isabelle's hand. When she holds it out, he traces her lifeline, tells her there is a dark handsome stranger in her future.

She pulls her hand away, frowning. "I think you are inventing things."

He laughs. Never has Sabine heard a man laugh so easily, so frequently.

Is he dangerous? Or genuine? She makes a note

to ask Monsieur Rodin what he thinks of this man. She knows what Mademoiselle Claudel would say: that even though she likes the look in his eye, he is no good, like any man.

Monsieur Lombardi walks them to the top of the steps, thanks them both for coming. He kisses Isabelle's hand, and then he does the same with Sabine. Lingering just slightly too long with his mouth against her freshly washed skin.

Isabelle is blessedly ignorant of what has passed between them. She will report to her brother that all was business, that Monsieur Lombardi is a dedicated artisan interested only in casting and sculpting. Isabelle does not have the imagination to think otherwise.

As Sabine and Isabelle walk back through the busy streets of the Rive Gauche, full of poor students and artists, flower vendors and soup carts, Sabine tries to force her mind from the mold-maker: from his eyes, his hands, his mouth.

She asks Isabelle about the main character in the novel she is reading.

"*Elle s'est noyée*," Isabelle says with a sad shake of her head. "She is drowned."

"Drowned?" Sabine stops walking at the base of the bridge, the Pont Neuf, and stares at her.

"Do you want to read it?" Isabelle asks, holding the book out to her. "I'm done."

"No, thank you." Sabine shakes her head. "I don't like tragic endings. How did she drown?"

"She had no choice," Isabelle says with a shrug. "She was pregnant and spurned by her wealthy lover, who had slain the noble boy she truly loved. She had to kill herself, so she threw herself into the Seine."

"That's horrible," said Sabine. They are on the bridge now, and she looks down into the river's dark waters.

"Sometimes there is no choice," says Isabelle.

"There is always a choice."

"*No.* No, there is not. To drown oneself is sometimes the only noble thing to do." Isabelle gives Sabine a sidelong glance. "The Seine claims hundreds of women every year, did you know? That is why they say: *Ce n'est rien; c'est une femme qui se noie.* It's nothing, just a woman drowning."

Sabine wonders whether Isabelle is implying that this will be Sabine's future as well. That she will share that watery fate—that she *should* drown—and thus leave Maurice to Isabelle. He is the only man Isabelle will ever love, Sabine thinks. That is her tragedy.

"According to Monsieur Lombardi, I will live a long life and have many children," Sabine says, trying to make light of Isabelle's harsh words.

"*Non*," Isabelle says, shaking her dark head. "You will be *une femme noyée.* You will drown. Your kind always does."

48

Dear Uncle Remy,
You'll never guess who's learning to swim!

I am splashing this envelope with a little pond water, but of course it will have dried by the time this reaches you. But perhaps if you lift it to your nose and inhale deeply you will catch a whiff of the pond: it smells of earth and rich green water, with a little fishiness thrown in for good measure.

There are frogs and tiny fishes no bigger than my fingernail. Dragonflies colored with greens and purples, depending on how the light hits them. It is hot and humid here, a lot like home.

And tomorrow will be the grande fête, the party for Delphine and Pierre-Guillaume Fontaine, to celebrate sixty-five years of marriage. My hands smell of lavender from all the sachets I've been making. I am sending you a few blossoms as well.

Invitations to Delphine and Pierre-Guillaume's sixty-fifth-anniversary party had been sent to virtually everyone in town. Preparations began early the morning of the party. The courtyard of the huge stone house was emptied of cars; dozens of tables were set up end to end in long rows, then covered with white tablecloths and sheets. Neighbors lent chairs and plates and silverware for the occasion. The aunts—and Armand—remained in the kitchen, chopping and cooking. The baked goods, fruit tarts, chocolate and emon mousses, and several pâtés and salads had been prepared the day before, but now was the time to make the cassoulets and casseroles and to marinate the meats for grilling.

The young people helped haul cases of wine up from the basement and brought bags of ice from town for sodas and juices. Even the little children helped, scouring the surrounding fields and woods for wildflowers to put into wide-mouthed mason jars they distributed on the tables. The huge iron gates were left open but decorated with garlands of crêpe paper and roses, the gravel was raked, and every windowsill held pots bursting with pink and red geraniums.

Claire was put to work as sous-chef—apparently Armand was satisfied with her chopping skills at this point—and then as chief pot washer. She didn't mind. It was wondrous to be in the middle of the action, to see how the family came together, teasing and laughing and determined to properly fête Grand-père and Grand-mère.

Once the guests arrived and festivities began in

earnest, the wine flowed, speeches were made, the food was savored, the music played, and the afternoon whizzed by.

At one point Claire noticed Pierre-Guillaume resting in the shade. He had been holding court all afternoon and seemed a bit weary, but happy. Delphine, for her part, was indefatigable. She moved through the crowd like a princess entertaining her subjects, regal and smiling.

"She's beautiful," said Claire, going to sit with him under the tree.

"She always has been," said Pierre-Guillaume. "I am a lucky man. You think I don't remember, but I remember your father. He was a sign."

"My great-grandfather, actually. He was a sign of what?"

"He told me I would marry my Delphine. And then *L'Inconnue* brought you to Paris, to my grandson. You see, it is all as it should be."

Claire searched the crowd for Armand. He was leaning against the wall on the other side of the courtyard, smoking a cigarillo. Children and dogs ran past him; old people clucked around him. But his gaze seemed to be for Claire only.

Had he been watching her, or had he somehow felt her gaze upon him, as she so often did when he looked at her? What was this sense of connection she felt with the grumpy sculptor? Was it simply their shared well of sadness and loss? Or something more?

Pierre-Guillaume lifted himself out of his chair with effort, leaning on his cane.

"May I help you?" Claire asked, jumping up to hold his arm.

"I remember when others took my arm for strength. Now I lean on a young woman! *C'est fou.* Aging, it is not pretty. Listen to me, young lady: life goes faster than you think. Savor it."

"*Oui, Grand-père,*" Claire said.

"You are staying in my old room at the studio, the apprentice room?"

"Yes—I mean . . . I was."

Claire wondered what would happen upon their return to Paris. Part of her wished she could be back with Armand in the workshop, pouring and sanding and making dinner, just the two of them. But another part of her wondered whether the magic she felt with him was somehow connected to the château, to the feeling of being somewhere out of time and place.

Pierre-Guillaume smiled. "I know it is not anything for young people today, but after the war that little room was like a haven, a sanctuary. I was so happy and proud to work for the Moulage Lombardi."

"It's very cozy."

"Now that's a good word for it!" He let out a raspy chuckle. *"Cozy."*

"You know, with everything going on, I forgot

until this minute: I found a box there, in your room."

"A box?"

"Behind a loose stone in the wall? I thought perhaps I found your hiding place."

Pierre-Guillaume cast his mind back. The notes he had found, which he'd read to himself like a love story. He nodded. He remembered. "Ah! Yes. Tell me, do you know who they belonged to?"

"No, we didn't open the box. I hope Armand remembered to bring it with him—he wanted to ask you about it. We thought it might be private."

"They are a series of love notes, I believe."

"Love notes? Between whom?"

"I don't know. They were already old when I was young! My master, Delphine's father, Marc-Antoine Lombardi, he said they were old family papers but that they were useless. I was supposed to use them to pack the mask of *L'Inconnue*, but I kept them instead. I tried to pack her carefully. Tell me, did she arrive safely?"

"Yes," Claire said. "She's beautiful."

"I remember that like it was yesterday. Packing her and sending her off to America."

"Would it be all right if Armand and I open that tin box and look inside?"

"*Mais oui*—of course! Bring it to me after the party and we can look together. You are curious, I see. This is good. It is good to be curious."

"You know, there was an odd old note included in the crate with *L'Inconnue*. That's what brought me to Paris: the note and the face together."

"It brought you here, to my grandson?" he said with a nod. "You see, it is as I like to say: it is all connected."

49

SABINE

The next day, another letter arrived from the Left Bank.

Thank you, was all it said.

Thank you for what? Sabine wrote at the bottom of the page and sent it back.

It returned: *For sharing a glimpse of the beauty of your soul.*

Fear washed over Sabine.

She sent the note back without answering.

50

Claire helped Pierre-Guillaume to a more comfortable chair and then sought out Armand, still leaning against the wall. He put his arms around her from behind and she leaned back against him, looking out over the festive court-yard. Loic had brought out an accordion; another uncle was strumming the guitar.

Armand smelled of tobacco.

"I thought you didn't approve of smoking," said Claire.

"These are not cigarettes. They are cigarillos. It is different."

"If you say so," she said with a smile. "Hey, I nearly forgot: did you bring the box I found in the apprentice's room?"

"I did, yes. It's with my things."

"I asked Pierre-Guillaume about it, and he says inside there's a series of love notes, but they don't belong to him. Maybe they're like the note that brought me to you."

"You've been listening to old men."

"I happen to like old men. I hang around you, don't I?"

"I'm not that old."

"You *act* old," she teased. "Or at least you did until you met *me*."

He smiled down at her, kissed her.

"Anyway, let's show him that box. I'd love to hear his stories of the old days."

Armand went to get it, and as the party wound down he and Claire brought the box to Pierre-Guillaume and helped him to pry off the rusted metal top.

Inside was a cache of notes, folded once, on thick linen paper.

"Yes, you see, I even numbered them," Pierre-Guillaume said, nodding as he started to paw through the slips. Numbers had been written at the top in pencil. "I remember now. I was trying to figure out the order. And this is what I came up with."

Each note had two different scripts on it, as though one was answering the other.

#1
Will you come sit for me?
You must ask Maurice.

#2
Thank you.
Thank you for what?
For sharing a glimpse of the beauty of your soul.

#3
I can't stop thinking about you. Please say you'll meet me.
I must go to the market in the morning.
I will find you.

#4
You are like the moon. You glow brilliantly, then disappear, then return to light up the dark sky once again. The tide of my soul rises to meet you and ebbs when you are far away. You are my moon.

#5

It pains me when you send my notes back without a response. But I understand. Still, I want you to know I will never give up. We will find a way.

All I can think of is you. You crowd my thoughts. It frightens me.

When can I see you next?

Tomorrow I will buy bread at the boulangerie at nine. I will try to go without my shadow, but if I am not alone you must not approach.

#6

I am sending this note with a kiss. Can you feel it?

I feel your kisses every moment of every day, and in my dreams when I close my eyes.

He will be at the Academy event tonight. Meet me?

In the plaza in front of the Cathédrale de Notre Dame. I will go to light candles for my mother and brother.

#7

I don't know if I can live this way anymore. You fill every part of me, my mind and my soul. I carry the taste of you with me in my heart and on my lips.

I am working on a plan. I believe my
friend Olivier will be able to help us.

<u>#8</u>
We have our plan. I know it is extreme, but
we must act. I can't stand that he hurts
you. And I fear what would happen,
should he ever discover us.
  *I am ready. Tell me when. I will meet you
  at the quai. Nothing will keep me away.*
Do not be afraid.
  *As long as you are waiting for me, I will
  never be afraid.*

There were a few other references to secret
assignations that were not numbered, but the gist
was clear.

"I like to think they lived happily ever after,"
said Pierre-Guillaume. "What do you think?"

Claire hesitated; she wasn't sure whether to
share with him the last note, the one she'd found
in the crate.

  My love, my dearest, Olivier has agreed to
  help. We can wait no longer. We must act.
  I will be waiting. Take nothing with you.
    He will never let me go alive.

Finally, Claire decided to keep it to herself.
"You don't have any idea who the notes

belonged to, Grand-père?" asked Armand.

Pierre-Guillaume shook his head. "You know my master was Marc-Antoine Lombardi, Delphine's father. Your great-grandfather."

Armand nodded. "Yes, my great-grandfather taught you the business, and you taught my father, and he me."

Pierre-Guillaume nodded. "Exactly! Which is why there are Fontaines in charge now, instead of Lombardis. But you are also a Lombardi deep inside, are you not?"

"Yes, Grand-père," Armand said with a slight smile.

"You have heard all of this before—of course you have. Sometimes I lose track, with so many grandchildren and grandnieces and -nephews. I forget who I told what. I am a lucky man, I think."

"I agree," said Armand. "So are you saying these notes belonged to Delphine's father, Marc-Antoine?"

"No, they were older than that. I think it was his father, Jean-Baptiste. Tell me, *Américaine*, did the face arrive safely? I was supposed to use those notes to pack her."

"Yes, she arrived just as she should have," said Claire. "She's perfect."

"Why do these notes matter so much to you, Claire?" Armand asked later that night. She had spread them out on the walnut desk in the

421

crowded farmhouse library and was inspecting them under a strong lamp. "Whatever happened— or didn't happen—was more than a century ago."

"But what if this note really was written by *L'Inconnue*? It might mean she didn't kill herself at all. That she was murdered by whoever this was who wouldn't let her go."

"Is that any less tragic?"

Excellent question. Was being murdered less awful than if she had chosen to kill herself?

"Suicide is the worst, don't you think?"

"I think you're thinking of your mother. In her case, an accident might seem less tragic than a suicide. But a murder . . . ?"

She shook her head, studied the notes.

"Claire, what I don't understand is why you think these notes belonged to the woman who posed for that death mask, *L'Inconnue*. Where's the connection?"

"I don't have one, not really. Just that the note was with the face when I first found it in my grandmother's attic. So maybe that's why I associate it with her. But why would *L'Inconnue*'s face be hanging on the wall of family masks?"

"I told you, Claire, she hung on a lot of walls. The Moulage Lombardi must have sold thousands of copies of her over the years."

"Everyone else on that wall was family."

"So you think someone—Jean-Baptiste, I

suppose—was in love with her and wrote her those notes?"

"Jean-Baptiste told Pierre-Guillaume he knew her. The dates are right, aren't they? He would have been a man in his late twenties right before the turn of the twentieth century, and *L'Inconnue* was probably still a teenager or in her early twenties when the mask was made."

Armand looked at her for a long moment. "You're saying he was called in to make the death mask of the woman he loved, who was killed by her boyfriend?"

"Maybe."

Armand blew out a breath and stared at Claire for a long moment.

"And I thought the mask was sad before. This just makes it worse."

"What I can't figure out is how to prove it, how to make the connection. The morgue didn't keep any records back then, and I haven't found a name or an address . . . nothing, really."

"When did you check with the morgue?"

"When you pulled your disappearing act in Paris. By the way, don't do that again, please. I don't like it."

He made a snorting noise.

"Come on, Claire. Let's go do something useful. Like make something with clay."

Claire had spent a couple of hours a day out in the studio ever since Armand had shown it to her. She couldn't get enough of the feeling of the wet earth. As she caressed the clay, she could feel emotions rise to the surface and relished the fact that she didn't have to put a name to them. She could simply let them come: the grief over Mammaw's death, the pain of her mother's loss, the anguish of the treatment she had suffered at the hands of her father. The joy she experienced in Armand's arms.

In the studio, Claire felt simultaneously removed from the world but also exquisitely present. One of these days she was going to pick up a hammer and chisel and have a go at a block of marble Once she figured out what she wanted to free from the stone.

"What I really want to sculpt is *you,*" she told Armand. "I have from the moment I first saw you. But I could never pull it off. At least not yet."

"Why not?" Armand asked, apparently amused and, she thought, pleased that she wanted to sculpt him.

"Your face . . . there's something about it that's so . . . unusual."

A terrible look passed over his countenance. Claire immediately regretted her words.

"Oh, Armand, I'm so sorry—I didn't mean—"

"I broke my jaw, nose, and eye socket in the accident."

"I didn't mean that! I mean, now that you say it, it's clear . . . Yes, your face is a little out of balance.

But that's what's so intriguing about it . . ." The last thing she wanted to do was hurt him. "All I'm saying is I think it would be hard to capture your spirit in clay, much less stone. It's intriguing, fascinating. You're so . . . you leave so much unsaid, and yet there is such tenderness and pain, so many emotions apparent on your face."

"On my broken face?"

"Your beautiful, broken face. Would you sit for me so I can sketch you?"

He agreed, sitting still and allowing her to study him at her leisure.

Claire remembered a time when she had been afraid of Armand. But now . . . he had asked her to trust him, and he led her into the pond. With his strong arms around her, she let the waters close over her head, fighting the panic, believing in Armand, and in herself. She learned how to hold her breath, to stay calm, to keep her head above water.

She was learning to swim.

51

After sharing one last long, drawn-out dinner with the family on their final day in the countryside, Armand and Claire slipped away with a bottle of wine, flashlights, and the sleeping bag. They spent their final night in the château, making love and holding each other in their little fort among the ruins.

The room was dark but for the glow of a single candle perched atop the pile of books. Crickets filled the fragrant night air with their chirping, but otherwise all was still, the mansion's ghosts quiet on this summer's eve.

"Do you know the Irish poet called Yeats?" Armand played with a lock of Claire's hair, watching it run through his fingers.

"A little. I'm not great at literature; I studied computer science in college, remember?"

"I believe that even on the computer one can read Yeats."

"I'm sure that's true," she said with a laugh.

He recited in English: " 'I came on a great house in the middle of the night, Its open lighted doorway and its windows all alight . . . But I woke in an old ruin that the winds howled through.' "

"That's beautiful," Claire said. "But . . . very sad."

He nodded. "It makes me think of this château. At night it seems filled with magic, somehow, but during the day it all slips away."

Claire leaned over him on her elbow. "Why are we here, Armand? Are you really going to fix up this place?"

"I thought you liked it."

"I *love* it. But . . . in a way I love it just as it is. There's something about the vines growing through the windows, the way nature is slowly reclaiming it . . ."

He snorted.

"I mean," Claire continued, "it would be wonderful if you had the resources to fix it up, but then what? Would you want to live here as lord of the manor? It's a little much for a single person, or even a couple, isn't it?"

"I suppose I always hoped it would be full of children, and the aunts."

"And a stray black cat?"

He smiled and brushed the hair out of her eyes.

"Yes, and a cat named Gertrude."

Said cat was awfully happy to see him upon their return to Paris. Claire had taken the train back with Armand; their departure from Lods was long and drawn out, an affair attended by extended family and neighbors exhorting them to stay another week. But Armand had insisted they had to get back to get the studio in shape to open for business by the first of September. In actuality, Claire decided, he had reached a saturation point with family time.

Now they were back, just the two of them, in the little garden behind the shop. They were sipping wine and enjoying the quiet evening when the feline came trotting over and wound herself around Armand's legs, mewling. He lifted her into his lap and stroked her, scratching behind her ears.

"Well, hello there, my beauty," he said in a sweet, quiet voice. "*Ça va?*"

"Seems like Quentin took good care of her while we were away."

Armand nodded.

"Armand . . . is your wife, Odile, with Quentin?"

He nodded. "Yes. It's better this way. She couldn't . . . she couldn't stand it. She's had a very hard time, and being around me made it even more difficult."

"I'm sorry." It was all Claire could think to say.

"And you should know, Odile is no longer my wife. The divorce was final a year ago. It's been three years since the accident."

"But surely she doesn't blame you?"

"She didn't blame me—at least, she didn't *mean* to blame me. I blame myself more. But she is staying in Provence, rarely comes to Paris anymore. Quentin sees her often. I'm glad to know she's all right. What we went through, it is . . ."

"Unimaginable."

He nodded.

Claire thought how Mammaw would say, *Time heals all wounds*. But she wasn't so sure. Perhaps it merely hardened the scars, calcifying over them like barnacles, like hard water stains that crust over and might, just might, crack off one day. But she doubted the wounds would ever fully heal; Armand's face showed them every day, his heart even more so.

But perhaps that was as it should be. Should one ever forget a beloved child, lost in one violent moment?

Perhaps the scars were like the golden lines of *kintsugi*, holding the memories together.

Claire thought about her own mother, lost to her in infancy. She must have witnessed the accident, but she was far too young to remember. At least consciously. Sean once suggested she get hypnotized to dig up the memory. But she wasn't sure she *wanted* to remember; the memories of what happened with her father were painful enough.

After *apéro* they went back upstairs. A huge stack of mail had arrived while they were gone; Armand started sorting through it, separating junk mail and advertisements, bills, and personal correspondence.

"Do you still get a lot of orders by mail?" Claire asked.

"Yes. I suppose one of these days I'll have to join the modern world, but I am enjoying being anachronistic. A man out of time."

Claire smiled. "An old crank, you mean."

He smiled back, tugged her ponytail gently.

"I should tell you—I started making some changes to your Web site."

"Changes?" He pulled back, looked worried.

"Nothing serious. I just fixed some links,

cleaned a few things up. But I made a list of questions for you, and have some suggestions, including a form so people could order over the Internet. Maybe we could sit down and go over them. You could join the modern world."

He gave her a reluctant smile and nodded. "How could I refuse?"

He glanced up at the old clock on the wall. "You know, we don't have groceries—why don't you let me take you out tonight?"

"You? Eat out? I didn't think you ate out."

"Paris is the city for lovers—don't you know this? Besides, I have something I want to show you."

First they had dinner at one of his favorite bistros, around the corner from where Ernest Hemingway—"one of yours"—used to live. After their two-hour meal—the proprietor knew Armand and kept refilling their wineglasses—they walked along the Seine. Even though the proximity of the river still made her nervous, it was comforting to know that if the worst happened—if she somehow tumbled in—she would be able to keep her head above water. She would never earn any medals for swimming form, but she could dog-paddle with the best of them.

They stopped to paw through some antiquarian books at a few of the *bouquinistes* that lined the Seine between the quai de la Tournelle and the quai Voltaire. Then they walked by a gathering of people of all ages—from high schoolers to the very old, from beginners to experts—dancing the tango.

Claire stopped to watch for a moment. The strains of the music were exotic, and the dance dramatic and romantic. It was charming.

"Turn around," Armand said, placing his hands on her shoulders and rotating her gently.

The Eiffel Tower, already majestic against the night sky, started to twinkle.

"Oh!" Claire said, catching her breath.

"I thought you'd like that."

"It's like a really, really tall disco ball." She looked over her shoulder at Armand and smiled. "This is awfully romantic."

He shrugged.

"And a little bit—or maybe a *lot*—touristy."

Now he barked out a laugh, and she joined him, wrapping her arms around his waist and pulling him tight.

"So you see, not everything touristy is bad."

There was a long pause as he searched her face and held her gaze.

"I seem to be developing a certain appreciation for American tourists, as a matter of fact."

The next morning Claire awoke in Armand's big bed. He was in a deep sleep, his chest falling and rising very subtly.

She watched him for a minute. They hadn't

spoken about the future; would she be leaving in a few days, going back to Louisiana or Chicago or elsewhere, looking for a job, relocating? Or should she put her energy into getting a job in Paris?

Claire had been so caught up with Armand that she hadn't thought much about one difficult truth: the face she had searched for she had found, but there had been no mystery there. No exciting secret about her life. She hadn't even figured out the note she had found in the crate. She felt it was connected to the others in Pierre-Guillaume's tin box, and her gut—or her imagination—told her it might have been correspondence between *L'Inconnue* and Jean-Baptiste Lombardi, but so what?

Armand was right. The idea that *L'Inconnue* and Jean-Baptiste had fallen in love, but she had been murdered, and then Jean-Baptiste had crafted her death mask . . . it was all too maudlin to consider. Better *L'Inconnue* be remembered as a suicide, and let it go at that.

Armand still didn't stir. Claire slipped out of bed as carefully as she could, hoping to let him sleep. He needed it.

Out in the kitchen, Claire decided she would make coffee for him for a change. She took the jar down from the shelf, scooped fragrant grounds into the basket, poured in water, turned on the machine. She smiled to herself when imagining Armand complaining that it was not strong enough, or perhaps too strong. That it was burned or not hot enough or something else.

For some strange reason, she found it adorable.

On the counter the letters Armand had sorted last night were in their neat piles: junk, bills, correspondence.

One item was addressed to Lisette Villeneuve. The woman who used to work there.

But the really odd thing was that Claire could have sworn the address was written in her Mammaw's hand.

She picked it up to study it. Postmarked Louisiana. Minerva Duval Paquet as the return address.

Minerva Duval Paquet. Otherwise known as Mammaw.

52

SABINE

The boy brings Sabine another note:

I am sending this note with a kiss. Can you feel it?

Sabine holds the note, reads it thrice. Remembering when Jean-Baptiste pulled her behind a produce cart outside the market, heedless of the smells of rotting vegetables and refuse. It was just the two of them, no one else in this world. She looked into his eyes and leapt, unafraid, into their depths.

He kissed her.

It was a revelation. She had enjoyed the horse trainer's lips on hers, but it was not this. Nothing like this. This was sunlight and fire. It was the relief of cool rain in summer, the warmth of a hearth in winter. As bright and disorienting as the electric bulbs the city was using to replace the gas flames in the streetlamps on the boulevards.

This kiss was everything.

Monsieur Rodin had sculpted this, Sabine realized with a shock. This was what he was attempting to portray in his sculpture called *The Kiss*—the one many people found vulgar, uncouth. The passion, the craving, the ache. The sensation that in this vast world full of people, there are now, in this moment, only two.

Sabine sits down with the note, dips her quill in ink, and dares to write the truth:

> I feel your kisses every moment of every day, and in my dreams when I close my eyes.

Maurice returns shortly after, arranges her in an uncomfortable position on the divan, and Sabine remains as still as the dead for hours. Thinking only of Jean-Baptiste's lips on hers, the mingling of their breath, their tongues, the sensation of his hands on her body.

"You look very beautiful today, Sabine," says Maurice. "You are wearing your *Mona Lisa* smile."

"*Merci, monsieur*," she says. She would not share the reason, even if she could, even if Maurice were a different sort of man. It is private, a secret heat.

After the sculpting session, Maurice leaves to meet some friends in a bar. He tells her to stay in, as her eye is still swollen from the night before last, when he lost his temper when she voiced an opinion about the Nabis.

"I had hoped to light candles for my mother and brother, and go to confession," she says. "I could wear my scarf around my head."

He hesitates a moment, but finally nods. "All right, but there and back, that is all."

"*Oui, monsieur.*"

The boy arrives at her door once Maurice has turned the corner.

The note reads: *He will be at the Academy event tonight. Meet me?*

Sabine writes: *In the plaza in front of the Cathédrale de Notre Dame. I will go to light candles for my mother and brother.*

53

Claire couldn't wrap her mind around what she was seeing. Mammaw had passed away weeks ago. When did she write such a letter? And why?

How on earth did *Mammaw* know *Lisette Villeneuve?*

This made no sense.

Claire stared at the envelope, fighting the nearly overwhelming temptation to open it.

According to the big clock above the sink, it was barely seven, which would make it midnight in Plaquemines Parish. But her cousin stayed up late, and it would be Saturday night there.

She called Jessica.

"Why, if it isn't cousin Chance," she said, her voice dripping with the familiar condescension. "Still working retail?"

"Do you know anything about a letter being sent from Mammaw to Paris?"

"What you talkin' about? You're losing it, girl. You know she passed before you even left."

"No, no, I know—I realize that. The thing is, the letter wasn't addressed to me, but to a woman named Lisette Villeneuve. Have you heard of her?"

"No."

"She's American, but she speaks fluent French. Could she have been a neighbor or something . . . ? Do we know any Villeneuves?"

There was a long pause.

"Jessica?"

She cleared her throat and Claire could hear a shuffle of papers. Was she even paying attention?

"Yeah, um . . ." Jessica was rarely at a loss for words. "You know how Mammaw was—she knew all sorts of people through church and all. Could be anyone."

"Yes, but it's awfully coincidental that this Villeneuve worked at the same place I ended up, isn't it?"

"Didn't you say Mammaw told you to go track down some package from Paris? Prob'ly that's why, 'cause she knew someone there."

That made sense, Claire supposed. Still . . .

"It must have been Uncle Remy mailed the letter," Jessica continued. "He's been cleaning up, probably found it with her things and mailed it. He also mailed a bunch of checks she'd written for bills, which really steams me 'cause I'm trying to sort everything out with her finances. Thank you so much, Mammaw, for making me executrix of your will."

"Executrix? There's a word you don't hear very often."

She laughed. "Right? Anyway, I guess this is what I get for taking that bookkeeping class at the community college. I tell you what: between the two of us, I don't think we're exactly the poster children for higher education. I'm thinkin' 'bout going back to waitressing and you're workin' as a shopgirl. Anyway, what did the letter say?"

"I don't know. It isn't addressed to me."

"You didn't read it?"

"No." Claire gazed at it, clutched tightly in her hand.

"I tell you what—you've got more willpower than me. If a letter arrived from a ghost at my address, I'd open it no matter the name on the envelope."

"Hey, you know Uncle Remy won't answer the phone, but would you go over and ask him? Call me if you find out anything?"

"Sure thing. I'll just go on over there and grill him in all my spare time."

"I know you're busy, Jessica. But I would really appreciate it."

She sighed. "He's a night owl like me. I'll go on by there on the way home. I'm at cousin Jeff's right now. He fell off that damned motorcycle again."

Claire offered to help with Jeff's medical bills and thanked Jessica for her help.

Armand came out into the kitchen, looking sleepy and luscious in nothing but boxer shorts. "I smell coffee."

"What is this?" Claire demanded, waving the letter in his direction.

"What's what?" he asked, rearing back slightly and trying to focus on what was in her hand. This clearly wasn't the response he had been expecting.

"There's a letter here for Lisette Villeneuve."

"She's still getting a few things here. Did you ask her to change her address?" he asked, moving over to the counter and pouring himself a cup of coffee.

"What *is* it about this woman?"

"How do you mean?"

"Did you and she . . . Were you lovers?"

He chokcd on his coffee, sputtering. "*What?* Claire, what are you talking about?"

"I know *something's* going on. Something's off about her, about this whole situation. Why didn't you tell me she was from Louisiana? How does she know my grandmother?"

"She knows your grandmother?"

"This letter she received is from my Mammaw. My grandmother."

"You said your grandmother told you to come here, right? Isn't it possible she sent you here because she already knew someone here? Instead of just out of the blue?"

Jessica had said the same thing. It was the only thing that made sense.

"Open it if you're so curious," he said, leaning

back against the counter and taking another sip of his coffee.

She looked down at the envelope, inscribed with Mammaw's familiar spidery scrawl, now slightly wrinkled from being clutched so tightly.

"You're not supposed to open other people's mail," Claire mumbled.

He laughed. "You, Claire Broussard, are such a strange mélange of rebel and saint."

"I'd hardly say saint."

She gazed down at it. The truth was, she was afraid of what she might find inside.

When he spoke again, his tone was gentle. "If you don't want to open it, why don't you take it to Lisette and ask her about it? Surely she can tell you how she knows your grandmother."

Claire didn't answer.

Stories. Her family made up stories. Where did Claire think she got it from, this propensity for mimicking, for pretending, for storytelling?

Tell me again, Mammaw. Tell me about my mama, when the car went off the road. Why didn't I die too?

It was a miracle, Chance. And you *are a miracle.*

"You said Villeneuve used to sculpt when she was here," said Claire. "Could I see something she made?"

"She smashed everything. She had a flair for the dramatic."

Armand had used that phrase with regard to her once, Claire remembered.

Claire dropped to her hands and knees, looking under the worktables, hoping to find some shards that could tell her something. Heedless of the grit that dug into her knees and palms.

"Claire, what are you doing? What's going on?"

"I have to . . . My family always said how my mother wanted to be a sculptor, wanted to run away to Europe. And . . . Mammaw knew her." Still kneeling on the floor, she looked up at Armand. "She didn't leave anything at all that she'd made?"

He blew out a breath, ran a hand through his already mussed hair. Then he headed into his bedroom and brought out a beat-up old Barbie case.

"All I have leftover are these little pieces she made for Léonor."

He opened the case.

Three little animals looked up at Claire. A bear, an alligator, and a cat. Fat clay balls stuck together, smiles on their faces. Just like the animals Claire had held in the palm of her hands back when she was a child, when she used to hide behind the couch.

The little sculptures that had moved in the palm of her hand, that had whispered to her:

You are not alone. You will be okay. You are a miracle.

54

"I s it possible my mother didn't die in the crash?" Claire heard herself asking, her voice sounding hollow and far away, as though someone else were talking. "Or even . . . that there wasn't a crash at all?"

"Claire, come sit down," Armand said, leading her to his wooden work stool. "You look a little shaky."

"Could they have lied about this? Could my mother have lived, and moved to Paris to become a sculptor, and no one ever *told* me?" She shook her head. "I know my family makes up stories, but this is— *Wait.* You knew her for years. She must have told you she was from Louisiana, where I'm from. How is it you've never mentioned that to me?"

"She didn't speak with a strong accent like you do. She had been living here in Paris for decades before she came to the *moulage.*"

"Are you saying you had no inkling, no idea?" When he didn't answer immediately, she pushed: "Armand?"

"I didn't know for sure, of course not." He shook his head. "But every once in a while . . . there are a few mannerisms of yours that put me in mind of her, but at first I assumed that was because you were both American. But then in Lods you made those little animals out of clay, so similar to these. And I noticed the shape of your ear."

"The shape of my *ear?*"

"It's very distinctive—I told you . . ." He trailed off with a shrug. "I'm a mold-maker. I notice these things."

"You knew but you didn't tell me?"

"What was I going to say, Claire? That perhaps the mother who died in a car crash has been living here in Paris working for the Moulage Lombardi? That she abandoned you?"

"Yes, that's precisely what you could have told me."

"You have to admit, it sounds pretty fantastical."

Indeed. It also sounded true.

"Tell me everything you can about her."

"There's not much to tell. Unlike you, she didn't seem to want to make a connection. She was only with us part-time for the last few years."

"That's long enough to learn something about someone."

"I'm sorry to tell you, Claire, but she was silent and irritable. She looked down on our work as not worthy of her, and frankly she never appeared to enjoy Léonor or Giselle's children. She did her work and translated for us and went home. No *apéro*, no shared meals. The only time she was truly kind was immediately after the accident. I

443

couldn't work for several months and she stepped in, ran things for a while."

"I can't believe everyone lied to me about this. What was Mammaw thinking? And now you too?" She held her head in her hands. "Everyone in my life is a liar."

"Pardon me, Claire. I did not lie to you about this. I noticed a similarity in your ear—that's a long way from having proof of anything so far-fetched. It crossed my mind, but I dismissed it as unbelievable."

"It doesn't matter," Claire said as she stood. "I'll be leaving soon anyway."

"Leaving? What does any of this have to do with us? With you and me?"

She let out a humorless laugh. "What did you think—that I was going to stay in France and pour masks with you forever? I was a temporary hire, remember?"

"And a temporary lover as well?"

"I have to leave, Armand. We both know that."

"Why? Why do you have to go back? You have no job, no close family."

"What am I supposed to do—stay around here and try to humor you while you grumble at the tourists? And then what? This isn't a life."

"You aren't living a life *now*. You're chasing phantoms from your past. You just got finished telling me your whole life is based on the fact that your mother died in a car crash that never happened. If she didn't die, Claire, she abandoned you to an alcoholic father."

"Yes, thank you for that valuable insight. I think I had figured that part out."

Her phone beeped and Armand threw up his hands. Claire checked a text message from Jessica: *Remy sent you a letter by e-mail, using my account.*

She opened the e-mail and read:

Dear Chance,
Jessica is helping me use this e-mail. You know I don't like computers. I hope it gets to you.

Jessica told me I shoud not of sent that letter. Sorry. Mammaw always sent a letter to that lady every few months or so. I remember sometimes she sent photos of you from school and all. And so I found that letter already to go and figgered she meant to send it. It goes to the same address where your letters come from so it seemed like it made sense but Sorry if I done the wrong thing.

Things are good here. Jessica says I shoud not stay alone in the house but maybe cousin Jeff needs a place to stay to get better so he can come here. The shrimp is still not come in so thats bad news for the boys.

I hope you are good and not mad at your uncle Remy. I like the letters you send. Please send more I miss you and love you,

Remy

P.S. I am very happy you learned to swim!

55

Let me go with you, Claire," Armand said. "We'll go talk to Lisette together."

"No," she said, backing away from him. "No, I don't want you to."

"Claire—"

"No. Thank you. I want to go by myself."

The whole way—as she ran to the metro, switched trains, ran to the apartment building— thoughts whirred through Claire's brain. *My mother is alive. My mother never died. My whole life has been based on a lie.*

She still couldn't quite believe it; it seemed so far-fetched, so impossible.

Was she about to meet her mother face-to-face? Had she already met her—twice—and yet Lizzie—*Lisette*—had said nothing?

Instead of driving into the bayou and killing herself, and nearly Chance, had Lizzie run off to Paris and abandoned Claire to her drunken father?

All these years, she could have known her mother? And how had the family kept the secret? She had always known they were good at telling stories, but why had no one—not one person— told Claire the truth? Was it possible they didn't know themselves? When Mammaw told everyone her daughter had died in that swamp and that Chance had survived by the grace of a miracle, had the story taken on a life of its own? Or had Lizzie feared Chance's father would follow her if he knew she had run off? Because surely he at least would have blurted out the truth under the influence of alcohol at some point, had he known the truth.

And why tell Chance she was saved by a miracle when all she was, in fact, was an abandoned child?

Nothing miraculous about that.

When Claire arrived at the apartment building, she passed the same young tattooed woman coming down the stairs.

"Oh, hi. How are you?" she said. "Your friend moved out, I think."

"She did?"

"Yeah, the landlord was pissed; she didn't give any notice. She left a note on her door—are you Chance Broussard, by any chance?"

Claire nodded.

"Here, I'll let you in," said the woman. "Are you okay?"

Claire nodded again. She couldn't bring herself to speak. She walked down the hallway to apartment 110. There, taped on the door, was an envelope addressed to Chance Broussard.

Her hands shook as she read the letter.

Dearest Claire (Chance?),

It seems awkward to say, "Sorry for abandoning you." But I really am. Sorry, that is. In all senses of the word, I suppose.

I was so young when I had you, Claire. Heartbreakingly young. All I had ever wanted was to run away to some beautiful city and become an artist. So I did. I found the mask in the attic—just as you did years later, according to what Mom (Mammaw) wrote me (she said you used to go in the attic and talk to it!)—and I wondered about her, dreamed about where she was from, and then I hunted her down.

Just as you did.

I knew you would have plenty of family to take care of you—perhaps too many, right?! I'm sorry to hear that your dad turned out to be a dud. This will probably sound strange, but I didn't really know him that well. Can hardly remember him, to tell the truth. We were just kids when I got pregnant; I was still in high school. Anyway, I'm sorry about that too—I always thought he would be a much better dad than I would be a mom. He was so excited to have you.

And then you went to live with my mom, which wasn't my plan for you. But she wrote me that you escaped, that you went to school in Chicago. So I suppose you really are my daughter!

Mom said she told you and everybody else I died in a car crash. Seems like she kept that secret just about to her grave; she always was good at holding her tongue when she made a point of it. I guess it was better that way, so you wouldn't think I'd abandoned you. So you wouldn't try to find me. I even changed my name: New life, new identity.

This is embarrassing to admit, but I always imagined I would make it big. That my talents would be recognized, that I would create more than these silly little animals (that always sold well, by the way!). I've been trying all my life, and then I wound up working in that god-forsaken mold-making shop, squandering my talents. I can't believe you're working there!

I thought one day maybe I'd come home triumphant and all would be forgiven. But I am just what I am: a failure. Camille

Claudel was never adequately recognized for her work when she was alive either, not to mention Vincent van Gogh, or even Vermeer until recently. I console myself with thoughts like that. Paris is a good place for a failed artist.

Please don't try to find me.

I'm sorry I left you. But I thought it was for the best. I still do.

Lisette (Lizzie). Your mom.

Claire could barely see through the tears when she finally tore open the letter from Mammaw. To Claire's mother.

Lizzie,

I'm not long for this world. So I'm sending her to you. She asked about where that mask come from, so it seemed like fate. You'd best tell her the truth, own up to what you done. Chance is the best part of you.

It's like I always say: she's a miracle.

Maman

Claire leaned back against the wall, then let herself slide all the way down until she sat with a thud on the dirty carpet.

Her head lolled back against the wall.

She had no idea how long she sat there staring

into space. Imagining her life, built on a foundation of lies. Remembering what she had asked Armand: *Am I so impossible to love?*

Boots and jeans appeared in her field of vision.

Armand stood in front of her. He crouched down, brushed a lock of hair out of her face.

"You okay?"

She nodded.

"Is it true?" he asked, glancing at the crumpled letter from Lisette still clutched in her hand.

She offered it to him and he read it through. Armand took a seat next to her on the floor, back against the wall. He put his arm around her shoulders but remained quiet for a long time. A few neighbors passed by, casting them strange looks, but no one said anything.

"Well, look on the bright side," Armand said after a long pause. "At least you know she wasn't trying to kill you in that swamp."

Claire started to chuckle, then to laugh. Her laughter soon ceded to crying, and then she couldn't stop. Great, wrenching sobs racked her body; she turned her face into Armand's chest, collapsed there, and cried for her childhood, for her mother and her father and Mammaw and the deluge of lies that washed over her.

56

SABINE

February 27, 1898

Sabine runs through the streets. Makes it as far as the quai du Louvre, to the beautiful Pont Neuf.

She is fished out of the river by the mold-maker, who had gone to meet her there. A boy helps him. It is the boy Jean-Baptiste had paid to run notes back and forth between the two of them.

"What is her name?" asks the boy solemnly. It is so early in the morning it is still dark, and he has never been party to such an undertaking.

"She has no name," says Jean-Baptiste with a sad shake of his head. "She is *inconnue*."

The boy stares at him wide-eyed, sure he will never understand the ways of grown-ups, or a man in love.

They carry the poor unfortunate girl to the morgue behind the Cathedral of Notre Dame. Olivier Delen is on duty; he attends to her early that morning. She is brought to the morgue with no identification, no possessions. Her clothes are poor quality, threadbare.

She is still beautiful and she smiles so sweetly.

The mold-maker casts her face, her final portrait, her death mask.

She is put on display alongside a homeless old man who died on a bench in the park in the night, and another young woman, hit by a carriage. There are a dozen other unidentified bodies in the frigid room already; they will remain a month or more, in the hopes that relatives might notice them missing, come looking for their wayward aunt, a beloved uncle. As is customary, the bodies are displayed with their clothes hanging beside them—sometimes the injuries are so grievous the family must recognize their loved one's garments rather than the face. Small cloths are strategically placed for modesty.

Jean-Baptiste sends the boy with a note to an address he knows well: the studio of Monsieur Maurice Desmarais.

Though it is still morning, Maurice arrives drunk. There is a long line at the morgue; people crowd in like they are looking into department store windows. Jean-Baptiste waits with him.

"Are you sure it's her?" Maurice demands.

"Are there two who look like her?" Jean-Baptiste answers, his voice shaking. "The morgue worker called me to make her death mask. I am very sure. Do you know her full name, so we can notify the family?"

Maurice shakes his head, muddled. "What could have possessed her? Why would she *do* such a thing? I gave her a place to live and plenty to eat, even chocolate. You should have seen how skinny the little country mouse was when I first knew her."

The line of visitors shuffled slowly past the panes of cold glass.

She was in the middle. Maurice throws himself at the glass, staring at her.

"But she is so beautiful still," he says. "How is it possible?"

"*Excusez-moi, monsieur.* Do you know who she is?" asks a man in the crowd. "If you know her, you should tell the authorities."

Jean-Baptiste whispers to Maurice, "If you claim her, you will be responsible for the expense of her burial. If you leave her, the state will take care of it. Bury her in a pauper's grave in Père Lachaise."

"That's true," Maurice says with a nod. He seems to be having difficulty making sense of what is happening. "But . . . I can't believe she would do this to me; why would she do this to me?"

"Some might suggest it was not a suicide," murmurs Jean-Baptiste as they file past, as he tries to keep his heart from breaking. He has made her death mask, the face of the woman he loved. "People have seen the bruises; they might think perhaps it is something else entirely. It might create a scandal if you were associated with this in any way."

"What are you saying?" Maurice rears back, looks horrified. "None of this is my fault! None of it! I had nothing to do with this girl's death . . . Perhaps it was Clément—he was always jealous I would not allow her to sit for him. The authorities should look to him, not me. I hardly know her; I don't even know her last name."

They come out the other side of the morgue into a cold but sunny day. Pigeons fly overhead; the bells toll at the cathedral. Children run by; two university students stop them and ask:

"Anything good on display today?"

Maurice and Jean-Baptiste exchange a glance.

"*Il n'y a rien*," says Maurice. "There is nothing, just a drowned woman."

57

Gumbo was bubbling on the stove, sending its spicy aroma through the atelier. Armand had tracked down sassafras filé and okra in some obscure corner of a Parisian farmers' market, and tonight Giselle and Thiérry and the children would be joining them for the exotic dinner, along with Delphine and Pierre-Guillaume, who had arrived by train for what they were calling their "honeymoon, sixty-five years late" in Paris.

Armand had even invited Quentin as a thank-you for taking care of his cat. Gertrude, for her part, was now happily ensconced in the Moulage Lombardi, a shop cat who slinked around with a liberal sprinkling of plaster dust on her formerly sleek black coat.

It was two weeks since they had returned from the countryside, since Claire's world had turned upside down. She tried calling her father, which went about as well as it usually did: he was drunk and belligerent and called her crazy. Then she tried Jessica.

"Yeah, I always thought there was something fishy about the whole mom-died-in-a-car-accident story."

"How so?" Claire asked.

"There was no funeral. I was old enough to remember—you know what a big deal funerals are around here. And no one talked about her much. Just seemed strange, that's all. Anyway, doesn't really matter anymore, does it? She's dead to you."

"I suppose you're right. Hey, would you do me a favor and ask Remy to send me the mask in the crate?"

"The what now?"

"He'll know what I mean. It's a sculpture of a face I found in Mammaw's attic a long time ago. Mammaw asked me to get it fixed, and now I think I know how. Remy has my address on all the letters—care of the Moulage Lombardi."

"Are you staying in Paris, then?"

"For a while anyway. Seems I can pick up some freelance Web-based work here, people looking for native English speakers who speak French."

"But you're actually gonna live overseas? What, did you fall in love?"

Claire gazed through the windows at Armand hunched over a project on his workbench. She noted her own reflection on the glass super-imposed on the scene: white coat, plaster-stained hands.

As if Armand felt the heat of her gaze through the windows, he looked up from his work, met her eyes, and smiled his slow, simmering smile.

"It's early yet, but . . . yes," said Claire. "Yes, I did."

Knowing the French weren't used to a lot of hot spices, Claire had made the gumbo extremely mild. They ate out in the garden; Delphine and Pierre-Guillaume had difficulty with steps, so they came through the little side alley. Pierre-Guillaume and Delphine kept them entranced with stories of World War II and the immediate aftermath, of Paris in the fifties and sixties.

When Armand brought out the cheese plate and the children asked permission to leave the table and play, Delphine made an announcement.

"Pierre-Guillaume and I have been thinking about it, Armand," she said, her hand holding her husband's arm, "and we have decided we want you to make our death masks and place them with the rest of the family."

Giselle made a little *miew* of distress and Thiérry wrapped his arm around her.

"Would you?" Armand asked.

"Please," said Delphine with a nod.

He nodded solemnly. "It will be my honor."

They all sat silently for a long moment, the knowledge of mortality an uninvited guest at the table.

"Claire very much wanted to replace all the missing masks, to restore the collection at the château," said Armand. "We found several here in the storage closet, but not the one for Mélusine, the wife of Jean-Baptiste."

"My grandmother would not allow anyone to make her mask," said Delphine.

"Why not?"

She shrugged. "Perhaps she found it *larmoyant*, like Armand's father. I knew my grandmother when I was young, you know. She was very kind; nothing ever rattled her. Not even the war. She gave birth to six children and raised her younger brother as well. And she was a very fine artist."

"I saw some of her work at the farmhouse in Lods," said Claire. "It was lovely. And Armand showed me her art studio. I take it she didn't care for Paris?"

Delphine shook her head. "She lived here for a

few years as a young woman but vowed she would never go back."

Pierre-Guillaume brought a rolled canvas out of his bag.

"This one is my favorite of hers," said Delphine. "We have had it hanging in our bedroom for many years, but Pierre-Guillaume and I agree it should hang here instead, in the Moulage Lombardi. It involves sculpture, after all."

Victorine and David ran back to the table to see what it was.

The oil painting portrayed the myth of Galatea and Pygmalion, but with a twist.

"Do you know this myth?" Delphine asked the children. "Pygmalion was a sculptor who fell in love with his own creation, Galatea, more beautiful than any real woman. And then she was brought to life."

"But in this painting, she is freeing herself," said Claire.

"*Exactement*," said Pierre-Guillaume. "Perhaps she has become her own muse, eh?"

In the painting Galatea stood on a dais, her feet still part of a block of white Carrara marble; the sculptor Pygmalion was sprawled asleep on the floor, as though sated from lovemaking. Galatea had availed herself of his hammer and chisel and was leaning over, freeing her feet from the block of stone. Carving her own escape.

She was partially turned away from view, but

she had a very slight serene smile on her pretty face.

"It is the smile of *La Joconde*," said Pierre-Guillaume, pointing. "It is the smile of a woman who knows."

"Knows what?" Victorine asked him.

"What only a woman can know," he said.

"You are a sweet old fool, my Pierre-Guillaume." Delphine kissed him on his grizzled cheek.

That evening, after their visitors had left and Claire and Armand were doing the dishes, Claire said, "I have a crazy idea."

Armand gave her a pained look. "I'm afraid to ask."

"What if *L'Inconnue* didn't die at all?"

"Then how do we have her death mask?"

"What if she and Jean-Baptiste Lombardi fell in love, but her husband or lover was abusive and they somehow cooked up a scheme so she could escape?"

Armand wiped his hands on a dish towel, then hung it up to dry. "Claire, I think you have a wonderful imagination—and a talent for giving a tragic story a happy ending."

"Maybe he spirited her away to the country-side, where she changed her name to that of a mermaid—Mélusine—because she nearly drowned in the river!"

Armand laughed.

"Wait, I'm serious. *That* would explain why his colleague named Olivier Delen, a non-Lombardi, ran the shop for many years. It wasn't because Jean-Baptiste loved the countryside, but because he was keeping Mélusine safe. And their oldest son, Marc-Antoine, went on to run the shop, and then Pierre-Guillaume married Delphine, who was Marc-Antoine's daughter."

Armand was still chuckling.

Claire gasped. "So that would make *you* a direct descendent of *L'Inconnue*!"

"Who, according to Claire Broussard, is *inconnue* no more," he said softly. "She was known as Mélusine Lombardi, and she lived a long, apparently happy life in the countryside and had many children."

"If it's true, she might still have been alive when my great-grandfather bought a copy of her mask here at the Moulage Lombardi in World War II and sent it back to Louisiana."

"And it arrived cracked and languished in the attic."

"Until my mother found it and followed the address here."

"As did you."

"As did I. And you know, at least in this, Mammaw didn't lie: she told me I would find a secret here, and I did."

"Several, in fact."

Claire blew out a long breath. "I just wish there

was a way to know for sure about *L'Inconnue*. How can I prove it?"

"I don't think you can. But you know, Claire, sometimes it's all right to live with mystery. To embrace the not knowing."

"First *kintsugi*, now this. You're quite the philosopher."

"All the best philosophers are French," he said, jutting out his chin. "Everyone knows this."

"The Germans and the Chinese might argue that point with you. But since I'm a guest in your country, I'll let it go."

Armand gently pulled her to him, wrapped his arms around her.

"All I know for sure, Claire, is that *L'Inconnue* brought you here, to the Moulage Lombardi, and to me. *And* she taught you the truth about your mother. Isn't that enough for one simple young woman from the countryside? Let's let her rest now. Let's leave her her secrets."

58

SABINE

She is cold.
Deeply cold, profoundly cold.
The display room morgue is kept frigid with blocks of ice and a system of ammonia coursing

through the pipes. There are plenty of dead here: homeless and friendless and abandoned. Suicides and murder victims, street dwellers killed by weather and old age.

How many times did Maurice tell her: *Be still as the dead?*

Sabine listened and learned. She knows how to be still as the dead. This is another thing she learned from Maurice: Sabine is not ashamed to be put on display, virtually naked, to strangers. She has been trained as a *modèle de profession* after all. Her naked body might be on display, but her soul is her own.

Last night she panicked when she heard footsteps behind her. She ran the rest of the way to the quai du Louvre, searching the shadows for Jean-Baptiste. He was there somewhere; she knew he was.

She made it to Pont Neuf, the beautiful bridge constructed by royalty centuries ago, decorated with sculptures of mermaids and other creatures of the sea.

And then she spotted him, her love, waiting for her under the bridge.

She threw herself in.

Cold. The waters pulled at her skirts. She had learned to swim in the pond outside her village, but that was in the warmth of summer in still water. But now the fall had taken her breath; the cold made it hard to move her arms and legs.

The current was stronger than she had imagined. The river's icy fingers reached for her, welcomed her into its depths.

Strong hands grasped her, pulled her to the shore.

It was not hard to play dead. She was so cold, her thoughts as frozen as her body, that Sabine had a moment of wondering whether she was in fact slipping from this life.

A pair of hands under her arms, another pair holding her ankles. They carried her to the nearby morgue. Jean-Baptiste's friend Olivier Delen opened the door for them, ushered them in.

They laid her out on the slab. Jean-Baptiste took off her sodden clothes, wrapped her in warm blankets, held her. Olivier brought her cup after cup of hot tea. The boy sat in the corner, wide-eyed. Part of a conspiracy now.

"He will come with us to the countryside?" she managed to utter.

"I'm sorry, my love?"

"The boy. If Maurice discovers him . . ."

Jean-Baptiste looked at the young fellow.

"He reminds me of my brother," said Sabine.

"Then he shall be your brother," said Jean-Baptiste. "He shall come with us to the country-side, if he pleases. You shall choose new names, and there we will live a beautiful life. There we will sketch and sculpt and grow our grapes and make our wine."

"In the countryside." Sabine closed her eyes and smiled.

"Now," said Jean-Baptiste in a voice as soft as summer rain, "close your eyes for me, my love, and I shall make your death mask."

She must survive the cold for a while longer, until Jean-Baptiste has made sure Maurice has seen her. The boy ran to bring him a note. He must think she is dead or he will never give up searching for her, for his reluctant muse.

A muse cannot be held captive, Camille Claudel had told her. *A muse must be free.*

It is the muse who chooses her artist, not the other way around.

As she lies there, eyes closed, still as the dead, Sabine decides her new name will be Mélusine. Because she has been created from the river, from the mud, from the wet plaster Jean-Baptiste stroked upon her face.

Sabine Moreau died in the Seine, abandoned and unknown, on February 27, 1898.

Mélusine Lombardi will go on to live a long and happy life.

With the artist of her choosing.

59

Claire opened the crate, pushing aside the packing material to show the broken face of *L'Inconnue*.

Armand studied the fragments.

"Are you sure you want to repair it? You happen to have some influence at Paris's famous Moulage Lombardi. I could get you a new one, cheap."

"We do not hide but rather make a *feature* of the scars—remember, Monsieur Lombardi Fontaine? Besides, she was my childhood friend. She can't be replaced."

He smiled and they cleaned the old glue and tape off the jagged pieces. Then Armand sprinkled gold powder into a bowl of wet lacquer and Claire mixed it in, creating a gleaming gold glue.

Standing side by side at the worktable, Claire and Armand pieced *L'Inconnue*'s broken face back together, bit by bit. Her apple cheeks, her closed eyes, the curls at the side of her face. In the jagged lines of gold Claire could see her own wounds reflected; she knew the scars that held her soul together, however unsightly, were stronger than the tissues they replaced.

Claire no longer feared the water. She was ready to plunge in.

They dabbed on the last of the gold glue, fitted together the final shards, and Armand and Claire stood back to admire their handiwork.

"Will you stay in Paris, Claire?" Armand asked in a quiet, gentle voice.

And *L'Inconnue* smiled, as though she knew.

AUTHOR'S NOTE

L'Inconnue is an actual mask of a young woman who lived during the late nineteenth century. No one knows for sure whether the model was French, English, German, Russian, or otherwise. The most common story told is that she committed suicide by throwing herself into the Seine, and that a morgue worker, who felt she was too beautiful not to commemorate, called for a mold-maker from the Lorenzi family to make her death mask. You can still buy a copy of her visage from the wonderful *Lorenzi Moulage d'Art*, now located on the outskirts of Paris.

Over the years, some experts have claimed the sculpture could not have been a true *death* mask; instead, they say, her skin tone and smile are indications that the mold must have been taken from a live woman. Some speculate that she might have been a mold-maker's daughter or a sculptor's model.

What we know for sure is that *L'Inconnue*'s sweet visage became wildly popular and was hung on the wall of many an artist, writer, and bohemian thinker throughout Europe around the turn of the twentieth century, up until the first World War. Also true is that Dr. Peter Safar, upon developing a method to teach CPR to the masses, worked with the Belgian toymaker Asmund Laerdal, and together they decided to use *L'Inconnue*'s face for the CPR training mannequin known as Resusci-Annie.

So in a way, the poor drowned woman has been resuscitated millions of times. Or perhaps she never drowned at all. My story for *L'Inconnue*, whom I named Sabine/Mélusine, is entirely an invention.

—Juliet Blackwell

A CONVERSATION WITH JULIET BLACKWELL

Q. In what ways did her childhood growing up in Plaquemines Parish affect Claire's outlook on the world?

A. Claire grew up with some of the best and worst aspects of a small town: on the one hand, she knew a sense of belonging, rich cultural traditions, and the love and support of a large extended family; but on the other her dreams were defined—and often limited—by her humble background and a narrow perspective on the world. Even after she manages to attain an education and do well in Chicago, Claire has the recurring fear that she might be "too big for her britches"—making her feel guilty about (or at least self-conscious of) the external success she has achieved, as well as her dreams of a different kind of life. Her experiences in Paris and the Franche-Comté allow her to feel culturally comfortable at a certain level, while opening her eyes to a whole new world.

Q. Claire suffers two tremendous losses in her life. Did one of them hit her harder than she was expecting? How long do you think it really took

471

Claire to recognize the impact her mother's death at such a young age had on her developing personality?

A. I think Claire largely dismissed the trauma of losing her mother so young because of the way the story was told—that Claire was a miracle for having survived—and because she had other family members to care for her. In many ways her father's alcoholism was even more traumatic than the early "car accident," since it was an ongoing betrayal, capped by a moment of true brutality. But it is not until she arrives in Paris and begins to confront her own fears—that perhaps her mother had intended to kill her as well as herself—that Claire understands she must learn to swim, figuratively as well as literally.

Q. Did your own artistic background influence Claire's interest in art and sculpture? What do you find most fascinating about the art of sculpting?

A. Yes! I love to write about art. I was trained as a painter (and it's still my first love), but when I took a sculpting class, I was enamored. It was like a whole new world: the sensuality of the curves and voids and spaces, the transformative play of shadows and light on different planes, the building up and breaking down in three dimensions. It was so physical.

Now that I'm a writer, and so much of my life is centered around words, I am particularly aware and appreciative of the nonverbal aspects of painting and sculpture, the pure connection between unspoken emotions and the result of one's hands. I adore art!

Q. Have you always been fascinated by the existence of death masks? When and how did you first come across the story of L'Inconnue? *Did you recognize immediately that there might be an idea for a novel there?*

A. The moment I heard about *L'Inconnue de la Seine*, I knew I wanted to use her story in a novel! I first learned about her when researching mold-making in Paris, and I stumbled across the phenomenon of death masks. Some consider death masks to be maudlin, but I find them fascinating—they were an attempt to capture "true" faces at a time when photography was nonexistent or rare. And because of their three-dimensionality, they can appear incredibly lifelike, bringing one face-to-face with the likes of Napoléon or Beethoven.

When I visited the *Lorenzi Moulage d'Art* on the outskirts of Paris, my ideas for the novel developed further. And while *L'Inconnue* appears in several stories from the Belle Epoque, I found surprisingly little mention of her in modern literature.

Finally, I couldn't resist the temptation to imagine a different kind of ending for the young model known only as *L'Inconnue*.

Q. How much do you think Claire and Armand's shared sense of loss provided a window through which they could connect to each other?

A. A great deal. I was influenced by the experiences of several friends who have gone through traumatic events, after which they found it difficult—even painful—to be around "shiny, happy people" all the time. Some sorrows run so deep that the only way one can open up is with someone who truly understands the pain without the need for explanation or description.

Q. What do you think Claire was truly looking for when she set off for Europe? Do you think she had found it by book's end?

A. I think Claire was looking for home. Like so many of us! She no longer feels comfortable in the town where she grew up, and she isn't happy in Chicago. When she falls in love with Paris, with sculpture, and with Armand, she finds a place where she can truly be who she wants to be. Where she doesn't have to hold herself back anymore. As Camille Claudel says in the book, "sometimes the artist you choose is yourself."

QUESTIONS FOR DISCUSSION

1. Claire finds herself at a crossroads in life and takes off to Paris. Do you find her actions precipitous? Could you imagine picking up and starting over in a foreign land? What factors made it possible for her to do so?

2. Have you ever felt that you just didn't belong—whether in your new circumstances or when you went back home or both? If so, did you adjust over time, or did you take steps to change your situation?

3. Have you ever been so intrigued by an item—a piece of art, a letter, an old journal— that you were compelled to trace its history? Do you find it believable that Claire went to Paris to research *L'Inconnue*'s mask?

4. In what ways did the themes of Sabine's and Claire's stories intersect in the novel, and in what ways are they different?

5. Sabine and Claire both come from humble backgrounds. Claire was able to move to a big city and do well for herself, while Sabine's

choices were very limited. Still, Sabine was lucky to be in Paris during a time when artists were hungry for models. If Sabine were living in contemporary times, how might her experiences (and opportunities) have been different?

6. When Claire is first touring Paris, she finds the city disappointing. How does she come to love it? Have you ever had a similar experience?

7. What do you think of the concept of *kintsugi*? Are there broken things in your life— physically or metaphorically—that you are inspired to repair with gold lacquer to make a feature of the breakage?

8. Several times Claire reflects on the sentence: "Who knows the truth? It is the story that is told." Are there family stories in your life that you question? How might such tales take on lives of their own?

9. Had you ever heard of the sculptor Camille Claudel? How do you think her sculpting career might have developed differently had she been a man? In what ways do you think Claudel influenced Sabine?

10. Why do you think so many people have been enamored with the *"Mona Lisa* smile"? What do you think it was about *L'Inconnue*'s smile—or her story—that has made people respond so strongly to her mask?

11. Do you have the sense that Claire's fear of water is symbolic? What might it mean for her to "learn to swim"?

12. Toward the end of the novel, Delphine and Pierre-Guillaume bring a painting of Galatea to the studio. In it, the statue is freeing herself from a block of marble. How does this relate to Sabine's earlier experiences?

13. Camille Claudel points out to Sabine that a muse chooses her artist rather than the other way around. In the later part of her life, do you think Sabine chose Jean-Baptiste as the "artist of her choosing" or herself?

14. Do you think Armand and Claire will go on to renovate the family château? Why or why not? Do you think it would be worth it to do so?

15. What do you suppose happened to the real model for the *L'Inconnue* death mask?

Juliet Blackwell was born and raised in the San Francisco Bay Area, the youngest child of a jet pilot and an editor. She graduated with a degree in Latin American studies from the University of California, Santa Cruz, and went on to earn master's degrees in anthropology and social work. While in graduate school, she published several articles based on her research with immigrant families from Mexico and Vietnam, as well as one full-length translation: Miguel León-Portilla's seminal work *Endangered Cultures*. Juliet taught medical anthropology at SUNY–Albany, was producer for a BBC documentary, and worked as an elementary school social worker. Upon her return to California, she became a professional artist and ran her own decorative painting and design studio for more than a decade. In addition to mainstream novels, Juliet pens the *New York Times* bestselling Witchcraft Mysteries and the Haunted Home Renovation series. As Hailey Lind she wrote the Agatha Award–nominated Art Lover's Mysteries series. She makes her home in northern California, but spends as much time as possible in Europe and Latin America.

Connect Online

julietblackwell.net

facebook.com/julietblackwellauthor

twitter.com/julietblackwell

Center Point Large Print
600 Brooks Road / PO Box 1
Thorndike, ME 04986-0001 USA

(207) 568-3717

US & Canada:
1 800 929-9108
www.centerpointlargeprint.com